JOSQUIN DES PREZ

GARLAND COMPOSER
RESOURCE MANUALS
(Vol. 2)

GARLAND REFERENCE LIBRARY
OF THE HUMANITIES
(Vol. 330)

Volume 2

Garland Composer
Resource Manuals

Advisory Editor:
Barry S. Brook

General Editor:
Guy A. Marco

JOSQUIN DES PREZ
A Guide to Research

Sydney Robinson Charles

GARLAND PUBLISHING, INC. • NEW YORK & LONDON
1983

Library of Congress Cataloging in Publication Data

Charles, Sydney Robinson.
  Josquin des Prez : a guide to research.

  (Garland composer resource manuals ; v. 2)
(Garland reference library of the humanities ; v. 330)
  Discography: p.
  Includes index.
  1. Josquin des Prez, d. 1521—Bibliography.
I. Title. II. Series. III. Series: Garland reference
library of the humanities ; v. 330.
ML134.J773C5 1983   016.784′092′4   81-48418
ISBN 0-8240-9387-9

Printed on acid-free, 250-year-life paper
Manufactured in the United States of America

GARLAND
COMPOSER RESOURCE MANUALS

In response to the growing need for bibliographic guidance to the vast literature on significant composers, Garland is publishing an extensive series of Resource Manuals. It is expected that this series, which will appear over a ten-year period, will encompass more than a hundred composers; they will represent Western musical tradition from the Renaissance to recent times.

Each Resource Manual will offer a selective, annotated list of writings—in all European languages—about one or more composers. There will also be lists of works by the composers, unless these are available elsewhere. Biographical sketches and guides to library resources, organizations, and specialists will be presented. As appropriate to the individual composers, there will be maps, photographs or other illustrative matter, and glossaries and indexes of various sorts. These volumes are being compiled by musical and bibliographical specialists, under the general editorial direction of Dr. Guy A. Marco. Advisory editor for the series is Dr. Barry S. Brook.

CONTENTS

PREFACE

Josquin research is presently in a stage of change and growth, in which older conclusions are being challenged and new approaches are being tried in an effort to bring to the twentieth century a fuller understanding of the creative output of this great composer. The present volume seeks to present a record of this research, old and new, in the hope of assisting further study of Josquin by assembling references which must now be sought in widely scattered sources. The record covers materials available by mid-1981.

The information on editions of separate works found in some basic and readily available reference works has not been duplicated here. The third edition of Heyer covers editions of individual works in collections thoroughly; earlier nineteenth-century editions are well indexed in EitnerV; Hilton indexes the short historical anthology editions, and CMP covers the host of current octavo editions. I have tried to list editions that do not fall within the coverage of these works, plus those of special interest or value.

It is a pleasure to have this opportunity to thank those who have helped to make this work possible: the University of California, Davis, for a generous leave of absence; my colleagues Richard Swift and D. Kern Holoman for encouragement and support; and most especially three wonderfully knowledgeable and helpful music librarians: John Emerson of the Music Library of the University of California, Berkeley, Marlene Wong of the Shields Library of the University of California, Davis, and Jean Lokie of the Music Library, University of California, Davis.

Sydney Robinson Charles
Davis, California
December 1981

ABBREVIATIONS

att. = attributed to
B (before date) = print no. in BrownI
cop. = copyright
CW = complete works edition, of Josquin unless other-
    wise specified.
diss. = doctoral dissertation
E (before date) = print no. in EitnerV
J (before date) = a Josquin print listed in section IIIB1
M. = *Missa*
st = sexti toni
svm = super voces musicales
Bibliographical citations are given in the bibliography in
    alphabetical order of abbreviation.

IOSQVINVS PRATENSIS.

1. Josquin des Prez, from Petrus Opmeer, *Opus chronographicum orbis universi* (Antwerp, 1611), p. 440.

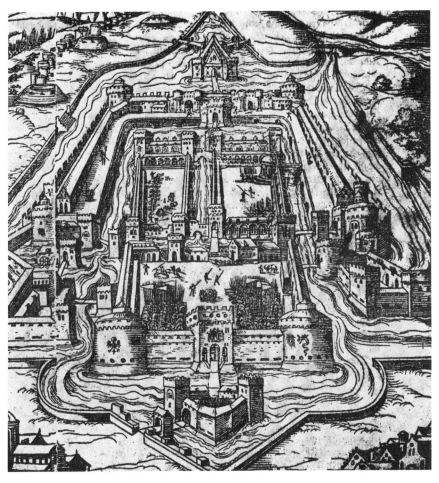

2. The Sforza Castle, Milan in the sixteenth century.

3. St. Peter's, Rome in Josquin's time.

4. The Sistine Chapel in Josquin's time.

5. Singer's Gallery in the Sistine Chapel.

6. The Ducal Palace at Ferrara.

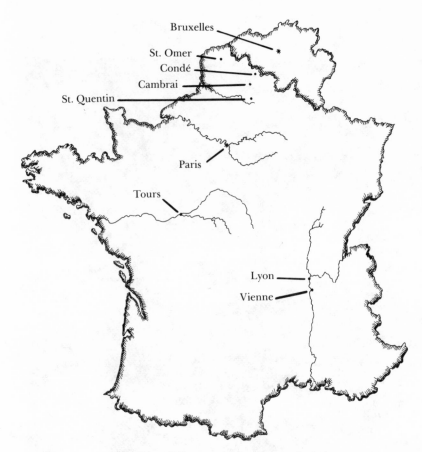

7. Map of France in Josquin's time.

Josquin des Prez

I. BIOGRAPHY

The facts about Josquin's life which are known at present offer only an incomplete account. Therefore all biographies are obliged to rely on a series of hypotheses and inferences to fill in the gaps. Important evidence discovered in the last twenty-five years has shown that many inferences of earlier writers are questionable or erroneous. For this reason the following account distinguishes the proven documentary evidence by arabic numbers in chronological order, each followed by a brief account of the hypotheses concerning the period in question.

Literature: The most extensive and thorough study of Josquin's life is still the indispensable Osthoff 1:3-100, which amplifies and largely supersedes his earlier MGG article. ReeseJ is an excellent and up-to-date summary account, and the combined studies in J: LowinskyA, NobleN, LockwoodJ, and KellmanJ offer valuable detail and documentation for the period from around 1473 to 1521. The reader of earlier writing on Josquin should evaluate it in the light of these studies.

Virtually every encyclopedia, biographical dictionary, and history of music gives some account of the life and works of Josquin, and no complete listing of these is attempted here. Osthoff 1:94-100 reviews chronologically the most significant literature from J.G. Walther's *Musikalisches Lexicon* (1732) to 1961. In addition the especially thorough account in PirottaD may be singled out. A special category is GhislanzoniD; see the comments in Osthoff 2:305. I have been unable to find any further information about books by Ghislanzoni on Josquin either dated 1976 (as in ReeseJ 737) or 1956 (as in GhislanzoniD, supplementary bibliography p. 580). Nor have I seen his 1958 recording notes, cited AMMM 15:XIII.

Shorter separate studies devoted to a survey of Josquin's life and works are BlumeJD, BlumeJJ, Delpuech, SmijersJ, Ursprung, and Werner. Larger studies including Josquin sections are listed below and in section II as pertinent.

A. DOCUMENTS AND HYPOTHESES

1. **1459, July.** Josquin ("Judocho de frantia") is named in
   the records of Milan cathedral as a newly employed
   "biscantor" (SartoriJ 57).

   Date of birth. This record, by using the word *biscantor*
   rather than *puer*, shows that Josquin was considered
   adult at this date. He therefore must have been
   born around 1440, instead of the later dates (most
   commonly *ca.* 1450) given in accounts prior to
   Sartori's 1956 publication.

   Place of birth and nationality. Many different theories
   have been offered, depending on the author's
   evaluation of one or more of the following factors:
   (1) the shifting political boundary between France
   and Burgundian territories in the fifteenth century;
   (2) conflicting statements of Josquin's nationality
   in sixteenth-century sources; and (3) the meaning of
   the acrostic letters in the last part of the text of
   Illibata Dei virgo nutrix. The most recent evidence
   (KellmanJ 208; see 1521 below) suggests that he was
   French.

   Salient points are summarized in ReeseJ 713-4
   and Osthoff 1:3-4; a review of earlier discussions
   is in Clarke. See also BorrenH, ClercxI 116-20,
   LenaertsC 107-9, SmijersK, Van der Linden, and
   Titcomb (with comments by Osthoff 2:305-6).

   Name. Both old and modern sources use a variety of for-
   mats. The given name is most often Josquin (a
   diminutive), but may appear as Josse, or in the
   Latin forms Jodocus/Judocus. The family name may
   be given as one word or two, with variant spellings:
   de/des/dez Pres/Prés/Prez, or in the Latin forms de
   Prato or Pratensis. Present preference is to spell
   the last name as it appears in the acrostic of
   Illibata Dei virgo nutrix: D(ES)PREZ, but there is
   no consensus between the forms des Prez (as in J)
   and Desprez (as in Osthoff and G). Proponents of
   the form Desprez rely on the contention that Josquin
   himself must have examined the 1508 document below,
   which uses this form. Kellman's reinterpretation
   of this document (KellmanJ 185-6, 207-8) may bear
   on this point. Many American publications still use
   the form Depres, Josquin, established by the Library
   of Congress.

   This surname was fairly common in Burgundian/
   northern French territories in this period. Osthoff

1:4 cites two other musicians: Philippet de pres
(with works in Seville 5-I-43 and Florence BR229),
and Pasquier Desprez (active 1467-77 at the Burgundian
court). HammM 48 suggests that it is the latter,
rather than Josquin, who is named in the text of
Compère's *Omnium bonorum plenum*, dated before 1474.
Early life. No documentation is known. Writing in 1633,
Claude Hémeré, a native of St. Quentin, stated
Josquin had been a choir boy in St. Quentin (Raugel,
quoted and discussed Osthoff 1:5-6; a historical
account of the St. Quentin choir is Gomart).
In 1558 ZarlinoI (Book 3:66), followed by many
other writers, stated that Josquin was a pupil of
Ockeghem. The texts of poetic laments on the death
of Ockeghem (MolinetF, CrétinD, and CrétinO) have
also been interpreted as indicating a pupil-teacher
relationship.
Literature: Recent books with good bibliographies
on the historical background in France and Burgundy
are ValeC and VaughnV. The latter also has helpful
maps, as does Clarke 73.

2. 1459-72. Josquin's employment as a Milan cathedral singer
continued through December, 1472, though with the
following absences: 9/59-4/60, 11/60-4/61, 1/62-1/63,
8/63-11/63, 5/64-6/64, 5/67-10/67, 5/68-10/68, 4/69-
5/69, 12/69-1/70. (Complete documentation and
further details in SartoriJ. On the Milan cathedral
choir see SartoriC.)

3. 1473? An undated list names Josquin among the chapel
singers of Galeazzo Maria Sforza, Duke of Milan
(LowinskyA 34).

4. 1473, September 20. Letter from the Duke of Milan to the
Cardinal of Novara regarding the benefice of Gozzano,
which the Duke had granted to Josquin at some pre-
vious date (LowinskyA 33-4).

5. 1474, February 25. Another letter about the stipend of
the Gozzano benefice (LowinskyA 35-6).

6. 1474, July 15; 1475, December 2. Josquin is included in
lists of ducal chapel singers (first published in
MottaM, later in SartoriJ 64-5).

7. 1475, October 1. Josquin is given four quires of paper to
prepare a manuscript for the ducal chapel (Vander-

straeten 6:21, CesariM 196, Osthoff 1:15, 203).
On December 26, 1476, Duke Galeazzo was assas-
sinated. See AdyM 112-27 for a convenient summary
of the ensuing unsettled period in Milanese govern-
ment which ended when Lodovico (Il Moro) Sforza,
Duke of Bari, became the leader, ostensibly in the
name of his nephew, Duke Gian Galeazzo Sforza.
The effects of this unsettled period on the court
musicians is discussed in LowinskyA 40-42 and
CesariM 194-7.

8. 1479, April 12. Josquin is given a travel pass from the
ducal chapel in Milan for a three-month votive
pilgrimage to St. Anthony of Vienne.
No documentation about Josquin is available
from this date until 1486. LowinskyA 42-60 shows
the probability that he entered the service of
Ascanio Sforza (1455-1505), younger brother of
Galeazzo Maria and Lodovico Sforza, created cardinal
by Pope Sixtus IV on March 3, 1484. Lowinsky dates
Ascanio's employment of the poet and musician Serafino Ciminelli dall'Aquila from 1484 to 1490/91.
Serafino's poem "Ad Iusquino suo compagno musico
d'Ascanio" (Menghini no. LXXIV, p. 112; discussed
and translated LowinskyA 51-7) cannot be more pre-
cisely dated.
Literature: CesariM is a well-illustrated account of Milanese music in this period, and the
larger collection of which it is a part, Malaguzzi-
Valeri, studies a broad range of cultural aspects
at the Sforza court of Milan. See also Gatti-PererA
and MilanoD. Another local history of music in this
period is Barblan, part of a detailed general history.

9. 1486, September. Josquin is named as a member of the papal
chapel choir in Rome each month from September,
1486, through January, 1487, and again in September,
1487, at a salary of 8 florins monthly (HaberlR
243ff., Osthoff 1:24-31, NobleN 76-8).
LowinskyA 60-61 suggests that the gap between
this document and the next can be filled by assuming
that Josquin accompanied Ascanio on his extended
visit to Milan during a serious illness of Lodovico
Sforza.

10. 1489, June-1494, April. Josquin is named as a member of
the papal chapel choir every month (NobleN 76-8,

emending Haberl and Osthoff). From April, 1494, the records of the papal choir are lacking until February, 1501. BurckardC 2:189 gives a list apparently from the end of 1499 which is identical with Haberl's 1501 list.

Josquin served under two Popes: Innocent VIII (Giovanni Battista Cibo), 1484-92, and Alexander VI (Roderigo Borgia), 1492-1503. The papal musicians from 1492 are studied in SherrP. A primary source on the activities of the papal chapel from 1483 to 1506 is the diary of Johannes Burckard or Burchard, Master of papal ceremonies (in two modern editions, BurckardC and BurckardT). A cursory and incomplete account of Burckard's musical information is ScheringM, amplified by SchulerS. Music practice in Italian chapels in this period is discussed in D'AcconeP.

The literature on the historical background of this period is truly voluminous, for the Borgias have never ceased to fascinate historians. Among more recent books, Mallett gives a good starting bibliography, and Sacerdote is particularly detailed and well illustrated. Old but still valuable in their respective areas are Pastor (on the papacy) and Gregorovius (on Rome). The French presence in Italy is well covered by Bridge, which has extensive bibliographies and useful appendices and maps.

11. 1489, September 9. Josquin receives by papal grant a canonry at St. Omer in the diocese of Therouanne. It is not known whether he took up this benefice (NobleN 80-84, 93-5).

(12?) 1493, April, May, or June. A "Josquin chantre" and other singers receive payment for performing at the court of Lorraine (Osthoff 1:21). It is not certain that this refers to Josquin des Prez, who was on the salary rolls of the papal court during these months.

13. 1493, November 8. A papal order is issued for the investigation of charges made by Josquin that the present chaplain of the altar of St. Theobald in the parish church of "Bassatea" in Cambrai diocese obtained the position by simony (NobleN 84-5, 98-100).

14. 1494, November 9.   Josquin receives by papal grant the
        canonry and prebend of St. Géry, Cambrai diocese.
        He apparently did not take up this benefice (NobleN
        88-9, 93, 100-101).
            It is generally inferred that Josquin remained
        in Rome for some years after 1494; LowinskyA sug-
        gests that he remained there until Ascanio left
        Rome, shortly before the French invasion of Milan
        in August, 1499. Without suggesting precise dates,
        ReeseJ and Osthoff turn to Glareanus's stories
        about Josquin and Louis XII (reigned 1498-1515).
        These are: (1) that Josquin wrote *Memor esto verbi
        tui* to remind the king of a neglected promise of
        reward, and *Bonitatem fecisti* on fulfillment of
        the promise (GlareanusD 440, GlareanusM 2:271,
        and Osthoff 1:41-2 where the authenticity of
        Bonitatem is negated); and (2) that Josquin art-
        fully composed a piece which a monotone could per-
        form, in response to the king's desire to partici-
        pate in a performance (GlareanusD 468, GlareanusM
        2:284, Osthoff 1:42, 207-8). Osthoff cites other
        versions of (1) in which the same incident is told
        of Josquin and King Francis I, and of the composer
        Dionisio Memmo and King Henry VIII. Clinkscale
        has identified the composition of (2), textless in
        Glareanus, with *Guillaume s'en va chauffer* of St.
        Gall 462, where it is stated that Louis XI (reigned
        1461-83) was the king involved.
            The only dated references to Josquin between
        11/9/1494 and 12/13/1501 presently known do not
        state where he is. They are:
    1499, December 19.   Letter of Johannes Vivaysius, a singer
        of the Duke of Ferrara, who is sending a "canto"
        by Josquin to the Duke of Mantua (GallicoJG). (The
        Duke of Mantua was the son-in-law of the Duke of
        Ferrara, being the husband of Isabella d'Este.)
    1501, September 25.   Letter to the Duke of Ferrara from
        one of his representatives at the French royal
        court in Lyons saying that Verbonnet is sending
        the Duke a new work by Josquin (LockwoodJ 122,
        Osthoff 1:45).

15. 1501, December 13.   A letter to the Duke of Ferrara from
        his representative at the French court in Lyons.
        He reports a conversation with Josquin, who has
        been in Flanders recruiting singers for the Duke,
        has left the money in the bank at Bruges, and has

been invited to accompany Archduke Philip the Fair of Burgundy on his trip to Spain (Osthoff 1:51, translated StevensonJ 217).

1502, February 24. Count Sigismundo Cantelmo, in "Sancto Mattheo," sends the Duke of Ferrara a *Salve regina* by Josquin (Osthoff 1:51, 211).

1502, August 14. Letter from Girolamo da Sestola (Il Coglia) in Ferrara to the Duke of Ferrara, then in Milan, recommending the employment of Josquin (LockwoodJ 112-3, 130-31).

1502, September 2. Letter from Gian di Artiganova in Ferrara to the Duke of Ferrara in Milan recommending the employment of Isaac as more suitable for the duke's service than Josquin (originally published partially by Vanderstraeten 6:87-8 and cited in most biographical accounts since then. Dated, amplified, discussed, and translated in LockwoodJ 113-4, 132-3; also discussed in Osthoff 1:51-2).

16. 1503, April 12. Letter to the Duke of Mantua from his ambassador in Lyons stating that Coglia, Josquin, and Verbonnet have arrived there from Paris (Osthoff 1:53, citing earlier publications; GallicoJG in a slightly different reading).

17. 1503, April 13. Letter to the Duke of Ferrara from his ambassador in Lyons mentioning Josquin's arrival (Osthoff 1:53).

18. 1503, April 28. Memorandum of letter from the Duke of Ferrara to his ambassador in Lyons, stating that Josquin has not yet arrived but is expected soon (LockwoodJ 133-4).

19. 1503, June-1504, April 22. Monthly payments to Josquin as "Maistro della Capella" at the Court of Ferrara (summarized LockwoodJ 137).

Thorough studies of Josquin's connections with the Ferrara court and further information on its musical establishment are Osthoff 1:50-60, 215-6, LockwoodMF, and LockwoodJ. See also LockwoodJM 192-6.

20. 1504, May 3. The Church of Notre Dame in Condé-sur-l'Escaut records the reception of four new canons, among them "Monsieur le prevost messire Josse de pres" (KellmanJ 207).

21. 1508, May 23. Letter from the Chapter of Notre Dame in
           Condé to Marguerite of Austria, Regent of the
           Netherlands, stating that Josquin is in good health
           (Delporte 54-6, Osthoff 1:69-70; reinterpreted by
           KellmanJ 185-6, 207-8).
               Documents which are considered to refer to
           other musicians named Josquin are:
    1516-17. A "Josquino cantore" was in the service of
           Cardinal Ippolito d'Este (LockwoodJ 120).
    1520, June 3. A Josquin arrived in Ferrara from Budapest
           with Cardinal Ippolito d'Este (*Ibid.* Lockwood
           suggests these references could be to Josquin Dor
           or Doro).
    1520, September. Two singers, one named "Joskin," paid
           by Charles V in Brussels or Malines for new songs
           (Osthoff 1:73-4, questioned by KellmanJ 186-9,
           defended by PickerJG 454).

22. 1521, August 3. Josquin is visited by city officials of
           Condé for the purpose of legitimizing his claim for
           bequeathal rights. The record of this visit is
           dated September 19, 1521. It describes Josquin as
           a priest, and says he described himself as foreign
           (i.e., to the Empire of Charles V, in which Condé
           was then situated. KellmanJ 208).

23. 1521, August 27. Death of Josquin in Condé. This date
           was on a tombstone in Notre Dame in Condé that is
           no longer in existence, but the inscription of
           which was copied in the seventeenth century (first
           published by Fétis; quoted Osthoff 1:74, ReeseJ
           716). KellmanJ 208 describes his will, by which he
           left a house and land in Condé to the church for
           costs of memorial services, including the singing
           of his *Pater noster.*
               Suggestions of a later date of death found in
           earlier biographies (following Gomart and Fétis,
           both summarized Osthoff 1:74ff.) are no longer
           considered valid in the light of Kellman's dis-
           covery of document 22 above.
               A summary of the statements from the sixteenth
           century onwards, that Josquin served as Kapell-
           meister at the court of Maximilian I, is found in
           Osthoff 1:70-71.

B. SUPPLEMENTARY DETAILS

1. Personal appearance.

The widely reproduced woodcut portrait comes from a
1611 publication (Opmeer; cited Osthoff 1:87,
ReeseJ 717) where it is said to have been made
after a now-lost painting in the Church of St.
Gudule, Brussels. (The different portrait given as
frontispiece of PAPTM 6 appears to be a nineteenth-
century rendering of the woodcut.) Osthoff 2:309
cites another possible portrait by Jean Perréal.
Clercx-LejeuneF gives a thorough study of these and
other putative pictures of Josquin, including the
well-known portrait of a musician by Leonardo da
Vinci?/Ambrogio de Predis? (Ambrosiana, Milan) which
has also been thought to depict Gafurius, among
others.

A contemporary description, first published by
Vanderstraeten (6:73-4), was formerly thought to
apply to Josquin. LockwoodMG shows that it refers
to a different individual, a contrabass singer of
Antwerp named "Gossino" (Gosswin? Cossin?). Josquin,
however, was a bass singer if Glareanus's story of
Guillaume s'en va chauffer (see no. 14 above) is
accepted, for it recounts that he himself sang the
bass to reinforce the king's tenor.

2. Josquin as teacher.

Only later sixteenth-century sources name pupils of
Josquin, and modern scholars are chary of interpret-
ing these statements as evidence of a direct pupil-
teacher relationship rather than the writer's belief
in a general influence of the distinguished senior
composer. A 1560 list of Josquin's *"disciples"* by
Ronsard is quoted in EitnerB 159; see further Osthoff
1:77-8, 2:308, and Rokseth. Adrian Petit Coclico
claimed to be a pupil of Josquin and described his
teaching (quoted and discussed in Osthoff 1:83-5;
English translation ReeseMR 229-30 and ReeseJ 717-8).

3. Reputation.

The most complete account of references to Josquin
by contemporary and later writers is found in Osthoff 1: Crétin (6-7), Molinet (6-7, 64), Eloi
d'Amerval (46), Jean Lemaire (64-8), Cortese (37-8),
anonymous epitaphs (75-7), Patrizzi (59-60), and a
chronological discussion from Luther onwards (87-

100). Other references are PirottaM 147-61 (Cortese),
LowinskyMRM 3:49 (Rabelais, Folengo) and 73 (anony-
mous Moulu text), DisertoriF 61-2 (Folengo),
DunningJ (Jachet de Mantova work), ReeseMR 259
(Bartoli), and a remark by Luther on Josquin is
explored in WioraJ. A twentieth-century reference
in Pfitzner's *Palestrina* is discussed by Rectanus.
BoormanJ examines Josquin's musical influence.
Studies which trace the spread of Josquin's music
in specific geographical areas are KirschJ (Germany),
Snížková (Czechoslovakia), and StevensonJ (Spain
and Portugal).

II. COMPOSITIONS

A. HISTORICAL AND STYLISTIC STUDIES

1. General studies of Josquin's works.
    The only detailed study of the totality of Josquin's
    output is Osthoff (for a review see LowinskySR).
    The most recent summary overview is NobleJ; the
    collection of studies in J covers a large proportion
    of the works, as listed in the excellent index.

2. Josquin's works in broader historical context.
    Ambros 3:203-37 is still of interest, as are
    BesselerM 230-80 and Pirro 171-92. More recent
    period histories are WolffM, BridgmanA 239-302,
    ReeseMR 228-60, and BrownMR 117-50. A general
    social and cultural background is given in BridgmanV.
    Studies centering on specific aesthetic concepts
    are EldersST (symbolism) and EldersSY (symbolism
    in Josquin), ManiatesC (mannerism), and WioraR
    (religion). Shorter studies tracing aspects of
    the cultural background are LowinskyMC, LowinskyMV,
    and PirrottaM.

3. Studies of specific categories and stylistic traits.
    (*N.b.* Listed here are studies of broader work
    categories; studies of individual works are cited
    under those works in section IIC below.)
  a. Mass. A valuable recent survey of the mass is Lock-
    woodG; LockwoodV studies the parody mass and Lock-
    woodS reports on computer analysis. Older general
    books are ScheringN (largely superseded) and WagnerG;
    also more general is Krings; Schmidt-Görg offers a
    brief survey. For other general works see the bib-
    liography of LockwoodG. Studies devoted entirely
    to Josquin's masses are BorrenA, DahlhausS, LovellM,
    PerkinsM, and PatrickC. RubsamenU compares masses
    of Josquin and La Rue, and PerformanceJMa examines
    performance and interpretation problems.

13

b. Motet. A valuable recent survey of the renaissance
   motet is PerkinsG with extensive bibliography.
   Leichtentritt (1908) is still the only general
   motet history; Stephan studies the late fifteenth
   century; Hüschen is a brief survey. More recent
   studies with special emphases are DammannS (iso-
   rhythm), DunningS (ceremonial motet), Han (Marian
   antiphon), KirschM (Andreas de Silva), Columbro
   (ostinato), WardTP (hymns), and GerberR (hymn
   cycles). Works in preparation are Ware (5+-voice
   motets) and WardTPC (polyphonic hymn catalogue).
   Studies devoted entirely to Josquin's motets are:
   DahlhausO and Rosen (dissonance); EldersP and MattfeldC and S (plainchant and cantus firmus);
   FinscherZ, OsthoffP, and Obst (psalm motets);
   GodtM (motivic integration); SparksP (authenticity);
   RuffS, RuffP, and Tiersot (general). Performance
   and interpretation are studied in FinscherH and
   PerformanceJMt. Magnificats are surveyed in KirschQ.
c. Secular works. An overview of the polyphonic chanson,
   with good bibliography, is BrownGC. See also BrownPC
   (Parisian chanson); BrownMF (theatrical chanson);
   BrownTC, IO, OP, and IV; HeartzC. The 3-voice
   chanson ("*chanson rustique*") is studied in AdamsT
   and BernsteinC; chanson texts are studied in
   JefferyC. Studies devoted to Josquin are Reiffenstein, BenthemJ (3-voice chanson), BenthemZ (5- to
   6-voice chanson), BlackburnJ (contrafacta), GallicoJ
   (frottola), JefferyL (texts), and PerformanceJS.
d. Instrumental ensembles. These are discussed in BrownIV,
   Kämper, and Ravizza.
e. Intabulations. General studies of vocal intabulations
   are WardJP and WardJU. Intabulations of Josquin are
   studied in BrownA, HoneggerM, ThibaultI, and Yong.
   See further Sources: Intabulations (IIID below).
f. Harmony, mode. A recent survey with good bibliography
   is PowersG. Other general studies are BergquistM,
   LowinskyT, and DahlhausT. Studies especially on
   Josquin are OsthoffB, PerkinsM, NovackT, and
   NovackF (on Josquin and Isaac). Discussions and
   studies of harmony especially as it is affected by
   musica ficta are LowinskySC, CrevelS, CrevelV,
   LowinskySCR, and BenthemF.
g. Musica ficta. In addition to the studies just cited,
   LockwoodGM is a useful summary with a good bibliography by Boorman. See further Bernet Kempers,
   DahlhausZ, and section IIB2a below. A study in
   progress is HallM.

h. Cantus firmus. The most complete study of cantus
   firmi in sacred music of this period is SparksC.
   Josquin's treatment is further studied in EldersP,
   FinscherZ, MattfeldC and S (with comments in
   Shepherd), MattfeldU (on the use of Ambrosian
   chant), and BernsteinC (3-voice chansons).
i. Rhythm. Rhythmic considerations are discussed in
   Bank, CollinsC and P, and KirschZ.
j. Other compositional features.
   Cadences: BrockhoffK, PerkinsM; *Dissonance*: Dahl-
   hausO, Patrick, Rosen; *Imitation*: FinscherZV,
   Williams; *Melody*: AntonowyczC, CrevelV, GodtM,
   MeierM (on melodic quotations), WioraS; *Ostinato*:
   Columbro, LenaertsZ; *Structure*: LenaertsM, NovackF,
   DammannS, PerkinsM; *Text setting*: FinscherZV.
k. Performance practice. BrownGP is a recent survey
   with good bibliography; D'AcconeP and WrightP re-
   port regional historical practices; other studies
   are BridgmanO, NobleS, and BrownPE (on recordings),
   BrownIO, IV, OP, and CM (chansons); Collins; EldersZ;
   FinscherH; LenaertsM; LitterickP; and the valuable
   Performance sections in J 646-719.

B. CHRONOLOGY, AUTHENTICITY, COMPLETE EDITIONS

Chronology and authenticity of Josquin's works are the
greatest problems under investigation in present Josquin research, with many areas in which no agreement has been
reached.

1. Chronology. The most complete approach to establishment
   of a chronological arrangement is found throughout
   the studies of individual works in Osthoff (indexed
   in his list of works 2:266-97). A summary account,
   offering some revisions to Osthoff's proposals,
   is in NobleJ. The dimensions of the problem are
   outlined in BlumeJJ; LowinskyJ and A propose different dates for some masses and motets. An earlier
   study is OsthoffZ; suggestions for computer assis-
   tance are given in MendelT.

2. Lists of compositions. There are several lists of Josquin's
   complete works, no two of which are identical as to
   which works are doubtful/spurious: OsthoffMGG;
   PirottaD; Osthoff 2; CW supp., NobleJ, and Report 3.
   All these are arranged by type: mass, mass movement,

motet, secular; Osthoff 2 includes a separate
listing of instrumental ensemble works. PirottaD
includes first publication dates; Osthoff 2 serves
as index to his commentary; CW supp. is also an
index; NobleJ is by far the most complete list of
doubtful/spurious works with source references;
Report 3 arranges the works by further classifica-
tions within the larger divisions.

3. Criteria for authenticity. Two general types of evidence
        are offered, usually in combination: source studies
        and stylistic studies. Separate source studies are
        listed in section III below; studies on the authen-
        ticity of individual works are listed under those
        works in the following list. Studies concerned
        with several works, and with the establishment of
        criteria for authenticity in general are: Osthoff
        (especially in the references cited 2:287-97);
        AntonowyczC, PS, and Z; BenthemE and Z; MaasJ;
        MendelT; SparksM and P; StaehelinM; and Report 1
        23ff.

4. Editions. Separate modern editions are cited under in-
        dividual compositions in the list below. An indexed
        list of editions prior to 1871 is found in EitnerV.
        The following refer to complete editions.
    a. A second edition of the complete works has been dis-
        cussed since 1971. Accounts of these discussions
        are J 724-54 and Report 1-4; see also TVNM 31 (1981)
        93. These discussions, especially Report 1, contain
        valuable commentary on editorial practice.
    b. The present complete edition is frequently mentioned
        in the discussions just cited. Other commentaries
        are AntonowyczJ, JustR, SmijersU, Ursprung, and
        Werner. The arrangement of this edition as it was
        issued from 1922 to 1969 is complex. It appeared
        in fifty-five consecutively numbered *Aflevering*,
        nos. 2-54 of which were assigned *Bundel* numbers
        indicating their positions within volumes. Volume
        numbers are non-consecutive throughout the set,
        with separate numbering systems for Masses (CW Ma
        below), Motets (CW Mt), and Secular works (CW W).
        In addition each composition was separately num-
        bered within these categories; compositions in the
        Supplement (CW supp.) are numbered in that order.
        Citations of this set usually give volume numbers,
        but vary as to further numbers given. Tables 1 and

2 correlate these numbering systems. Aflevering
(hereafter afl.) 1-44 were edited by Smijers; afl.
45-53 by Antonowycz; afl. 54-5 by Antonowycz and
Elders.

C. JOSQUIN'S COMPOSITIONS LISTED

List 1 below is arranged in a single alphabetical order,
and includes (1) cross-references to all known variant texts
(*contrafacta*), to the beginning texts of all separate sections of compositions other than masses and magnificats,
and to the beginning text of all separately texted vocal
parts; (2) references to all known fifteenth- and sixteenth-
century sources of the composition; (3) other bibliographical
references as pertinent. The lists which follow under 2
below give the titles of compositions arranged in textual
and musical categories.

These lists comprise all Josquin compositions published
in the CW, plus a few others considered authentic in one or
more of the lists cited above. Not included are: (1) works
misattributed to Josquin from the sixteenth through nine-
teenth centuries but rejected by Smijers, and (2) works not
ascribed to Josquin in any known extant source, but proposed
as his on stylistic grounds by modern scholars. Both these
categories are well covered in NobleJ.

The numerous inclusions in the CW which have been ques-
tioned or rejected as works of Josquin by one or more modern
scholars are indicated here by parentheses placed around
the title. This indication simply means that a question
has been raised: in many cases there is no agreement among
scholars, as indicated by the references given. The titles
of works which are given in lower-case letters rather than
capitals are considered genuine but are not extant in complete form. Unless otherwise stated, all works are for four
voices.

1. Alphabetical list with sources.

A custodia matutina = De profundis, part 2
A LA MORT
    Tenor: Monstra te esse matrem
    Source: FlorenceC Bas.2439
    Edition: Osthoff 2:163, mm. 1-11
A L'EURE QUE JE VOUS P.X.   CW W2 B4 (afl.53) no.41, p.12
    35 mm.
    Canon: Ad nonam canitur bassus hic tempore lapso

TABLE 1: CW by Aflevering

Order of citation: afl. no., vol. no., *Bundel* no., date, later ed. or reprint (R)

1. [Laments on Josquin] 1922	20. Ma2:9 1940; R1969	39. Mt3:15 1954
2. Mt1:1 1923; R1969	21. Mt1:8 1942; R1969	40. Mt3:16 1955
3. W1:1 1923; R1969	22. Ma2:10 1948	41. Mt4:17 1955
4. Mt1:2 1924	23. Ma2:11 1950	42. Mt4:18 1955
5. W1:2 1924; R1969	24. Mt2:9 1950	43. Ma4:20 1956
6. Mt1:3 1925	25. Mt2:10 1950	44. Ma4:Mf1 1956
7. Mt1:4 1925	26. Ma3:12 1950	45. Mt5:19 1957
8. W1:3 1925; R1969	27. Ma3:13 1951	46. Mt5:20 1957
9. Mt1:5 1926	28. Ma3:14 1951	47. Mt5:21 1958
10. Ma1:1 1926; *Opera omnia*, editio altera, 1957	29. Ma3:15 1951	48. Mt5:22 1959
11. Ma1:2 1927; *Opera omnia*, editio altera, 1957	30. Ma3:16^1 1952	49. Mt5:23 1961
12. Ma1:3 1927	31. Ma3:16^2 1952	50. Ma4:Mf2 1963
13. Ma1:4 1929	32. Ma3:17 1952	51. Mt5:24 1963
14. Ma1:5 1931	33. Ma4:18 1952	52. Mt5:25 1964
15. Ma2:6 1935; R1969	34. Ma4:19 1953	53. W2:4 1965
16. Mt1:6 1936; R1969	35. Mt3:11 1954	54. W2:5 1968
17. Ma2:7 1937; R1969	36. Mt3:12 1954	55. supp. 1969
18. Mt2:7 1938; R1969	37. Mt3:13 1954	
19. Ma2:8 1939; R1969	38. Mt3:14 1954	

TABLE 2: CW by volume (*Deel*) no.

A. MASSES AND SEPARATE MASS MOVEMENTS

Each complete mass carries the same number as its *Bundel* (B) no.

Vol.1: B1, afl.10
B2, afl.11
B3, afl.12
B4, afl.13
B5, afl.14
Vol.2: B6, afl.15
B7, afl.17
B8, afl.19
B9, afl.20
B10, afl.22
B11, afl.23
B12, afl.26
Vol.3: B13, afl.27
B14, afl.28
B15, afl.29
B16, afl.30/31
B17, afl.32
Vol.4: B18, afl.33
B19, afl.34
B20, afl.43
Mf B1, afl.44
Mf B2, afl.50

(Mf = separate mass movements)

B. MOTETS

Vol.1: B1, afl.2, no.1-9
B2, afl.4, no.10-14
B3, afl.6, no.15-19
B4, afl.7, no.20-24
B5, afl.9, no.25-9
Vol.2: B6, afl.16, no.30-32
B7, afl.18, no.33-5
B8, afl.21, no.36-9
B9, afl.24, no.40-41
B10, afl.25, no.42-4
Vol.3: B11, afl.35, no.45-8
B12, afl.36, no.49-51
B13, afl.37, no.52-4
B14, afl.38, no.55-7
B15, afl.39, no.58-61
Vol.4: B16, afl.40, no.62-5
B17, afl.41, no.65-7
B18, afl.42, no.68-70
Vol.5: B19, afl.45, no.71-3
B20, afl.46, no.74-6
B21, afl.47, no.77-8
B22, afl.48, no.79-81
B23, afl.49, no.82-5
B24, afl.51, no.86-9
B25, afl.52, no.90-96

C. SECULAR WORKS

Vol.1: B1, afl.3, no.1-12
B2, afl.5, no.13-23
B3, afl.8, no.24-34
Vol.2: B4, afl.53, no.35-49
B5, afl.54, no.50-65

Text: incipit only
Source: 1504[3]
Edition: ScheringG 61
Recording: see section IV
A l'ombre *see* En l'ombre
A une dame j'ay fait vue (Busnois) = tenor of Missus est ...
    a Deo
ABSALON FILI MI. CW supp. no.5, p.22 (low range)
    85 mm.
    Text: 2 Samuel 18:33; Genesis 37:35
    Sources: London Roy.8.G.VII (anon.; low range); 1540[7] and
        1559[2] (both high range)
    Intabulation: 1558[20]
    Discussion: LowinskyJ 20 (date), LowinskySC 24-7 *et
        passim*, J 654-8
    Editions: PAPTM 6:57 (high), Wooldridge 229 (high),
        Osthoff 2:382 (low); octavo ed. see CMP
    Recordings: see section IV
(ABSOLVE, QUAESUMUS, DOMINE, 6 v.). CW Mt5 B23 (afl.49)
    no.82, p.109.
    107 mm.
    Tenor: Requiem (L.U.1807)
    Text: Burial service (L.U.1821)
    Source: Toledo 21
    Discussion: JustR (questions authenticity), AntonowyczZ,
        EldersP 528-9, PickerJ 255ff., DunningS 101-2
Accede nuncia = Mittit ad virginem, part 2
Ach unfal, was zichstu mich = Qui belles amours
ADIEU MES AMOURS. CW W2 B4 (afl.53) no.35, p.1
    60 mm.
    Text: JefferyL 408-9
    Sources: Bologna Q 17, Bologna Q 18, Florence BR.229,
        Florence Magl.XIX 107[bis], Florence Magl.XIX 178,
        FlorenceR 2794, Munich 1516, Paris Res.Vm[7]504 (I)
        (superius only; anon.), Regensburg C.120, Rome
        Giul.XIII.27, RomeC 2856, St. Gall 462, St. Gall 463,
        Washington M2.1 M6 (anon.), 1501
    Intabulations: 1507[5] (anon.; ed. J 456-8), B1533[1] (anon.;
        ed. J 459-61), 1536[12] (anon.), 1556[32], Berlin 40026
        (att. Isaac; ed. J 462-3), Munich 272
    Discussion: J 663-74; cf. BrownMF no.181; AtlasC 1:
        61ff.
    Editions: Ambros 5:131-3, FellererA, HewittO, J 665,
        SmijersV 5:156, SMd 5
    Recordings: see section IV
Adieu mes amours, 7 v.; only 3 v. known, with text Ave Maria.
    CW supp. no.25, p.85 (superius only)
    Sources: Bologna R 142 (superius), Piacenza (tenor, bass)
    Discussion and edition (3 v.): PickerJ 247-55

Adjuro vos, o filiae Syon = Plus nulz regretz
Adjuva nos = Domine non secundum, part 4
(ALLEGEZ MOY, 6 v.). CW W1 B3 (af1.5) no.14, p.36
    46 mm.
    Sources: Copenhagen 1872, Hamburg Hans.III 12-16, 1540^7
        (att. Barbe in music, Lebrin in index), 1545^{15}, J1550,
        1572^2 (att. Josquin in music, Willaert in index)
    Intabulation: 1552^{29} (anon.; ed. J 471-4)
    Discussion: Osthoff 2:218 (questions authenticity);
        BrownMF no.9
    Recordings: see section IV
ALMA REDEMPTORIS MATER. CW Mt2 B4 (af1.21) no.38, p.77
    2. Tu quae genuisti
    117 mm.
    Text: Marian antiphon (L.U.273)
    Sources: Bologna Q 18, Florence II.I.232, 1519^2
    Recording: see section IV
ALMA REDEMPTORIS MATER/AVE REGINA. CW Mt1 B4 (af1.7) no.21,
    p.105
    2. Tu quae genuisti/Gaude virgo
    158 mm.
    Texts: Marian antiphons: *Alma* (L.U.273) in superius and
        bass, *Ave* (L.U.274) in tenor and alto
    Sources: Cortona 95/6, Florence II.I.232, Milan 2267,
        Rome Sist.15, 1505^2
    Discussion: AMMM 15:XXVIII-XXX
    Edition: AMMM 15:86 (after Milan 2267)
    Recordings: see section IV
Audi, auditui meo = Miserere mei, part 2
Audi virgo = O virgo prudentissima, part 2
Ave caro Christi cara = Ave Christe
(AVE CHRISTE, IMMOLATE IN CRUCIS ARA). CW Mt5 B20 (af1.46)
    no.76, p.45
    2. Salve lux mundi
    227 mm.
    Text: Rhymed prayer (Osthoff 2:96)
    Sources: Rome Pal.1at.1976-9, Toledo 22 (att. Bauldeweyn),
        Vienna 15941 (att. Bauldeweyn), 1564^5
    Discussion: SparksM 98ff. (suggests Bauldeweyn as com-
        poser)
    Editions: Bordes 1 (motets):41, Chorwerk 18, octavo ed.
        [1938?] in U. of Pennsylvania Choral Series 87
    Recordings: see section IV
AVE MARIA ... BENEDICTA. CW Mt1 (af1.2) no.2, p.12
    67 mm.
    Text: Marian antiphon with additional text
    Sources: Bologna R 142 (superius), 1504^1
    Intabulation: 1507^5 (ed. DisertoriF 243)

Edition: DisertoriF 243
Recording: see section IV
Ave Maria ... benedicta, 6 v. = Pater noster, part 2
AVE MARIA ... VIRGO SERENA.   CW Mtl Bl (afl.2) no.1, p.1
    155 mm.
    Text: see Benoit-Castelli.   On variants see Osthoff 2:86
        and CW Mtl p.XIII
    Sources: Barcelona 454, BarcelonaOC 5 (anon.), Berlin
        40013, Berlin 40021 (as "Verbum incarnatum"), Florence
        II.I.232, Florence Magl.XIX 164-7, Gotha A98, Hradec
        Krǎlové II A 7 (anon.), LeipzigU 1494 (superius, bass,
        anon., textless), LondonR 1070, Milan 2266, Modena IX,
        Munich 19, Munich 3154, MunichU 322-5, MunichU 326,
        Nürnberg 83795 (tenor, bass), Rome Sist.42, St. Gall 463,
        Segovia, Ulm 237 (anon.), WarsawU 58 (anon.), 1502[1].
        Theorist: GlareanusD 346, 358
    Intabulation: St. Gall 530 ("Das lang Ave Maria")
    Other arrangements: 6 v. version in Munich 41 (ed. CW Mtl
        no.1a, p.5), 8 v. version using Josquin superius in
        VeronaF 218; see further Osthoff 2:86
    Discussions: DahlhausT 18-9, EldersP 537-8, FinscherZ
        69-72, MattfeldS 171-3.   Especially relating to date:
        JustM 1:274, LowinskyA 68-9, NoblittD (with disagree-
        ment in NobleJ)
    Editions: Bordes 1 (Motets):92, Casimiri 2, GlareanusM 2:
        436, Muller-Blattau 2; numerous octavo editions:
        Dessoff Choir Series 74, U. of Pennsylvania Choral
        Series 90; see further CMP for complete editions and
        editions of *Ave vera virginitas* (m. 94 to end)
    Recordings: see section IV
Ave Maria ... Virgo serena, 7 v. *see* Adieu mes amours, 7 v.
Ave Maria (chant) = tenor of Virgo salutiferi
AVE MARIS STELLA, 3-4 v.   CW supp. no.1, p.1
    1. Ave maris stella: chant
    2. Summens illud ave, 3 v. by Dufay (23 mm.)
    3. Solve vincla: chant
    4. Monstra te esse matrem, 4 v. (55 mm.)
    5. Virgo singularis (chant)
    6. Vitam praesta puram, 4 v. (22 mm.)
    7. Sit laus Deo, 4 v. (48 mm.)
    Text: Marian hymn (L.U.1259)
    Source: Rome Sist.15 (part 4 att. Josquin)
    Discussion: J 645-54
    Recordings, part 4: see section IV
AVE MARIS STELLA.   CW Mt5 B25 (afl.52) no.94, p.203
    2. Virgo singula
    199 mm.

Source: Bologna Q 20
Discussion: EldersP 536
Edition: see CMP

Ave munda spes, Maria (4 v.; only 3 extant). CW supp. no.15, p.72
2. Ave gemma
3. O castitatis lilium
302 mm.
Text: Marian sequence
Source: Vienna 15941 (alto, tenor, bass)
Discussion and complete edition with reconstructed superius: GodtR

AVE NOBILISSIMA CREATURA, 6 v. CW Mt2 B7 (afl.18) no.34, p.29
2. Tibi, domina gloriosa
Tenor: Benedicta tu in mulieribus
Text: not otherwise known
Sources: Bologna R 142 (tenor), MunichU Art.401, Toledo 13, 1519[2]
Discussion: DammannS 20-23, EldersZ 67-73
Recording: see section IV

Ave regina *see* Alma redemptoris mater/Ave regina

Ave sanctissima virgo, canon, 1 v. extant
Source: 1540[7]
References: Osthoff 2:133, 268; HarránB 173-4

Ave vera virginitas = Ave Maria ... virgo, from m. 94

AVE VERUM CORPUS, 2-3 v. CW Mt1 B2 (afl.4) no.12, p.48
1. Ave verum (2 v.); Vere passum (3 v.)
2. Cuius latus (2 v.); Esti nobis (3 v.)
3. O dulcis O pia (3 v.)
121 mm.
Text: Trope, between Sanctus and Benedictus
Sources: Basel F.X.22-4, MunichU 322-5, St. Gall 463, 1503[1]. Theorists: GlareanusD 288-99; Wilphlingseder (text: Miserere mei).
Editions: GlareanusM 2:361. Older octavo: by Frank Damrosch (G. Schirmer, cop.1899), Concord Series of Music ... 31 (E.C. Schirmer, 1922); see further CMP
Recordings: see section IV

(AVE VERUM CORPUS, 5 v.). CW Mt5 B22 (afl.48) no.80, p.90
2. Cuius latus perforatum
3. O dulcis Jesu
Canon in tenor: Fuga in epidiapente
145 mm.
Sources: 1545[2], 1568[7]
Discussion: SparksP 352-3 (questions authenticity)

Ave virginum decus hominem = Illibata Dei, part 2

BAISEZ MOY, MA DOULCE AMYE.   CW Wl B2 (afl.5) no.20a, p.53
   39 mm.
   Text: HewittC 68
   Sources: Brussels/Tournai, Cortona/Paris (lacking bass),
      Paris Res.Vm^7 504 (= [1535]^{14}), 1502^2, 1520^3
   Discussion: HewittC ix-x, 68-9
   Edition: HewittC 186-7; for octavo eds. see CMP
   Recordings: see section IV
(BAISEZ MOY, MA DOULCE AMYE, 6 v.).   CW Wl B2 (afl.5) no.20,
      p.51
   39 mm.
   Canon in superius: Fuga in diatessaron; Canon in bass:
      Fuga
   Sources: Copenhagen 1848, 1502^2, 1545^{15}, J1550
   Discussion: BlumeJD, HewittC ix-x, 71-2 (both question
      authenticity)
   Edition: HewittC 195
   Recordings: see section IV
Beata mater et intacto virgo = tenor of O virgo prudentissima
(BEATI QUORUM REMISSAE SUNT INIQUITATES, 5 v.).   CW Mt4 B16
      (afl.40) no.62, p.1
   2. Verum tamen in diluvio
   3. In camo et freno
   264 mm.
   Text: Psalm 31 (English 32)
   Sources: Berlin 40031, 1538^6, 1553^4
   Discussion: Osthoff 2:229-31 (questions authenticity)
BELLE, POUR L'AMOUR DE VOUS
   38 mm.
   Sources: Brussels 11239 (anon.), Florence Magl.XIX 178
   Edition: PickerC 428
Benedic, Domine, domum istam = Stetit autem Salomon, part 2
BENEDICITE OMNIA OPERA DOMINI.   CW Mt3 B13 (afl.37) no.53,
      p.86
   201 mm.
   Text: Canticle, Daniel 3:57-74
   Sources: Zwickau LXXXI 2, 1537^1, 1553^6, 1559^2
   Discussion: LowinskyT 20-25
   Recording: see section IV
BENEDICTA ES, CAELORUM REGINA, 6 v.   CW Mt3 B11 (afl.35)
      no.46, p.11
   2. Per illud ave (2 v.)
   3. Nunc mater ex ora (6 v.)
   175 mm.
   Text: Marian sequence. See BesselerA
   Sources: Bologna R 142 (quintus v.), Copenhagen 1872
      (anon.), Edinburgh 64 (anon.), Louvain 163, Munich 1536,

MunichU Art.401, Padua A17 (anon.), Rome Sist.16, Rome
SMM 26, Seville 1, Toledo 18, Toledo 22, Uppsala 76c,
Utrecht, Valladolid 255 (tenor), 1520[4], 1537[1], 1553[1],
J1555, 1558[4]. Sources of part 2 only: Munich 260,
Regensburg B.220-2, 1546[6], 1590[18]. Theorists:
GlareanusD 347, 1591[26]
Intabulations: 1547[22] (anon.), 1547[23] (anon.), 1552[29]
(anon.), 1554[32], 1558[20], B1558[6], 1562[28], B1563[12] (anon.),
1574[13], 1578[29], Munich 264. Parts 1, 3: 1553[33].
Part 2: 1547[25], 1551[22], 1556[32] (anon.), B1556[5-6]
(anon.)
Other arrangement: 12 v., att. J. and Johannes Castille-
tus: Munich 1536, 1558[4], 1589[17]
Discussion: AntonowyczM
Editions: BesselerA, MonteCW 38, SmijersV 5:146
Recordings: see section IV
Benedicta tu in mulieribus = tenor of Ave nobilissima
creatura
BERGERETTE SAVOYENNE. CW W2 B4 (afl.53) no.36, p.3
55 mm.
Text: JefferyL 409-10; BrownMF no.36
Sources: Florence Magl.XIX 107[bis], St. Gall 463, Segovia,
1501
Editions: HewittO no.10; octavo eds. see CMP
Recordings: see section IV

CAELI ENNARUNT GLORIAM DEI. CW Mt3 B15 (afl.39) no.61,
p.146
2. Lex Domini immaculata
3. Dilecta quis intelligit
362 mm.
Text: Psalm 18 (English 19)
Sources: Kassel 24, 1538[6], 1553[4]
(CANTATE DOMINO CANTICUM NOVUM, 5 v.). CW Mt5 B19 (afl.45)
no.72, p.8
2. Tollite hostias
224 mm.
Text: Psalm 95 (English 96)
Sources: 1539[9] (anon.), 1553[4], 1553[5]
Discussion: FinscherZ (questions authenticity)
CE PAUVRE MENDIANT (Fortune d'estrange plummaige), 3 v.
CW W2 B4 (afl.53) no.46, p.22
Tenor: Pauper sum ego (Psalm 87:16)
45 mm.
Sources: Brussels 228 (anon.), FlorenceC Bas.2439 (text:
Fortune d'estrange ...), London Add. 35087 (anon.;
text: Pauper sum in all parts)
Editions: Osthoff 2:385, PickerC 389

CELA SANS PLUS, 3 v.   CW W2 B4 (afl.53) no.44, p.18
     57 mm.
     Text: incipit only.   Cf. BrownMF no.61
     Sources: Paris Res.Vm[7] 504 (III), St. Gall 461, Verona
          757, Zwickau LXXVIII,3, 1501
     Editions: HewittO no.61, BoerC 82, Giesbert 2:100
     Recording: see section IV
(CENT MILLE REGRETS, 5 v.).   CW W1 B3 (afl.8) no.26, p.68
     62 mm.
     Sources: Rome Pal.1at 1982 (att. LaRue), Vienna 18746
          (anon.), J1550
     Reference: Osthoff 2:185 (questions authenticity)
Chant du soldat = Scaramella
Christi, fili Dei = Vultum tuum, part 7
CHRISTUM DUCEM.   CW Mt1 B1 (afl.2) no.4, p.21
     (Part 6 of Qui velatus, q.v.)
     129 mm.
     Sources: Hradec Králové II A 6, II A 7; Padua A17; 1514[1]
(CHRISTUS MORTUUS EST, 6 v.).   CW Mt5 B24 (afl.51) no.87,
          p.146
     Tenor: Circumdederunt me.   Osthoff 2:94 suggests this
          work is part 2 of a 3-part work of which each part
          uses the same tenor (part 1: *Videte omnes*; part 3:
          Sic Deus dilexit).   NobleJ considers *Videte* a contra-
          factum of *Nymphes, nappés*, and questions the authenticity
          of *Christus mortuus* and *Sic Deus*.
     Sources: Zwickau LXXIII, 1564[3]
     Discussion: CrevelA 103-34; see further *Nymphes, nappés*
          below
Circumdederunt me = Nymphes, nappés
Circumdederunt me (chant) = tenor of Christus mortuus est,
          Nymphes, nappés, and Sic Deus dilexit
Clama ne cesses = Canon in M. l'homme armé svm: Agnus 3
COEUR LANGOREULX, 5 v.   CW W1 B1 (afl.3) no.1, p.1
     61 mm.
     Sources: 1545[15], J1550, 1572[2]
     Intabulation: Munich 266 (anon.)
     Recording: see section IV
(COEURS DESOLEZ, 4 v.).   CW W1 B3 (afl.8) no.32, p.81
     61 mm.
     Sources: Munich 1516 (anon.), 1528[6]
     References: Osthoff 2:184-5, HeartzP 215 both consider
          Appenzeller the composer
     Editions: Chorwerk 3, PAPTM 6; octavo eds. see CMP
     Recording: see section IV
COEURS DESOLEZ, 5 v.   CW W1 B3 (afl.8) no.28, p.72
     Tenor: Plorans ploravit
     52 mm.

Text: JefferyL 411
Source: J1550
Discussion: PickerJG, Osthoff 1:65ff.
Recordings: see section IV
Comme femme desconfortée = tenor of Stabat mater
COMMENT PEULT HAVER IOYE. CW W2 B5 (af1.54) no.56, p.18
    59 mm.
    Canon in tenor: Fuga duorum temporum per dyapason
    Sources: Bologna Q 17, Florence Magl.XIX 178, Paris
      Res.Vm^7 504 (= [1535]^{14}; anon.), Rome Giul.XIII.27,
      1502^2. Theorist: GlareanusD 356 (Text: O Jesu fili David)
    Intabulation: 1507^6 (anon.)
    Discussion: AtlasC 1:60, HewittC 46-8, OsthoffW
    Editions: HewittC 145, Chorwerk 30 as O Jesu, GlareanusM
      434 as O Jesu. Octavo eds. CMP
    Recordings: see section IV
Cor meum conturbatus est = Domine ne in furore (Ps.37),
      part 2
(CREDO). CW Ma4 B2 (af1.50) no.6, p.132
    2. Et incarnatus est
    239 mm.
    Source: Cambrai 18
    Reference: Osthoff 1:200
CREDO CHIASCUN ME CRIE. CW Ma4 B2 (af1.50) no.5, p.124
    2. Crucifixus
    3. Et unam sanctam
    205 mm.
    Sources: Cambrai 18, Munich 53 (att. Brumel), Rome Sist.
      23 ("des rouges nez"), Rome SMM JJ III.4 (anon.), Vienna
      11778, 1505^1
CREDO DE TOUS BIENS PLAYNE. CW Ma4 B1 (af1.44), no.2, p.94
    2. Et incarnatus
    3. Et in spiritum (2 v.; canon: Duo in carne una)
    4. Qui cum patre
    Based on Hayne van Ghizeghem chanson (Odhecaton no.20)
    206 mm.
    Recording: see section IV
CREDO VILAYGE (I). CW Ma4 B1 (af1.44) no.3, p.102
    2. Qui propter
    3. Crucifixus
    4. Et in spiritum
    5. Qui cum Patre
    391 mm.
    Based on Credo 1 (L.U.64)
    Source: 1505^1
    Discussion: BorrenE
(CREDO VILAYGE (II)). CW Ma4 B2 (af1.50) no.4, p.118
    2. Crucifixus

Compositions

148 mm.
Sources: Munich 53 (att. Brumel), Rome Sist.23 (anon.),
     Vienna 11778, 1505^{1}
Credo Vilayge, 5 v. = M. de beata virgine: Credo
Cuius gloriam = Verbum caro factum est, part 3
Cuius latus perforatum = Ave verum corpus, part 2
Cum ergo cognovissit = Responsum acceperat Simeon, part 2

Da siceram mentibus = Je ne me puis tenir
Date siceram moerentibus = Je ne me puis tenir
(DE PROFUNDIS CLAMAVI [Mixolydian]). CW Mt5 B25 (afl.52)
     no.91, p.177
     2. A custodia matutina
     174 mm.
     Sources: Kassel 24, 1539^{9}
     Editions: Chorwerk 33; Dessoff Choir Series 48
DE PROFUNDIS CLAMAVI (Phrygian). CW Mt3 B11 (afl.35) no.47,
     p.20
     2. A custodia matutina
     167 mm.
     Text: Psalm 129 (English 130)
     Sources: Dresden 1/D/6 (bass), Erlangen 473/4, Kassel 24,
          Regensburg C.120 (anon.), Vienna 15941 (att. Champion),
          1520^{4}, 1521^{3}, $[1521]^{7}$ (altus), 1539^{9}. Theorist:
          GlareanusD 374
     Discussion: Hoffman-ErbrechtP 289-91
     Editions: Chorwerk 57, PAPTM 6, RiemannH 2/1:260
     Recordings: see section IV
DE PROFUNDIS CLAMAVI, 5 v. CW Mt5 B24 (afl.51) no.90, p.170
     117 mm.
     Text: Psalm 129 (English 130) with added Requiem ...
          Kyrie ... Pater noster
     Sources: Kassel 24, Rome Sist.38 (with canon: Les trois
          estas sont assemblés pour le soulas des trespasses),
          1521^{4}
     Discussion: KellmanJ 189-90, DunningS 102-4
     Edition: Chorwerk 57
DE TOUS BIENS PLAYNE, 3 v.
     60 mm.
     Superius of Hayne van Ghizeghem chanson with textless
          lower parts. Tenor canon: Fuga per semibrevem in
          netesinemenon
     Source: 1502^{1}
     Edition: Osthoff 2:395
DE TOUS BIENS PLAYNE. CW W2 B4 (afl.53) no.49b, p.31
     60 mm.
     Superius and tenor of Hayne van Ghizeghem chanson; bass
          and alto in canon: "Petrus et Johannes current in puncto"

Sources: 1501, GlareanusD 460 ("Fuga ad minimam")

Reference: BrownMF no.73

Edition: GlareanusM 529

Recordings: see section IV

De tous biens playne (Hayne superius) = Superius of Victimae
  paschali laudes, part 2; superius of Scimus quoniam;
  see also Credo De tous biens playne

Delevi ut nubem = Faulte d'argent

Déploration *see* Nymphes des bois

(DESCENDI IN ORTUM MEUM). CW supp. no.6, p.26

  93 mm.

  Text: Song of Solomon 6:10, 12, alleluia

  Sources: London Roy.8.G.VII (anon.), Rome Pal.lat.1976-9
    (anon.), Vienna 15941 (lacks superius)

  Discussion: NobleJ 734 (questions authenticity)

  Edition: Osthoff 2:378

Deus autem noster in caelo = In exitu Israel, part 2

Deus custodit te = Levavi oculos meos, part 2

(DEUS, IN NOMINE TUO SALVUM ME FAC). CW Mt2 B10 (af1.25)
  no.44, p.127

  2. Voluntarie sacrificabo

  253 mm.

  Sources: Rome Sist.46 (att. Carpentras), 1519[3] (anon.),
    1553[5]

  Edition: CarpentrasCW 5

(DEUS PACIS REDUXIT A MORTUIS). CW Mt3 B14 (af1.38) no.57,
  p.116

  2. Is absolutos et perfectos

  217 mm.

  Sources: Budapest Pr.6 (anon.), Zwickau LXXXI 2 (att.
    Stolzer), 1538[3]

Dic nobis, Maria = Victimae paschali laudes, part 2

Dilecta quis intelligit = Caeli ennarrunt, part 3

Diligam te, Domine = Text of Agnus 2, M. Ave maris, in 1545[7]

Doleo super te = Planxit autem David, part 4

DOMINE, DOMINUS NOSTER, 5 v. CW Mt5 B24 (af1.51) no.89,
  p.161

  159 mm.

  Text: Psalm 8

  Tenor canon: Crescite et multiplicamine

  Sources: Dresden Gr.59a, Halle Ed.1147, Kassel 24 (anon.),
    1553[4]

  Discussion: EldersZ 102-4

  Edition: Chorwerk 64

DOMINE, EXAUDI ORATIONEM MEAM. CW Mt5 B25 (af1.52) no.92,
  p.189

  2. Memor fui

  3. Spiritus tuus bonus

341 mm.
Text: Psalm 142 (English 143)
Sources: Kassel 24, 1553[6]
Edition: Chorwerk 64
Domine Jesu Christe *see* O Domine Jesu Christe
Domine, labia mea aperies = Miserere mei, Deus, part 3
Domine memineris = Domine non secundum peccata, part 2
DOMINE, NE IN FUORE TUO (Ps.37; English Ps.38). CW Mt2 B8
    (afl.21) no.39, p.81
    2. Cor meum conturbatum est
    208 mm.
    Sources: Heilbronn XCII/3-XCVI/3, Hradek Králové II A 21,
       Kassel 24, London Add. 19583/Modena/Paris, Regensburg
       C.120 (anon.), Zwickau LXXXI 2, 1519[2], 1538[6], 1553[4]
    Edition: Chorwerk 33
    Recordings: see section IV
DOMINE, NE IN FURORE TUO (Ps.6). CW Mt3 B15 (afl.39) no.59,
    p.131
    2. Turbatus est a furore
    168 mm.
    Sources: Bologna Q 20, Dresden 1/D/6 (bass; anon.),
       Heilbronn XCII/3-XCVI/3 (anon.), London Add. 19583/
       Modena, 1538[6], 1553[4]
DOMINE, NE PROJICIAS ME. CW Mt4 B16 (afl.40) no.64, p.23
    2. Sed tibi soli peccavi
    215 mm.
    Text: see Osthoff 2:135
    Sources: Berlin 40031, Heilbronn XCII/3-XCVI/3 (anon.),
       1538[6], 1553[5]
DOMINE, NON SECUNDUM PECCATA, 2-4 v. CW Mt1 B2 (afl.4)
    no.13, p.51
    1. Domine non secundum (2 v.)
    2. Domine memineris (2 v.)
    3. Quia paupere (4 v.)
    4. Adjuva nos (4 v.)
    248 mm.
    Text: Tract (L.U.527)
    Sources: BarcelonaOC 5, Berlin 40013, MunichU 322-5,
       Nürnberg 83795 (tenor, bass), Rome Sist.35 (parts 1,
       2, 4), Rome SP B 80, 1503[1], 1549[16] (parts 1-2),
       GlareanusD 246-50
    Edition: GlareanusM 311
Dominus memor fuit nostri = In exitu Israel, part 3
DOMINUS REGNAVIT. CW Mt4 B17 (afl.41) no.65, p.33
    2. Mirabiles elationes maris
    176 mm.
    Text: Psalm 92 (English 93)

Sources: Leipzig 51 (tenor, bass), 1539[9], 1553[5]
Editions: Chorwerk 33, NAWM 30
Recordings: see section IV
DOULEUR ME BAT, 5 v.   CW W1 B2 (af1.5) no.18, p.40
   62 mm.
   Sources: Vienna 18746 (anon., textless), 1545[15], J1550
   Recording: see section IV
DU MIEN AMANT, 5 v.   CW W1 B2 (af1.5) no.23, p.59
   Residuum: Or au facteur de toute creature
   94 mm.
   Sources: Vienna 18746, 1545[15], J1550
   Discussion: BenthemZ
DULCES EXUVIAE.   CW W2 B5 (af1.54) no.51, p.4
   85 mm.
   Text: Virgil, *Aeneid* IV:651-4 (death of Dido)
   Sources: London Roy.8.G.VII, 1559[2]
   Discussion: LowinskyJ 19, OsthoffV 88-94, SkeiD, StrunkV
      485-7
   Edition: Chorwerk 54
   Recordings: see section IV
Dum complerentur = Lectio actuum apostolorum
D'ung aultre amer (Ockeghem) = Superius of Victimae, part 1

Ecce Maria genuit nobis salvatorem = O admirabile, part 5
ECCE, TU PULCHRA ES, AMICA MEA.   CW Mt2 B6 (af1.16) no.30,
   p.1
   98 mm.
   Text: Song of Solomon excerpts; see Osthoff 2:113
   Sources: Bologna Q 19, Bologna R 142, Cortona 95/6,
      Florence II.I.232, Seville 1, Ulm 237, Verona 758,
      Verona 760, J1502
   Intabulation: 1552[35] (title: Tota pulchra es)
   Edition: Chorwerk 18
Ego sum ipse que deleo = Tenez moy
Eja ergo = Salve regina (no.48), part 2
EL GRILLO.   CW W2 B5 (af1.54) no.53, p.19
   35 mm.
   Source: 1505[4] (att. Josquin Dascanio)
   Discussion: GallicoJ 450-54, JeppesenF 3:18
   Editions: IM140, 50*; facsimile 144. ScheringG 71.
      Octavo eds. see CMP
   Recordings: see section IV
EN L'OMBRE D'UNG BUISSONET AU MATINET, 3 v.   CW W2 B5
   (af1.54) no.61, p.28
   77 mm.
   Text: BenthemJ 440-42, BrownMF no.97
   Sources: Paris f.fr.1597, St. Gall 461, 1536[1], 1578[15]

     Discussion: BenthemJ 426-8
     Edition: Giesbert 2:68
EN L'OMBRE D'UNG BUISSONET AU MATINET, 4 v.   CW W2 B5 (af1.54)
     no.59, p.24
     41 mm.
     Text: see above
     Sources: FlorenceC Bas.2442, Munich 1516 (anon.), Paris
        f.fr.2245, RomeC 2856, 1504^3, 1520^3 (anon.), 1536^1
EN L'OMBRE D'UNG BUISONNET TOUT AU LOING D'UNE RIVYERE, 3 v.
     CW W2 B5 (af1.54) no.60, p.26
     43 mm.
     Text: BenthemJ 437-40, BrownMF no.97
     Sources: Bologna Q 17, Brussels/Tournai, London Add.
        35087, Paris Res.Vm^7 504 (= [1535]^{14}), 1536^1, 1562^9,
        1578^{15}
     Intabulation: B1533$_1$
     Discussion: OsthoffJ
(EN NON SAICHANT, 5 v.).   CW W1 B1 (af1.3) no.9, p.21
     53 mm.
     Sources: Leipzig 49-50 (text: Venite ad me omnes),
        1545^{15}, J1550
     Discussion: BenthemZ (questions authenticity); BlackburnJ
        44-9 (defends authenticity, clarifies sources)
     Edition: Chorwerk 3
ENTRÉ JE SUIS EN GRANT PENSÉE, 3 v.   CW W2 B5 (af1.54) no.58,
     p.23
     45 mm.
     Text: BenthemJ 431-2
     Source: FlorenceR 2794
     Discussion: BenthemJ 427
     Editions: BenthemJ 432, PickerC 479
ENTRÉ JE SUIS EN GRANT PENSÉE, 4 v.   CW W2 B5 (af1.54) no.57,
     p.20
     55 mm.
     Sources: With above text: Augsburg 142a (anon.),
        Brussels 228 (Entrée suis en pensée; anon.), Cortona/
        Paris (anon.), FlorenceC Bas.2439 (Par vous je suis),
        Florence Mag1.XIX 164-7, MunichU 328-31 (anon.), Vienna
        18810. With text In meinen sinn: Basel F.X.1-4, 1535^{11},
        1535^{13}
     Discussion: BenthemC, PickerP
     Editions: Osthoff 2:393, PickerC 285, PAPTM 6 (In meinen
        synn)
     Recordings: see section IV
Et ecce terraemotus factus est = tenor of In illo tempore
     stetit
Et Jesum benedictum = Salve regina (no.48), part 3

Et post transmigrationem Babylon = Liber generationis, part 3
Et ut advertat indignationem = Recordare virgo mater, part 2
Et verbum caro factum est = In principio, part 3
Exaudi Domine (2 v.) = M. pange lingua: Agnus 2, text in
    1545[6]

Facta autem hac voce = Lectio actuum apostolorum, part 2
FACTUM EST AUTEM. CW Mt1 B3 (af1.6) no.16, p.70
    2. Qui fuit Heli
    3. Qui fuit Obed
    398 mm.
    Text: Luke 3:21-4:1
    Sources: LondonR 1070 (incomplete, anon.), 1504[1]
FAMA, MALUM. CW W2 B5 (af1.54) no.50, p.1
    83 mm.
    Text: Virgil, *Aeneid* IV:174-7
    Sources: London Roy.8.G.VII, St. Gall 463
    Discussion: LowinskyJ 19, OsthoffV 94-6
    Edition: Chorwerk 54
    Recordings: see section IV
Fanfare/Fanfare for Louis XII *see* Vive le roy
Fantazies de Joskin *see* Ile fantazies
(FAULTE D'ARGENT, 5 v.). CW W1 B2 (af1.5) no.15, p.38
    73 mm.
    Text: JefferyL 412-3, BrownMF no.131
    Sources: Augsburg 142a, Copenhagen 1873, FlorenceC
        Bas.2442, Leipzig 49 (anon.; text: Delevi ut nubem),
        Uppsala 76c, 1545[15], J1550, E1560c (= 1572[2])
    Intabulations: B1543[1], 1565[22], 1574[12]
    Discussion: BenthemZ (questions authenticity), Blackburn
        42, 49-50
    Editions: HAM 91; octavo editions listed CMP
    Recordings: see section 4
Fecit potentiam (2 v.) = Magnificat quarti toni, part 6
Felli sitim magni regis = Huc me sydereo, part 2
Filiae Jerusalem = O virgo virginum, part 2
(FORTUNA DESPERATA, 3 v.). CW W2 B4 (af1.53) no.48b, p.27
    57 mm.
    Uses superius and tenor of Busnois chanson; bass att. J
    Source: Segovia
FORTUNA D'UN GRAN TEMPO, 3 v. CW supp. no.13a-b, pp.62, 63
    47 mm.
    Text: incipit only
    Sources: Florence Pan.27 (anon.), Paris Res.Vm[7] 504
        (= [1535][14], anon.), 1501 (later eds.: 1503[2], 1504[2],
        anon.)
    Intabulations: 1507[5] (anon.), Basel F.IX.22, Basel
        F.VI.26(c), Berlin 40026 (WarburtonK 95, BenthemFE)

     Discussion: BenthemF; J 691-5, 751; JeppesenF 3:22ff.;
        LowinskyA 71-2; LowinskyF
     Editions: J 693, HewittO
     Recordings: see section IV
Fortune d'estrange plummaige = Ce povre mendiant
Fuit homo missus a Deo (4 v.) = In principio, part 2
Fuit homo missus a Deo (6 v.) = Inter natos mulierum, part 2

GAUDE VIRGO, MATER CHRISTI.   CW Mt1 B4 (af1.7) no.23, p.114
     107 mm.
     Text: Sequence (Dreves, *Analecta hymnica* 15:76)
     Sources: Brussels 9126, Ulm 237, 1505[2]
     Edition: Reeser
Germinavit radix Jesse = O admirabile, part 4
GLORIA DE BEATA VIRGINE.   CW Ma4 B1 (af1.44) no.1, p.85
     2. Qui tollis
     3. Cum sancto spiritu
     208 mm.
     Text: includes *Spiritus et alme* trope
     Sources: Florence II.I.232, 1505[1]
(GUILLAUME S'EN VA CHAUFFER)
     27 mm.
     Sources: St. Gall 462, GlareanusD 469 (without text)
     Discussion: Clinkscale, NobleJ 736 (questions authen-
        ticity); see also p. 8 above
     Editions: Clinkscale, GlareanusM 2:547, SMd5:92
     Recordings: see section IV

Haec dicit Dominus = Nymphes, nappés
HELAS MADAME, 3 (4) v.   CW supp. no.11, p.55
     144 mm.
     Text: incipit only; see BenthemJ 422n.
     Sources: Florence Mag1.XIX 178, Seville 5-I-43 (superius).
        4 v.: Florence BR.229, FlorenceR 2356
HOMO QUIDAM FECIT COENAM MAGNAM, 5 v.   CW Mt1 B5 (af1.9)
        no.28, p.147
     2. Venite, comedite
     132 mm.
     Text: Luke 14:16ff.
     Uses canonic c.f. (L.U.1856)
     Sources: LondonR 1070 (anon.), Rome Sist.42, Toledo 22,
        Zwickau LXXIII, 1508[1]
     Edition: LenaertsK
HONOR, DECUS, IMPERIUM.   CW supp. no.2, p.7
     19 mm.
     Text: verse 2 of *Nardi Maria pistici*, hymn for St. Mary
        Magdalene (Dreves, *Analecta hymnica* 51:73; MMMA 1:
        no.753)

Source: Rome Sist.15
Edition: Osthoff 2:377
Hora qui ductis tertia = Qui velatus, part 2
HUC ME SYDEREO DESCENDERE, 6 v. CW Mt2 B6 (af1.16) no.32,
     p.11
    2. Felli sitim magni regis
    194 mm.
    Tenor: Plangent eum (L.U.735)
    Text: by Mapheus Vegius; see LowinskyJ 18
    Sources: Bologna R 142, Brussels 9126, Budapest Pr.6,
       Copenhagen 1872 (anon.), Florence II.I.232, Leiden
       863, LondonR 1070 (anon.), Regensburg 893, Rome Sist.45,
       St. Gall 463-4, 1519[2], 1538[3], J1555, 1558[4]
    Discussion: DammannS 27; EldersP 526-7 and EldersZZ
       (suggest a link with Ave nobilissima); FinscherZ 67-8
    Recordings: see section IV

Il ne me chault = Plaine de dueil, part 3
ILE FANTAZIES, 3 v. CW W2 B4 (af1.53) no.43, p.16
    50 mm.
    Text: none
    Sources: RomeC 2856, St. Gall 462
    Editions: WolfS 19, SMd 5
    Recordings: see section IV
ILLIBATA DEI VIRGO NUTRIX, 5 v. CW Mt1 B5 (af1.14) no.27,
     p.140
    2. Ave virginum decus hominem
    193 mm.
    Tenor: "La mi la illibata"
    Text: J 558-9 (Eng. translation; see further below)
    Sources: Rome Sist.15 (anon.), 1508[1]
    Discussion: AntonowyczI, EldersJ; see further section
       IA1 (Place of birth) above, p.4
    Recordings: see section IV
Illumina oculos meos = Usquequo, Domine, part 2
In amara crucis ara = Qui velatus, part 4
In camo et freno = Beati quorum remissae, part 3
(IN DOMINO CONFIDO). CW Mt5 B19 (af1.45) no.73, p.20
    2. Oculi eius in pauperum
    178 mm.
    Text: Psalm 10 (English 11)
    Sources: Kassel 24 (anon.), 1538[6] (anon.), 1553[3], 1553[4]
    NobleJ 734 (questions authenticity)
    Recording: see section IV
IN EXITU ISRAEL DE EGYPTO. CW Mt3 B12 (af1.36) no.51, p.58
    2. Deus autem noster
    3. Dominus memor fuit nostri
    401 mm.

Text: Psalm 113 (English 114)
Sources: Dresden 1/D/6 (bass; anon.), Kassel 24, Rome
   Sist.38, Toledo 22, Vienna 15941, 1537[1], 1559[2]
Intabulations: 1553[35] (anon.), 1558[20], 1570[35], Munich
   272 (anon.)
Discussion: NovackT 329-32
Recording: see section IV
In flagellis potum felis = Qui velatus, part 3
In Idumeam extendam = Paratum cor meum, part 3
IN ILLO TEMPORE ASSUMPSIT JESUS DUODECIM DISCIPULOS. CW Mt5
   B22 (afl.48) no.79, p.85
   121 mm.
   Text: Matthew 20:17-19
   Sources: Königsberg 1740, Rome Sist.38, Toledo 13
   Discussion: NovackF 196-200
(IN ILLO TEMPORE STETIT JESUS, 6 v.). CW Mt3 B14 (afl.38)
   no.55, p.99
   123 mm.
   Tenor: Et ecce terraemotus (L.U.782)
   Text: Luke 24:36-41
   Sources: Bologna R 142, Copenhagen 1872, Copenhagen 1873,
      Stuttgart 25 (anon.), Wroclau 5, 1538[3], 1559[1]
   Discussion: SparksP 324-6 (questions authenticity)
   Edition: PAPTM 6
In meinem Sinn = Entré je suis
In pace in idipsum *see* Que vous madame
IN PRINCIPIO ERAT VERBUM. CW Mt3 B14 (afl.38) no.56, p.106
   2. Fuit homo missus a Deo
   3. Et verbum caro factum est
   256 mm.
   Text: John 1
   Sources: Modena IX, Munich 10, Regensburg 840, Regens-
      burg 940-41, Rome Sist.38, Toledo 22, Wroclau 6,
      1538[3] (parts 1-2), 1554[10]
   Intabulations: 1552[35], 1553[33]
   Edition: Chorwerk 23
   Recordings: see section IV
In principio erat verbum (5 v.) = Verbum caro factum est,
   part 2
IN TE DOMINI SPERAVI, PER TROVAR PIETA
   33 mm.
   Text: IM 19*
   Sources: Basel F.X.17-20 (anon.), Basel F.X.22-4,
      Bologna Q 18 (textless), Erlangen 473-4, Florence BR 337,
      Florence Pan.27, FlorenceC Bas.2441, Leipzig 51, London
      Eg.3051, Madrid 1335, MunichU 326-7 (anon.), Paderborn
      9822-3, Paris Res.Vm/ 676, Regensburg 940-41, Sion Tir.

84-7, St. Gall 463, 1504[4] (J. Dascanio), 1538[8] (text all Latin)

Intabulations: 1509[3] (ed. DisertoriF 401), 1544[24] (anon.)

Discussion: GallicoJ 450-51

Editions: IM 38 (facsimile CXXII), Barbieri 68, Schwartz 37, MME 5:84 (facsimile p.24), HAM 95b

Recordings: see section IV

INCESSAMENT LIVRÉ SUIS À MARTIRE, 5 v.   CW W1 B1 (afl.3)
   no.9, p.13

   68 mm.

   Sources: Vienna 18746 (anon., textless), 1545[15], J1550

   Discussion: BenthemZ

   Editions: Chorwerk 3, PAPTM 6

   Recording: see section IV

(INCESSAMENT MON POVRE CUEUR LAMENTE, 5 v.).   CW W1 B3 (afl.8)
   no.27, p.70

   53 mm.

   Sources: Bologna R 141 (anon.), Munich 1508 (anon.), St. Gall 461 (att. LaRue), Vienna 18746 (anon.), J1550, E1560c (= 1572[2], att. LaRue)

   Discussion: BenthemZ

   Recording: see section IV

Iniquos odio habui (only tenor extant).   CW supp. no.17, p.85
   Source: Bologna R 142

Intemerata virgo = Vultum tuum, part 3

(INTER NATOS MULIERUM, 6 v.).   CW Mt5 B23 (afl.49) no.84, p.125
   2. Fuit homo missus a Deo

   88 mm.

   Text: Matthew 11:11, John 1:6

   Sources: Bologna R 142 (tenor), Rome Sist.38 (anon.), RomeV San Borromeo II.55-60

   Discussions: AntonowyczZ, SparksP 356-7

INVIOLATA, INTEGRA ET CASTA ES, MARIA, 5 v.   CW Mt2 B10 (afl.25) no.42, p.111
   2. Nostra ut pura

   3. O benigna regina

   147 mm.

   Text: LowinskyMRM 3:180 (with Eng. translation)

   Based on chant (L.U.1861; cf. EldersP 551-2)

   Sources: Barcelona 681, FlorenceM 666, London Add. 19583/ Paris, Modena IX, MunichU 326, Regensburg 891-2, Regensburg C.120, Rome Sist.24, St. Gall 463, Seville 1, Toledo 10, 1519[3], 1520[4], 1521[3], [c1521][7], 1538[3], J1555, 1559[1]

   Intabulations: B1533[1] (anon.), 1547[25], 1558[20], 1578[24], Munich 267

Discussion: EldersP 551-2, LowinskyMRM 3:180-82, 104
Editions: LowinskyMRM 4:231-40, PAPTM 6
Recordings: see section IV
(INVIOLATA, INTEGRA ET CASTA ES, MARIA, 12 v.).   CW supp.
   no.10, p.45
  48 mm.
Tenor: O Maria flos virginum
Source: Kassel 38
Discussion: EldersP 539-40
Ipsum regem angelorum = Nesciens mater, part 2
Is absolutos et perfectos = Deus pacis reduxit, part 2

J'AY BIEN CAUSE DE LAMENTER, 6 v.   CW W1 B3 (afl.8) no.33,
   p.83
  44 mm.
Sources: Hamburg s.s., 1540[7]
Discussion: Osthoff 2:226-7 suggests text was later
  added to an instrumental work.
Edition: Ambros 5:125
Recordings: see section IV
J'ay bien nourri sept ans = J'ay bien rise tant
(J'AY BIEN RISE TANT, 3 v.)
  54 mm.
Sources: Florence BR 229 ("J'ay bien nori," att.
  Japart), Florence Magl.XIX 178, Rome Giul.XIII.27
  (anon.), Segovia ("J'ay bien norri," att. Joye)
Discussion: AtlasC 1:79-81
Edition: AtlasC 2:14
JE ME ..., 3 v.
No further text known
Source: Florence Magl.XIX 178
Edition: Osthoff 2:167, mm. 1-9
JE ME COMPLAINS, 5 v.   CW W1 B1 (afl.3) no.11, p.26
  57 mm.
Sources: Munich 1508, Vienna 18746 (anon., textless),
  1545[15], J1550, E1560c (= 1572[2])
Discussion: Curtis, BenthemZ
Edition: octavo ed. see CMP
Recordings: see section IV
JE NE ME PUIS TENIR D'AIMER, 5 v.   CW W1 B3 (afl.8) no.31, p.78
  79 mm.
Text: BlackburnJ 40
Sources: Munich 1508 (anon.), J1550, E1560c (= 1572[2]).
  With text *Date siceram moerentibus*: Budapest 23,
  MunichU 326 (alto; anon.), Regensburg 1018 (anon.),
  Regensburg B.211-5 (anon.), Wroclaw 12 (anon.)
Intabulations: London Add. 29247 (att. Gombert). With
  title *Date siceram*: Krakow 1716 (att. N.C.), 1558[20]

(att. Claudin), 1562^{24} (anon.). With title *Respice in me*: $B1546_{14}$ (att. Gombert). With title *Lauda Syon*: 1554^{32} (att. Gombert)

    Discussion: BenthemZ, BlackburnJ 30–42, J 683–91
    Editions: BlackburnJ 68, J 685; octavo ed. see CMP
    Recordings: see section IV
Je ne veultz mary = La belle se siet, part 2
Je ne vis oncques la pareille = tenor of L'amye a tous
JE N'OSE PLUS, 3 v.
    Text: incipit only
    Source: Florence Magl.XIX 178
    Edition: Osthoff 2:189
Je prens congié *see* Tulerunt Dominum
JE RIS ET SI AY LARME. CW supp. no.12, p.61
    37 mm.
    Sources: FlorenceC Bas.2442, St. Gall 463 (anon.),
      Ulm 237 (anon.)
JE SEY BIEN DIRE. CW W2 B4 (afl.53) no.38, p.7
    57 mm.
    Text: incipit only
    Source: 1504^{3}
    Edition: Ambros 5:129
Je te requiers = Plaine de dueil, part 2
JUBILATE DEO OMNIS TERRA. CW Mt4 B17 (afl.41) no.66, p.41
    2. Laudate nomen ejus
    124 mm.
    Text: Psalm 99 (English 100)
    Sources: Dresden 1/D/6 (bass), Dresden 1/D/501 (superius;
      anon.), Vienna SM 15500 (anon.), 1539^{9}
    Recording: see section IV
Justus es, Domine = Mirabilia testimonia tua, part 2

LA BELLE SE SIET, 3 v. CW W2 B5 (afl.54) no.62, p.30
    2. Je ne veultz mary
    150 mm.
    Text: BenthemJ 442
    Source: 1536^{1}
    Edition: Osthoff 2:387
LA BERNARDINA, 3 v. CW W2 B4 (afl.53) no.42, p.14
    47 mm.
    Text: incipit only
    Sources: Bologna Q 18, Munich 1516 (anon.), 1504^{3}, 1538^{9}
    Intabulations: 1507^{5} (solo and duet; ed. ScheringG 62b),
      1536^{13}
    Recordings: see section IV
LA PLUS DES PLUS, 3 v. CW W2 B4 (afl.53) no.45, p.20
    57 mm.
    Text: incipit only

Sources: Paris Res.Vm^7 504 (III) (anon.), Zwickau LXXVIII 3,
    1501, 1538^9
Intabulation: 1536^{13}
Edition: Hewitt0 no.64
Recordings: see section IV
(LA SPAGNA, 5 v.). CW W2 B5 (afl.54) no.52, p.8
    90 mm.
    Sources: Copenhagen 1872 (anon.). With text *Propter pec-
        cata* (Baruch 6:1-6): Dresden 1/D/6, Hradec Krălové 22a
        (tenor), Rokyzany (bass), 1537^1, 1559^1
    NobleJ 736 (questions authenticity)
    Recording: see section IV
L'AMYE A TOUS, 5 v. CW W1 B3 (afl.8) no.25, p.65
    83 mm.
    Tenor: Je ne viz oncques la pareille
    Source: J1550
    Discussion: BenthemZ
Latius in numerum canit = Ut Phoebi radiis, part 2
Lauda Syon *see* Je ne me puis tenir
Laudate nomen eius = Jubilate Deo, part 2
LAUDATE, PUERI, DOMINUM. CW Mt4 B18 (afl.42) no.68, p.61
    2. Ut collocet eum Dominus
    203 mm.
    Text: Psalm 112 (English 113)
    Sources: Kassel 24, Verona 760 (anon.), 1539^9 (anon.),
        1553^5
    Edition: PAPTM 6
    Recording: see section IV
Le povre mendiant = Ce povre mendiant
LE VILLAIN
    Text: incipit only (cf. JefferyL 415)
    Source: Augsburg 142a
    Edition: Osthoff 2:171, mm. 1-10
(LECTIO ACTUUM APOSTOLORUM, 5 v.). CW Mt2 B9 (afl.24) no.41,
    p.99
    2. Facta autem hac voce
    260 mm.
    Tenor: Dum complerentur dies pentecostes (L.U.884)
    Text: Acts 2:1-11
    Sources: MunichU Art.401, Rome Sist.42 (att. Viardot),
        1519^3, 1520^4 (anon.), 1526^4
LEVAVI OCULOS MEOS IN MONTES. CW Mt4 B18 (afl.42) no.70,
    p.83
    2. Dominus custodit te
    183 mm.
    Text: Psalm 120 (English 121)
    Source: 1539^9
    Analysis: NovackT 330-33

Lex Domini immaculatà = Caeli ennarrunt, part 2
L'HOMME ARMÉ. CW W2 B5 (afl.54) no.55, p.17
    19 mm.
    Canon: Et sic de singulis
    Source: 1502^2
    Discussion: DisertoriS, HewittC 23; on the melody and
      other settings see LockwoodA
    Editions: HewittC 91; others cited p.23
    Recordings: see section IV
LIBER GENERATIONIS JESU CHRISTI, 3-4 v. CW Mt1 B3 (afl.6)
    no.15, p.59
    2. Salomon autem genuit Reboam (3 v.)
    3. Et post transmigrationem Babylon (4 v.)
    384 mm.
    Text: Matthew 1:1-16
    Sources: Cortona 95/6, Dresden 1/D/505 (anon.), Florence
      II.I.232, Florence Magl.XIX 107bis, LondonR 1070 (anon.),
      Munich 10, Rome Sist.15, Toledo 22, Uppsala 76c, 1504^1,
      1538^3, J1555, 1559^2. Theorist: GlareanusD 376-87
    Edition: GlareanusM 2:454
    Recording: see section IV
Ludovici Regis Franciae jocosa cantio = Guillaume s'en va
    chauffer
Lugebat David Absalon *see* Tulerunt Dominum meum

MA BOUCHE RIT ET MON CUEUR PLEURE, 6 v. CW W1 B2 (afl.5)
    no.19, p.47
    Residuum: same text
    84 mm.
    Uses superius of Ockeghem, *Ma bouche rit* (cf. Osthoff
      2:213f.)
    Sources: Uppsala 76b (5 v.); 1545^{15}, J1550
    Discussion: Kohn
(MA DAME, HELAS, 3 v.)
    Sources: Bologna Q 16 (att.? "Dux Carlus"), Verona 757
      (anon.), Zwickau LXXVIII 3, 1501 (att. J; anon. in
      1503^2, 1504^2)
(MAGNIFICAT). CW supp. no.7, p.30
    1. Et exultavit (4 v.); 2. Quia fecit mihi magna (2 v.);
      3. Fecisti potentiam (4 v.); 4. Esurientes (3 v.)
    Source: Segovia
MAGNIFICAT QUARTI TONI. CW Mt5 B21 (afl.47) no.77, p.62
    1. Anima mea; 2. Et exultavit; 3. Quia respexit; 4. Quia
      fecit; 5. Et misericordia; 6. Fecit potentiam;
      7. Deposuit potentes; 8. Esurientes; 9. Suscepit
      Israel; 10. Sicut locutus est; 11. Gloria Patri;
      12. Sicut erat in principio
    531 mm.

Music the same in verses 2, 7, 9; in verses 4, 10; verses
6, 11; verses 3, 12
Canon, verse 10: Si cantas, numerum numera minuendo qua-
ternum
Sources: Leipzig 49 (att. Brumel), Rome Sist.44. Even
no. verses only: Modena 3 (att. LaRue), Modena 4 (att.
Agricola)
Intabulation: 1554[32] (part 6)
Discussion: KirschQ, LagasM, MaasJ, OsthoffM
Arrangement by Bruno Maderna for chorus and orchestra
MAGNIFICAT TERTII TONI, 3-4 v. CW Mt5 B21 (afl.47) no.77,
p.54
1. Et exultavit (4 v.); 2. Quia fecit (4 v.); 3. Fecit
potentiam (3 v.); 4. Esurientes (4 v.); 5. Sicut
locutus est (3 v.); 6. Sicut erat in principio (4 v.)
188 mm.
Source: Berlin 40021
Discussion: OsthoffM
MAGNUS ES TU, DOMINE. CW Mt1 B3 (afl.6) no.19a-b, p.88
2. Tu pauperum refugium (69 mm.). Part 1, version a:
43 mm.; Part 1, version b: 125 mm.
Sources: version a: Regensburg B.211-5 (att. Josquin,
"alii H.F."), 1504[1] (anon.), 1538[3] (att. Finck).
Version b: MunichU 322-5, St. Gall 463, Vienna SM 15500
(anon.), GlareanusD 272-5
Discussion, analysis: JosephA, SalzerC 402-9
Editions: GlareanusM 2:341; Part 2 only: BesselerA,
HAM 90; octavo ed.: Concord Series of Music no.62;
see further CMP
Recordings, Part 2 only: see section IV
MEMOR ESTO VERBI TUI. CW Mt2 B6 (afl.16) no.31, p.3
2. Portio mea, Domine
228 mm.
Text: Psalm 118 (English 119):49-64
Sources: Bologna R 142, Florence II.I.232, Kassel 24,
LondonR 1070 (anon.), Modena IV (anon.), Munich 19,
MunichU 322-5, Rome Sist.16, St. Gall 463, 1514[1],
1539[9], 1539[2]
Intabulation: 1536[13]
See section IA14 above
Memor fui = Domine, exaudi, part 2
Mente tota tibi supplicamus = Vultum tuum, part 5
(MI LARES VOUS TOUSJOURS LANGUIR, 5 v.). CW W1 B3 (afl.8)
no.34, p.85
43 mm.
Discussion: BenthemZ (questions authenticity)
MILLE REGRETZ. CW W1 B3 (afl.8) no.24, p.63
41 mm.

Text: JefferyL 416; HeartzC 200, 222; PickerJG 451-2
Sources: Basel F.IX.59-62 (anon.), Basel F.X.17-20
  (anon.), Berlin 40194 (anon.), Cambrai 125-8 (anon.),
  Gdansk 4003 (anon.), Munich 1501 (anon.), Munich 1516
  (anon.), 1533 (H41, att. Lemaire); 1549^{29} (with Re-
  sponse: *Les miens aussi brief* by Susato; see SillimanR),
  Ganassi 1535
Intabulations: $B1533_1$ (anon.), 1536^{13} (ed. J 466), 1538^{22}
  ("Canción del emperador"; ed. J 464, NAWM 95b), 1546^{21},
  $B1551_8$, 1552^{29} (anon.), $B1556_{5-6}$, Munich 266 (anon.),
  Munich 272 (anon.)
Discussion: BrownPC, HeartzC, PickerJG
Editions: BrownPC 143, Chorwerk 3, NAWM 45, PAPTM 6; for
  octavo eds. see CMP
Recordings: see section IV
Mirabiles elationes maris = Dominus regnavit, part 2
MIRABILIA TESTIMONIA TUA, DOMINE. CW Mt4 B18 (af1.42) no.69,
  p.69
  2. Justus es, Domine
  313 mm.
  Text: Psalm 118 (English 119):129-44
  Sources: 1539^9, 1553^3
Miserator et misericors Dominus *see* Se congié prens
Miserere mei, Deus (3 v.) = Text of Ave verum corpus in
  Wilphlingseder
MISERERE MEI DEUS, 5 v. CW Mt2 B5 (af1.21) no.37, p.58
  2. Audi, auditui meo
  3. Domine labia mea aperies
  425 mm.
  Text: Psalm 50 (English 51)
  Sources: Dresden 1/D/3, Dresden Gr.59a, FlorenceM 666,
    London Add. 19583/Modena, Munich 10, MunichU 327
    (anon.), Rome Sist.38, St. Gall 463 (with optional
    2nd bass by Bidon), 1519^2, 1520^4, 1521^3, 1537^1, 1553^4,
    1559^1
  Discussion: GlareanusD 320 (GlareanusM 2:260), Ott
    (1538^3 preface, quoted Osthoff 1:216, 2:122), LowinskyMRM
    3:95ff. and 194-9, NovackF 251-4
  Editions: LowinskyMRM 5:41, BordesA (Motet 1) 122. Oc-
    tavo ed. Frank Damrosch (G. Schirmer, *ca*. 1900); see
    also CMP
  Recordings: see section IV
Miserere nostri, Domine = Misericordias Domini, part 3
MISERICORDIAS DOMINI IN AETERNUM CANTABO. CW Mt2 B10 (af1.25)
  no.43, p.118
  2. Quoniam est Dominus suavis
  3. Miserere nostri, Domine
  284 mm.

Text: Psalm excerpts (see Osthoff 2:123)
Sources: Cortona 95-6/Paris, Florence II.I.232 (mm. 1-
    159), 1519[3], 1537[1] (anon.), 1559[2]
Discussion: J 746-7
MISSA AD FUGAM. CW Ma3 B14 (afl.28) no.14, p.61
    I. 1. Kyrie; 2. Christe; 3. Kyrie (62 mm.). II. 1. Et in
    terra; 2. Qui tollis (135 mm.). III. 1. Patrem; 2. Et
    incarnatus (205 mm.). IV. 1. Sanctus; 2. Pleni (3 v.);
    3. Hosanna (125 mm.); 4. Benedictus (3 v., 51 mm.).
    V. 1. Agnus (45 mm.); 2. Agnus (3 v., 40 mm.)
    Sources: Jena 31 (anon.; lacks Credo), Toledo 9, J1514.
    Theorist: GlareanusD (Benedictus, 218; GlareanusM
    2:292). The M. ad fugam in 1516[1] is M. sine nomine
    (see below). Rome Sist.49 contains this mass (anon.)
    with different versions of IV and V, printed separately
    CW 87-91.
    Intabulation: 1547[25] (Cum sancto spiritu), 1552[35]
(MISSA ALLEZ REGRETZ). CW Ma4 B20 (afl.43) no.20, p.61
    I. 1. Kyrie-Christe; 2. Kyrie (63 mm.). II. 1. Et in
    terra; 2. Qui tollis (81 mm.). III. 1. Patrem;
    2. Crucifixus; 3. Resurrexit (134 mm.). IV. 1. Sanctus;
    2. Pleni (2 v.); 3. Hosanna (117 mm.); 4. Benedictus
    (2 v., 57 mm.). V. 1. Agnus Dei (30 mm.); 2. Agnus
    Dei (59 mm.)
    Sources: Jena 21, Leipzig 51 (tenor, bass), Stuttgart 45
    (anon.). See further NobleJ 733 where the mass is
    listed with doubtful works.
    Based on Hayne van Ghizeghem chanson (ed. CW as above,
    p.83)
MISSA AVE MARIS STELLA. CW Ma2 B6 (afl.15) no.6, p.1
    I. 1. Kyrie; 2. Christe; 3. Kyrie (55 mm.). II. 1. Et in
    terra; 2. Qui tollis (108 mm.). III. 1. Patrem; 2. Et
    incarnatus (163 mm.). IV. 1. Sanctus; 2. Pleni (3 v.);
    3. Hosanna (121 mm.); 4. Benedictus (2 v.); 5. Qui venit
    (2 v., 36 mm.). V. 1. Agnus Dei (24 mm.); 2. Agnus
    Dei (2 v., 22 mm.); 3. Agnus Dei (38 mm.)
    Sources: Basel F.IX.25, Brussels 9126 (anon.), Frank-
    furt 2, Jena 3, Milan 2267, MilanA E 46, Rome Sist.41,
    Rome SMM JJ III 4, Stuttgart 44 (anon.), Toledo 9,
    Vienna 1783, Vienna 4809 (Agnus 2), J1505, 1539[1], 1545[7]
    (Agnus 2 with text Diligam te)
    Intabulation: 1547[25]
    Edition: AMMM 15
    Recordings: see section IV
Missa choral de Maria = Missa de beata virgine
Missa coronata = Missa de beata virgine
(MISSA DA PACEM). CW Ma4 B19 (afl.34) no.19, p.29
    I. 1. Kyrie; 2. Christe; 3. Kyrie (64 mm.). II. 1. Et in

terra; 2. Qui tollis (123 mm.). III. 1. Patrem; 2. Et
incarnatus; 3. Crucifixus (2 v.); 4. Et resurrexit
(2 v.); 5. Et iterum (202 mm.). IV. 1. Sanctus;
2. Pleni; 3. Hosanna (145 mm.); 4. Benedictus (59 mm.).
V. 1. Agnus Dei (52 mm.); 2. Agnus Dei (6 v., 47 mm.)
Sources: Königsberg 1740 (att. Mouton), Munich 7 (att.
Bauldeweyn; with variant Agnus 1, CW 58), Stuttgart 46
(lacks Agnus 1), Toledo 19 (Kyrie, part of Gloria),
1539[2]
Discussion: SparksM 34-98, attributing work to Bauldeweyn
and surveying earlier literature
Edition: Chorwerk 20
Recording: see section IV
MISSA DE BEATA VIRGINE, 4-5 v.   CW Ma3 B16[1-2] (af1.30-31)
no.16, p.125
I. 1. Kyrie; 2. Christe; 3. Kyrie (109 mm.). II. 1. Et
in terra; 2. Qui tollis; 3. Cum sancto spiritu (250 mm.).
The other movements are for 5 v. except as noted:
III. 1. Patrem; 2. Crucifixus; 3. Et in spiritum (248
mm.). IV. 1. Sanctus; 2. Pleni; 3. Hosanna (118 mm.);
4. Benedictus (39 mm.). V. 1. Agnus Dei; 2. Agnus Dei
(2 v.); 3. Agnus Dei (87 mm.)
Sources: Complete mass: Berlin 40014, Bologna Q 25 (alto,
tenor), Budapest 20, Budapest 24, Budapest Pr.6,
Cambrai 4 (anon.), Cambrai 18, Jena 7, MilanA E 46,
Munich 510 (anon.), Munich C, Nürnberg 83795, Rome
Giul.XII.2, Rome Sist.45, Rome Sist.160 (alto, bass),
Rostock 49, Stuttgart 44, Toledo 16, Toledo 22,
Uppsala 76b, Uppsala 76c, Vienna 4809, Weimar (partly
att. LaRue), Wolfenbüttel A, J1514, 1516[1], 1539[1].
Kyrie and Gloria: Dresden Gr.53, Eisenach, Rostock 40.
Gloria and Credo: Rome Sist.23. Gloria: Florence
II.I.232, GlareanusD 392. Cum sancto spiritu: Basel
F.X.21, Cambrai 125-8, Dresden 1/E/4, Greifswald,
St. Gall 463, Ulm 237, Uppsala 89. Credo: BolognaS
A.XXXI, Jena 36, Modena a.N.1.2. Agnus Dei 2: 1543[19],
1545[6], GlareanusD 305
Intabulations: 1552[35] (with omissions). Kyrie: B1546[14],
1547[25], B1557[2]. Cum sancto spiritu: KrakowS (2),
Munich 272, 1536[13], B1546[14], 1547[25], 1552[29], 1558[20],
1578[24], 1583[22]. Credo: 1547[25], 1554[32]. Benedictus:
1547[25], 1552[29]. Agnus Dei 2: Zurich Z.XI.301
Discussions: Haarlem, HallS, J 712-8, JosephsonM, ReeseP
Editions, complete: Chorwerk 42. For keyboard intabula-
tions see WarburtonK.
Recordings: see section IV
Missa de venerabilis sacramento = Missa pange lingua

MISSA DI DADI.   CW Ma3 B15 (afl.29) no.15, p.93
    I. 1. Kyrie; 2. Christe; 3. Kyrie (58 mm.).   II. 1. Et
    in terra; 2. Domine Deus, rex (3 v.); 3. Domine Fili
    unigenite (2 v.); 4. Domine Deus, agnus (3 v.); 5. Qui
    tollis (204 mm.).   III. 1. Patrem; 2. Crucifixus (225
    mm.).   IV. 1. Sanctus; 2. Pleni (3 v.); 3. Hosanna
    (85 mm.); 4. Benedictus ... Hosanna (2 v., 58 mm.).
    V. 1. Agnus Dei (68 mm.); 2. Agnus Dei (2 v., 54 mm.);
    3. Agnus Dei (80 mm.)
   Based on *N'auray ie iamais mieulx* by Robert Morton (CW
   as above, p.124)
   Source: J1514
MISSA D'UNG AULTRE AMER.   CW Ma2 B11 (afl.23) no.11, p.121
    I. 1. Kyrie; 2. Christe; 3. Kyrie (49 mm.).   II. Et
    in terra (47 mm.).   III. 1. Patrem; 2. Et resurrexit
    (107 mm.).   IV. 1. Sanctus ... hosanna (47 mm.); 2. Tu
    solus qui facis mirabilia (70 mm.).   V. 1. Agnus Dei
    (21 mm.); 2. Agnus Dei (15 mm.); 3. Agnus Dei (16 mm.)
   Variants: IV.2 in 1505[1] is *Tu lumen, tu splendor Patris*
   (verse 2 of Christmas hymn, *Jesu redemptor*; edition
   p.139).   Rome Sist.41 has a different Sanctus and
   Benedictus (edition pp.136-8), with Tu solus following
   the mass.
   Based on Ockeghem chanson (edition p.140)
   Sources: Modena IV, Rome Sist.41, J1505.   Sanctus: 1505[1]
Missa Elizabeth = Missa faisant regretz
MISSA FAISANT REGRETZ.   CW Ma3 B13 (afl.27) no.13, p.33
    I. 1. Kyrie; 2. Christe; 3. Kyrie (61 mm.).   II. 1. Et
    in terra; 2. Qui tollis (96 mm.).   III. 1. Patrem;
    2. Et incarnatus; 3. Et in spiritum (160 mm.).
    IV. 1. Sanctus; 2. Pleni (3 v.); 3. Hosanna (100 mm.);
    4. Benedictus (46 mm.).   V. 1. Agnus Dei (16 mm.);
    2. Agnus Dei (31 mm.); 3. Agnus Dei (55 mm.)
   Based on motive from part 2 of Frye, *Tout a par moy* (ed.
   CMM 19. Agricola setting ed. CW p.56)
   Sources: Jena 3 (Missa Elizabeth), Munich 510, Rome
   Sist.23, Rome Pal.lat.1980/81, Toledo 9, Vienna 4809,
   Vienna SM 15495, J1514, 1516[1]
   Intabulated excerpts: 1528[22], B1546[14], 1547[25], 1552[35],
   1554[32]
   Discussion: FellererJ (intabulations)
MISSA FORTUNA DESPERATA.   CW Ma1 B4 (afl.13) no.4, p.81
    I. 1. Kyrie; 2. Christe; 3. Kyrie (73 mm.).   II. 1. Et
    in terra; 2. Qui tollis (160 mm.).   III. 1. Patrem;
    2. Et incarnatus; 3. Et in spiritum (280 mm.).
    IV. 1. Sanctus; 2. Pleni (3 v.); 3. Hosanna (163 mm.);
    4. Benedictus (46 mm.).   V. 1. Agnus Dei (60 mm.);
    2. Agnus Dei (62 mm.)

Based on (Busnois?) chanson (2 versions pp.106-7)
Sources: Barcelona0 5, ModenaE a.M.1.2, Munich 3154,
   Rome Sist.41, Vienna 11778, J1502, 1538[9] (Pleni),
   1539[1], 1539[2]. Theorists, Agnus Dei 1: GlareanusD 220
   (GlareanusM 469), Wilphlingseder (1563), Zanger (1554)
Intabulated excerpts: 1552[35]
Discussion: OsthoffR
Recording: see section IV
Missa Fridericus dux Saxonie = Missa Hercules (in Jena 3)
MISSA GAUDEAMUS. CW Ma1 B3 (af1.12) no.3, p.57
   I. 1. Kyrie; 2. Christe; 3. Kyrie (66 mm.). II. 1. Et
   in terra; 2. Qui tollis (159 mm.). III. 1. Patrem;
   2. Et incarnatus (3 v.); 3. Et in spiritum; 4. Et unam
   catholicam (279 mm.). IV. 1. Sanctus; 2. Pleni (3 v.);
   Hosanna (89 mm.); 4. Benedictus (2 v.); 5. Qui venit
   (2 v.); 6. In nomine (2 v., 57 mm.). V. 1. Agnus Dei 1
   (29 mm.); 2. Agnus Dei (40 mm.); 3. Agnus Dei (66 mm.)
Based on Marian introit (CW introduction; cf. L.U.1556)
Sources: Basel F.IX.25, Cambrai 18 (anon.), Jena 32
   (anon.), Regensburg B211-5 (Agnus 2), Rome Sist.23,
   Stuttgart 46, Toledo 27, Vienna 11778 (att. Ockeghem),
   J1502, 1539[1], GlareanusD 220 (Benedictus; GlareanusM
   2:293)
Intabulated excerpts: 1547[25], 1552[35]
Recordings: see section IV
MISSA HERCULES DUX FERRARIAE. CW Ma2 B7 (af1.19) no.7, p.19
   I. 1. Kyrie; 2. Christe; 3. Kyrie (55 mm.). II. 1. Et
   in terra; 2. Qui tollis (102 mm.). III. 1. Patrem;
   2. Et incarnatus; 3. Et in spiritum (162 mm.).
   IV. 1. Sanctus; 2. Pleni; 3. Hosanna (91 mm.);
   4. Benedictus; 5. Qui venit; 6. In nomine (17 mm.).
   V. 1. Agnus Dei (47 mm.); 2. Agnus Dei (3 v., 51 mm.);
   3. Agnus Dei (6 v., 52 mm.)
Sources: Basel F.IX.25, Bologna R 142 (Agnus 3),
   BolognaS A.XXXI, Brussels 9126 (M. Philippus rex
   Castiliae), Jena 3 (M. Fridericus dux Saxonie), Milan
   2267, Rome Sist.45, St. Gall 463 (Agnus 3), Toledo 27,
   Vienna 4809 (anon.), J1505, 1545[6] (Pleni, with text:
   Numquid iustificari potest). Theorists: Heyden (1537,
   Pleni), GlareanusD (Agnus 2, p.221; Pleni p.242;
   GlareanusM 2:294, 307), Faber (1550, Et in spiritum),
   Wilphlingseder (1563, Agnus 2), Paix (1590, Pleni,
   Agnus 2)
Intabulated excerpts: 1538[22], 1552[35], 1554[32]
Discussion: JacksonT, JohnsonM
Editions: AMMM 15 (Milan 2267), BankH, Monnikendam
Recordings: see section IV
Missa in diatessaron sequentia signis = Missa sine nomine

MISSA LA SOL FA RE MI. CW Ma1 B2 (af1.11) no.2, p.42
    I. 1. Kyrie; 2. Christe; 3. Kyrie (61 mm.). II. 1. Et
    in terra; 2. Qui tollis (112 mm.). III. 1. Patrem;
    2. Et incarnatus (242 mm.). IV. 1. Sanctus; 2. Pleni;
    3. Hosanna (75 mm.); 4. Benedictus; 5. Qui venit (3 v.,
    56 mm.); 6. Hosanna (37 mm.). V. 1. Agnus Dei (19 mm.);
    2. Agnus Dei (22 mm.)
    Sources: Berlin 40091, BolognaS A.XXXI, MilanA E 46,
    Paris Res.Vma 851, Regensburg B220-22 (Agnus 2),
    Regensburg C.100, Rome Sist.41, Rome SMM JJ III 4,
    Stuttgart 44 (lacks Agnus), Toledo 19, Vienna 11778,
    Vienna 11883 (Kyrie, Gloria), J1502, 1539[1], Zanger
    (1554, Hosanna 1)
    Intabulated excerpts: B1546[14], 1552[35], 1554[32]
    Discussion: HaarR
    Recordings: see section IV
MISSA L'AMI BAUDICHON. CW Ma2 B9 (af1.20) no.9, p.67
    I. 1. Kyrie; 2. Christe; 3. Kyrie (65 mm.). II. 1. Et
    in terra; 2. Qui tollis (2 v.); 3. Qui sedes (169 mm.).
    III. 1. Patrem; 2. Et incarnatus (2 v.); 3. Crucifixus
    (2 v.); 4. Et resurrexit (288 mm.). IV. 1. Sanctus;
    2. Pleni (2 v.); 3. Hosanna (93 mm.); 4. Benedictus
    (2 v.); 5. Qui venit (2 v.); 6. In nomine (2 v., 48 mm.).
    V. 1. Agnus Dei miserere/dona (17 mm.); 2. Agnus Dei
    (3 v., 59 mm.)
    Sources: Regensburg B220-22 (Qui tollis), Rome Sist.23,
    Verona 761 (anon.), J1505
MISSA L'HOMME ARMÉ SEXTI TONI. CW Ma1 B5 (af1.14) no.5,
    p.109
    I. 1. Kyrie; 2. Christe; 3. Kyrie (74 mm.). II. 1. Et
    in terra; 2. Qui tollis (152 mm.). III. 1. Patrem;
    2. Et resurrexit; 3. Et unam catholicam (258 mm.).
    IV. 1. Sanctus; 2. Pleni (2 v.); 3. Gloria tua (2 v.);
    4. Hosanna (79 mm.); 5. Benedictus (2 v.); 6. Qui
    venit (2 v.); 7. In nomine (30 mm.). V. 1. Agnus Dei
    (27 mm.); 2. Agnus Dei (3 v., 50 mm.); 3. Agnus Dei
    (76 mm.)
    Sources: Casale Monferrato M, Jena 31, Leipzig 51,
    Milan 2267 (lacks Benedictus, Agnus Dei), Rome
    Chig.VIII.234 (Kyrie, Gloria, Credo), Segovia, Stutt-
    gart 47 (lacks Agnus), Vienna 11778, J1502, J1558-60.
    Theorists: Heyden (1537, Agnus 3), GlareanusD 220
    (Benedictus, GlareanusM 2:293), Wilphlingseder (1563,
    Benedictus)
    Intabulated excerpt: Chicago C
    Discussion: LockwoodA (on *L'homme armé* and its polyphonic
    use, summarizing earlier literature)

Editions: AMMM 15 (Milan 2267), Darvas
Recordings: see section IV
MISSA L'HOMME ARMÉ SUPER VOCES MUSICALES. CW Ma1 B1 (af1.10)
    no.1, p.1
    I. 1. Kyrie; 2. Christe; 3. Kyrie (87 mm.). II. 1. Et
    in terra; 2. Qui tollis (141 mm.). III. 1. Patrem;
    2. Et incarnatus (omits text "Et in spiritum ...
    ecclesiam," found in Rome Sist.154; CW p.36); 3. Con-
    fiteor (180 mm.). IV. 1. Sanctus; 2. Pleni (3 v.);
    3. Hosanna (126 mm.); 4. Benedictus (2 v.); 5. Qui
    venit (2 v.); 6. In nomine (2 v., 49 mm.). V. 1. Agnus
    Dei (35 mm.); 2. Agnus Dei (3 v., 25 mm.); 3. Agnus
    Dei ... dona (124 mm.)
    Canons (not identical in all sources; see CW pp.IXff.):
    II. 2. Cancrizet et supra dicta notet. III. 2. Can-
    crizet; 3. Aequivalet. IV. 3. Gaudet cum gaudentibus.
    V. 2. Tria in unum; 3. Clama ne cesses
    Sources: Barcelona0 5, Basel F.IX.25, BolognaS A.XXXI,
    Frankfurt 2, Jena 32, ModenaE a.M.1.2, Paris Res.Vma 851,
    Regensburg 878-82, Rome Sist.154 (includes optional
    quintus v., Agnus 3, by Jo. Abbat.; CW p.XIV), Rome
    Sist.197, Rome Giul.XII 2, Toledo 9, Toledo 21 (Agnus 3),
    Uppsala 76c, Vienna 11778, J1502, 1539[1], 1539[2], Intarsia
    in San Sisto, Piacenza (Agnus 2). Theorists: Anon.,
    Berlin th.1175 (Agnus 2), Heyden (1537, Kyrie 1,
    Hosanna, Benedictus 4-6, Agnus 2), GlareanusD (1547,
    p.144 Benedictus 4; p.442 Agnus Dei 2 with resolution,
    CW 40; GlareanusM 2:521ff.), Faber (1550, Christe,
    Hosanna, Agnus 2), Zanger (1554, Agnus 2), Dressler
    (1571, Christe, tenor of Sanctus, Hosanna), Paix (1590,
    1594, Agnus 2)
    Intabulated excerpts: 1547[25], 1552[35], 1578[24]
    Discussion: BenthemM, StamJ, BenthemK, CollinsP,
    HeikampZ, J 706-9. On the melody see LockwoodA
MISSA MALHEUR ME BAT. CW Ma2 B8 (af1.19) no.8, p.39
    I. 1. Kyrie; 2. Christe; 3. Kyrie (85 mm.). II. 1. Et
    in terra; 2. Qui tollis (154 mm.). III. 1. Patrem;
    2. Et incarnatus; 3. Et in spiritum (217 mm.).
    IV. 1. Sanctus; 2. Pleni (2 v.); 3. Hosanna (178 mm.);
    4. Benedictus (2 v.); 5. Qui venit (2 v.); 6. In nomine
    (2 v., 24 mm.). V. 1. Agnus Dei (84 mm.); 2. Agnus
    Dei (2 v., 50 mm.); 3. Agnus Dei (6 v., 89 mm.)
    Canon, Agnus 1: De minimis non curat prector (Leipzig:
    Multi sunt vocati, pauci vero electi; Brussels: Canon
    ad longam)
    Sources: Basel F.IX.25 (anon.; Kyrie, Gloria, Agnus),
    BolognaS A.XXXI, Brussels 9126, Jena 3, Leipzig 51,

MilanA E 46, Modena IV, Munich 260 (Benedictus, Agnus 2), Regensburg B220-22 (Pleni), Rome Sist.23, Rostock 40 (title: M. Quae est ista), Toledo 9, Vienna 4809, Vienna 11883, J1505, 1549[16] (Pleni, with text *Quid tam solicitis*). Theorists: Anon., London Add. 4911 (Agnus 2); Heyden (1537, Agnus 2); GlareanusD 450 (Agnus 2; GlareanusM 2:528)

Based on chanson by ?Ockeghem (edition CW as above, p.66; further on the chanson see AtlasC 1:149ff.)

Discussion: J 710-12

MISSA MATER PATRIS. CW Ma3 B12 (afl.26) no.12, p.1

I. 1. Kyrie; 2. Christe; 3. Kyrie (85 mm.). II. 1. Et in terra; 2. Qui tollis; 3. Cum sancto spiritu (108 mm.). III. 1. Patrem; 2. Crucifixus; 3. Et in spiritum; 4. Et vitam venturi (179 mm.). IV. 1. Sanctus; 2. Pleni (2 v.); 3. Hosanna (136 mm.); 4. Benedictus (2 v., 58 mm.). V. 1. Agnus Dei (30 mm.); 2. Agnus Dei (2 v., 35 mm.); 3. Agnus Dei (5 v., 73 mm.)

Sources: Regensburg B220-22 (Agnus 2), J1514. Theorists: Heyden (1537, Benedictus), GlareanusD (1547, Pleni, p.446; Benedictus, p.448; Agnus 2, p.257; GlareanusM 2:526, 527, 341)

Based on 3 v. Brumel motet (CW as above, p.20)

Discussion: Some scholars have raised questions about the authenticity of this mass (e.g., PirroH 137, Osthoff 1:151ff.) but have refrained from decisive negation. AntonowyczMP defends the authenticity. See also AntonowyczP. Analysis: NovackF 200-206

Complete edition: Forbes (New York: G. Schirmer, 1966)

Recordings: see section IV

Missa n'auray je = Missa di dadi

MISSA PANGE LINGUA. CW Ma4 B18 (afl.33) no.18, p.1

I. 1. Kyrie; 2. Christe; 3. Kyrie (70 mm.). II. 1. Et in terra; 2. Qui tollis (109 mm.). III. 1. Patrem; 2. Et incarnatus; 3. Crucifixus; 4. Et in spiritum (215 mm.). IV. 1. Sanctus; 2. Pleni (2 v.); 3. Hosanna (138 mm.); 4. Benedictus (2 v., 48 mm.). V. 1. Agnus Dei (25 mm.); 2. Agnus Dei (2 v., 56 mm.); 3. Agnus Dei ... dona (J1558-60 has text: Agnus Dei, Pange lingua; 77 mm.)

Sources: Brussels IV 922, Budapest 8, Jena 21 (anon.; with Benedictus by Gascongne), Leipzig 49, MilanA E 46, Munich 260 (Pleni, Benedictus, Agnus 2; anon.), Munich 510 (anon.), Regensburg C.100, Rome Giul.XII.2 (anon.), Rome Sist.16, Rome Pal.lat.1980/81, Rome SMM JJ III 4, Toledo 16, Vienna 4809, 1539[2], 1545[6] (Pleni, with text

Quis separabit nos; Agnus 2 with text *Exaudi Domine*),
  J1558-60
Intabulated excerpts: B1546$_{14}$, 1547^{25}, 1552^{32}, Chicago C
Based on hymn chant (CW p.V; L.U.957)
Analysis: NovackF 206-31
Complete editions: Ambros 5:79 (1539^2), BankP, Chorwerk 1,
  Dessoff Choir Series 25, WarburtonE (Sistine 16),
  U. of Pennsylvania Choral Series 89
Recordings: see section IV

Missa Philippus rex Castiliae = Missa Hercules, in Brussels
  9126
Missa quae est ista = Missa malheur me bat, in Rostock 40
MISSA SINE NOMINE. CW Ma3 B17 (afl.32) no.17, p.167
  I. 1. Kyrie; 2. Christe; 3. Kyrie (57 mm.). II. 1. Et
  in terra; 2. Qui tollis; 3. Cum sancto spiritu (132
  mm.). III. 1. Patrem; 2. Et incarnatus; 3. Crucifixus;
  4. Et in spiritum (194 mm.). IV. 1. Sanctus; 2. Pleni
  (2 v.); 3. Hosanna (98 mm.); 4. Benedictus (2 v.);
  5. Qui venit (2 v.); 6. In nomine (2 v., 30 mm.).
  V. 1. Agnus Dei (28 mm.); 2. Agnus Dei (2 v., 18 mm.);
  3. Agnus Dei ... dona (59 mm.)
The tenor is derived by canon in each movement: I. Quaere
  in suprano. In diatessaron. II. In basso. In diapente.
  III. In suprano. In diatessaron. IV. In alto. In dia-
  pente. V. In basso. In diapente
Sources: Jena 3, ModenaE a.N.1.2 (Credo), Vienna 4809,
  J1514, 1516^1 (title: M. ad fugam), 1545^6 (Benedictus,
  with text: Nunquid oblivisci), GlareanusD 258 (Pleni;
  GlareanusM 2:325)
Intabulation: 1538^{22} (Cum sancto spiritu)
Edition: LenaertsK (Sanctus)
Recordings: see section IV
MISSA UNA MUSQUE DE BISCAYA. CW Ma2 B10 (afl.22) no.10,
  p.93
  I. 1. Kyrie; 2. Christe; 3. Kyrie (88 mm.). II. 1. Et
  in terra; 2. Qui tollis; 3. Qui sedes (133 mm.).
  III. 1. Patrem; 2. Et iterum (272 mm.). IV. 1. Sanctus;
  2. Pleni; 3. Hosanna (130 mm.); 4. Benedictus (58 mm.).
  V. 1. Agnus Dei (17 mm.); 2. Agnus Dei (39 mm.);
  3. Agnus Dei ... dona (27 mm.)
Sources: Berlin 40021, Vienna SM 15495, J1505
Discussion: J 743-5
Recording: see section IV
(MISSUS EST GABRIEL ANGELUS A DEO, 5 v.). CW Mt2 B9 (afl.24)
  no.40, p.89
  2. Hic erit magnus
Tenor: Busnois, *A une dame j'ay fait veu* (tenor)

195 mm.

Text: see LowinskyMRM 3:219

Sources: FlorenceM 666 (att. Mouton; text: Missus est
angelus Gabriel), MunichU Art.401, Rome Giul.XII.4,
Rome Sist.19, 1519[3], 1520[4] (att. Mouton), 1559[1] (att.
Mouton)

Discussion: LowinskyMRM 3:219-28, EldersZ 100-102

Recording: see section IV

MISSUS EST GABRIEL ANGELUS AD MARIAM.   CW Mt1 B3 (af1.6)
no.17, p.82

86 mm.

Sources: Augsburg 142a, Bologna R 142, Brussels 9126,
Cortona 95/6, Florence II.I.232, Florence Mag1.164-7
(anon.), London Roy.8.G.VII (anon.), Rome Sist.63
(anon.), Toledo 10, Ulm 237 (anon.), Uppsala 76c,
1504[1]

MITTIT AD VIRGINEM.   CW Mt1 B1 (af1.2) no.3, p.14
2. Accede nuncia

240 mm.

Text: sequence by Peter Abelard

Sources: LondonR 1070 (anon.), Rome Sist.46, 1504[1], J1555

Discussion: Werner

Recording: see section IV

MON MARY M'A DIFFAMÉE, 3 v.

34 mm.

Text: BenthemJ 434

Sources: Brussels IV 90/Tournai, London Add. 35087,
1578[15]

Discussion: BenthemJ

Edition: BenthemJ 444-5

Monstra te esse matrem = Ave maris stella, part 4; also
tenor of A la mort

Montes Gelboe = Planxit autem David, part 2

Nardi Maria pistici *see* Honor, decus, imperium

Nay biem no rise tans = J'ay bien rise tant

(NESCIENS MATER VIRGO VIRUM, 5 v.).   CW Mt5 B19 (af1.45)
no.71, p.1

2. Ipsum regem angelorum

126 mm.

Text: Marian antiphon (see EldersP 538)

Sources: Hradec Krălové II A 26, Hradec Krălové II A 29
(1 v.), 1545[3]

Discussion: SparksP 350ff., *passim* (questions authenticity)

N'ESSE PAS UNG GRANT DESPLAISIR, 5 v.   CW W1 B1 (af1.3) no.8,
p.17

44 mm.

Sources: Copenhagen 1872, Copenhagen 1873, Halle Ed.1147
(anon.; no text), 1540[7] (N'esse point ...), 1544[13],
1545[15] (with Response: *Si vous n'avez aultre desir*,
6 v. by Jo. Le Brung; ed. CW no.8a), 1549[29], E1560c
(= 1572[2]), 1568[7] (text: *O pater omnipotens*)
Discussion: BenthemZ
Edition: PAPTM 6
Recordings: see section IV
Nobis esset falacia = Tu solus, qui facis mirabilia, part 2
Non accedat ad malum = Qui habitat (4 v.), part 2
Nostra ut pura = Inviolata, integra, part 2
Nunc caeli regina = Virgo salutiferi, part 3
Nunc dimittis, 6 v. = Responsum acceperat Simeon, part 2
(NUNC DIMITTIS SERVUM TUUM, DOMINE). CW Mt5 B25 (afl.52)
    no.93, p.198
    122 mm.
    Text: Canticle of Simeon (Luke 2:29-32)
    Source: Bologna Q 20
    Discussion: Osthoff 2:67 (questions authenticity)
Nunc mater ex ora = Benedicta es, part 3
Nunquid iustificari potest = M. Hercules: Pleni, in 1545[6]
Nunquid oblivisci = M. sine nomine: Benedictus, in 1545[6]
NYMPHES DES BOIS, 5 v. CW W1 B2 (afl.5) no.22, p.56 (as
    "Requiem": CW Mt1 B5 (afl.9) no.29, p.152)
    159 mm.
    Tenor: Requiem aeternam (L.U.1807)
    Text: LowinskyMRM 3:213-4
    Sources: FlorenceM 666, 1508[1] (text only in tenor: the
        source for CW Mt1 version), 1545[15]
    Discussion: LowinskyMRM 3:66-8, 213-17. Review of a per-
        formance 2/22/1875 in MfMg 7 (1875), 62
    Editions: LowinskyMRM 4:338-46
    Recordings: see section IV
NYMPHES, NAPPÉS, 6 v. CW W1 B1 (afl.3), no.21, p.54
    67 mm.
    Tenor: Circumdederunt me
    Sources, text *Nymphes, nappés*: 1545[15], J1550. *Circum-
        dederunt*: MunichU Art.401 (5 v.). *Haec dicit Dominus*:
        Berlin 40013, Gotha A98, Nürnberg 83795, Regensburg
        B.211-5, Zwickau LXXIV, 1537[1], 1558[4]. *Videte omnes
        populi*: Bologna R 142, 1502[2]
    Intabulations: "Circumdederunt": 1547[22], Munich 266.
        "Haec dicit": Munich 267
    Discussion: CrevelA 103-34 and BlackburnJ 53 argue that
        Nymphes is the original text. Osthoff 2:94-5 argues
        that *Videte* is the original text, and the first part of
        a cycle: 2. *Christus mortuus*, 3. *Sic Deus dilexit*, each
        part using the same tenor. Cf. Christus mortuus.
    Edition: PAPTM 6

O ADMIRABILE COMMERCIUM.   CW Mt1 B1 (af1.2) nos.5-9, p.24
   2. Quando natus es
   3. Rubum quem viderat Moyses
   4. Germinavit radix Jesse
   5. Ecce Maria genuit nobis salvatorem
   102 mm., 91 mm., 64 mm., 66 mm., 73 mm.
   Text: 5 antiphons for circumcision of Our Lord (L.U.442);
     see LowinskyMRM 3:129-30
   Sources: Cambridge 1760, Florence II.I.232, FlorenceM
     666, Paris Res.41 (parts 1, 2, 5), Rome Sist.46 (anon.),
     1521[2], 1538[3]
   Discussion: LowinskyMRM 3:129-34
   Edition: LowinskyMRM 4:28
   Recording: see section IV
O benigna regina = Inviolata, integra, part 2
(O BONE ET DULCIS DOMINE JESU).   CW Mt1 B3 (af1.6) no.18,
   p.85
   Tenor: Pater noster
   Bass: Ave Maria
   95 mm.
   Text (tenor, bass): EldersP 538-9
   Sources: Cortona 95/6-Paris (anon.), Florence II.I.232,
     Florence Magl.XIX 164-7 (anon.), Verona 756, 1504[1]
   Discussion: Osthoff 2:296 (questions authenticity)
O BONE ET DULCISSIME JESU. CW Mt5 B25 (af1.53) no.96, p.216
   2. Si ego commisi
   203 mm.
   Sources: BolognaS A.XXIX, Leiden 865, Munich 41 (with 2
     added voices, printed separately CW as above pp.XLVff.),
     Rome Sist.45, St. Gall 463, [1521][7]
   Edition: Chorwerk 57
   Recording: see section IV
O DOMINE JESU CHRISTE. CW Mt1 B2 (af1.4) no.10, p.35
   2. O Domine ... cruce vulneratum
   3. O Domine ... in sepulcro
   4. O Domine ... pastor bone
   5. O Domine ... propter illam amaritudinem
   345 mm.
   Text: Osthoff 2:81
   Source: 1503[1]
   Edition: Octavo ed. see CMP
   Recordings: see section IV
(O DULCIS AMICA). 1 v. canon "cuiusvis toni"
   Source: 1540[7]
O dulcis, O pia = Ave verum corpus, part 3
O Jesu fili David = Comment peult
O lux beatissime = Veni sancte spiritus, part 2

O Maria, nullam tam gravem = Vultum tuum, part 4
O Maria, virgo sanctissima = Si congié prens
O mater Dei et homines = Tu solus qui facis mirabilia
O pater omnipotens = N'esse pas
O virgo genetrix = Plusieurs regretz
O VIRGO PRUDENTISSIMA, 6 v. CW Mt3 B11 (af1.35) no.45, p.1
    2. Audi virgo
    Alto, tenor: Beata mater et intacta virgo
    190 mm.
    Text: by A. Poliziano (Osthoff 2:93)
    Tenor: L.U.1681
    Sources: Leiden 862, Munich 1536, MunichU Art.401, Rome
       Sist.24, 1520^4, 1535^3, 1558^4
O VIRGO VIRGINUM, 6 v. CW Mt5 B23 (af1.49) no.83, p.114
    2. Filiae Jerusalem
    187 mm.
    Text: Marian antiphon (EldersP 538)
    Sources: Bologna R 142, Rome Giul.XII.4, Rome Sist.46,
       Rome SMM 26, J1555
    Edition: Chorwerk 57
    Recordings: see section IV
Oculi eius in pauperem = In Domino confido, part 2
Ora pro nobis = Vultum tuum, part 6

Par vous je suis = Entré je suis
PARATUM COR MEUM, 3-4 v. CW Mt4 B17 (af1.41) no.67, p.46
    2. Salvum fac dextera tua (3 v.)
    3. In Idumaeam extendam
    325 mm.
    Text: Psalm 107 (English 108)
    Sources: Cortona 95/6-Paris, Florence Magl.XIX 164-7,
       1539^7, J1555
PARFONS REGRETZ, 5 v. CW W1 B1 (af1.3) no.3, p.5
    67 mm.
    Sources: Vienna 18746 (anon.), 1545^{15}, J1550, E1560c
       (= 1572^2)
    Discussion: KellmanJ 184 (commenting on Osthoff 1:68)
    Edition: Octavo eds. see CMP
    Recordings: see section IV
PATER NOSTER, QUI ES IN CAELIS, 6 v. CW Mt3 B12 (af1.36)
    no.50, p.47
    2. Ave Maria
    198 mm.
    Sources: Berlin 40013, Berlin 40043 (anon.), Copenhagen
       1872, Dresden G1.5, Gotha A98, Hradec Králové II A 22,
       Leipzig 49-50, Modena IX (part 2), Munich 12, Munich
       1536, MunichU Art.401, Nürnberg 83795, Padua A17 (anon.),

Rome Sist.55, RomeV SB II.55-60, Saragossa 17 (part 2),
   Seville 1 (part 2), Toledo 18, Utrecht (part 2),
   Valladolid 6 (part 2), Valladolid [15] (part 2), 1537[1],
   J1555, 1558[4]
Intabulations: 1536[11], 1546[29], 1547[22] (anon.), 1547[25]
   (part 2), 1547[23], 1552[29], 1558[20], B1563[12], 1578[24] (part
   2; anon.)
Discussion: BrownA 504-20 (intabulations); see section
   IA23 above

Patrem *see* Credo
Pauper sum ego = Tenor of Ce povre mendiant
Per illud ave = Benedicta es, part 2
Per omnia seculum seculorum = Tenor of Scimus quoniam
PETITE CAMUSETTE, 6 v. CW W1 B2 (af1.5) no.17, p.43
   42 mm.
   Text: see JefferyL 417
   Sources: Bologna R 142, Copenhagen 1873, Leipzig 49
      (anon.; text: Petite et accipietis), Rome Pal.lat
      1980/81, 1545[15], J1550, E1560c (= 1572[2])
   Discussion: BlackburnJ 42ff., BenthemZ
   Edition: SmijersV 5:155
   Recordings: see section IV
Petite et accipietis = Petite camusette
Pie Jesu Domine (from Dies irae) = Tenor of Proch dolor
PLAINE DE DUEIL, 5 v. CW W1 B1 (af1.3) no.4, p.7
   2. Je te requiers
   3. Il ne me chault
   52 mm.
   Sources: Brussels 228 (anon.), Vienna 18746 (anon.),
      1545[15], J1550
   Discussion: KellmanJ 183-4 (commenting on Osthoff 1:68),
      PickerC 73-4, BenthemZ
   Editions: PickerC 361, Chorwerk 3
   Recordings: see section IV
Plangent eum = Tenor of Huc me sydereo
PLANXIT AUTEM DAVID. CW Mt1 B3 (af1.6) no.20, p.95
   2. Montes Gelboe
   3. Sagitta Jonathae
   4. Doleo super te
   337 mm.
   Text: 2 Kings 1:17-27
   Sources: Dresden 1/D/505 (anon.), Florence II.I.232
      (att. Ninot in index), Rome Sist.38, St. Gall 463,
      1514[1] (anon.), J1555. Theorist: GlareanusD 418
      (GlareanusM 2:499)
   Recordings: see section IV

PLUS N'ESTES MA MAITRESSE. CW W1 B3 (af1.8) no.30, p.76
    68 mm.
    Source: J1550
PLUS NULZ REGRETZ. CW W1 B3 (af1.8) no.29, p.74
    74 mm.
    Text: by Jean Lemaire de Belges. See PickerJG 455
    Sources: Augsburg 142a, Basel F.X.1-4, Bologna R 142
      (text: Adjuro vos), Brussels IV 90/Tournai, Florence
      Magl.XIX 117, Florence Magl.XIX 164-7 (anon.),
      FlorenceC Bas.2442, London Roy.App.41, Munich 1508,
      Munich 1516 (anon.), Paris Res.Vm^7 504 (anon.),
      Regensburg C.120 (lacks text), Rome lat.11953,
      Uppsala 76c, Vienna 18810, 1540^7, J1550
    Intabulations: Krakow 1716, Munich 266, Munich 1511d,
      B1533$_{11}$, 1536^{13}, B1556$_{5-6}$ (anon.), 1562^{24} (anon.)
    Discussion: BenthemZ, BrownTC 83ff., J 674-83, KellmanJ
      182-3, PickerJG 447-8
    Editions: PickerC 280, J 675; Octavo: Dessoff Choir
      Series 48
    Recordings: see section IV
PLUSIEURS REGRETZ. CW W1 B1 (af1.3) no.7, p.15
    60 mm.
    Text: JefferyL 418
    Sources: Copenhagen 1848 (anon.), Leipzig 49 (text:
      Sana me, Domine), Uppsala 76b, Vienna 18746 (anon.),
      1545^{15}, J1550, 1559^1 (text: O virgo genetrix), E1560c
      (= 1572^2)
    Discussion: BenthemZ, BlackburnJ 42ff., PickerJP
    Editions: Chorwerk 3, PAPTM 6 "O virgo genetrix"
    Recordings: see section IV
Portio mea, Domine = Memor esto, part 2
Posuisti in nervo = Responde mihi, part 2
(POUR SOUHAITTER, 6 v.). CW W1 B1 (af1.3) no.10, p.23
    46 mm.
    Sources: Copenhagen 1873, 1545^{15}, J1550
    Discussion: Osthoff 2:225 (questions authenticity)
PRAETER RERUM SERIEM, 6 v. CW Mt2 B7 (af1.18) no.33, p.21
    2. Virtus sancti spiritus
    129 mm.
    Text: see Osthoff 2:72, EldersP 534
    Sources: Bologna R 142, Budapest 2, Copenhagen 1872,
      Dresden G1.5, Dresden Gr.57, FlorenceD 11, Gotha A98,
      Leiden 863, Leiden 865, LondonR 1070 (anon.), Louvain
      163, MunichU Art.401, Regensburg C.120, Rokycany, Rome
      Giul.XII.4, Rome Sist.16, Rome SMM 26, RomeMas,
      RomeV SB II.55-60, St. Gall 463, Seville 1, Toledo 22,
      Uppsala 76b, Wroclaw 6, Wroclaw 11, Wroclaw B40,

Wroclaw B54, Zwickau XCIV 1, 1519^2, 1520^4, 1537^1, J1555
Intabulations: 1547^{22}, 1554^{32}, 1555^{36}, 1558^{20}, Munich 272
Discussion: BrownA 491-504 (intabulations), DunningS 327
Edition: Chorwerk 18
Recordings: see section IV
(PROCH DOLOR, 7 v.). CW supp. no.14, p.66
    Tenor: Pie Jesu Domine (from Dies irae)
    Canon, alto: Celum, terra mariaque succurrite pio
    87 mm.
    Source: Brussels 228 (anon.)
    Discussion: DunningS 65-8, EldersST 22-4, PickerC 89-90
    Edition: PickerC 304
Propter peccata = La Spagna

Quando natus est = O admirabile commercium, part 2
QUANT JE VOUS VOYE, 3 v. CW W2 B5 (afl.54) no.65, p.40
    39 mm.
    Text: BenthemJ 434-5, JefferyL 418
    Sources: London Add.35087, 1536^1, 1542^8
    Discussion: BenthemJ 426-8, 434-6
    Recording: see section IV
Que fuit Heli/Obed = Factum est autem, parts 2, 3
(QUE VOUS, MA DAME, 3 v.). CW W2 B4 (afl.53) no.47, p.23
    Tenor: In pace in idipsum
    63 mm.
    Sources, with text *Que vous* ...: London Roy.A.XVI, Paris
        1597 (anon.), 1503^4 (att. Agricola, with optional 4th
        voice, ed. CW p.XV). Text or incipit *In pace* ...:
        Bologna Q 17, Brussels 11239, Florence BR 229, Florence
        Magl.XIX 178, Rome Giul.XIII.27, RomeC 2856, Segovia
        s.s., St. Gall 463, Warsaw 58 (anon., text incipit
        only), Washington M2.1 M6, 1542^8 (att. Agricola)
    Intabulations: Basel F.IX.22 (att. Isaac), 1507^6
    Discussion: AtlasC 1:70-73 (reviewing earlier writing),
        PickerC 85-7
    Editions: AgricolaCW 5, AtlasC 2:11, BesselerC, PickerC
        461
    Recording: see section IV
QUI BELLES AMOURS
    Sources: Basel F.X.21 (tenor only; text: *Ach unfal was
        ziehstu mich*), MunichU 328-31 (anon.), Vienna 18810
    Intabulation: Wertheim 6
    Edition: mm. 1-11 in Osthoff 2:173
    Recording: see section IV
QUI HABITAT IN ADJUTORIO ALTISSIMI. CW Mt3 B13 (afl.37)
        no.52, p.75
    2. Non accedat ad malum
    282 mm.

Text: Psalm 90 (English 91)

Sources: Cambrai 125-8, Dresden Gr.57, Gotha A98, Hradec Králové II A 21, Kassel 24, Munich 10, Regensburg 863-70, Regensburg 940-41, Rome Sist.38, Toledo 22, Vienna 15441, Zwickau XLI 73, 1537[1], J1555, 1559[2]

Intabulations: B1553[1] (anon.), 1558[20], 1565[22], Munich 267, Munich 272

Discussion: BrownA 481-91 (intabulations). CummingsT 47n. cites a 1616 performance.

QUI HABITAT IN ADJUTORIO ALTISSIMI, 24 v.

"Est fuga bis trina quaevis post tempora bina"

Sources: Heilbronn IV/2-V/2 (tenor, quintus), Kassel 24 (anon.), 1542[6], 1568[7]

Discussion: StamV, LowinskyO 178-80

Editions: Exempla VI, RiemannH 238

Qui jacuisti mortuus = Qui velatus, part 5

(QUI REGIS ISRAEL, INTENDE, 5 v.). CW Mt4 B16 (af1.40) no.63, p.16

110 mm.

Text: MattfeldS 164n.

Sources: Dresden 1/D/3, 1538[6], 1553[5]

Discussion: Osthoff 2:129ff. (questions authenticity)

QUI VELATUS FACIE FUISTI. CW Mt1 B2 (af1.4) no.11, p.41

2. Hora qui ductis tertia

3. In flagellis potum felis

4. In amara crucis ara

5. Qui jacuisti mortuus

6. Christum ducem (see separate entry above)

383 mm. (parts 1-5)

Text by St. Bonaventura (see Osthoff 2:81)

Sources: Wroclaw I.F.428 (part 4), 1503[1] (parts 1-5)

Discussion: MattfeldS 175-6, Werner

Edition: Chorwerk 23

Recording: see section IV

Quia pauperes facti sumus = Domine non secundum, part 3

Quid tam solicitus = M. malheur, Pleni, in 1549[16]

Quis separavit nos = M. pange lingua, Pleni, in 1545[6]

Quoniam est Dominus suavis = Misericordias Domini, part 2

RECORDANS DE MY SEGNORA. CW W2 B4 (af1.53) no.39, p.9

36 mm.

Canon: Omnia probate, quod bonum est tenete

Text: incipit only. The list in TVNM 26 (1976) p.34 states it is a contrafactum of a 4 v. Si congié prens.

Sources: Florence Magl.XIX 178, Rome Giul.XIII.27

Discussion: AtlasC 1:123-4

Edition: Osthoff 2:402

Recordings: see section IV

(RECORDARE, VIRGO MATER).   CW supp. no.8, p.35
   2. Et ut avertat indignationem
   Source: 1520[1]
   Discussion: Osthoff 2:80 (questions authenticity)
REGINA CAELI.   CW supp. no.3, p.8
   2. Resurrexit sicut dixit
   164 mm.
   Text: Marian antiphon with alleluia (L.U.275)
   Sources: Bologna Q 20, Königsberg 1740, J1555
(REGINA CAELI, 6 v.)
   Source: Rome Sist.46 (att. J. in table of contents)
   Discussion: NobleNM
   Edition: NobleNM
   Recording: see section IV
REGRETZ SANS FIN, 6 v.   CW W1 B1 (af1.3) no.5, p.9
   129 mm.
   Sources: 1545[15], J1550
   Discussion: Osthoff 2:222-3
   Recording: see section IV
Requiem, 5 v.   (CW Mt1 (af1.9) no.29) *see* Nymphes des bois
Requiem (L.U.1807) = Tenor of Absolve, quaesumus, and of
   Nymphes des bois
Respice in me Deus = Je ne me puis tenir
RESPONDE MIHI.   CW Mt5 B20 (af1.46) no.75, p.37
   2. Posuisti in nervo pedem meum
   155 mm.
   Text: Job 13:22-8 (see Osthoff 2:57)
   Sources: Leiden 463 (anon.), 1545[2]
(RESPONSUM ACCEPERAT SIMEON, 3-6 v.).   CW Mt5 B23 (af1.49)
   no.85, p.131
   2. Cum ergo cognovisset (3 v.)
   3. Nunc dimittis (6 v.)
   202 mm.
   Text: Luke 2:26, 28-30
   Source: 1545[3]
   Discussion: SparksP (questions authenticity)
Resurrexit sicut dixit = Regina caeli (4 v.), part 2

Sagitta Jonathae = Planxit autem David, part 3
Salomon autem genuit Reboam = Liber generationis, part 2
SALVE REGINA.   CW Mt5 B25 (af1.52) no.95, p.211
   125 mm.
   Text: Marian antiphon (L.U.276)
   Sources: Dresden 1/D/505 (anon.), Rome Sist.42, Verona
   759
SALVE REGINA, 5 v.   CW Mt3 B11 (af1.35) no.48, p.26
   2. Eja ergo
   3. Et Jesum benedictum

177 mm.
Canon in tenor: Qui perseverat salvus erit
Sources: BarcelonaO 7, Barcelona 681, ModenaS IX, Munich
    34, Rome Sist.24, Saragossa 17, Seville 1, Vienna 15941,
    1521[5], 1535[4], J1555
Intabulations: 1546[23], 1552[35], Coimbra M.M.48
Discussion: Ingram
Editions: Treize livres 12, DavidS
Recording: see section IV
(SALVE, SANCTA FACIES). CW supp. no.4, p.15
    160 mm.
Sources: Bologna Q 20, Milan 2267
Salvum fac dextera tua = Paratum cor meum, part 2
Sana me, Domine = Plusieurs regretz
Sancta Dei genetrix = Vultum tuum, part 2
(SANCTA MATER, ISTUD AGAS). CW supp. no.9, p.41
    87 mm.
Sources: Barcelona 454, Seville 5-5-20 (att. Peñalosa)
Discussion: StevensonJ 219-20 citing further sources with
    attribution to Peñalosa
(SANCTI DEI OMNES). CW Mt5 B20 (afl.46) no.74, p.27
    232 mm.
Sources: LondonR 1070 (anon.), Milan 2267 (anon.), Rome
    Sist.42 (att. Mouton), Rome Sist.86 (att. Mouton),
    Toledo 13, Verona 758, Verona 760, 1504[1], Mouton 1555
Analysis: NovackF 95-6
SANCTUS DE PASSIONE. CW Ma4 B2 (afl.50) no.7, p.142
    1. Sanctus; 2. Pleni (2 v.); 3. Hosanna; 4. Honor et
    benedictio sit crucifixo filio; 5. Benedictus
    70 mm.
Source: 1505[1]
Edition: Osthoff 1:242 (parts 1-3)
Recording: see section IV
Sanctus d'ung aultre amer *see* M. d'ung aultre amer
SCARAMELLA VA ALLA GUERRA. CW W2 B5 (afl.54) no.54, p.16
    37 mm.
Sources: Florence BR 229, Florence BR 337, Florence
    Magl.XIX 164-7
Intabulations: B1532[2], 1544[24]
Discussion: GallicoJ 447-50, JeppesenF 3:18-19
Edition: Ambros 5:134
Recordings: see section IV
Sed tibi soli peccavi = Domine, ne projicias me, part 2
Sepulcrum Christi = Victimae paschali laudes, part 2
Si congié prens (4 v.) *see* Recordans de my segnora
SI CONGIÉ PRENS, 6 v. CW W1 B1 (afl.3) no.12, p.28
    100 mm.
Text: see JefferyL 419

Sources: Bologna A 71, Bologna R 142 (text: O Maria virgo sanctissima), Leipzig 49-50 (text: Miserator et misericors Dominus), Rome Pal.lat.1980-81, St. Gall 463-4, 1545[15], J1550, E1560c (= 1572[2])

Discussion: BenthemZ, BlackburnJ 42ff., Osthoff 2:220-22

Recording: see section IV

Si ego commisi = O bone et dulcissime Jesu, part 2

SI J'AVOYE MARION, 3 v.   CW W2 B5 (afl.54) no.63, p.36

Also: Si j'eusse Marion

Source: 1536[1]

Discussion: BenthemJ 430-31

SI J'AY PERDU MON AMY, 3 v.   CW W2 B5 (afl.54) no.64, p.37
72 mm.

Text: BenthemJ 437, CW p.XIV

Sources: Paris 1597 (anon.), St. Gall 461, 1536[1], 1578[15]

Discussion: BenthemJ

Edition: Giesbert

Recordings: see section IV

(SI J'AY PERDU MON AMYE, 4 v.)

Sources: Florence Magl.XIX 164-7 (anon.), FlorenceC Bas.2442, St. Gall 461 (anon.)

Edition: Giesbert, Osthoff 2:175, mm. 1-7

Si j'eusse Marion see Si j'avoye Marion

(SIC DEUS DILEXIT MUNDUM, 6 v.).   CW Mt5 B24 (afl.51) no.86, p.143

Tenor: Circumdederunt me
68 mm.

Sources: Zwickau LXXIII 3, 1564[3]

See above: Christus mortuus, Nymphes nappés

Sit laus Deo = Ave maris stella (3-4 v.), part 7

Spiritus tuus bonus = Domine, exaudi orationem meam, part 3

STABAT MATER, 5 v.   CW Mt2 B8 (afl.21) no.36, p.51

2. Eia mater fons amoris

Tenor: Comme femme desconfortée (Binchois)

Text: Marian sequence (L.U.1634)

Sources: Brussels 215-6, Brussels 9126, Copenhagen 1848, Copenhagen 1872-3, Florence II.I.232, Hradec Králové II A 26, Hradec Králové II A 41, Leiden 863, LondonR 1070 (anon.), Louvain 163, Munich 12, MunichU 327, MunichU Art.401, Regensburg 892, Rokycany, Rome Chig.C.VIII.234, Rome lat.11973, RomeMas, Toledo 10, Uppsala 76c, Valladolid 16/17, Wroclaw 11, 1519[2], 1520[4], 1538[3], 1538[7], J1555, 1559[1]. Theorist: Faber (1553)

Intabulations: 1536[11] (anon.), 1546[29], 1547[22], 1553[33], 1558[20], B1563[12] (anon.), 1568[23] (anon.), 1571[16] (anon.), 1578[24] (2 versions)

 Discussion: BrownA 479-81 (intabulations), J 479-81
 Editions: Ambros 5:61, PedrellM
 Recordings: see section IV
STETIT AUTEM SALOMON. CW Mt3 B15 (afl.39) no.58, p.125
 2. Benedic, Domine, domum istam
 140 mm.
 Text: 1 Kings 8:22-4
 Sources: Leipzig 51 (anon.), Regensburg 888, 1538[7]

TANT VOUS AIMME, BERGERONETTE
 Source: FlorenceC Bas.2442
 Edition: Osthoff 2:176, mm. 1-6
TENEZ MOY EN VOZ BRAS, 6 v. CW W1 B2 (afl.5) no.13, p.33
 77 mm.
 Sources: Bologna R 142 (text: Vidi speciosam), Leipzig 49
 (anon.; text: Ego sum ipse que deleo), Nürnberg 83795
 (anon.; text: Ego sum ...), Munich 1508 (anon.), 1545[15],
 J1550, E1560c (= 1572[2])
 Discussion: BlackburnJ 42ff., BenthemZ
 Edition: EngelM
Tibi, domina gloriosa = Ave nobilissima creatura, part 2
Tollite hostias = Cantate Domino, part 2
(TRIBULATIO ET ANGUSTIA INVENERUNT ME). CW Mt3 B13 (afl.37)
 no.54, p.95
 57 mm.
 Text: Psalm excerpts: see MattfeldS 164
 Sources: Berlin 40031 (anon.), Dresden 1/D/6, Leipzig 49,
 London Roy.VIII.G.7 (anon.), 1526[5] (att. Verdelot),
 1537[1], 1559[2]
 Intabulations: 1552[29], Krakow 1716
 NobleJ 735 (questions authenticity)
 Editions: PAPTM 6, Hüschen
 Recordings: see section IV
Tu pauperum refugium = Magnus es tu, part 2
Tu potis es primae = Virgo salutiferi, part 2
Tu quae genuisti = Alma redemptoris mater (no.38), part 2
TU SOLUS, QUI FACIS MIRABILIA. CW Mt1 B2 (afl.4) no.14,
 p.56
 2. Nobis esset falacia (Superius, bass: D'ung aultre
 amer)
 90 mm.
 Cf. Missa d'ung aultre amer
 Sources: Florence Pan.27, ModenaS IV, St. Gall 463,
 Washington (with text: O Mater Dei), 1503[1], 1508[3]
 (with text: O Mater Dei)
 Edition: NAWM 29; octavo eds. listed CMP
 Recordings: see section IV

(TULERUNT DOMINUM MEUM, 8 v.)
>   Sources: Dresden Gl.5 (anon.), Dresden Gr.55 (anon.),
>   Dresden Lob.50, Leipzig 49, London Roy.App.44-50 (att.
>   Gombert; text: Je prens congié), Munich 1536 (no.50.
>   As Lugebat David: no.3), Regensburg 786 (text: Lugebat
>   David Absalon), VeronaF 218 (att. Gombert; text:
>   Sustinuimus pacem), 1554[10], 1564[1] (text: Lugebat ...)
>   Intabulation: 1552[35] (att. Gombert)
>   Discussion: Hertzmann
>   Edition: Chorwerk 23
>   Recordings: see section IV

Turbatus est a furore = Domine, ne in furore (Ps.6), part 2

UNA MUSQUE DE BUSCGAYA.   CW W2 B4 (afl.53) no.37, p.5;
>   CW Ma2 B10 (afl.22) no.37, p.119
>   Text: see CW W2 p.XI
>   Canon, superius: Quiescit qui super me volat, Venit post
>   me qui in puncto clamat
>   Sources: Bologna Q 17, Bologna Q 18 (anon.), Cortona
>   95/6-Paris, Florence BR 229, Florence Magl.XIX 178,
>   Rome Giul.XIII.27, RomeC 2856, Seville 5-I-43, 1504[3]
>   Discussion: AtlasC 1:88
>   Edition: Bordes
>   Recordings: see section IV

USQUEQUO, DOMINE, OBLIVISCERIS ME.   CW Mt3 B15 (afl.39) no.60,
>   p.138
>   2. Illumina oculos meos
>   193 mm.
>   Text: Psalm 12 (English 13)
>   Sources: Dresden 1/D/501, Heilbronn XCII/3-XCVI/3 (anon.),
>   1538[6], 1553[4]

Ut collocet eum Dominus = Laudate pueri, part 2

UT PHOEBI RADIIS.   CW Mt1 B4 (afl.7) no.22, p.110
>   2. Latius in numerum canit
>   150 mm.
>   Text: Callahan
>   Sources: Ulm 237, 1505[5]

VENI, SANCTE SPIRITUS, 6 v.   CW Mt3 B12 (afl.36) no.49, p.37
>   2. O lux beatissime
>   177 mm.
>   Text: Pentecost sequence (L.U.880)
>   Sources: Berlin 40013, Bologna R 142 (anon.), Dresden
>   Gl.5 (anon.), Dresden Gr.55 (anon.), Dresden Pirna 8
>   (anon.), Gotha A98, Hradec Králové II A 22, Hradec
>   Králové II A 29, Nürnberg 83795, Regensburg 879,
>   Stuttgart 36, Uppsala 76b (att. Forestier), 1537[1],
>   J1555, 1558[4]

Discussion: BlackburnJ 52n.
Edition: Chorwerk 18
Recording: see section IV
Venite ad me omnes = En non saichant
Venite, comedite = Homo quidam fecit coenam magnam, part 2
(VERBUM CARO FACTUM EST, 5 v.). CW Mt5 B24 (af1.51) no.88,
   p.149
   2. In principio (2 v.)
   3. Cuius gloriam (5 v.)
   Sources: Zwickau LXXIII, 1546[7] (att. Appenzeller)
Verbum incarnatum *see* Ave Maria ... virgo serena (4 v.)
Verum tamen in diluvio = Beati quorum remissae, part 2
VICTIMAE PASCHALI LAUDES. CW Mt1 B5 (af1.9) no.26, p.136
   2. Dic nobis, Maria
   121 mm.
   Text: Easter sequence (L.U.780)
   Sources: MunichU 322-5, St. Gall 463, 1502[1]. Theorist:
      GlareanusD 368 (GlareanusM 2:442)
   Intabulation: St. Gall 530
   Edition: SmijersV 5:140
(VICTIMAE PASCHALI LAUDES, 6 v.). CW Mt5 B22 (af1.48)
   no.81
   2. Sepulcrum Christi
   193 mm.
   Sources: Florence Mag1.XIX 125bis (anon.), Rome Sist.24
      (att. Brunet), RomeV SB E II.55-60, Toledo 10
   Discussion: SparksP 346-9
Videte omnes populi *see* Nymphes, nappés
Vidi speciosam = Tenez moy en voz bras
VIRGO PRUDENTISSIMA. CW Mt1 B5 (af1.9) no.25, p.133
   74 mm.
   Text: Antiphon (L.U.1600[2])
   Sources: Hradec Králové II A 7, MunichU 322-5, St.
      Gall 463, 1502[1], 1537[1] (att. Isaac), 1559[2] (att.
      Isaac)
   Recording: see section IV
VIRGO SALUTIFERI, 5 v. CW Mt2 B7 (af1.18) no.35, p.42
   2. Tu potis es
   3. Nunc caeli regina
   Tenor: Ave Maria
   216 mm.
   Text: by Ercole Strozzi. LowinskyMRM 3:199f.
   Sources: FlorenceM 666, LondonR 1070 (anon.), MunichU
      Art.401, Rome Sist.16, Rome Sist.42, 1519[2], 1534[6], 1557[1]
   Intabulation: 1578[24] (part 3)
   Discussion: Hoffmann-ErbrechtO 292-3, LowinskyMRM 3:87,
      199-201
   Editions: Treize livres 4, LowinskyMRM 5:42

Virgo singula = Ave maris stella, part 2
Virtus sancti spiritus = Praeter rerum seriem, part 2
Vitam praesta puram = Ave maris stella (3-4 v.), part 6
VIVE LE ROY.   CW W2 B4 (af1.53) no.40, p.10
    41 mm.
    Canon, tenor: Finite vocales modulis apteque subinde
      vocibus his vulge nascitur unde tenor. Non varis
      pergit cursu totumque secundum subvehit ad primam per
      tetracorda modum (see Osthoff 2:234-5)
    Source: 1504^3
    Edition: ScheringG 62a
    Recordings: see section IV
(VIVRAI-JE TOUSJOURS EN TELLE PAINE)
    Source: Cambrai 125-8
    Listed as authentic only in TVNM 26 (1976) 35
    Edition: Maldeghem Trésor (profane), 14:12
Voluntarie sacrificabo = Deus, in nomine tuo, part 2
(VOUS L'AREZ, S'IL VOUS PLAIST, 6 v.). CW W1 B2 (af1.5)
    no.16, p.41
    50 mm.
    Sources: 1545^{15}, J1550, E1560c (= 1572^2)
    Discussion: BenthemZ, Osthoff 2:223f.
(VOUS NE L'AUREZ PAS, 6 v.). CW W1 B1 (af1.3) no.2, p.3
    37 mm.
    Sources: 1545^{15}, J1550
    Discussion: BenthemZ, Osthoff 2:223f.
VULTUM TUUM DEPRECABUNTUR. CW Mt1 B4 (af1.7) no.14, p.117
    2. Sancta Dei genetrix
    3. Intemerata virgo
    4. O Maria, nullam tam gravem
    5. Mente tota tibi supplicamus
    6. Ora pro nobis
    7. Christe, fili Dei
    586 mm.
    Text: see Osthoff 2:83-4
    Sources: Barcelona 454 (parts 3-4), Berlin 40021 (anon.,
      part 5), Cambrai 125-8 (anon., part 3), Milan 2266
      (parts 3-6), Munich 19 (anon., part 5), Padua A17
      (parts 1, 3, 5, 7), Regensburg C.120 (part 5), Rome
      Sist.26 (part 5), St. Gall 463 (anon., part 5), Segovia
      (part 3), Ulm 237 (anon., parts 2-6), 1505^2, 1539^2
      (part 5)
    Intabulations: Berlin 40026 (part 5; ed. WarburtonK),
      St. Gall 530 (anon., part 5)
    Analysis: NovackT 318-21, 323-4
    Recording: see section IV

2. Summary categorical lists.

a. Masses. See the entries under the word MISSA in List 1
   above.

b. Separately composed Mass movements. See the entries under
   CREDO, GLORIA, and SANCTUS in list 1 above.

c. Magnificats. See the entries under the word MAGNIFICAT
   in list 1 above.

d. 4-voice works with Latin text
        Absalon fili mi
        Alma redemptoris mater (2 settings)
        (Ave Christe immolate)
        Ave Maria
        Ave Maria ... virgo serena
        Ave maris stella (2 settings)
        Ave munda spes (incomplete)
        Benedicite omnia opera
        Caeli ennarunt
        Christum ducem
        De profundis
        (De profundis)
        (Descendi in ortum meum)
        (Deus in nomine tuo)
        (Deus pacis reduxit)
        Domine exaudi
        Domine ne in furore (2 versions)
        Domine ne projicias
        Domine non secundum peccata
        Dominus regnavit
        Dulces exuviae
        Ecce tu pulchra es
        Facta est autem
        Fama, malum
        Gaude virgo
        Honor, decus, imperium
        (In Domino confido)
        In exitu Israel
        In illo tempore assumpsit
        In principio
        Jubilate Deo
        Laudate pueri
        Levavi oculos meos
        Liber generationis
        Magnus es tu

     Memor esto verbi tui
     Mirabilia testimonia tua
     Misericordias Domini
     Missus est Gabriel
     Mittit ad virginem
     (Nunc dimittis)
     O admirabile commercium
     (O bone et dulcis Domine)
     O bone et dulcissime Jesu
     O Domine Jesu Christe
     Paratum cor meum
     Planxit autem David
     Qui habitat in adjutorio altissimi
     Qui velatus
     (Recordare virgo)
     Regina caeli
     Responde mihi
     Salve regina
     (Salve sancta facies)
     (Sancta mater)
     (Sancti Dei omnes)
     Stetit autem Salomon
     (Tribulatio et angustia)
     Tu solus qui facis mirabilia
     Usquequo Domine
     Ut Phoebi radiis
     Victimae paschali laudes
     Virgo prudentissima
     Vultum tuum

e. 5-voice works with Latin text
     (Ave verum corpus)
     (Beati quorum remissae)
     (Cantate Domino canticum novum)
     De profundis
     Domine Dominus noster
     Homo quidam
     Illibata Dei
     Inviolata, integra et casta
     (Lectio actuum apostolorum)
     Miserere mei Deus
     (Missus est Gabriel)
     (Nesciens mater)
     (Qui regis Israel)
     Salve regina
     Stabat mater
     (Verbum caro factum est)
     Virgo salutiferi

f. 6-voice works with Latin text
    (Absolve quaesumus)
    Ave nobilissima creatura
    Benedicta es, caelorum regina
    Christus mortuus est
    Huc me sydereo
    (In illo tempore stetit)
    (Inter natos mulierum)
    O virgo prudentissima
    O virgo virginum
    Pater noster
    Praeter rerum seriem
    (Regina caeli)
    (Responsum acceperat Simeon)
    (Sic Deus dilexit mundum)
    Veni sancte spiritus
    (Victimae paschali laudes)

g. Other works with Latin text
    Ave verum corpus (2-3 v.)
    (Proch dolor, 7 v.)
    (Tulerunt Dominum meum, 8 v.)
    (Inviolata, integra et casta, 12 v.)
    Qui habitat in adjutorio altissimi (24 v.)

h. 3-voice works with French text or title
    A la mort
    Ce povre mendiant
    Cela sans plus
    De tous biens playne
    En l'ombre d'ung buissonet au matinet
    En l'ombre d'ung buissonet tout au loing
    Entré je suis en grant pensée
    (Fortuna desperata)
    Helas madame
    (J'ay bien rise tant)
    Je me
    Je n'ose plus
    Je sey bien dire
    La belle se siet
    Ma dame, helas
    Mon mary
    Quand je vous voye
    (Que vous, ma dame)
    Se j'avoye Marion
    Si j'ay perdu

i. 4-voice works with French text or title
    A l'eure
    Adieu mes amours
    Baisez moy
    Belle, pour l'amour
    Bergerette savoyenne
    (Coeurs desolez)
    Comment peult avoir joye
    De tous biens playne
    En l'ombre d'ung buissonet au matinet
    Entré je suis
    (Guillaume s'en va)
    Helas madame
    Je ris et si ay larme
    Je sey bien dire
    Le villain
    L'homme armé
    Mille regretz
    Plus n'estes ma maitresse
    Plus nulz regretz
    Qui belles amours
    (Si j'ay perdu)
    Tant vous aimme
    Una musque de Buscgaya
    Vive le roy
    (Vivrai je tousjours)

j. 5-voice works with French text or title
    (Cent mille regretz)
    Coeur langoreulx
    Doleur me bat
    Du mien amant
    (En non saichant)
    (Faulte d'argent)
    Incessament livré suis
    (Incessament mon povre cueur lamente)
    Je me complains
    Je ne me puis tenir
    L'amye a tous
    Mi lares vous
    N'esse pas ung grant desplaisir
    Nymphes des bois (Déploration)
    Parfons regretz
    Plaine de dueil
    Plusieurs regretz

k. 6-voice works with French text or title
>   (Allegez moy)
>   (Baisez moy)
>   J'ay bien cause
>   Ma bouche rit
>   Nymphes, nappés
>   Petite camusette
>   (Pour souhaitter)
>   Regretz sans fin
>   Si congié prens
>   (Vous l'arez)
>   (Vous ne l'aurez pas)

l. Works with Italian text or title
>   El grillo
>   Fortuna d'un gran tempo
>   In te, Domini (macaronic Latin/Italian)
>   La Bernardina
>   La Spagna
>   Recordans de my segnora
>   Scaramella va alla guerra

m. Works generally considered to be instrumental
>   Ile fantazies (3 v.)
>   La Bernardina (3 v.)
>   La plus des plus (3 v.)
>   La Spagna (5 v.)
>   Vive le roy (4 v.)

n. Works intabulated for keyboard instruments
>   Adieu mes amours
>   Ave Maria ... virgo serena
>   Benedicta es
>   Bergerette savoyenne
>   (Faulte d'argent)
>   Fortuna d'un gran tempo
>   Inviolata, integra
>   Je ne me puis
>   Magnificat quarti toni
>   Mass excerpts:
>   M. de Beata Virgine
>   M. faisant regretz
>   M. Hercules
>   M. l'homme armé svm
>   Mente tota (Vultum, part 5)
>   O admirabile commercium
>   Plus nulz regretz
>   Que vous madame

Salve regina (5 v.)
Scaramella
Stabat mater
(Tribulatio et angustia)
Veni sancte spiritus
Victimae paschali laudes
Virgo prudentissima
Virgo salutiferi

o. Works intabulated for lute/vihuela/guitar
Absalon fili mi
Adieu mes amours
(Allegez moy)
Ave Maria ... benedicta
Benedicta es
Coeur langoreulx
Comment peult haver joye
Ecce tu pulchra es
En l'ombre d'ung buissonet tout au loing
(Faulte d'argent)
(Fortuna desperata)
Fortuna d'un gran tempo
In exitu Israel
In principio
In te Domini
Inviolata, integra
Je ne me puis tenir
La Bernardina
La plus des plus
Magnificat, tertii toni (excerpt)
Mass excerpts:
  M. ad fugam
  M. ave maris
  M. de Beata Virgine
  M. faisant regretz
  M. fortuna
  M. gaudeamus
  M. Hercules
  M. la sol fa re mi
  M. l'homme armé st
  M. l'homme armé svm
  M. pange lingua
  M. sine nomine
Memor esto
Mille regretz
Miserere mei
Nymphes, nappés

Pater noster
Plus nulz regretz
Praeter rerum
Que vous ma dame
Qui belles amours
Qui habitat (4 v.)
Salve regina (5 v.)
Scaramella
Stabat mater
(Tribulatio et angustia)
(Tulerunt Dominum)

III. SOURCES

A. MANUSCRIPT SOURCES

The following list cites only literature which is basic,
recent, and/or especially pertinent to Josquin compositions.
Fuller references are given in the invaluable CC (of which
only vol. 1 is available at present writing). Further useful
recent references are given in G articles: *Libraries* and
Sources, manuscript. This list, following the practice of
CC, is arranged by city, with RISM sigla given in parentheses
following each library entry. Compositions listed are either
(1) attributed to Josquin in that source or (2) anonymous in
that source (indicated by an asterisk), but included in section II above. Compositions not included in section II are
italicized. Bibliographic references cite pertinent but
incomplete information about the source unless otherwise
indicated.

AUGSBURG. STAATS- UND STADTBIBLIOTHEK (D-Brd-As)
    Catalogue: GottwaldM
    MS 142a (*olim* 18, *olim* Cim.43). 1505-14, Augsburg
      Entré je suis (4 v.)*, Faulte d'argent, Le villain,
        Missus est ... ad Mariam, Plus nulz regretz*, Text-
        less duo
      CW W1 B2, BenteW 230-42

BARCELONA. BIBLIOTECA CENTRAL DE CATALUÑA (E-Bc)
    Catalogue: PedrellC
    MS 454. Late 15th-early 16th century, Spain
      Ave Maria ... virgo, Intemerata virgo, O Maria (Vultum
        3-4), Sancta mater istud
      AngésMME 1:112-5, StevensonJ 219-20
    MS 681. 1st half of 16th century, from Vich
      Inviolata, Salve regina (5 v.)
      AngésMME 1:134-5

Barcelona0: BARCELONA. BIBLIOTECA ORFEÓN CATALÁN (E-Boc)
    MS 5. Late 15th-early 16th century
        Ave Maria ... virgo*, Domine, non secundum (incomplete)*,
            M. Fortuna*, M. l'homme armé svm (Kyrie, Agnus)
        CW Mal Bl, AnglésMME 1:115, StevensonJ 220
    MS 7. 1583, Barcelona
        Salve regina (5 v.)

BASEL. UNIVERSITÄTS-BIBLIOTHEK (CH-Bu)
    Catalogue: Richter
    MS F.IX.25. 7 partbooks, from 3 different original sets.
        16th century
        M. ave maris, M. gaudeamus, M. Hercules (alto, tenor),
            M. l'homme armé svm, M. malheur (alto, tenor)
        CW Mal Bl
    MS F.IX.59-61. 4 partbooks: 1543^{24} with ms additions
        Mille regretz*
    MS F.X.1-4. 4 partbooks, containing dates 1522, 1524
        In mynem sinn (= Entré je, 4 v.), *Lordault, Mon seul
        plaisir*
        CW Wl B3
    MS F.X.17-20. 4 partbooks, after 1550
        (All contents anon.) Mille regretz*, In te, Domini,
        speravi*
        CW Wl B3
    MS F.X.21. Tenor partbook, containing dates 1521-75
        Ach unfal (= Qui belles amours)*, Cum sancto spiritu
            (M. de Beata Virgine)
    MS F.X.22-24. 3 partbooks: 1535^{11} with ms additions
        Ave verum corpus (2-3 v.), In te Domine speravi
        CW Mtl Bl

BERLIN. DEUTSCHE STAATSBIBLIOTHEK (D-Ddr-Bds), and BERLIN.
    STAATSBIBLIOTHEK PREUSSISCHER KULTURBESITZ (D-Brd-B)
        MS 40013 (*olim* Z13). *ca.* 1540, Torgau. Missing since 1945
            Ave Maria ... virgo serena, Domine non secundum, Haec
                dicit (= Nymphes, nappés), Missa coronata (= de Beata
                Virgine), Pater noster, Veni sancte spiritus
            CW Mtl Bl, Gerhardt 21-5
        MS 40021 (*olim* Z21; D-Brd-B). *ca.* 1490-1500, Nürnberg
            Magnificat 3. toni, Mente tota (Vultum 5), M. una
                musque, Verbum incarnatum (= Ave Maria ... virgo
                serena)
            JustM
        MS 40031 (*olim* Z21). 16th century. Missing since 1945
            Domine ne projicias, Tribulatio et angustia*
            CW Mt3 B13

MS 40043 (*olim* Z43). *ca.* 1542-4, Torgau. Missing since
   1945
  Pater noster*
  Gerhardt 37-40
MS 40091 (*olim* Z91; D-Brd-B). *ca.* 1516, Rome
  M. la sol fa re mi
  CW Mal B2, StaehelinZS
MS 40194 (D-Brd-B). 16th century
  Mille regretz*
MS 40634. 1st half of 16th century. Missing since 1945
  M. allez regretz (?) (att. N. Scomtianus)

BOLOGNA. CIVICO MUSEO BIBLIOGRAFICO MUSICALE (I-Bc)
  Catalogue: GaspariC
  MS A 71 (*olim* 159). 1510-15
    Si congié prens
    AnglésMME 1:91, 128
  MS Q 16 (*olim* 109). 1487-*ca.* 1510
    Ma dame, helas ("Dux Carlus Burgensis")
    AtlasC 1:235-6, JeppesenF 2:10-16, Pease
  MS Q 17 (*olim* 148). *ca.* 1500
    Adieu mes amours, Comme peult, En l'ombre (no.60),
      In pace (= Que vous), Una musque
    AtlasC 1:236-7, WexlerN
  MS Q 18 (*olim* 143). Early 16th century, Bologna
    (All contents anon.) Adieu mes amours*, Alma redemptoris
      (no.38)*, In te Domine*, La Bernardina*, Una musque*
    AtlasC 1:237, JeppesenF 2:10, 108-9
  MS Q 19 ("Rusconi Codex"). Contains date 1518
    Ecce tu pulchra
    CW Mt2 B6, LockwoodJM 234-41, LowinskyMRM 3:52-60
  MS Q 20. 4 partbooks, *ca.* 1530
    Ave maris (no.94), Domine ne in furore (no.59), Nunc
      dimittis, Regina caeli (CW supp.)
    LowinskyMRM 3:197, Osthoff 2:16
  MS Q 25. 2 partbooks (alto, tenor), 1525-50
    M. de Beata Virgine*
  MS R 141 *see* section B below: [1521][4]
  MS R 142. Partbook, before 1550, northern Italy
    Adjuro vos (= Plus nulz regretz), Ave Maria ... bene-
    dicta, Ave nobilissima, Benedicta es, Ecce tu pulchra,
    Huc me sydereo, In illo tempore stetit, Iniquos odio
    habui, Inter natos, Memor esto, M. Hercules: Agnus 3,
    Missus est ... ad Mariam, O Maria virgo (= Si congié
    prens), Petite camusette, *Salva nos*, Veni sancte
    spiritus*, Videte omnes (= Nymphes, nappés), Vidi
    speciosam (= Tenez moy)
    BenthemZ 187, BlackburnJ 50-54

BolognaS: BOLOGNA. ARCHIVIO MUSICALE DELLA FABBRICERIA DI SAN
    PETRONIO (I-Bsp)
    MS A.XXIX (*olim* B). 1512-27, Bologna
        O bone et dulcissime Jhesu*
        FratiP 464-6, TirroE, TirroG
    MS A.XXXI (*olim* D)
        Me de Beata Virgine: Credo, M. Hercules, M. la sol fa
        re mi, M. l'homme armé svm, M. malheur
        Frati 464-6, J 712ff., TirroG

BRUSSELS. BIBLIOTHÈQUE ROYALE (B-Br)
    General survey: BorrenI
    MS 215/216. 1512-6, Brussels/Mechlin. Scribe Alamire
        Stabat mater*
        CW Mt2 B8, KellmanJ 209, 211-3, Robijns
    MS 228. 1516-23, for Marguerite of Austria
        Ce povre mendiant*, Entré je suis, Plaine de deuil*,
        Proch dolor*
        CW W1 B1, KellmanJ 213, PickerC
    MS 9126. 1505, Brussels/Mechlin
        Gaude virgo, Huc me sydereo, M. ave maris, M. Hercules,
        M. malheur, Missus est ... ad Mariam, Stabat mater
        CW Mt3 B11, KellmanJ 210, KellmanO 10-12
    MS 11239. *ca.* 1500, for Marguerite of Austria
        Belle pour l'amour, Que vous madame
        PickerC
    MS IV 90. Superius partbook; Tournai 94 is the matching
        tenor partbook. Early 16th century, Bruges
        Baisey moy, En l'ombre (no.60), Mon mary m'a defamée*,
        Plus nulz regretz
        BenthemJ 422, 424, 429, Faider 96-8
    MS IV 922 ("Occo Codex"). *ca.* 1530-34, Brussels/Mechlin
        M. pange lingua (with Gascongne Benedictus, from his
        M. es hat ein Sinn)
        Huys, KellmanJ 215-6; *Facsimilia musica neerlandica 1*

BUDAPEST. ORSZÁGOS SZÉCHÉNYI KÖNYVTÁRA (H-Bn)
    Catalogue (in prep.): Murányi
    MS Bártfa 2. 6 partbooks, *ca.* 1550 and later
        Praeter rerum
    MS Bártfa 8. 4 partbooks, *ca.* 1550
        M. pange lingua*
    MS Bártfa 20. 2 partbooks (superius, tenor), after 1603
        M. de Beata Virgine
    MS Bártfa 22. Tenor partbook, after 1550
        Magnificat 7. toni, Te Deum
    MS Bártfa 23. Bass partbook, after 1550
        Da siceram mentibus (= Je ne me puis tenir; att. Claudin)
        AlbrechtZ

(MS) Bártfa Pr.6. 4 partbooks: Rhau 1544 print (Resinarius
    works), with ms additions made after 1558
    Deus pacis reduxit, Huc me sydereo, M. de Beata Virgine
    Fox

CAMBRAI. BIBLIOTHÈQUE MUNICIPALE (F-Ca)
    Survey: CoussemakerN
    MS 4. *ca.* 1526-30, Cambrai
      (All contents anon.) M. de Beata Virgine*
      CW Ma3 B16
    MS 18 (20). *ca.* 1520, Cambrai
      M. de Beata Virgine, Credo (m.f. no.6), M. gaudeamus
      CW Mal B3
    MS 125-8 (*olim* 124). 4 partbooks, 1542, Bruges
      Cum sancto spiritu (M. de Beata Virgine), Mille regretz*,
        Qui habitat, Vivrai-je tousjours
      CW Wl Bl, BarthaB, Diehl

CAMBRIDGE. MAGDALENE COLLEGE (GB-Cmc)
    Catalogue: James
    MS Pepys 1760. 1498-1516
      O admirabile commercium
      LowinskyMRM 3:133-5; numerous refs. in CC 128-9

CASALE MONFERRATO. ARCHIVIO E BIBLIOTECA CAPITOLARE, DUOMO
  (I-CMac)
    Catalogue: CrawfordS
    MS M (D)
      (All contents anon.) M. l'homme armé st*
      StaehelinW

COPENHAGEN. DET KONGELIGE BIBLIOTEK (DK-Kk)
    MS 1848. *ca.* 1525, Lyons?
      Baisez moy (6 v.), Plusieurs regretz, Stabat mater,
        Tenez moy
      BenthemJ 422
    MS 1872. 7 partbooks, dated 1541-3, from Königsberg
      Allegez moy, Benedicta es*, Huc me sydereo*, In illo
        tempore stetit, La Spagna*, N'esse pas un grant dis-
        plaisir, Pater noster, Praeter rerum, Stabat mater
      Foss
    MS 1873. 5 partbooks, with date 1556
      Faulte d'argent, In illo tempore stetit, N'esse pas
        un grant displaisir, Petite camusette, Pour souhaitter,
        Stabat mater
      CrevelA 337-44

CORTONA. BIBLIOTECA COMMUNALE (I-CT)
    MS 95/6. 2 partbooks (superius, alto) of original set
      of 7. Tenor of set is Paris n.a.fr.1817. Late 15th-

early 16th century, Italy
Alma redemptoris/Ave, Baisez moy*, Ecce tu pulchra,
  Entre je suis*, Liber generationis, Misericordias,
  Missus est ... ad Mariam, O bone et dulcis Domine,
  Paratum cor, Una musque*
CW W1 B2, AtlasC 1:240-41, NowackiL 162

DANZIG *see* GDANSK

DRESDEN. SÄCHSISCHE LANDESBIBLIOTHEK (D-ddr-Dlb)
  Catalogue: SteudeM
  MS 1/D/3 (*olim* B.1270). 6 partbooks, *ca.* 1550-60
    De profundis (att. "Henricus Josquin"; by Senfl),
      Miserere mei, Qui regis Israel
    CW Mt2 B8, Steude no.5
  MS 1/D/6 (*olim* Oels 529). Bass partbook, *ca.* 1560-70
    De profundis (no.47)*, Domine ne in furore (no.59)*,
      Judica me (by Caen), In exitu Israel, Propter peccata
      (= La Spagna), *Te Deum*, Tribulatio et angustia
    CW Mt3 B11, Steude no.7
  MS 1/D/501. Superius partbook, *ca.* 1560
    Jubilate Deo*, Usquequo*
    Steude no.9
  MS 1/D/505 (*olim* Annaberg 1248). Late 1520's, Annaberg
    Liber generationis*, Planxit David*, Salve regina
      (no.95), *Scimus quoniam diligentibus*
    Kindermann, NoblittMD
  MS 1/E/24 (*olim* B265). 5 partbooks, dated 1571, Germany
    Cum sancto spiritu (M. de Beata Virgine)
    Steude no.12
  MS Glashütte 5. Superius and alto partbooks, 1583-8
    Pater noster, Praeter rerum, Tulerunt Dominum*, Veni
      sancte spiritus*
    Steude no.21
  MS Grimma 53. 5 partbooks, *ca.* 1560-75, Meissen
    M. de Beata Virgine (Kyrie, Gloria). Steude no.41
  MS Grimma 55. 7 partbooks, *ca.* 1560-80, Meissen
    Tulerunt Dominum, Veni sancte spiritus*
    Steude no.43
  MS Grimma 57. 4 partbooks, *ca.* 1560-86, Meissen
    Praeter rerum*, Qui habitat*
    Steude no.45
  MS Grimma 59a. Superius partbook, *ca.* 1560, Meissen
    Domine Dominus noster, Miserere mei
    Steude no.48
  MS Löbau 50. 7 partbooks: prints with ms additions, *ca.*
    1610-60
    Tulerunt Dominum
    Steude no.66

MS Pirna VIII. *ca.* 1560-70, Pirna
Veni sancte spiritus*
CW Mt3 B12, Steude no.101

EDINBURGH. UNIVERSITY LIBRARY (GB-Eu)
MS 64 ("Dunkeld Antiphoner") *ca.* 1557, Scotland
Benedicta es*
Elliot

EISENACH. STADTARCHIV (D-ddr-EIa)
MS s.s. ("Eisenacher Kantorenbuch"). *ca.* 1550, Eisenach
M. de Beata Virgine (Kyrie, Gloria), *Sancta trinitas*
(by Févin?)
CW Ma3 B16, SchröderE

ERLANGEN. UNIVERSITÄTSBIBLIOTHEK (D-brd-ERu)
Catalogue: FischerK
MS 473/4. 1540-41, Heilbronn
De profundis (no.47), In te Domine
KrautwurstH

FLORENCE. BIBLIOTECA NAZIONALE CENTRALE (I-Fn)
Catalogue: BecheriniC. Study of several MSS: RifkinS
MS II.I.232 (*olim* Magl.XIX 58). *ca.* 1515-20, Florence
Alma redemptoris, Alma redemptoris/Ave, Ave Maria ...
virgo serena, Ecce tu pulchra, Huc me sydereo, Liber
generationis, Memor esto, Misericordias (incomplete),
M. de Beata Virgine (Gloria), Missus est ... ad Mariam,
O admirabile commercium, O bone et dulcis Domine,
Planxit autem, Stabat mater
CW Mt1 B1, CummingsF, EitnerH, LowinskyM, NowackiL
MS Banco Rari (BR) 229 (*olim* Magl.XIX 59). 1492-3,
Florence
Adieu mes amours, Helas ma dame*, In pace (= Que vous),
J'ay bien nori (= J'ay bien rise; att. Japart),
Scaramella, Una musque
AtlasC 1:248, BragardM, BrownMRM, Jeppesen 2:53-4,
146-7, JustM 1:125-8
MS Banco Rari (BR) 337 (*olim* Pal.1178). Bass partbook,
ca. 1520
In te Domine (att. Dascanio), Scaramella
JeppesenF 2:43-5, 126-31
MS Magl.XIX 58 *see above* MS II.I.232
MS Magl.XIX 59 *see above* MS BR 229
MS Magl.XIX 107bis. Before 1513, Florence
Adieu mes amours, Bergerette Savoyenne, In pace (4 v.;
= Que vous), Liber generationis
CW Mt1 B3, AtlasC 1:243
MS Magl.XIX 117. *ca.* 1505-20
Plus nulz regretz (incomplete)
AtlasC 1:244-5

MS Magl.XIX 125bis. Alto partbook, 1530-34, Florence
  Victimae paschali (6 v.)*
  LowinskyN 206-24
MS Magl.XIX 164-7. 4 partbooks, *ca*. 1505-40
  (All contents anon.) Ave Maria ... virgo*, Entré je
  suis (no.57)*, Missus est ... ad Mariam*, O bone et
  dulcis Domine*, Paratum cor meum*, Plus nulz regretz*,
  Scaramella*, Si j'ay perdu*
  CW Mtl B1, AtlasC 1:246, PannellaC, RifkinS
MS Magl.XIX 178. *ca*. 1492-4, Florence
  Adieu mes amours, Belle pour l'amour, *Cela ne plus* (by
  Lannoy?), Comment peult, Helas ma dame, In pace
  (= Que vous), Nay biem (= J'ay bien rise), Je me,
  Je n'ose, *O Venus bant* (by Weerbeke?), Recordans de
  my segnora, Una musque
  AtlasC 1:247
MS Palatino 1178 *see above* MS BR 337
MS Panciatichi 27. Early 16th century, Northern Italy
  Fortuna d'un gran tempo*, In te Domine, Tu solus
  CW Mtl B2, AtlasC 1:252, JeppesenF 2:37-42, 122-5

FlorenceC: FLORENCE. BIBLIOTECA DEL CONSERVATORIO DI MUSICA
  LUIGI CHERUBINI (I-Fc)
  Survey: BecheriniM
  MS Basevi 2439. *ca*. 1508, Brussels/Mechlin
    A la mort, Fortune d'estrange plummaige (= Ce povre
    mendiant), Par vous je suis (= Entré suis, no.57)
    KellmanJ 211, NewtonF
  MS Basevi 2441. Early 16th century, Milan
    In te Domine (att. Dascanio)
    Jeppesen 2:50, 140-43, RifkinS 306
  MS Basevi 2442 ("Strozzi Chansonnier"). 3 partbooks
    (superius, altus, tenor), *ca*. 1510-28
    En l'ombre (no.59), Faulte d'argent, Je ris*, Plus
    nulz regretz, Si j'ay perdu, Tant vous aime
    BrownCF, BrownMS

FlorenceD: FLORENCE. DUOMO (I-Fd)
  MS 11. Includes date 1557, Florence
    Praeter rerum*

FlorenceM: FLORENCE. BIBLIOTECA MEDICEA-LAURENZIANA (I-Fm)
  MS acq. e doni 666 (*olim* Olschki, *olim* coll. Sra. Alida
    Varsi; "Medici Codex"). 1518
    Inviolata, Miserere mei, O admirabile commercium,
    Nymphes des bois
    LockwoodJM, LowinskyM, LowinskyMRM 3-5 (commentary,
    facsimile, edition), StaehelinR (with bibliography
    of earlier discussion)

FlorenceR: FLORENCE. BIBLIOTECA RICCARDIANA E MORENIANA (I-Fr)
  MS 2356. *ca.* 1480-1500, Florence
    Helas ma dame (4 v.)
    AtlasC 1:256, PlamenacP, PlamenacS
  MS 2794. *ca.* 1480-90
    Adieu mes amours, Entré suis
    JonesF, RifkinP

FRANKFURT AM MAIN. STADT- UND UNIVERSITÄTSBIBLIOTHEK (D-brd-F)
  MS Mus.fol.2. *ca.* 1510-20, Belgium
    M. ave maris, M. l'homme armé svm
    Hoffmann-ErbrechtF, Hoffmann-ErbrechtM

GDÁNSK. BIBLIOTEKA POLSKEIJ AKADEMII NAUK (PL-GD)
  MS 4003. 4 partbooks, *ca.* 1554-63
    Mille regretz*, Tenez moy*

GOTHA. FORSCHUNGSBIBLIOTHEK GOTHA (D-ddr-GO1)
  MS Chart.A98 (Gothaer Chorbuch; Codex Gothanus). 1545,
    Torgau
    Ave Maria ... virgo*, Haec dicit (= Nymphes, nappés)*,
    Pater noster*, Praeter rerum*, Qui habitat*, Veni
    sancte spiritus*
    CW Mt2 B1, Gerhardt 29-37, LowinskyMRM 3:128

GÖTTINGEN. STAATLICHES ARCHIVLAGER (D-brd-Ga), MS 7 *see*
  KÖNIGSBERG 1740

GREIFSWALD. UNIVERSITÄTS-BIBLIOTHEK (D-ddr-GRu)
  MSS BW 640-41 (*olim* Eb 1 33). 2 partbooks (superius,
    bassus) bound with 1538[8]
    Cum sancto spiritu (M. de Beata virgine)

HALLE. SEKTION GERMANISTIK UND KUNSTWISSENSCHAFTEN DER MARTIN-
  LUTHER UNIVERSITÄT, FACHBEREICH MUSIKWISSENSCHAFT (D-ddr-
  HAmi)
    MS Ed.1147, App. 5 partbooks: 1540[6] and 1550[2] with ms
      additions
    Domine Dominus noster, Plusieurs regretz*, N'esse pas*
    CW W1 B1

HAMBURG. STAATS- UND UNIVERSITÄTSBIBLIOTHEK (D-brd-Ha)
  MS Hans.III 12-16 (= III,4 IV). 5 partbooks, *ca.* 1554.
    Missing since 1945
    Allegez moy
    CW W1 B3
  MS s.s.
    J'ay bien cause
    CW W1 B3

HEILBRONN. STADTARCHIV, MUSIKSAMMLUNG (D-brd-HB)
   Catalogue: Siegele
   MS IV/2-V/2. 2 partbooks (tenor, quintus) of 1539[8] with
      ms additions, after 1575
      Qui habitat (24 v.)
   MS XCII/3-XCVI/3. 4 partbooks (prints of 1545 and 1566
      with ms additions, evidently copied from 1538[6])
      Domine, ne in furore (2: no.39 and no.59*), Domine ne
      projicias*, Usquequo*

HRADEC KRÁLOVÉ. KRAJSKE MUZEUM, KNIHOVNA (CS-Hk)
   Catalogue: ČernýS; survey BoormanC
   MS II A 6. 1st half of 16th century
      Christum ducem, Virgo prudentissima
   MS II A 7 ("Codex Speciálnik"). Late 15th-early 16th
      century
      Ave Maria ... virgo, Christum ducem, Virgo prudentissima
      JustM 1:121-2
   MS II A 21. 16th century
      Domine ne in furore (no.39), Qui habitat
   MS II A 22. 2 partbooks (superius, tenor), late 16th
      century
      Pater noster (with Czech. translation), Propter peccata
      (= La Spagna), Veni sancti spiritus
      SnížkováJ 280-84
   MS II A 26. 2nd half of 16th century
      Nesciens mater (1 v.), Stabat mater (2 v.)
      SnížkováJ 280-84
   MS II A 29. 2nd half of 16th century
      Stabat mater (1 v.), Nesciens mater (1 v.), Veni
      sancte spiritus (1 v.)
   MS II A 41, App. 2nd half of 16th century
      Stabat mater (2 v.)

JENA. UNIVERSITÄTS-BIBLIOTHEK (D-ddr-Ju)
   Catalogue: RoedigerG
   MS 3. 1518-20, Brussels/Mechlin; for Frederick of Saxony
      M. ave maris, M. Elizabeth (= M. faisant regretz),
      M. Fridericus dux Saxonie (= M. Hercules), M. Malheur,
      M. sine nomine
      CW Ma2 B6, KellmanJ 213
   MS 7. *ca.* 1516, Brussels/Mechlin
      M. de Beata Virgine
      CW Ma3 B16, KellmanJ 212
   MS 21. *ca.* 1521-5, Brussels/Mechlin, scribe Alamire, for
      Frederick of Saxony
      M. allez regretz, M. pange lingua*
      CW Ma4 B18, KellmanJ 213

MS 31. Early 16th century, for Wittenberg
Missa ad fugam*, M. l'homme armé st*
CW Ma3 B14

MS 32. *ca.* 1500-1520, for Wittenberg
(All contents anon.) M. Gaudeamus*, M. la sol fa re mi*,
M. l'homme armé svm*
CW Ma1 B1

MS 36. Early 16th century; for Wittenberg
M. de Beata Virgine (Credo)
CW Ma3 B16

KALININGRAD *see* KÖNIGSBERG

KASSEL. MURHARD'SCHE UND LANDESBIBLIOTHEK (D-brd-Kl)
Catalogue: Israel
MS 4° Mus. 24. 4 partbooks, after 1550
Beati omnes (by Champion), *Bonitatem fecisti* (by Carpentras), Caeli ennarunt, *Clamavi: ad Dominum*, De
profundis (no.90), De profundis (no.91), *Deus in ad-*
jutorium (by Senfl), Domine Dominus noster*, Domine
exaudi, Domine ne in furore (no.39), *Domine ne in*
furore (by Verdelot), *Domine quis habitat*, *Domini*
est terra (by Appenzeller? Vinders?), *Illumina oculos*
meos, In Domino confido*, *Lauda Jerusalem* (by Maitre
Jan), Laudate pueri, Memor esto, Miserere mei, Qui
habitat, Qui habitat (24 v.)*
Osthoff 2:19-20, NagelJ 102-5
MS 4° Mus. 38. *ca.* 1566
Inviclata (12 v.)
NagelJ 105, Osthoff 2:19

KÖNIGGRÄTZ *see* HRADEC KRÁLOVÉ

KÖNIGSBERG. STAATS- UND UNIVERSITÄTSBIBLIOTHEK (USSR-KA)
Survey: Müller-BlattauM
MS 1740. 5 partbooks, *ca.* 1537-43, copied by Matthias
Krüger. 4 of the set missing since 1945; the Bassus
is now Göttingen. Staatliches Archiv, MS 7 (cf.
CC 1:250, 439)
Alleluia: Laudate Dominum, In illo tempore assumpsit,
Ite in mundum, M. da pacem (att. Mouton), *Petre tu*
es pastor, Regina caeli (CW supp.)
CW Ma4 B19, LogeM, SparksM 70

LEIDEN. GEMEENTE-ARCHIEF (NL-Lu)
MS 862. 1559, for Leiden
Benedicta es, O virgo prudentissima
CW Mt3 B11, LandK
MS 863 ("Choirbook C"). 1559, for Leiden
Huc me sydereo, *M. tous les regretz* (by LaRue), *M. sub*

tuum praesidium (by LaRue), *Requiem, 6 v.* (by Richafort), Stabat mater
CW Mt2 B6, LandK

MS 865. 1559

O bone et dulcissime*, Praeter rerum
LandK

LEIPZIG. UNIVERSITÄTS-BIBLIOTHEK (D-ddr-LEu)
Thomaskirche MSS 49/50 (III A alpha 17-21). 5 partbooks,
1558
Beati omnes (by Champion), *Conserva me* (by Wolff or
Finck), Delevi ut nubem (= Faulte d'argent), *Ecce
sacerdos magnus*, Magnificat 4. toni (att. Brumel),
Magnificat 7. toni, Miserator et misericors (= Si
congié prens), M. pange lingua, Pater noster, Petite
et accipete (= Petite camusette), Sana me (= Plusieurs
regretz), Tribulatio et angustia, Tulerunt Dominum,
Venite ad me (= En non saichant)
CW Ma4 B18, BlackburnJ 42-50, OrfM, YouensM, YouensR
Thomaskirche MS 51 (III A alpha 22-23). 2 partbooks,
tenor and bass, 1555
Dominus regnavit*, In te Domine*, M. allez regretz,
M. l'homme armé, Phrygian mode, M. malheur, *M. mon
seul plaisir*
CW Ma1 B5, NoblittR, OrfM
MS 1494 ("Nikolas Apel Codex"). *ca.* 1492-1504
Ave Maria ... virgo (2 v., lacks text)
EDM 32-4 (commentary, transcription; does not include
Ave Maria)

LONDON. BRITISH LIBRARY (*olim* British Museum) (GB-Lbm)
Catalogue: Hughes-Hughes
MS Add. 19583. One of a set of partbooks for the Este
family, around 1530. Two others are extant: Modena
a.F.2.29 and Paris n.a.fr.4599
Domine ne in furore (no.39), Domine ne in furore (no.
69), Inviolata, Miserere mei
BraithwaiteI, LockwoodJM 234n., LowinskyMRM 3:117,
NowackiL 163
MS Add. 35087. Compiled for H. Laurinus (d.1509)
En l'ombre (no.60), Mon mary*, Pauper sum ego (= Ce
povre mendiant)*, Quant je vous voye, *Vrai dieu
d'amours*
BenthemJ 422, 434ff., 439, BernsteinCF 13n., Braith-
waiteI, McMurtryB
MS Egerton 3051. Late 15th century. Originally part of a
larger MS of which Washington is another part
In te Domine (att. Dascanio)
JeppesenF 2:64-7, 154-7, StaehelinF

MS Roy.8.G.VII. 1516-22, Brussels/Mechlin, scribe Alamire
   Absalon fili mi, Descendi in hortum*, Dulces exuviae*,
   Fama malum*, Missus est ... ad Mariam
   BraithwaiteI, KellmanJ 212, TirroRG, Walker
MS Roy.20.A.XVI. *ca.* 1500-1510
   L'eure est venue, Que vous madame, *Mes pensées*
   LitterickM
MS Roy.App.41-4
   Plus nulz regretz
MS Roy.App.49-54
   Je prens congié (= Tulerunt; att. Gombert)

LondonR: LONDON. ROYAL COLLEGE OF MUSIC (GB-Lcm)
   MS 1070. *ca.* 1535
   (All contents anon.) Ave Maria ... virgo*, Factum est
      autem (incomplete)*, Homo quidam*, Huc me sydereo*,
      Liber generationis*, Memor esto*, Mittit ad virginem*,
      Virgo salutiferi*
   LowinskyMB, LowinskyMRM 3:115-6, NowackiL 164

LOUVAIN. BIBLIOTHÈQUE DE L'UNIVERSITÉ (B-LVu)
   MS 163. Dated 1546; now destroyed
   Benedicta es, Praeter rerum, Stabat mater
   Prod'homme 486-7

MADRID. BIBLIOTECA REAL (E-Mp)
   MS 1335 (*olim* 2-I-5; "Cancionero de Palacio")
   In te Domine (later addition to MS; facsimile MME 5,
      p.34)
   AnglésMME 1, 5, 10, 14, BarbieriC

MILAN. ARCHIVIO DELLA CAPPELLA MUSICALE DEL DUOMO (I-Md)
   MS 2266 (Librone IV). Late 15th-early 16th century; a
      Gaffurius codex. Partially destroyed by fire
   Ave Maria ... virgo, Vultum tuum (parts 3-6)
   AMMM 15:pp.II-III, AMMM 16 (facsimile), FinscherZV 62,
      JeppesenD, SartoriC, SartoriQ
   MS 2267 (Librone III). Late 15th-early 16th century; a
      Gaffurius codex.
   Alma redemptoris/Ave, M. ave maris, M. Hercules (Gloria,
      Credo, Sanctus), M. l'homme armé st (lacks Benedictus,
      Agnus), Salva sancta facies, Sancti Dei omnes
   AMMM 15, JeppesenD, SartoriC

MilanA: MILAN. BIBLIOTECA AMBROSIANA (I-Ma)
   MS Mus. E 46. After 1530
   M. ave maris, M. de Beata virgine, *M. dirige* (by LaRue),
      M. la sol fa re mi (incomplete), M. pange lingua,
      M. quem dicunt homines
   CW Mal B2, J 712

MODENA. ARCHIVIO CAPITOLARE DEL DUOMO (I-MOd)
   General study: CrawfordV
   MS III. ca. 1520-24
     Magnificat 4. toni (att. LaRue)
     NowackiL 164
   MS IV. ca. 1513-20
     Magnificat 4. toni (att. Agricola), Memor esto*, M. d'ung
       aultre amer, M. malheur (Kyrie, Gloria, Agnus)*, Tu
       solus
     CW Ma2 B11, NowackiL 164-5
   MS IX. ca. 1510-30
     Ave Maria ... virgo, Ave Maria (= Pater noster, part 2),
       In principio, Inviolata, Salve regina (5 v.)
     CW Mt2 B10, LowinskyMRM 3:61, RubsamenM 77-80

ModenaE: MODENA. BIBLIOTECA ESTENSE (I-MOe)
   Catalogue: LodiC
   MS alpha.F.2.29 see London. British Library. MS Add.
     19583
   MS alpha.M.1.2 (olim L457). Early 16th century
     M. fortuna, M. l'homme armé svm
     CW Ma1 B1
   MS alpha.N.1.2 (olim L.452, 502). 1534, Ferrara
     Patrem vilayge, Credo (from M. de Beata virgine)
     CW Ma3 B16, J 712ff.

MUNICH. BAYERISCHE STAATSBIBLIOTHEK (D-brd-Mbs)
   Catalogue: MaierM; catalogue (partbooks, tablatures):
     GöllnerB
   MS 7. ca. 1495-1534, Brussels/Mechlin, scribe Alamire
     M. da pacem (att. Bauldeweyn)
     CW Ma4 B19, Bente 196-7, KellmanJ 209, SparksM 71ff.,
       96-8
   MS 10. ca. 1525-30
     In principio, Liber generationis, Miserere mei, Qui
       habitat
     Bente 66-70
   MS 12. ca. 1520-30
     Pater noster, Stabat mater
     Bente 63-6
   MS 19. 1st half of 16th century
     Ave Maria ... virgo, Memor esto, Mente tota (= Vultum
       tuum, part 5)*
     Bente 166-71
   MS 34. ca. 1520-30, for William IV of Bavaria, scribe
     Alamire
     (All contents: Salve regina settings) Salve regina
       (5 v.)
     CW Mt3 B11, Bente 197-8, KellmanJ 215

MS 41. Mid-16th century
  Ave Maria ... virgo (with 2 added voices), O bone et
    dulcissime Jesu (with 2 added voices)
  Bente 191-3
MS 53. *ca.* 1510
  Credo chiascun (att. Brumel), Credo villayge II (att.
    Brumel)
  Bente 62-3
MS 260. A collection of *Bicinia*
  M. malheur (Benedictus, Agnus 2), M. pange lingua
    (Pleni, Benedictus, Agnus 2), Per illud ave (Benedicta
    es, part 2)*
  RRMR 16-17 (edition)
MS 510. Before 1519, belonged to Cardinal Matthäus Lang
  M. de Beata Virgine (Gloria, Credo), M. faisant
    regretz, M. pange lingua
  CW Ma3 B13, Bente 206-7, HallS 46ff.
MS 1501. 4 partbooks, mid-16th century
  Mille regretz*
  CW W1 B3
MS 1508. 6 partbooks, mid-16th century
  Incessament mon povre cueur*, Je me complains, Je ne
    me puis*, Plus nulz regretz*, Tenez-moy*
  Taricani
MS 1516. 4 partbooks, *ca.* 1530-40
  Adieu mes amours, Coeurs desolez (4 v.)*, En l'ombre
    (no.59)*, La Bernardina*, Mille regretz*, Plus nulz
    regretz*
  CW W1 B3, Göllner 92ff., WhislerM
MS 1536. 5 partbooks (of original set of 7), before 1583
  Benedicta es (12 v. version, att. J. and Johannes
    Castilletus), *In nomine Jesu* (by Mouton?), Lugebat
    David (= Tulerunt Dominum), O virgo prudentissima,
    Pater noster, Tulerunt Dominum, Veni sancte spiritus
  Göllner 101-32
MS 3154 ("Chorbuch des Nicolaus Leopold"). *ca.* 1466-1511,
    Innsbruck
  Ave Maria ... virgo, *O Venus bant* (by Weerbeke?), M.
    fortuna
  CW Mt1 B1, JustM 1:120-21, NoblittC, NoblittD
MS C (*olim* Cim.210). 1538
  M. de Beata virgine
  CW Ma3 B16, Bente 198-206

MunichU: MUNICH. UNIVERSITÄTS-BIBLIOTHEK (D-brd-Mu)
  Catalogue: GottwaldMM
  MS 322-5 (*olim* Cim.44a). 4 partbooks dated 1527, belonged
    to Glareanus

Ave Maria ... virgo, Ave verum corpus (2-3 v.), Domine
non secundum, Magnus es tu, Memor esto, *Tulerunt
Dominum* (4 v.), Victimae paschali laudes, Virgo
prudentissima
  CW Mt1 B1
MS 326 (*olim* Cim.44b, part 1). Altus partbook, 1543
  Ave Maria ... virgo*, Date siceram (= Je ne me puis;
  possibly att. Leonhard Zinnsmeister), In te Domine*,
  Inviolata*
  CW Mt1 B1, FinscherW
MS 327 (*olim* Cim.44b, part 2). Tenor partbook
  Miserere mei*, Stabat mater
MS 328-31 (*olim* Cim.44c). 4 partbooks, copied by Lukas
  Wagenrieder *ca.* 1520-30
  Qui belles amours*
  Bente 255-68, EitnerF, SmithersT
MS 4° Art.401, Appendix (*olim* Cim.44i). 4 partbooks:
  1520^1, 1520^2 with ms additions made from 1536 to
  1540
  Ave nobilissima, Benedicta es, Circumdederunt (= Nymphes,
  nappés), Lectio actuum, Missus est ... a Deo, O virgo
  prudentissima, Pater noster, Praeter rerum, Stabat
  mater, *Verbum bonum*, Virgo salutiferi
  CW Mt2 B9, LowinskyMRM 3:118-9

NÜRNBERG. GERMANISCHES NATIONALMUSEUM (B-brd-Ngm)
  MS 83795. 2 partbooks, tenor and incomplete bassus, *ca.*
  1529-48
  Ave Maria ... virgo, Domine non secundum, Ego sum ipse
  (= Tenez moy)*, Haec dicit Dominus (= Nymphes,
  nappés), Veni sancti spiritus
  Gerhardt

PADERBORN. ERZBISCHÖFLICHE AKADEMISCHE BIBLIOTHEK (D-brd-PA)
  MSS 9822-3
  In te Domine

PADUA. BIBLIOTECA CAPITOLARE (I-Pc)
  Catalogue: Constant, Garbelotto
  MS A17. 1522, by Fr. Jordanus Pasetus Venetus
  Benedicta es, Christum ducem, *Congratulamini* (by Le
  Brun? Richafort?), Pater noster, Vultum tuum (parts
  1, 3, 5, 7)

PARIS. BIBLIOTHÈQUE NATIONALE (F-Pn)
  MS f.fr.1597. *ca.* 1500-1510
  (All contents anon.) En l'ombre (no.61), Que vous
  madame, Si j'ay perdu (no.64)
  Osthoff 2:165, ShippC

MS f.fr.2245. *ca.* 1496(?)
En l'ombre (no.59)
KellmanJ, Osthoff 2:164
MS n.a.fr.1817 *see* Cortona 95/6
MS n.a.fr.4379 *see* Seville 5-I-43
MS n.a.fr.4599 *see* London Add. 19583

PARIS. BIBLIOTHÈQUE NATIONALE, FONDS DU CONSERVATOIRE (F-Pc)
Rés. 41. 1532 print (Carpentras) with ms additions
O admirabile commercium (parts 1, 2, 5)
CW Mt1 B1
Rés.Vm⁷ 504 (I-III). 3 superius partbooks printed by
Egenolff, Frankfurt am Main, in the 1530's. I = RISM
[1535]¹⁴
I: Adieu mes amours*, Baisez moy*, Comment peult*,
Plus nulz regretz*. III: En l'ombre (no.61)*, For-
tuna d'un gran tempo*, La plus de la plus belle*
Berz, BridgmanC, StaehelinZ
Rés.Vm⁷ 676. Dated 1502, Italy
In te Domine
BridgmanM, JeppesenF 2:84-6, 176-81
Rés.Vma 851 ("Bourdeney MS"). Late 16th century; in
score notation
Benedicta es, M. la sol fa re mi, M. l'homme armé svm
BridgmanAL, MischiatiA

PIACENZA. ARCHIVIO DEL DUOMO (I-PCd)
Catalogue: Bussi
(Partbooks). Early 16th century
Ave Maria (= Adieu mes amours)
BussiP, PickerJ, WeidensauLE

REGENSBURG. BISCHÖFLICHE ZENTRALBIBLIOTHEK, PROSKE MUSIK-
BIBLIOTHEK (D-brd-Rp)
General description: HammS 698-9; catalogue in prep.:
Scharnagl
MS A.R.773 *see* MS C.100 below
MS A.R.786/837. 1578
Lugebat David (= Tulerunt Dominum)
MS A.R.840. *ca.* 1570
In principio
MS A.R.863-70. 5 partbooks, 2nd half of 16th century
Qui habitat
MS A.R.879. 1571
M. l'homme armé svm, Veni sancti spiritus*
J 732-3
MS A.R.888. 1577
Stetit autem Salomon

MS A.R.891-2. 5 partbooks, *ca.* 1575-80
   Inviolata, Stabat mater
   LowinskyMRM 3:120
MS A.R.893
   Huc me sydereo
MS A.R.940-41. 4 partbooks, 1557-60
   In principio, In te Domine, Qui habitat
   BrenneckeH
MS A.R.1018. 5 partbooks, 1562
   Date siceram (= Je ne me puis)*
MS B.211-15. *ca.* 1538
   Clamavi: ad Dominum, Date siceram (= Je ne me puis)*,
      Haec dicit (= Nymphes, nappés), Magnus es tu (att.
      Josquin, "*alii* H.F.")
   MohrH
MS B.220-22. 4 partbooks, *ca.* 1538
   M. gaudeamus (Agnus 3), M. la sol fa re mi (Agnus 2),
      M. l'ami Baudichon (Qui tollis), M. malheur (Pleni),
      Per illud ave (Benedicta es, part 2)
   MohrH
MS C.100 (*olim* A.R.773)
   M. la sol fa re mi, M. pange lingua
MS C.120 ("Pernner Codex"). Before 1522-3
   Adieu mes amours, De profundis (no.47), Domine ne in
      furore (no.39)*, Inviolata, Mente tota (Vultum, part
      5), Praeter rerum, Plus nulz regretz, *Tous les regretz*
      (by LaRue)
   KrautwurstC

ROKYCANY. CHURCH ARCHIVE
   MS A V 22a-b. 2 partbooks, 2nd half of 16th century
      Praeter rerum, Propter peccata (= La Spagna), Stabat
         mater
      SnížkováJ 284

ROME. BIBLIOTECA APOSTOLICA VATICANA (I-Rvat)
   Partial catalogues: HaberlV, LlorensC, LlorensO, SherrP;
      survey: AnglésT
   Cappella Giulia MS XII.2.C.48. *ca.* 1520
      M. de Beata Virgine, M. l'homme armé svm, M. pange
         lingua*
      CW Ma1 B1 and Ma4 B18, LlorensO 67-9, LowinskyMRM 3:
         60-61
   Cappella Giulia MS XII.4.E.1. Dated 1536
      Missus est ... a Deo, O virgo virginum, Praeter rerum
      LlorensO 48-51
   Cappella Giulia MS XIII.27 ("Codex Medici"). *ca.* 1490-94,
      for Giuliano di Medici
      Adieu mes amours, E comepeult (= Comment peult), In

pace (= Que vous ma dame), J'ay bien nori (= J'ay bien
rise)*, Recordans de my segnora, Una musque
AtlasC (commentary, edition), LlorensO 43-8

Cappella Sistina MS 15. Early 16th century
Alma redemptoris/Ave, Ave maris (3-4), Illibata Dei,
Honor decus
GerberR 50-58, J 649-50, LlorensC 21-9

Cappella Sistina MS 16. Early 16th century
Benedicta es, Memor esto, M. pange lingua, Praeter
rerum, Virgo salutiferi
LlorensC 29-31

Cappella Sistina MS 19. *ca.* 1534-49
Missus est ... a Deo
CW Mt2 B9, LlorensC 39-41

Cappella Sistina MS 23. Early 16th century
Credo de vilage (I)*, Credo de vilage (= M. de Beata
Virgine: Credo), Credo des rouges nes (= Credo
Chiascun mi crie), Gloria (M. de Beata Virgine),
M. faisant regretz, M. gaudeamus, M. l'ami Baudichon,
M. malheur
CW Ma1 B3, J 712-3, LlorensC 48-9, SherrN

Cappella Sistina MS 24. 1545
Inviolata, O virgo prudentissima, Salve regina (no.48)
CW Mt2 B10, LlorensC 50-52

Cappella Sistina MS 26. Early 16th century
Mente tota (= Vultum, part 5)
LlorensC 54-6

Cappella Sistina MS 35. Late 15th century
Domine non secundum (parts 1, 2, 4)
LlorensC 69-72

Cappella Sistina MS 38. 1563
De profundis (no.90), In exitu Israel, In illo tempore
assumpsit, In principio, Inter natos*, Miserere mei,
Planxit autem, Qui habitat
LlorensC 76-9

Cappella Sistina MS 41. Early 16th century
Credo de tous biens playne, M. ave maris, M. d'ung
aultre amer, M. la sol fa re mi, M. l'homme armé st,
Tu solus
HaarR 566-7, plate 41, LlorensC 81-3

Cappella Sistina MS 42. Beginning of 16th century
Ave Maria ... virgo, Homo quidam, Liber generationis*,
Salve regina (no.95), Virgo salutiferi
CW Mt1 B1, LlorensC 83-6, NowackiL 166

Cappella Sistina MS 44. Early 16th century
Magnificat 4. toni
LlorensC 90-92, Osthoff 2:61-2

Cappella Sistina MS 45. Early 16th century
  Huc me sydero, M. de Beata Virgine, M. Hercules, O bone
    et dulcissime Jesu
  J 712-13, Llorens 92-4
Cappella Sistina MS 46. Early 16th century
  Mittit ad virginem, O admirabile commercium*, O virgo
    virginum*. Llorens suggests that an anonymous Chris-
    to inclita candida may be by Josquin.
  CW Mt1 B1, LlorensC 94-8, LowinskyMRM 3:232, RifkinS
    317-9
Cappella Sistina MS 49. Early 16th century
  M. ad fugam*
  CW Ma3 B14, LlorensC 100-102
Cappella Sistina MS 55. *ca.* 1523-34
  Pater noster. (Also: M. de Beata Virgine by Josquin
    Dor, not the same as the work by J. des Prez)
  CW Mt3 B12, LlorensC 108-10, AntonowyczMP 58-9
Cappella Sistina MS 63. Late 15th-early 16th century
  Missus est ... ad Mariam*
  LlorensC 119-20
Cappella Sistina MS 154. 1550-55
  M. l'homme armé svm
  CW Ma1 B1, LlorensC 181-2
Cappella Sistina MS 160. *ca.* 1518-9, for Leo X, scribe
    Alamire
  M. de Beata Virgine
  KellmanJ 212, LlorensC 187-9
Cappella Sistina MS 197. Beginning of 16th century
  M. l'homme armé svm
  LlorensC 213
MS Chig.C.VIII.234. 1498-1503, Brussels/Mechlin
  M. l'homme armé st (Kyrie, Gloria, Credo), Stabat
    mater
  CW Ma1 B5, KellmanJ 195-6, KellmanO
MS lat.11953
  Plus nulz regretz, Stabat mater
MS Pal.lat.1976-79. 4 partbooks, 1528-31, for Marie of
    Hungary
  Ave Christe immolate*, Descendi in hortum meum
  KellmanJ 215, RubsamenM 72-4, Seeley
MS Pal.lat.1980-81. Tenor and bass partbooks, 1513-23
  M. faisant regretz, M. pange lingua, Petite camusette,
    Si congié prens
  LowinskyMRM 3:61-5, NowackiL 167, RubsamenM 74ff.
San Pietro B 80. Early 1480's, but J. work added later
  Domine non secundum
  HammM

Santa Maria Maggiore MS Archivium Liberianum 26. 16th century
  Benedicta es, O virgo virginum*, Praeter rerum
  RubsamenM 549
Santa Maria Maggiore MS JJ III.4. Altus partbook, 1520-50
  Credo Chiascun*, M. ave maris, M. la sol fa re mi,
    M. pange lingua
  HudsonN

RomeC: ROME. BIBLIOTECA CASANATENSE (I-Rc)
  MS 2856 (*olim* O.V.208). 1490-93; has Este and Gonzaga
    arms
    Adieu mes amours, En l'ombre (no.59), Ile fantazies de
      Joskin, In pace (= Que vous ma dame), Una musque
    AtlasC 1:239-40, LlorensCC, WolffC

RomeMas: ROME. BIBLIOTECA MASSIMO
  MS Lippmann no.143. Superius and tenor partbooks, *ca.*
    1532-4
    Praeter rerum, Stabat mater
    LippmannM, LippmannU

RomeV: ROME. BIBLIOTECA VALLICELLIANA (I-Rv)
  MS San Borromeo E II.55-60. 6 partbooks, 1530-31, Florence.
    (A new number has been given this MS. NowackiL 167
    gives it as MS Inc.107bis; Crawford in JAMS 32,
    p.152, cites a new shelf mark of S^1 35-40.)
    Inter natos, Pater noster, Praeter rerum, Veni sancti
      spiritus, Victimae paschali (no.81)
    LowinskyN, NowackiL 167

ROSTOCK. UNIVERSITÄTS-BIBLIOTHEK (D-ddr-ROu)
  Survey: Gaehtgens
  MS 40. 4 partbooks, mid-16th century
    M. de Beata Virgine (Kyrie, Gloria), *M. missus est
      angelus* (by Moulu), M. quae est ista (= M. malheur)
  MS 49. 6 partbooks, 1566, by Jacob Praetorius
    Magnificat 7. toni, M. de Beata Virgine, M. pange
      lingua, *M. veni sancte spiritus*, *Te Deum* (by de Silva?),
      Te Deum
    CW Ma3 B16, BolteC, Hoffmann-ErbrechtO

ST. GALL. STIFTSBIBLIOTHEK (CH-SGs)
  See Geering
  MS 461 (Fridolin Sicher Liederbuch). *ca.* 1500
    Cela sans plus, En l'ombre (no.61)*, Incessament mon
      povre coeur (att. LaRue), Si j'ay perdu*
    Giesbert (edition)
  MS 462 (Johannes Heer of Glarus Liederbuch). 1510-30
    Adieu mes amours*, Guillaume s'en va, Ile fantazies
    BrownP, Clinkscale, SMd 5 (edition, commentary)

MS 463-4. Superius and altus partbooks, 1517-20, compiled
by Egidius Tschudi
Adieu mes amours, Ave Maria ... virgo, Ave verum (no.12),
Bergerette savoyenne, *Bonitatem fecisti* (by Carpen-
tras), De profundis (no.47), Domine non secundum,
Fama malum, Huc me sydereo, In pace (= Que vous ma
dame)*, In te Domine, Inviolata, Je ris et si*, Magnus
es tu, Memor esto, Mente tota (Vultum, part 5),
Miserere mei (with 6th v. by Bidon), M. de Beata
Virgine (Gloria), M. Hercules (Agnus 2), O bone et
dulcissime, *O Venus bant* (by Weerbeke?), Planxit
autem, Praeter rerum, Tu solus, *Tulerunt* (4 v.),
Victimae paschali (no.26), Virgo prudentissima
CW Mt1 B1, Geering, LoachA

SARAGOSSA. BIBLIOTECA CAPITULAR DE LA SEO (E-Zs)
MS 17
Ave Maria (Pater noster, part 2), Salve regina (no.48)

SEGOVIA. CATEDRAL, ARCHIVIO CAPITULAR (E-SE)
MS s.s. Late 15th-early 16th century; belonged to Queen
Isabella
Ave Maria ... virgo, Bergerette savoyenne, Fortuna
desperata, In pace (= Que vous ma dame), Intemerata
virgo (Vultum, part 3), J'ay bien norri (= J'ay bien
rise; att. Joh. Joye), *Magnificat*, M. l'homme armé st
AnglésMI, BakerU, JustM 1:122-4, StevensonJ 224

SEVILLE. CATEDRAL, BIBLIOTECA CAPITULAR Y COLOMBINA (E-Sc)
MS 1. 1st half of 16th century
Ave Maria (Pater noster, part 2), Benedicta es, Ecce
tu pulchra es, Inviolata, Praeter rerum, Salve regina
(no.48)
CW Mt3 B11, AnglésMC, StevensonJ 223
MS 5-I-43. Early 16th century chansonnier, part of which
is Paris n.a.fr.4379
Paris: Helas ma dame*, Una musque
AtlasC 1:257, MoerkS, PlamenacR, PlamenacSP (facsimile)

SION (SITTEN). KAPITELARCHIV (CH-Sk)
MS Tiroir 87, Mappe 4
In te Domine (reference in TVNM 26, 1976, p.37)

STUTTGART. WÜRTEMBERGISCHE LANDESBIBLIOTHEK (D-brd-S1)
Catalogues: GottwaldH, Halm
MS 25. *ca.* 1542
In illo tempore stetit*
CW Mt3 B14, Bente 45
MS 36. 1548-50
Veni sancte spiritus
CW Mt3 B12

MS 44. *ca.* 1540
  (All contents anon.) M. ave maris, M. de Beata Virgine,
    M. la sol fa re mi
  CW Ma1 B3
MS 45. *ca.* 1538
  M. allez regretz*
  CW Ma4 B20
MS 46. 1539
  M. da pacem, M. gaudeamus
  CW Ma1 B3, SparksM 81ff.
MS 47. *ca.* 1507
  M. l'homme armé st (lacks Agnus)

TOLEDO. CATEDRAL, BIBLIOTECA CAPITOLAR (E-Tc)
  Descriptive lists: LenaertsMS, Rubio PiquerasC, Steven-
    sonT
  MS 9. *ca.* 1540-60
    M. ad fugam, M. ave maris, M. faysans regretz, M.
      l'homme armé svm, M. malheur
    CW Ma1 B1
  MS 10. *ca.* 1550
    Inviolata, Missus est ... ad Mariam, Stabat mater,
      Victimae paschali (no.81)
  MS 13. *ca.* 1540-60
    Ave nobilissima, In illo tempore assumpsit
  MS 16. 1542
    M. de Beata Virgine, M. pange lingua
    CW Ma4 B18
  MS 17. 1550
    In principio
  MS 18. *ca.* 1540-60
    Benedicta es, Pater noster
    CW Mt3 B11
  MS 19. 1543
    M. da pacem, M. la sol fa re mi
    CW Ma4 B19, SparksM 73ff.
  MS 21. 1549
    Absolve, quaesumus (in black notation), M. l'homme armé
      svm (Agnus 3)
  MS 22. Early 16th century, Netherlands*
    Benedicta es, Homo quidam, In exitu Israel, In prin-
      cipio, Liber generationis, M. de Beata Virgine,

---

*This MS, lost for many years, was recently located by Robert J.
Snow. It is in the office of the Obra y Fábrica of the Toledo
Cathedral and is now numbered Res.23. See *Abstracts of Papers
Read at the forty-eighth annual meeting of the American
Musicological Society*.... Ed. by D. Kern Holoman [Davis:
University of California, 1982], p. 19.

Praeter rerum, Qui habitat
SparksM 128, StevensonJ 222, plate 34
MS 27. 1550
M. gaudeamus, M. Hercules

TOURNAI. BIBLIOTHÈQUE DE VILLE, MS 94 *see* BRUSSELS IV 90

ULM. SCHERMAR'SCHE BIBLIOTHEK (D-Brd-Usch)
MS 237abcd. 4 partbooks, 1551
Ave Maria ... virgo*, Ecce tu pulchra, En non saichant*,
Gaude virgo, Je ris et si, M. de Beata Virgine (Cum
sancto spiritu), Missus est ... ad Mariam*, Ut
Phoebi, Vultum tuum (parts 2-6)*
CW Mtl Bl

UPPSALA. UNIVERSITETSBIBLIOTEKET (S-Uu)
MS Vok mus i hs 76b
Ma bouche rit, M. de Beata Virgine, M. fortuna, Plusieurs
regretz, Praeter rerum, Veni sancte spiritus (att.
Forestier)
StevensonT
MS Vok mus i hs 76c
Benedicta es, Faulte d'argent, Liber generationis,
M. de Beata Virgine, Missus est ... ad Mariam, Plus
nulz regretz
StevensonT
MS Vok mus i hs 89
M. de Beata Virgine (Cum sancto spiritu)

UTRECHT. BIBLIOTHEEK DER RIJKSUNIVERSITEIT (NL-Uu)
MS Lerma
Ave Maria (Pater noster, part 2), Benedicta es

VALLADOLID. CATEDRAL, ARCHIVIO MUSICAL
Catalogues: AnglésA, López-Calo
MS 6 (= Anglés 5)
Ave Maria (Pater noster, part 2)
CW Mt3 B12
MS s.s. (Anglés no.15). Tenor partbook
Ave Maria (Pater noster, part 2)
MS 17 (225)
Benedicta es, Stabat mater
MS 255. Tenor partbook, 2nd half of 16th century
Benedicta es

VERONA. BIBLIOTECA CAPITOLARE (I-VEcap)
Catalogue: TurriniP
MS 757
Cela sans plus*, Ma dame helas*
MS 758
Ecce tu pulchra es, O bone et dulcis Domine, Sancti Dei
omnes

MS 759
  Salve regina (no.95; superius only)
MS 760. *ca.* 1530
  De profundis (no.91), Laudate pueri, Sancti Dei omnes
  NowackiL 168
MS 761. Beginning of 16th century
  (All contents anon.) M. l'ami Baudichon
  SmijersVz 179

VeronaF: VERONA. BIBLIOTECA DELL'ACCADEMIA FILARMONICA (I-VEaf)
  Catalogue: TurriniC
  MS 218. 8 partbooks, *ca.* 1534-38
    Ave Maria ... virgo (8-v. version), Sustinuimus pacem
      (= Tulerunt Dominum)
    Böker-HeilZ, NowackiL

VIENNA. ÖSTERREICHISCHE NATIONALBIBLIOTHEK (A-Wn)
  Survey: Grasburger
  MS 1783. *ca.* 1500, gift of Philip the Fair to Manuel of
      Portugal; scribe Alamire
    M. ave maris stella
    DixonM, KellmanJ 210, RubsamenU 370
  MS 4809. *ca.* 1521-5, for R. Fugger
    M. ave maris, M. de Beata Virgine, M. faisant regretz*,
      M. Hercules*, M. malheur, M. pange lingua ("de
      venerabilii sacramento"), M. sine nomine ("in
      diatessaron sequentia signis")
    KellmanJ 201-4, 213
  MS 11778. Companion volume to MS 4809
    Credo Chiascun, Credo vilayge (II), M. fortuna, M. l'ami
      Baudichon*, M. l'homme armé st, M. l'homme armé svm
    CW Ma1 B1, KellmanJ 201-4, 214
  MS 11883. Beginning of 16th century
    M. la sol fa re mi (Kyrie, part of Gloria), M. malheur
  MS SM 15495 (*olim* Kunsthistorisches Staatsmuseum,
      Sammlung für Plastik und Kunstgewerbe, MS 5248).
      1493-1511, for Maximilian I
    M. faisant regretz, M. una musque
    CW Ma2 B10, KellmanJ 200, 211
  MS SM 15500. 1544
    Jubilate Deo, Magnus es tu
  MS 15941. 3 partbooks (altus, tenor, bassus) of original
      4, *ca.* 1521-31, for Fugger family
    Ave Christe, Ave munda spes, De profundis (no.47, att.
      Champion), Descendi in hortum, In exitu Israel, In
      principio, Qui habitat, Salve regina (no.48)
    KellmanJ 201ff., 214-5, NowackiL 168, SparksM 98-104
  MS 18746. 5 partbooks, *ca.* 1523, for R. Fugger, scribe
      Alamire
    (All contents anon.) Douleur me bat, Du mein amant,

Incessament livré suis, Je me complains, Parfons re-
gretz, Plaine de dueil, Plusieurs regretz
CW Wl B2, BenthemE, KellmanJ 184, 214
MS 18810. 5 partbooks with dates 1524, 1533, copied by
Lucas Wagenrieder
Entré je suis, Plus nulz regretz, Qui belle amours
CW Wl B3, Bente 264-8, RobisonV
MS 18832. 2 partbooks (complete set), *ca.* 1521-5, for
Fugger family
M. gaudeamus (Benedictus, Agnus 2), M. la sol fa re
mi (Agnus 2), M. pange lingua (Pleni, Benedictus,
Agnus 2)
Nowak

WARSAW. BIBLIOTEKA UNIWERSYTECKA (PL-Wu)
MS 58 (*olim* Breslau MS Mf.2016). *ca.* 1500, Bohemia/
Silesia?
Ave Maria ... virgo, Mente tota (Vultum, part 5)*,
Que vous madame
FeldmannA, FeldmannC, JustM 1:114-20

WASHINGTON, D.C. LIBRARY OF CONGRESS (US-Wc)
M2.1 M6 (*olim* Wolffheim collection). Late 15th century;
originally part of a larger collection, another part
of which is now London Egerton 3051
Adieu mes amours*, In pace (= Que vous madame)*,
O mater Dei (= Tu solus)
RifkinN, StaehelinF, WolffheimM 2:no.1262

WEIMAR. HAUPT- UND PFARRKIRCHE (D-ddr-WR...)
MS s.s. 1st half of 16th century
M. de Beata Virgine (att. LaRue)
CW Ma3 B16
Codex B (now in Jena, according to KirschJ 274). *ca.* 1542
Haec dicit (= Nymphes nappés)

WOLFENBÜTTEL. LANDEBIBLIOTHEK (D-brd-W)
MS A. *ca.* 1520
M. de Beata Virgine

WROCLAW. BIBLIOTEKA UNIWERSYTECKA (PL-Wu)
Catalogues: BohnM, KuhnB (Brieg MSS)
MS 2. 1572; copy in score of MS 5, q.v. Destroyed
MS 5. 6 partbooks, 2nd half of 16th century. Destroyed
Ave Jesu Christe (by Verdelot), *Congratulamini* (by
LeBrung? Richafort?), In illo tempore stetit,
Tulerunt
CW Mt3 B14, BohnM 20-22, SparksP 358, WarburtonK viii
MS 6. 1567, score notation
In principio, Praeter rerum
BohnM 22-26, WarburtonK viii

MS 11. 2nd half of 16th century
  Praeter rerum, Stabat mater
  BohnM 43-5
MS 12. *ca*. 1600. Destroyed
  Date siceram (= Je ne me puis)*
  BohnM 36-9
MS Brieg K40. 1 partbook (quintus), 2nd half of 16th
    century
  Praeter rerum
  KuhnB 24-5
MS Brieg K54. 4 partbooks (superius, altus, tenor, quin-
    tus), late 16th century
  Praeter rerum
  KuhnB 36-9
MS I F 428 (*olim* Frankfort an der Oder, Viadrina Library;
    "Grüne Codex der Viadrina"). *ca*. 1510-30, Germany
  In amara crucis (Qui velatus, part 4)
  StaehelinG

ZWICKAU. RATSSCHULBIBLIOTHEK (D-ddr-Z)
  Catalogue: Vollhardt. These MSS are sometimes cited by
    library numbers and sometimes by the simpler Voll-
    hardt numbers.
  MS XXXIII,34 (Voll.19). 5 partbooks, late 16th century
    Stabat mater
  MS XLI,73 (Voll.25). 4 partbooks, late 16th century
    Qui habitat
  MS LXXIII (Voll.4; "Schalreuter MS"). 6 partbooks, 1547
    Homo quidam, Verbum caro
  MS LXXIV,1 (Voll.11). 6 partbooks, 2nd half of 16th cen-
      tury
    Ecce Dominus veniet (by Senfl), Haec dicit (= Nymphes
      nappés)
  MS LXXVIII,2 (Voll.1). 4 partbooks, 1531
    Textless work
  MS LXXVIII,3 (Voll.12). 3 partbooks (superius, tenor,
      bass), before 1546
    Cela sans plus, La plus de plus, Ma dame helas
  MS LXXXI,2 (Voll.16). 3 partbooks (superius, tenor, bass),
      early 16th century
    Benedicite omnia opera, Deus pacis (att. Stoltzer),
      Domine ne in furore (no.39)*
  MS XCIV,1 (Voll.9). Alto, tenor partbooks, 1590
    Praeter rerum*, Tulerunt Dominum

B. PRINTED SOURCES

1. Printed collections devoted to Josquin alone (See Noble0)

J1502. *Misse Josquin. L'omme armé, super voces musicales.
La sol fa re mi. Gaudeamus. Fortuna desperata, L'omme
armé, sexti toni.* Venice: Petrucci, Sept. 27, 1502.

———. 2nd ed.: Fossombrone, March 1, 1514 (1515 n.s.).

———. 3d ed.: Fossombrone, May 29, 1516.

———. Reprint: Rome, Jacopo Giunta, Giovanni Giacomo Pasoti,
Valerio Dorico, 1526.

J1505. *Missarum Josquin liber secundus. Ave maris stella.
Hercules dux ferrarie. Malheur me bat. L'ami baudichon.
Una musque de buscaya. D'ung aultre amer.* Venice: Ottaviano
Petrucci, 1505. [Facsimile ed. PetrucciJ.]

———. 2nd ed.: Fossombrone, 1515.

———. Reprint: Rome: Jacopo Giunta, Giovanni Giacomo Pasoti,
Valerio Dorico, 1526.

J1514. *Missarum Josquin liber tertius. Mater patris. Faysans
regres. Ad fugam. Di dadi. De beata virgine. Missa sine
nomine.* Fossombrone: Petrucci, 1514.

———. 2nd ed.: Fossombrone, 1516.

———. Reprint: Rome: Giunta (& as above), 1526.

(1545 Susato see 1545[15] below)

J1550. *Trente sixiesme livre contenant xxx. chansons tres
musicales, a quatre cinq & six parties, en cinq livres
... le tout de la composition de feu Iosquin des prez....*
Paris: Attaingnant, March 14, 1549 (1550 n.s.).
HeartzP no.162
Allegez moy, Baises-moy (6 v.), Cent mille regretz,
Coeur langoreulx, Coeurs desolez (5 v.), Douleur me
bat, D'un mien amant, En non sachant, Faulte d'argent,
Incessament livré, Incessament mon povre, Je me complains, Je ne me puis tenir, L'amye a tous, Ma bouche
rit, Nesse pas un grand desplaisir, Nimphes nappés,
Parfons regrets, Petit camusete, Plaine de deuil,
Plus n'estes ma maitresse, Plus nulz regretz, Plusieurs
regretz, Pour souhaiter, Regretz sans fin, Si congié
prens, *Si vous n'avez aultre desir*, Tenez moy, Vous
l'aurez, Vous ne l'aures pas
Discussion: BlackburnJ 55-60

J1555. *Josquini Pratensis, musici praestantissimi, moduli,*
  ex sacris literis dilecti, et in 4, 5, et 6 vocis dis-
  tincti. Liber primus. Contratenor. Paris: A. Le Roy,
  R. Ballard, 1555.
    Benedicta es, Huc me sydereo, Inviolata, Liber genera-
      tionis, Mittit ad virginem, O virgo virginum, Pater
      noster, Paratum cor meum, Praeter rerum, Planxit
      autem, Qui habitat, Regina caeli, Salve regina (5 v.),
      Stabat mater, Veni sancte spiritus
    CW Mtl Bl gives introduction, contents

J1558-60. Isenburg prints of masses, no place, no publisher.
  Now in Wiesbaden Landesbibliothek. Includes M. l'homme
  armé st, M. pange lingua. See CW Mal B6, RISM A:I:4
  no.J676-7, MfMg 24 (1892) 157-8, MoserM

2. Anthologies. The numbers below follow RISM:RI; numbers
  prefaced by E refer to EitnerB. General works on pub-
  lishers are: Berz and BridgmanC on Egenolff; BoormanP,
  NobleO, and SartoriB on Petrucci; Meissner, Bain, and
  Forney on Susato; LesureA/Thibault on Le Roy-Ballard;
  Chapman and PickerM on Antico; Cusick on Dorico; see
  further the individual entries in G, Bautier-Regnier.

1501. *Harmonice musices odhecaton A.* Venezia: O. Petrucci,
  15 mai 1501. Later eds.: 1503², 1504².
    Adieu mes amours, Bergerette savoyenne, Cela sans plus,
      De tous biens playne, Fortuna d'un gran tempo, La
      plus de plus, Ma dame helas*, *O Venus bant* (anon.
      1503², 1504²)
    Edition: HewittO
    Discussion: BoormanF, AtlasC 1:250-52, ReeseH
    Facsimiles: MMMF 1:10, PetrucciH

1502¹. *Motetti A numero trentatre A.* Venezia: O. Petrucci,
  9 mai 1502.
    Ave Maria ... virgo, Victimae paschali (4 v.), Virgo
      prudentissima
    DrakeF

1502². *Canti B. numero cinquanta B.* Venezia: O. Petrucci,
  5 febr. 1501 (1502 n.s.). Later ed.: 1503³.
    Baises moy (4 v.), Baises moy (6 v.)*, Comment peult,
      L'omme armé
    Edition, commentary: HewittC
    Facsimile: MMMLF 1:23

1503[1]. *Motetti De passione De cruce De beata virgine et
    huius modi.B.* Venezia: O. Petrucci, 10 mai 1503.
        Ave verum, Domine non secundum, O Domine Jesu Christe,
        Qui velatus, Tu solus
    DrakeF, Barclay-Squire

1504[1]. *Motetti C.* Venezia: O. Petrucci, 15 set. 1504.
    4 partbooks.
        Ave Maria ... benedicta, Factum est autem, Liber
        generationis, Magnus es tu, Missus est ... ad Mariam,
        O bone et dulcis Domine, Planxit autem, Sancti Dei
        omnes*

1504[3]. *Canti C. N⁰ cento cinquanta.* Venezia: O. Petrucci,
    10 febr. 1503 (1504 n.s.).
        A l'eure, En l'ombre (no.59), Je sey bien dire, La
        Bernardina, Que vous ma dame (att. Agricola), Una
        musque, Vive le roy
    Facsimile: MMMF 1:25

1504[4]. *Frottole libro primo.* Venezia: O. Petrucci, 28 nov.
    1504.
        In te Domine speravi (Josquin Dascanio)
    JeppesenF 1:12-9, 78-81
    Editions: IM, Schwartz

1505[1]. *Fragmenta missarum.* Venezia: O. Petrucci, 31 oct.
    1505. 4 partbooks.
        Credo ciascun me crie, Credo de tous biens playne,
        Credo la belle se siet (by R. de Févin?), Credo
        villayge (I and II), Gloria de beata Virgine, *M.
        Ferialis*, Sanctus de passione, Sanctus d'ung aultre
        amer
    Osthoff 1:124, CW Ma2 B11

1505[2]. *Motetti libro quarto.* Venezia: O. Petrucci, 4 jun.
    1505. 4 partbooks.
        Alma redemptoris mater/Ave, Gaude virgo, Ut Phoebi,
        Vultum tuum

1505[4]. *Frottole libro tertio.* Venezia: O. Petrucci, 6 febr.
    1504 (1505 n.s.). Later ed.: 1507[2]
        El grillo (Josquin Dascanio)
    Edition: IM
    Discussion: JeppesenF 1:21-4, 84-7

1508[1]. *Motetti a cinque libro primo.* Venezia: O. Petrucci,
    1508. 4 partbooks extant.
        Homo quidam, Illibata Dei, Requiem (= Nymphes des
        bois)

1508[3]. *Laude libro secondo*. Venezia: O. Petrucci, 11 jan.
1507 (1508 n.s.).
O mater Dei (= Tu solus)
Edition: JeppesenM

[1513] (not RISM). *Quinquagena carminum*. Mainz: Schöffer,
1513. Tenor partbook.
Coment peult, Lomme arme
CW W2 B5 p.VI

1514[1]. *Motetti de la corona*. *Libro primo*. Venezia: O. Petruc-
ci, 17 aug. 1514. 4 partbooks. Later ed.: 1526[1].
Christum ducem, Memor esto
BoormanP, BoormanPD, GehrenbeckM

1516[1]. *Liber quindecim missarum electarum, quae per excel-
lentissimos musicos compositae fuerunt*. Rome: Andrea
Antiquum, mai, 1516.
M. de Beata Virgine, M. faisant, M. sine nomine (mis-
named M. ad fugam)
CW Ma3 B13, Chapman

1519[2]. *Motetti de la corona*. *Libro tertio*. Venezia: O.
Petrucci, 7 sept. 1519. 4 partbooks. Later eds.: 1526[3],
1527[2].
Alma redemptoris mater (no.38), Ave nobilissima,
Domine ne in furore (no.39), Huc me sydereo,
Miserere mei, Praeter rerum
See 1514[1]

1519[3]. *Motetti de la corona*. *Libro quarto*. Venezia: O. Petrucci, 31 oct. 1519. 4 partbooks. Later ed.: 1526[4]
Deus in nomine tuo, Inviolata, Lectio actuum, Misericordias Domini, Missus est ... a Deo
SparksM 21-3, 113; see 1514[1]

1520[1]. *Motetti novi libro secondo*. Venezia: A. Antico,
30 nov. 1520. 4 partbooks.
Recordare virgo
PickerM, Chapman

1520[3]. *Motetti novi e chanzoni franciose a quatro supra doi*.
Venezia: A. Antico, 15 oct. 1520.
Baisez moy (4 v.), En l'ombre (no.59)
RubsamenM 86f., Chapman, PickerM

1520[4]. *Liber selectarum cantionum quas vulgo Mutetas
appellant sex quinque et quatuor vocem*. Augsburg: Grimm
& Wyrsung, 1520.
Benedicta es, De profundis (no.47), Inviolata, Lectio
actuum*, Miserere mei, Missus est ... a Deo (att.

Mouton), O virgo prudentissima, Praeter rerum, Stabat mater
Bente 294-302, DunningS 44-5

1521[3]. *Motetti libro primo.* Venezia: A. Antico, aug. 1521. 4 partbooks.
De profundis (no.47), Inviolata, Miserere mei, O admirabile commercium
Chapman, PickerM

[1521][4]. *Motetti libro secondo.* [Venezia: A. Antico, 1521.] Only altus partbook extant.
De profundis (no.90)
JeppesenF 1:73, PickerM, Chapman

1521[5]. *Motetti libro quarto.* Venezia: A. Antico, aug. 1521. 4 partbooks.
Salve regina (5 v.)
Chapman, PickerM

[1521][7]. *Motetti et carmina gallica.* [Roma: A. Antico? s.d.] 4 partbooks.
De profundis (no.47)*, Inviolata, O bone et dulcissime Jesu
Chapman, PickerM

1522. *Missarum decem a clarissimis musicis compositarum nec dum antea exceptis tribus aeditarum. Liber primus.* Rome: G. Giunta, mag. 1522. 4 partbooks.
M. de Beata Virgine, M. faisant

[1528][6]. *Trente et quatre chansons musicales a quatre parties....* Paris: Attaingnant, Jan. 23, 1529 (n.s.). 4 partbooks.
Coeurs desolez (4 v.)
HeartzP no.5

[1533] (not RISM). *Chansons musicales a quatre parties....* Paris: Attaingnant, April, 1533. 4 partbooks.
Mille regretz (att. J. Lemaire)
HeartzP no.41, HeartzC pp.200-201

1534[6]. *Liber quartus XXIX musicales quatuor vel quinque parium vocum modulos habet....* Paris: Attaingnant, June 1534. 4 partbooks.
Virgo salutiferi
HeartzP no.50
Edition: Treize livres, v.4

1535[4]. *Lib. duodecimus xvii musicales ad virginem Christiparam salutationes habet....* Paris: Attaingnant, mart. 1535. 4 partbooks.

    Salve regina (5 v.)
    HeartzP no.64
    Edition: Treize livres, v.12

1535[11]. *Reutterliedlein.* Frankfurt am Main: C. Egenolff,
    1535. 4 partbooks.
    In meinem synn (= Entre je suis)

[*ca.* 1535][13]. *Gassenhawer und Reutterliedlin.* [Frankfurt am
    Main: C. Egenolff, s.d.] 4 partbooks; 3 extant.
    In meinem synn (= Entre je suis)
    Facsimile, MoserG

[*ca.* 1535][14] see section IIIA: Paris ... Rés. Vm[7] 504 (I, III)

1536[1]. *La courone et fleur de chansons à troys.* Venezia:
    A. Antico (A. dell'Abbato), 1536. 3 partbooks.
    En l'ombre (no.60), En l'ombre (no.61), La belle se
      siet, Quant je vous voye, Si j'avoye Marion, Si j'ay
      perdue
    BernsteinC, BernsteinCF

1537[1]. *Novum et insigne opus musicum, sex, quinque, et
    quatuor vocum, cuius in Germania hactenus nihil simile
    usquam est editum.* Nürnberg: H. Grapheus (Formschneider),
    1537. 6 partbooks ed. J. Ott.
    Benedicite omnia opera, Benedicta es, Haec dicit
      (= Nymphes nappés), In exitu Israel, Miserere mei,
      Misericordias Domini, Pater noster, Propter peccata
      (= La Spagna), Praeter rerum, *Quam pulchra es* (by
      Moulu or Mouton), Qui habitat, Tribulatio et
      angustia, Veni sancte spiritus, Virgo prudentissima
      (att. Isaac)
    Osthoff 2:10-11, SparksM 125-6

1538[3]. *Secundus tomus novi operis musici, sex, quinque et
    quatuor vocum, nunc recens in lucem editus....* Nürnberg:
    H. Grapheus, oct. 1538. 5 partbooks ed. J. Ott.
    Deus pacis reduxit, Huc me sydereo, In illo tempore
      stetit, In principio, Inviolata, Liber generationis,
      Magnus es (att. Finck), O admirabile commercium, O
      virgo prudentissima, Stabat mater

1538[6]. *Tomus primus psalmorum selectorum praestantissimis
    musicis in harmonias quatuor aut quinque vocum redactorum.*
    Nürnberg: J. Petreius, 1538. 4 partbooks.
    Beati quorum, Caeli ennarrant, Domine ne in furore
      (no.39), Domine ne in furore (no.59), Domine ne
      projicias, In Domino confido, *Judica me* (by A. Caen),
      Qui regis Israel, Usquequo

1538[7]. *Modulationes aliquot quatuor vocum selectissimae,*
quas vulgo modetas vocant, a praestantiss. musicis com-
positae, iam primum typis excusae. Nürnberg: J. Petreius,
sept. 1538. 4 partbooks.
> *Dilectus Deo* (by A. Févin?), Stabat mater, Stetit autem
> Salomon

1538[8]. *Symphoniae iucundae atque adeo breves quatuor vocum,*
ab optimis quibusque musicis compositae.... Wittenberg:
G. Rhaw, 1538. 4 partbooks.
> In te Domine

1538[9]. *Trium vocum carmina a diversis musicis composita.*
Nürnberg: H. Formschneider, 1538. 3 partbooks.
> La Bernardina, La plus des plus, M. fortuna (Pleni)
> HolzmannH

1539[1]. *Liber quindecim missarum, à praestantissimis musicis*
compositarum.... Nürnberg: J. Petreius, 1539. 4 partbooks.
> M. ave maris, M. de Beata Virgine, M. fortuna, M.
> gaudeamus, M. la sol fa re mi, M. l'homme armé svm

1539[2]. *Missae tredecim quatuor vocum a praestantiss.*
artificib. compositae. Nürnberg: H. Grapheus, 7 febr.
1539. 4 partbooks ed. J. Ott.
> M. da pacem, M. fortuna, M. l'homme armé svm, M. pange
> lingua, *M. sub tuum praesidium* (by LaRue)
> SparksM 94ff.

1539[9]. *Tomus secundus psalmorum selectorum quatuor et*
quinque vocum. Nürnberg: J. Petreius, 1539.
> Cantate Domino*, De profundis (no.47), De profundis
> (no.91), Dominus regnavit, Jubilate Deo, Laudate
> pueri, Levavi oculos, Memor esto, Mirabilia testi-
> monia, Paratum cor meum

1540[7]. *Selectissimae necnon familiarissimae cantiones, ultra*
centum vario idiomate vocum, tam multiplicium quam etiam
paucar. Fugae quoque, ut vocantur. Besonder ausserlessner
künstlicher lustiger Gesanng mancherlay Sprachen ... von
acht Stymmen an bis auf zwo; ... sinngen und auf Instrument
zubrauchen. Augsburg: M. Kreisstein, 1540. 5 partbooks.
> Absalon fili mi, Agnus Dei (fuga), Ave sanctissima
> virgo (fuga), J'ay bien cause, Mi lares vous, N'esse
> point un gran displaisir, O dulcis amica (fuga), Plus
> nulz regretz

1542[6]. *Tomus tertius psalmorum selectorum.* Nürnberg: J.
Petreius, 1542. 4 partbooks.
> Qui habitat (24 v.)

1542[8]. *Tricinia. Tum veterum tum recentiorum in arte musica symphonistarum, latina, germanica, brabantia & gallica, ante hac typis nunquam excusa....* Wittenberg: G. Rhaw, 1542. 3 vols.
> In pace (= Que vous madame; att. Agricola), Quant je vous voy

1543[19]. *Il primo libro a due voci di diversi autori novamente stampato et con ogni diligentia corretto.* Venezia: A. Gardane, 1543. 2 partbooks.
> M. de Beata Virgine: Agnus 2

1544[13]. *Le cincquiesme livre contenant trente et deux chansons a cincq et a six parties composées par maistre Nicolas Gombert et aultres excellens autheurs convenables et propices a jouer de tous instrumentz.* Antwerpen: T. Susato, déc. 1544. 5 partbooks.
> N'esse pas ung grant desplaisir
> Facsimile: CEMF 6

1545[2]. *Concentus octo, sex, quinque & quatuor vocum.* Augsburg: P. Ulhard, 1545. 4 partbooks ed. Salbinger.
> Ave verum (5 v.), Responde mihi. SparksP 349.

1545[3]. *Cantiones septem, sex et quinque vocum.* Augsburg: Kreisstein, 1545. 5 partbooks ed. Salbinger. 2nd ed.: 1546[5].
> Nesciens mater, Responsum acceperat Simeon

1545[6]. *Bicinia gallica, latina, germanica, ex praestantissimis musicorum monumentis collecta, & secundum seriem tonorum disposita. Tomus primus....* Wittenberg: G. Rhaw, 1545. 2 partbooks.
> Exaudi Domine (= M. pange lingua: Agnus 2), Nunquid justi (= M. Hercules: Pleni), Nunquid (= M. sine nomine: Benedictus), Per illud ave (Benedicta es, part 2), Quis separavit nos (= M. pange lingua: Pleni)
> Edition: Rhaw 6
> Discussion: AlbrechtZ

1545[7]. *Secundus tomus biciniorum ... Additae sunt quaedam, ut vocunt, fugae, plenae artis et suavitatis.* Wittenberg: G. Rhaw, 29 mai 1545. 2 partbooks.
> Benedictus (canon), Diligam te Domine (= M. ave maris: Agnus 2)
> AlbrechtZ

1545[15]. *Le septiesme livre contenant vingt et quatre chansons a cincq et a six parties, composées par feu de bonne memoire et tres excellent en musicque Josquin des Prez, avecq troix epitaphes dudict Josquin, composez par*

divers aucteurs.... Antwerpen: T. Susato, 1545. 5 part-
books.
  Allegez moy, Baisez moy (6 v.), Coeur langoreulx,
  Douleur me bat, Du mien amant, En non saichant,
  Faulte d'argent, Incessament livré suis, Je me com-
  plains, Ma bouche rit, N'esse pas ung grant desplaisir,
  Nymphes nappés, Nymphes des bois, Parfons regretz,
  Petite camusette, Plaine de dueil, Plusieurs regretz,
  Pour souhaitter, Regretz sans fin, Si congié prens,
  Tenez moy, Vous l'arez, Vous ne l'aurez pas
  Facsimile: CEMF 8

1549[16]. *Diphona amoena et florida, selectore Erasmo Roten-*
  buchero, boiaro. Nürnberg: J. Montanus & U. Neuber,
  1549.
  Agnus Dei, Crucifixus, Et incarnatus est, *In principio*
  (contrafactum?), Domine non secundum (parts 1-2),
  Quid tam solicitis (= M. malheur: Pleni)

1549[29]. *L'unziesme livre contenant vingt et neuf chansons*
  amoreuses a quatre parties, propices a tous instrumentz
  musicaulx.... Antwerpen: T. Susato, oct. 1549. 4 partbooks.
  Mille regretz (and Response by Susato, "Les miens
  aussi brief"), N'esse pas un grant* (and Response
  by Le Brung)

1553[2]. *Liber primus collectorum modulorum (qui moteta vulgo*
  dicuntur) quae iam olim a praestantissimis et musicae
  peritissimis emissa, ac variis voluminibus dispersa, nunc
  primum iudicio exacto, hoc libro (qui vere motetorum
  thesaurus dici potest) in unum redacta.... Paris: N. du
  Chemin & C. Goudimel, 1553. Only superius partbook extant.
  Benedicta es
  LesureN

1553[4]. *Psalmorum selectorum a praestantissimis huius nostri*
  temporis in arte musica artificibus in harmonias quatuor,
  quinque et sex vocum redactorum. Tomus primus. Nürnberg:
  J. Montanus & U. Neuber, 1553. 4 partbooks.
  Beati quorum, Caeli ennarrant, Domine Dominus noster,
  Domine ne in furore (no.39), Domine ne in furore
  (no.59), In Domine confido*, *Judica me* (by Caen),
  Miserere mei, Usquequo

1553[5]. *Tomus secundus Psalmorum selectorum, quatuor et*
  plurium vocum. Nürnberg: J. Montanus & U. Neuber, 1553.
  4 partbooks.
  Cantate Domino, *Deus in nomine tuo* (by Carpentras?),
  Domine ne projicias, Dominus regnavit, Laudate pueri,
  Quam dilecta (by Certon), Qui regis Israel

1553[6]. *Tomus tertius Psalmorum selectorum, quatuor et plurium vocum.* Nürnberg: J. Montanus & U. Neuber, 1553. 4 partbooks.
Benedicite omnia opera, Domine exaudi, Mirabilia testimonia

1554[10]. *Evangelia dominicorum et festorum dierum musicis numeris pulcherrime comprehensa & ornata. Tomi primi continentis historias & doctrinam, quae solent in ecclesia proponi. De nativitate. De epiphanijs. De resurrectione Jesu Christi.* Nürnberg: J. Montanus & U. Neuber, 1554. 5 partbooks.
In principio, Tulerunt Dominum

1558[4]. *Novum et insigne opus musicum, sex, quinque, et quatuor vocum, cuius in Germania hactenus nihil simile usquam est editum. Nunc quidem locupletatum plus centum non minus elegantibus carminibus, tum Josquini, tum aliorum clarissimorum symphonistarum tam veterum quam recentiorum, quorum quaedam antehac sunt edita, multa nunc primum in lucem exeunt.* Nürnberg: J. von Berg & U. Neuber, 1558. 6 partbooks.
Benedicta es, Haec dicit (= Nymphes, nappés), Huc me sydereo, *In nomine Jesu* (by Mouton?), O virgo prudentissima, Pater noster, Praeter rerum, Veni sancte spiritus

1559[1]. *Secunda pars magni operis musici continens clarissimorum symphonistarum tam veterum quam recentiorum....* Nürnberg: J. von Berg & U. Neuber, 1559.
In illo tempore stetit, Inviolata, Miserere mei, Missus ... a Deo, O virgo genetrix* (= Plusieurs regretz), Propter peccata* (= La Spagna), Stabat mater, Virgo salutiferi

1559[2]. *Tertia pars magni operis musici....* Nürnberg: J. Montanus & U. Neuber, 1559.
Absalon fili mi, Benedicite omnia opera, Dulces exuviae, In exitu Israel, Liber generationis, Memor esto, Mente tota (Vultum, part 5), Misericordias Domini, *Quam pulchra es* (by Moulu? Mouton?), Qui habitat, Tribulatio et angustia, Virgo prudentissima (att. Isaac)

E1560c. *Livre de Meslanges contenant sixvingtz chansons des plus rares et plus industrieuses qui se trouvent soit des autheurs antiques, soit des plus memorables de nostre temps. Composées a cinq, six, sept, & huit parties....* Paris: Le Roy & Ballard, 1560. Only the superius partbook in Berlin was known to Eitner; it has been missing since 1945. Later ed.: 1572[2].

     Faulte d'argent, Incessament mon povre (att. LaRue),
     Je ne me puis tenir, N'esse pas un grand desplaisir,
     Petite camusette, Plusieurs regretz, Si congié prens,
     Tenez moy, Vous l'aurez

1562[9]. *Il terzo libro delle muse a tre voci. Di canzon
francese di Adrian Willaert nuovamente e con alcune
d'altri autori insieme ristampato et con somma diligentia
corrette.* Venezia: G. Scotto, 1562. Only tenor, superius
partbooks extant.
     En l'ombre (no.60)

1564[1]. *Thesaurus musicus continens selectissimas octo, septem, sex, quinque et quatuor vocum harmonias, tam a
veteribus quam recentioribus symphonistas compositas....
Tomi primi continentis cantiones octo vocum.* Nürnberg:
J. Montanus & U. Neuber, 1564. 8 partbooks.
     Lugebat David (= Tulerunt Dominum)

1564[3]. *Thesauri musici tomus tertius ... sex vocum.* Nürnberg: J. Montanus & U. Neuber, 1564.
     Christus mortuus est, *In nomine Jesu* (by Mouton?), Sic
       Deus dilexit

1564[5]. *Thesauri musici tomus quintus, et ultimus, continens
sacras harmonias quatuor vocibus compositas....* Nürnberg:
J. Montanus & U. Neuber, 1564. 4 partbooks.
     Ave Christe immolate
     SparksM 98ff.

1568[5]. *Novi et catholici thesaurus musici. Liber quartus
quo selectissime atque plane novae, neque unquam ante in
lucem editae moteta ... summo studio atque labore Petri
Ioannelli de Gandino bergomensis collectae....* Venezia:
A. Gardano, 1568. 6 partbooks.
     Benedicta es (12 v., att. Castilleti)

1568[7]. *Cantiones triginta selectissimae: quinque, sex,
septem: octo: duodecim et plurium vocum ... editae, per
Clementem Stephani: buchaviensem.* Nürnberg: U. Neuber,
1568. 4 partbooks.
     Ave verum (5 v.), Qui habitat (24 v.)

1572[2]. *Mellange de chansons tant des vieux autheurs que des
modernes, a cinq, six, sept, et huict parties.* Paris: Le
Roy et Ballard, 1572. 6 partbooks. See E1560c above
     Coeur langoreulx, Faulte d'argent, Incessament mon
       povre (att. LaRue), Je me complains, Je ne me puis
       tenir, N'esse pas, Parfons regretz, Tenez moy

1578[15].   *Second livre de chansons a trois parties composé par*
     plusieurs autheurs. Paris: A. Le Roy et R. Ballard, 1578.
     3 partbooks.
          En l'ombre (no.60), En l'ombre (no.61), Mon mary, Si
          jay perdu

1590[19].   *Bicinia, sive cantiones suavissime duarum vocum, tam*
     divinae musices tyronibus, quam eiusdem artis peritioribus
     magno usui futurae ... *ex praeclaris huius aetatis auc-*
     toribus collectae. Antwerpen: P. Phalèse et J. Bellère,
     1590. Later ed.: 1609[18].
          Per illud ave (Benedicta es, part 2)

1591[27].   *Bicinia sacra, ex variis autoribus in usum iuventutis*
     scholasticae collecta, quibus adjuncta est compendiaria
     in artem canendi Introductio ... *edita a Frid. Lindnero.*
     Nürnberg: C. Gerlach, 1591.
          Per illud ave (Benedicta es, part 2)

          C. MUSIC EXAMPLES IN THEORY TREATISES

               Only complete compositions or
               complete sections are listed.

1. Manuscripts

Berlin. Deutsche Staatsbibliothek. MS theor.1175 (D–ddr–Bds)
     Explicatio compendiosa doctrinae de signis musicalibus,
          exemplis probatissimorum musicorum illustrata.
     M. l'homme armé svm: Agnus 2
     CW Mal B1, CC 1:38; Kiesewetter in *Allgemeine*
          musikalische Zeitung 32:716ff., CollinsP

London. British Library. MS Add. 4911 (GB–Lbm)
     The art of music, by an anon. Scottish author.
     M. malheur: Agnus 2

2. Prints

1537.   Sebaldus Heyden. *Musicae, id est artis canendi libro*
     duo. Nürnberg: Petreius, 1537.
          M. ad fugam: Benedictus; M. Hercules: Pleni; M. l'homme
          armé st: Kyrie 2, Agnus 3; M. l'homme armé svm:
          Kyrie 1, Christe, Osanna, Benedictus, Agnus 2; M.
          malheur: Agnus 2; M. mater patris: Pleni, Benedictus

1547. Heinrich Glareanus. *Dodecachordon*. Basel: H. Petrus,
   sept. 1547.
      Ave Maria ... virgo; Ave verum (parts 1-2); Benedicta
      es (part 2); De profundis (no.47); De tous biens
      playne; Domine non secundum (parts 1, 2); Guillaume
      s'en va (textless); Liber generationis; Magnus es tu;
      M. ad fugam: Benedictus; M. de Beata Virgine: Gloria,
      Agnus 2; M. fortuna: Agnus 1, 2; M. gaudeamus:
      Benedictus; M. Hercules: Pleni, Agnus 2; M. l'homme
      armé st: Benedictus; M. l'homme armé svm: Benedictus,
      Agnus 2; M. malheur: Agnus 2; M. mater patris: Pleni,
      Benedictus, Agnus 2; M. pange lingua: Pleni; M. sine
      nomine: Pleni; O Jesu fili David (= Comment peult);
      Planxit autem; Victimae paschali laudes
   GlareanusD (facsimile), GlareanusM (Eng. translation),
   PAPTM 16 (Ger. translation), Frei (partial music
   edition), Lichtenhahn, ScheringNG

1550. Heinrich Faber. *Ad musicam practicam introductio*.
   Nürnberg, 1550. (See also 1591 below)
      M. Hercules: Et in spiritus (= Credo, part 3); M.
      l'homme armé svm: Christe, Hosanna, Agnus 2

1554. Johann Zanger. *Praeceptis musicae practicae*. Leipzig,
   1554.
      M. fortuna: Agnus 1; M. la sol fa re mi: Hosanna;
      M. l'homme armé svm: Pleni, Benedictus, Agnus 2

1563. Ambrosius Wilphlingseder. *Erotemata musices practicae,
   continentia praecipuas eius artis praeceptiones, in gratiam
   & usum studiosae iuventutis*.... Nürnberg: C. Heussler,
   1563.
      Miserere mei (3 v.; = Ave verum corpus 1), M. fortuna:
      Agnus 2; M. Hercules: Agnus 2; M. l'homme armé st:
      Kyrie 2, Benedictus

1571. Gallus Dressler. *Musicae practicae elementa in usum
   scholae Magdeburgensis edita*. Magdeburg: W. Kirchner,
   1571.
      M. l'homme armé svm: Christe, Sanctus, Hosanna

1590. Jacob Paix. *Selectae, artificiosae et elegantes
   fugae*.... Lavingae: Leonardus Reinmichaelius, 1590.
      Examples from Glareanus: M. Hercules: Pleni, Agnus 2;
      M. l'homme armé svm: Agnus 2

1591. *Compendium musicae, pro illius artis tironibus. A.M.
   Henrico Fabro latine conscriptum, & a M. Christoforo Rid
   in vernaculum sermonem conversum, nunc praeceptis & exem-
   plis auctum studio & opera Adam Gumpelzhaimeri*. Augsburg:

V. Schönig, 1591. Many later eds.: 1595^{14}, 1600^{10}, 1605^{21}, etc.

   Per illud Ave (Benedicta es, part 2)

D. INTABULATIONS

   The following list cites only complete editions of the source listed. The composer named in most separate editions is the intabulator, about whom further information is readily available in G. Few studies of intabulations of Josquin exist: Yong is a useful list of printed intabulations derived from the indispensable BrownI, and WarburtonK lists keyboard intabulations. General stylistic studies are WardJP and WardJU, and Josquin intabulations are discussed in BrownA and ThibaultI.

1. Index of intabulators' names

Ammerbach, Elias Nikolaus	1583^{22}
Bakfark, Valentin Greff	1565^{22}
Barberis, Melchiore de	$B1549_1$
Borrono, Pietro Paolo	$B1548_{2-3}$
Bossinensis, Franciscus	1509^3
Brayssing, Grégoire	1553^{35}
Cabezon, Antonio de	1578^{24}
Canova, Francesco, da Milano	1536^{11}, 1546^{29}, 1547^{21}
Capirola, Vincenzo	Chicago
Cavazzoni, Girolamo	$B1543_1$
Drusina, Benedict de	1556^{32}
Fuenllana, Miguel de	1554^{32}
Ganassi dal Fontego, Sylvestro di	$B1535_1$
Gerle, Hans	$B1532_2$, $B1533_1$
Gintzler, Simon	1547^{22}
Gorlier, Simon	1551^{22}
Heckel, Wolff	$B1556_{5-6}$, 1562^{24}
Hör, Clemens	Zurich Z.XI.301
Holtzach, Oswald	Basel F.VI.26c
Jan of Lublin	Krakow 1716
Kleber, Leonhard	Berlin 40026
Kotter, Johannes	Basel F.IX.22
Mudarra, Alonso de	$B1546_{14}$
Narvaez, Luys de	1538^{22}
Newsidler, Hans	1536^{12-13}, 1540^{23}, 1544^{24}, 1549^{41}
Newsidler, Melchior	1574^{13}
Ochsenkuhn, Sebastian	1558^{20}

Paix, Jacob 1583^{23}, 1589^{17}
Pisador, Diego 1552^{35}
Rippe, Albert de 1555^{36}, $B1558_6$, 1562^{28},
                                            1574^{12}
Rühling, Johannes 1583^{24}
Sicher, Fridolin   St. Gall 530
Spinacino, Francesco 1507^5, $B1507^2$
Susato, Tylman $B1551_8$
Teghi, Pietro de 1547^{23}
Valderràbano, Enriquez de 1547^{25}
Venegas de Henestrosa, Luis $B1557_2$

2. Manuscripts

BASEL. UNIVERSITÄTS-BIBLIOTHEK
    MS F.VI.26(c). *Keyboard Fundamentum*. Oswald Holtzach,
        1515
        Fortuna d'un gran tempo*
    MS F.IX.22. Keyboard tablature of J. Kotter
        Adieu mes amours (att. Isaac), Fortuna d'un gran tempo*,
            In pace (att. Isaac)
        Both MSS, from Amerbach collection, ed. SMd 6:1, with
            further bibliography.

BERLIN. STAATSBIBLIOTHEK PREUSSISCHER KULTURBESITZ
    MS 40026 (*olim* Z 26). Keyboard tablature of Leonhard
        Kleber, 1524
        Adieu mes amours (ed. ThibaultI 462-3), Ave Maria ...
            virgo (ed. WarburtonK), Fortuna d'un gran tempo*,
            Inter natos (not the motet of II above), Mente tota
            (= Vultum, part 5. Ed. WarburtonK)
        KotterbaO, Löwenfeld

CHICAGO. NEWBERRY LIBRARY
    Case MSVM C.25. Lute tablature of Vincenzo Capirola, *ca.*
        1517, Venice
        M. l'homme armé st: Et resurrexit; M. pange lingua:
            Gloria
        Study, edition: GombosiC

COIMBRA. BIBLIOTECA GERAL DA UNIVERSIDADE
    MS M.M.48. Organ score, 1559
        Salve regina (no.48)
        Kastner

KRAKÓW. BIBLIOTEKA POLSKIEJ AKADEMIA NAUK
    MS 1716. Organ tablature of Jan of Lublin, mid-16th century
        Date siceram (att. N.C.; = Je ne me puis, dated 1542),

Plus nulz regretz, Tribulatio et angustia
Edition: CEKM 6:3

KRAKÓW. STAATSARCHIV
Organ tablature (*olim* Monastery of the Holy Spirit), 1548
M. de Beata Virgine: Cum sancto spiritu (2 versions)
See WarburtonK p.IX, InskoC

LONDON. BRITISH LIBRARY
MS Add. 29247. Lute tablature, early 17th century
Je ne me puis (att. Gombert)
See BlackburnJ 32

MUNICH. BAYERISCHE STAATSBIBLIOTHEK
MS 264. German organ tablature, 1596-8
Benedicta es
MS 266. Italian lute tablature, 1550-70
Circund dederund (= Nymphes nappés), Coeur langoreulx*,
Mille regretz*, Plus nulz regretz*
MS 267. Italian lute tablature, mid-16th century
Benedicta es, Haec dicit (= Nymphes nappés), Inviolata,
Qui habitat
MS 272. German lute tablature, mid-16th century
Adieu mes amours*, In exitu Israel*, Mille regretz*,
M. de Beata Virgine: Cum sancto spiritu, Praeter
rerum*, Qui habitat
MS 1511d. Italian lute tablature, mid-16th century
Plus nulz regretz

ST. GALL. STIFTSBIBLIOTHEK
MS 530. Organ tablature of Fridolin Sicher, *ca.* 1516-17
Adieu mes amours (ed. WarburtonK), Ave Maria ... virgo
("Das lang Ave Maria"), Bergerette savoyenne (ed.
WarburtonK), Magnificat 4. toni (ed. WarburtonK),
Mente tota (Vultum, part 5), O admirabile commercium
(complete; parts 4-5 ed. WarburtonK), Victimae
paschali laudes (no.26; ed. WarburtonK), Virgo
prudentissima (ed. WarburtonK)
CW Mt1 B1, p.vi, MarxN, Nef, WarburtonF

WERTHEIM AM MAIN. BIBLIOTHEK
MS 6. Lute tablature, *ca.* 1520-32
Ach unfal (= Qui belles amours)
Boetticher

WROCLAW. BIBLIOTEKA UNIWERSYTECKA
MSS 2, 6 *see* section B above

ZÜRICH. ZENTRALBIBLIOTHEK
MS Z.XI.301. Organ tablature of Clemens Hör, *ca.* 1535-40
M. de Beata Virgine: Agnus 2*, Scaramella*, 2 unidentified
works. Ed. SMd 7:1.

3. Prints

For consistency with section B above, RISM numbers are used when available. Numbers preceded by B are from BrownI.

1507^{5-6}, B1507$_{1-2}$. *Intavolatura de lauto. Libro primo, Libro secondo*. Venezia: Ottaviano Petrucci, 1507 (2 vols.).
By Francesco Spinacino
Libro 1: Adieu mes amours, Ave Maria ... benedicta, Fortuna d'un gran tempo*, La Bernardina (solo and duet versions), *O Venus bant*
Libro 2: Comment peult, *Fortuna desperata*, Que vous ma dame
See ThibaultI 456, DisertoriF 176, 184, 243, Schmidt

1509^{3}, B1509$_{1}$. *Tenori e contrabassi intabulati col sopran in canto figurato per cantar e sonar col lauto Libro primo. Francisci Bossinensis Opus*. Venezia: Ottaviano Petrucci, 27 mart. 1509.
In te Domine (J. Dascanio)
Edition: DisertoriF

B1532$_{2}$. *Musica teusch, auf die Instrument der grossen und kleinen Geygen, und Lautten, welcher massen die mit Grundt und Art jrer Composicion auss dem Gefang in die Tabulatur zu ordnen und zu setzen ist ... vormals in Truck nye und yke durch Hans Gerle Lutinist zu Nurenberg aussgangen*. 1532.
Scaramella* (for lute)
Facsimile ed.: MMMF 2:101

B1533$_{1}$. *Tabulatur auff die Laudten etlicher Preambel, teutscher, welscher und francösischer Stück, von Liedlein, Muteten, und schönen Psalmen, mit drey und vier Stymmen, durch Hans Gerle ... zu Nürnberg*. 1533.
Adieu mes amours, En l'ombre (no.60), Inviolata, Mile regres, Plus mile regres (= Plus nulz), Qui habitat

B1535$_{1}$. *Ganassi dal Fontego: Opera intitulata Fontegara*. Venezia, 1535.
In mensural notation, giving flute/recorder ornamentation for Mille regretz*
GanassiF, GanassiT

1536^{11}, B1536$_{3}$. *Intabolatura di liuto de diversi, con la bataglia, et altre cose bellissime, di M. Francesco da Milano....* Venezia: F. Marcolini, mag. 1538.
Pater noster, Stabat mater
FrancescoL, FrancescoO

1536^{12}, $B1536_6$. *Ein newgeordent künstlich Lautenbuch in zwen*
Theyl getheylt. Der erst für die anfahenden Schuler ...
durch mich Hansen Newsidler Lutinisten.... Nürnberg:
J. Petreius, 1536.
   Adieu mes amours*
   Facsimile ed.: Institutio pro Arte Testudinis, 1974

1536^{13}, $B1536_7$. *Der ander Theil des Lautenbuchs* ... *durch*
mich Hansen Newsidler Lutinisten und Bürger zu Nürnberg....
Nürnberg: J. Petreius, 1536.
   La Bernardina, La plus des plus, Memor esto, Mille
   regretz (ed. ThibaultI 466), M. de Beata Virgine:
   Cum sancto spiritu, Plus nulz regretz

1538^{22}, $B1538_1$. *Los seys libros del Delphin de musica de*
cifras para tañer vihuela. Hechos por Luys de Narbaez....
Valladolid: Hernandez de Cordova, oct. 1538. 6 vols.
   Mile regres ("La cancion del Emperador del quarto
   tono"); M. Hercules: Sanctus, Osanna (misnamed M.
   faisant); M. sine nomine ("Missa de la fuga"): Cum
   sancto spiritu
   Editions: MME 2, Torner

$B1543_1$. *Intavolatura cioe recercari canzoni hinni magnificati*
composto per Hieronimo [Cavazzoni] *de Marcantonio da*
Bologna.... Venezia, 1543.
   Faulte d'argent*
   CDMI 23-7

1544^{24}, $B1544_1$. *Das erst Buch: ein newes Lautenbüchlein mit*
vil feinen lieblichen Liedern für die jungen Schuler ...
durch mich Hansen Newsidler Lutennisten.... Nürnberg:
H. Günther, 1544. Later ed.: 1547^{26}.
   In te Domine*, Scaramella*

1546^{23}, $B1546_4$. *Intabulatura di lautto libro sesto di*
diversi motetti a quattro voce, intabulati, et accomodati
per sonar sopra il lautto dal reverendo messer pre
Merchiore de Barberijs de Padova suonatore eccellentissimo
di lauto.... Venezia: Scotto, 1546.
   Salve regina (no.48)

1546^{21}, $B1546_{18}$. *Les chansons reduictz en tabulature de luc*
a trois et quatre parties. Livre deuxième. Louvain: P.
Phalèse, 1546.
   Pavane Mille regretz*

1546^{29}, $B1546_7$. *Intabolatura de lauto di Francesco da Milano*
de motetti recercari et canzoni francese ... *Libro segondo.*
Venezia: A. Gardano, 1546. Later eds.: 1561^{17}, 1563^{20}.
   Pater noster, Stabat mater
   See 1536^{11} above

B1546$_{14}$. *Alonso Mudarra tres libros de musica en cifras para vihuela*.... Seville: Juan de Leon, 1546.
    M. de Beata Virgine: Kyrie 1, Cum sancto spiritu; M. faisant: Qui tollis, Pleni; M. la sol fa re mi: Benedictus; M. pange lingua: Kyrie; Respice in me (= Je ne me puis tenir; att. Gombert)
    MME 7, FellererJ

1547^{22}, B1547$_3$. *Intabolatura de lauto di Simon Gintzler musico del reverendissimo cardinale di Trento, de recercari motetti madrigali et canzon francese* ... *Libro primo*. Venezia: A. Gardano, 1547.
    (All contents anon.) Benedicta es*, Circumdederunt (= Nymphes nappés)*, Stabat mater*

1547^{25}, B1547$_5$. *Libro de musica de vihuela intitulado Silva de Sirenas* ... *compuesta por Enrriquez Valderravano*. Valladolid: F. Fernandez de Cordova, 1547. 7 vols.
    Ave Maria (= Pater noster, part 2); Benedicta es; Inviolata; M. ad fugam: Cum sancto spiritu; M. ave maris: Benedictus; M. de Beata Virgine: Kyrie, Cum sancto spiritu, Credo; M. faisant: Credo (partial); M. gaudeamus: Agnus; M. l'homme armé svm: Agnus; M. pange lingua: Qui tollis
    MME 22-3

1547^{26}, B1547$_4$. *Das erst Buch. Ein newes Lautenbüchlein mit vil feiner lieblichen Liedern* ... *durch mich Hansen Neusidler Lutennisten*.... Nürnberg: C. Gutknecht, 1547.
    In te Domine

1547^{23}, B1547$_{9-10}$. *Des chansons & motetz reduictz en tabulatur de luc, a quatre cinque et six parties, livre troixiesme. Composées par l'excellent maistre Pierre Teghi Paduan.* Louvain: P. Phalèse, 1547. Another ed. with Latin title: 1547^{10}. Later ed.: B1574$_5$.
    Benedicta es*, Pater noster

B1548$_{2-3}$. *Intavolatura di lauto dell'eccellente Pietro Paolo Borrono da Milano* ... *Libro ottavo*. Venetia: H. Scotto, 1548. Later ed.: 1563^{18}.
    Mala se ne

B1549$_1$. *Intabolatura di lauto libro nono intitolato il Bembo* ... *composte per* ... *Melchioro Barberis Padoano*.... Venezia: H. Scotto, 1549.
    Vray dieu damours

1551^{22}, B1551$_1$. *Le troysieme livre contenant plusieurs duos et trios* ... *mis en tabulature de Guiterne, par Simon*

Gorlier. Paris: Robert Grandjon & Michel Fezendat, 1551.
Per illud ave (= Benedicta es, part 2)*

B1551$_8$. *Het derde musyck boexken begrepen int ghet al van
onser neder duytscher spraken, daer inne begrepen syn
alderhande danserye*.... Antwerpen: T. Susato, 1551.
Later ed.: B1563$_{12}$.
Pavane Mille regretz*

1552^{35}, B1552$_7$. *Libro de musica de vihuela, agara nuevamente
compuesto por Diego Pisador, vezino de la ciudad de
Salamanca, dirigedo al muy alto y muy poderoso señor don
Philippe principe de Espana*.... Salamanca: D. Pisador,
1552.
For voice and vihuela: In principio, Miserere mei,
M. ad fugam (lacks Agnus 2), M. faisant (lacks Pleni,
Agnus 2-3), M. fortuna: Benedictus, M. Hercules (lacks
Pleni, Agnus), M. l'homme armé svm (lacks Hosanna,
Benedictus, Agnus 1-2), Tota pulchra es (= Ecce tu
pulchra), Tulerunt (att. Gombert). For vihuela: M. ave
maris (lacks Hosanna, Benedictus, Agnus 2-3), M. for-
tuna: Pleni, M. gaudeamus (lacks Hosanna, Benedictus,
Agnus 2-3), M. la sol fa re mi (lacks Pleni, Hosanna
2, Agnus 2-3), Salve regina (no.48)
HoneggerM, HoneggerT.
Facsimile: Minkoff, 1973

1552^{29}, B1552$_{11}$. *Hortus musarum in quo tanquam flosculi quidam
selectissimorum carminum collecti sunt ex optimis quibusque
autoribus ... collectore Petro Phalesio*.... Louvain: P.
Phalèse, 1552.
Allegez moy*; Benedicta es; Mille regretz; M. ave maris:
Benedictus; M. de Beata Virgine: Cum sancto spiritu,
Benedictus; Pater noster; Stabat mater; Tribulatio et
angustia*
Ed. of Allegez moy: ThibaultI 471

1553^{35}, B1553$_3$. *Quart livre de tabulature de guiterre,
contenant plusieurs fantasies, pseaulmes, & chansons ...
composées par M. Gregoire Brayssing de augusta*. Paris:
Le Roy & Ballard, 23 nov. 1553.
In exitu Israel*

1553^{33}, B1553$_{10}$. *Horti musarum seconda pars, continens selectissima quaedam ac iucundissima carmina testudine simul
et voce humana, vel alterius instrumenti musici adminiculo
modulanda*.... Louvain: P. Phalèse, 1553.
Benedicta es*, Stabat mater*

1554^{32}, B1554$_3$. *Libro de musica para vihuela, intitulado*
Orphenica lyra ... *compuesto por Miguel de Fuenllana*....
Seville: Martin de Montesdoca, 1554.
  Benedicta es; Lauda Sion (= Je ne me puis, att. Gom-
  bert); Magnificat 3. Toni (Part 4: Fecit potentiam);
  M. de Beata Virgine: Patrem, Crucifixus; M. faisant:
  Kyrie, Et in terra; M. Hercules: Pleni; M. la sol fa
  re mi: Kyrie; M. pange lingua: Benedictus; Praeter
  rerum
  Edition: JacobsO

1555^{36}, B1555$_4$. *Cinquiesme livre de tabulature de leut* ...
composées par feu messire Albert de Rippe de Mantoue....
Paris: Michel Fezandat, 1555.
  Praeter rerum
  Edition: VaccaroO
  Study: BuggertM

1556^{32}, B1556$_2$. *Tabulatura continens insignes et selectissimas*
quasdem fantasias: cantiones germanicas, italicas, ac
gallicas: passemezo; choreas. & mutetas. Iam primum in
lucem aeditas per Benedictum de Drusina Elbigensum.
Frankfurt a.d. Oder: Eichhorn, 1556.
  Adieu mes amours*, Per illud ave (Benedicta es, part 2)*

B1557$_2$. *Libro di cifra nueva para tecla, harpa y vihuela* ...
compuesto por Luys Venegas de Henestrosa. Alcala: Joan de
Brocar, 1557.
  M. de Beata Virgine: Kyrie 1, 2, Cum sancto spiritu;
  M. faisant: Kyrie 1, 2; M. pange lingua: Kyrie

1558^{20}, B1558$_5$. *Tabulaturbuch auff die Lauten von Moteten*
frantzösischen-welschen und teütschen geystlichen und
weltlichen Liedern ... *durch Sebastian Ochsenkhun* ...
zusammen ordinirt und gelesen.... Heidelberg: J. Kohlen,
1558.
  Absalon fili mi, Benedicta es, Date siceram (= Je ne
  me puis tenir; att. Claudin), In exitu Israel, Inviolata, M. de BVM: Cum sancto spiritu, Pater noster,
  Praeter rerum, Qui habitat, Stabat mater

B1558$_6$. *Sixiesme livre de tabulature de leut, contenant*
plusieurs chansons, fantasies, motetz, pavanes et
galliardes composées par feu messire Albert de Rippe....
Paris: Michel Fezandat, 1558.
  Benedicta es
  Edition: VaccaroO
  Study: BuggertM

1562^{24}, $B1562_3$. *Lautten Buch, von mancherley schönen und*
lieblichen Stucken mit zweyen Lautten zusamen zuschlagen,
und auch sonst das mehrer Theyl allein für sich selbst ...
durch Wolffen Heckel ... *in ein verstendige Tabulatur*
nach geschribner Art aussgesetzt und zusammen gebracht.
Strasbourg: Chr. Müller, 1562. 1 vol.
  Mille regres* (duet), M. de Beata Virgine: Cum sancto
    spiritu*, Plus nulz regres* (duet), Per illud ave*
    (duet)

1562^{28}, $B1562_{11}$. *Cinquiesme livre de tabelature de luth*
contenent plusieurs motetz, & fantasies. Par maistre
Albert de Rippe mantouan. Paris: Le Roy et Ballard, 1562.
  Benedicta es
  Edition: Vaccaro0

$B1563_{12}$. *Theatrum musicum in quo selectissima optimorum quo-*
rumlibet autorum ac excellentissimorum artificum cum
veterum tum etiam novorum carmina.... Louvain: P. Phalèse,
1563.
  Benedicta es, Mille regretz, Pater noster, Stabat
    mater

1565^{22}, $B1565_1$. *Valentini Greffi Bakfarci pannonii, har-*
moniarum musicarum in usum testudinis factarum, tomus
primus. Krakow: L. Andreae, oct. 1565. Later ed.: $B1569_1$.
  Faulte d'argent, Qui habitat
  GombosiB, Homoly0

1568^{23}, $B1568_7$. *Luculentum theatrum musicum in quo (demptis*
vetustate tritis cantionibus) selectissima optimorum
quorumlibet auctorum ac excellentissimorum artificum
tum veterum, tum praecipuè recentiorum carmina....
Louvain: P. Phalèse, 1568.
  Benedicta es, Stabat mater

1570^{35}, $B1570_4$. *Selectissima elegantissimaque gallica,*
italica in guiterna ludenda carmina.... Louvain: P.
Phalèse; Antwerpen: J. Bellère, 1570.
  In exitu Israel

1571^{16}, $B1571_6$. *Theatrum musicum, longe amplissimum qui*
(demptis quae vetustate viluerant) authorem praestantiss.
tum veterum, tum recentiorum carmina selectissimae sunt
inserta ... *universa propemodum nunc recenter à peritissimis*
quibusque translatae in testudinis usum, velut Iulio
Cesare paduano, Melchiore Neuslyder germano et Sixto
Kargl.... Louvain: P. Phalèse et L. Bellère, 1571.
  Benedicta es*, Stabat mater*

1574[13], B1574[5]. *Teütsch Lautenbuch, darinnenn kunstliche*
Muteten, liebliche italianische, frantzösische, teütsche
Stuck ... ausgesetzt ... durch Melchior Newsidler.
Strasbourg: B. Jobin, 1574.
  Benedicta es
  Discussion: Kopff

1574[12], B1574[7]. *Thesaurus musicus continens selectissima*
Alberti Ripae, Valentini Bacfari et aliorum praestantissi-
morum carmina ad usum chelys, vel testudinis accomodata....
Louvain: P. Phalèse et J. Bellère, 1574.
  Faulte d'argent*

1578[24], B1578[3]. *Obras de musica para tecla arpa y vihuela,*
de Antonio de Cabeçon, musico de la camara y capilla del
rey Don Philippe nuestro señor. Recopiladas y puestas en
cifra por Hernando de Cabeçon su hijo.... Madrid: F.
Sanchez, 1578.
  Ave Maria (Pater noster, part 2); Benedicta es (2 versions); Inviolata (2 versions); M. de Beata Virgine:
  Cum sancto spiritu; M. l'homme armé svm: Hosanna,
  Benedictus, Agnus 3 ("Clama ne cesses"); Nunc caeli
  regina (Virgo salutiferi, part 3), Stabat mater (2
  versions)
  Editions: MME 27-9, JacobsC
  Discussion: Barber

1583[22], B1583[2]. *Orgel oder Instrument Tabulaturbuch in sich*
begreiffende eine notwendig unnd kurtze Anlaitung, die
Tabulatur unnd Application zuverstehen, auch dieselbige
auss gutem Grund recht zu lernen. Darnach folgen auffs
allerleichtest gute deutsche lateinische welsche und
frantzösische Stücklein ... zusammengebracht ... durch
Eliam Nicolaum Ammerbach. Nürnberg: Gerlach, 1583.
  M. de Beata Virgine: Cum sancto spiritus

1583[23], B1583[4]. *Ein schön nutz unnd gebreüchlich Orgel*
Tabulaturbuch. Darinnen etlich der berümbten Componisten,
beste Moteten ... alle mit grossem Fleiss coloriert ...
vom Iacopo Paix augustano. Laugingen: L. Reinmichel, 1583.
  Veni sancte spiritus

1583[24], B1583[6]. *Tabulaturbuch auff Orgeln und Instrument*
darinne auff alle Sontage und hohe Fest durchs gantze
Jhar auserlesene, liebliche und künstliche Moteten ...
durch Johannem Rüling von Born ... Der erste Theil.
Leipzig: J. Beyer, 1583.
  O lux beatissima (Vene sancti spiritus, part 2)

1589[17], B1589[6]. *Thesaurus motetarum. Newerlessner zwey und
zweintzig herrlicher Moteten, recht kunst Stück* ... *von
Iacobo Paix augustano, organico lavingano*. Strasbourg:
B. Jobin, 1589.
   Benedicta es (12 v.; att. Josquin, Castilleti)

IV. DISCOGRAPHY

Since it is of interest to study changing approaches to the performance practice of renaissance music, approximate dates for recordings are suggested. Wherever a performance date is stated on the recording it is so listed. Other dates should be regarded as terminal dates, derived from Schwann (prefaced by S), library cards or record catalogues (given in parentheses), or copyright dates (prefaced by cop.). Record companies which specialize in reprints pose special problems, for their issues may be either complete reissues of entire earlier recordings, or composites of a number of earlier recordings of various ages. Thus all Schwann dates and dates in parentheses should be regarded as tentative, since the actual performance may have been from one to several years earlier.

I have tried to give American record labels where possible, with cross-references to other labels under which the same record is issued. The order within each label is numerical, disregarding the welter of prefatory letters dear to the hearts of manufacturers. All recordings are 12" 33 1/3 rpm unless otherwise stated.

A valuable survey of Josquin recordings is Bridgman0, citing numerous early reviews. The most helpful general source for recordings before 1951 is Clough; Schwann, Myers, and Maleady give thorough coverage within their date spans. The two editions of CooverM offer special coverage to 1971.

A. LIST OF RECORDINGS BY RECORD LABEL

ABC CLASSICS 67017 (S1977) 2 discs. *Missa la sol fa re mi; motets, chansons*. Capella Antiqua München; K. Ruhland. La Bernardina, Ile fantazies, Je ne me puis tenir, La plus de plus, Qui velatus, Sanctus de passione, Absalon, Adieu mes amours, Allegez moy, Fortuna d'un gran tempo, El grillo, Inviolata, Miserere mei, Planxit autem, Scaramella, Tu solus, M. la sol fa re mi

ACADEMY 30B (1950-52) 10" disc. *Courtly Music of the XVI Cen-
tury*. Harvard-Radcliffe Glee Clubs; Westergaard.
Mille regretz.
ADVENT *see* TELARC
ALLEGRO 14 (1949?). *Music of the Gothic Period*. The Vielle
Trio with Du Bose Robertson, tenor. Reissued 1964 as
Allegro 9019.
Ile fantazies
ALLEGRO 17 (1949) 10" disc. [French choral music]. Pro
Musica Chorus, Calder. (with: Ravel, Debussy, Jannequin,
Couperin) Reissued as Compagnie Industrielle du Disque
33007.
Coeurs desolez
ALTE WERK *see* TELEFUNKEN
AMADEO 5030 *see* MUSICAL HERITAGE 713
AMADEO 5043 *see* MUSICAL HERITAGE 929
AMADEO 6233 *see* MUSICAL HERITAGE 1716
AMADEO 6326 (1964-6?). *Internationale Woche für Chormusik in
Graz*.
Mille regretz. Ensemble Stephane Caillat.
ANGEL 36013 *see* CAPITOL 8460
ANGEL 36379 (S1963 original; this issue S1967). *Music for
Maximilian*. Originally issued as *Innsbruck. Die Hof-
kapelle Maximilians I (Musik in alten Stadten und
Residenzens)*, Odéon/Electrola 91 107.
Adieu mes amours (from RomeC 2856), J'ay bien cause,
Plus nulz regretz. RIAS Kammerchor; Günther Arndt.
ANGEL 36926 (cop.1972). *Music from the Court of Ferdinand and
Isabella*. The Early Music Consort of London; David
Munrow. Also issued as HMV 3738.
In te, Domine
ANTHOLOGIE SONORE. *L'Anthologie sonore*. [Record series direc-
ted by Curt Sachs and Felix Raugel] (*ca.* 1939-59).
Earlier nos. in 78 rpm, later reissued in 33 1/3 rpm
under Haydn Society label.
no. 73, vol. VIII (78 rpm; 1938; Haydn Society AS 5).
M. Hercules: Kyrie; Stabat mater. Paraphonistes de St.
Jean; Guillaume de Van.
nos. 107/8, vol. XI (78 rpm; 1940-42; Haydn Society AS 5).
Miserere mei, Vive le roy, Si congié prens. Paraphonistes
de St. Jean; G. de Van. Included on Haydn Society AS 5:
"Chant du soldat" (Scaramella), Raugel.
ARGO 90 (1963?). [Choral music]. Choir of Saint Eustache;
Emile Martin.
Miserere mei
ARGO 681 (cop.1971). *Josquin des Près, John Dunstable*. Purcell
Consort; Grayston Burgess.
Petite camusette, Coeurs desolez, Nymphes des bois, Vive

le roy, El grillo, La Bernardina, Baises moy, Fortuna
desperata, Ave Maria ... virgo (6 v. arrangement)
ARGO 793 (cop.1975). *Musica reservata.* Musica reservata:
Michael Morrow, director; Andrew Parrott, conductor.
Mille regretz (chanson, pavane), Scaramella, Adieu mes
amours, Plaine de deuil, In te Domine (frottola and
2 dances), Tenez moy en vos bras, Faulte d'argent,
Nymphes des bois, El grillo, Coeurs desolez (4 v.;
3 versions), Bergerette savoyenne, Recordans de my
segnora, Regretz sans fin
ARNO VOLK VERLAG 101-3 (1972). *Die Messe.* Pro Musica, Köln;
Johannes Hömberg.
M. sine nomine: Sanctus
AVANT GARDE 129 (cop.1967). *A Choral Tapestry, volume two.*
Ambrosian Singers; John McCarthy.
Ave vera virginitas

BACH GUILD 620/5042 (1961). *Josquin Desprez.* Musica Antiqua,
Wien; Wiener Kammerchor, Gillesberger.
M. Hercules, M. da pacem: Et incarnatus, Veni sancte
spiritus, In principio (parts 1, 3), De profundis
BACH GUILD 671/70671 (1969?). *Madrigal Masterpieces, Vol. 3:
The Renaissance in France, Italy, and England.* Deller
Consort. Also issued as Vanguard 298.
Nymphes des bois, Parfons regretz
BACH GUILD (Historical Anthology ...) *see* VANGUARD 3
BAM (Boîte à Musique) 022/9022 (1955). *Josquin des Prés,
Pierre Manchicourt.* Chanteurs de St. Eustache; Emile
Martin.
Miserere mei
BAM 040 (S1964). *Lassus, Des Pres, Reutter.* Chanteurs de St.
Eustache; Emile Martin.
Nymphes des bois
BAROQUE 9002 (1959?). *Josquin des Pres: Missa una musque de
Buscaya.* Renaissance Chorus of New York; Harold Brown.
BASF *see* HARMONIA MUNDI
BOÎTE À MUSIQUE *see* BAM

CAMERATE 30 031, recorded 1964. [Isaac, Des Prez]. Neder-
laandse Christelijke Radio Vereneging Vocaal Ensemble,
Hilversum; Marinus Voorberg.
O virgo virginum, Praeter rerum
CANTATE 658 236 (1973?). *Musica reservata.* Martin Luther
Kantorei, Detmold; Eberhard Popp.
O Jesu fili David, Dominus regnavit, De profundis,
Domine ne in furore
CAPITOL 8460 (S1959). *Echoes from a 16th Century Cathedral.*
Roger Wagner Chorale. Also issued as Angel 36013.
Ave vera virginitas

CARILLION 124, recorded 11/14/61. *Des Prez. Missa mater patris et filia*. Harvard Glee Club; Elliot Forbes.
   Also includes Brumel: *Mater patris et filia*
CHANT DU MONDE 540 (10" 78 rpm; between 1936 and 1950).
   Annecy Lycée Chorus.
   Ave vera virginitas
CHRISTSCHALL 119 (10" 78 rpm; before 1936). Munich Cathedral Choir, Berberich.
   M. pange lingua: Sanctus
CHS (Concert Hall Society) 47 (1949?). [Lassus, des Prez].
   Dessoff Choir; Paul Boepple.
   Ave Maria, De profundis
CLASSIC EDITION 1018 (1953?). *Music of Six Centuries*. Recorder Consort of the Musicians' Workshop.
   Si jay perdu
COLLEGIUM 102/3 (1975?) 2 discs. *Flemish and Burgundian Music in Honor of the Blessed Virgin Mary*. The Columbia University Collegium Musicum; Richard Taruskin.
   102: Virgo prudentissima, M. gaudeamus: Kyrie, M. de Beata Virgine: Credo. 103: Ave Maria ("after Josquin", by Senfl)
COLLEGIUM 109/10 (1975). *A Composite Missa L'homme armé*. The Columbia University Collegium Musicum; Richard Taruskin.
   109: L'homme armé
COLLEGIUM 111 (1975). *Motets for Christmas*. The Columbia University Collegium Musicum; Alexander Blachly.
   Liber generationis, O admirabile commercium (complete)
COLLEGIUM 116 (1975). *Musical Metamorphoses of the Renaissance*. The Columbia University Collegium Musicum; Alexander Blachly
   Fortuna desperata
COLUMBIA RFX 71 (78 rpm; 1939/40?). Strasbourg Cathedral Chorus; Hoch (coupled with Bruckner).
   Tu pauperum refugium
COLUMBIA RFX 73 (78 rpm; 1938/40?). Strasbourg Cathedral Chorus; Hoch (coupled with LaRue).
   O Domine Jesu Christe
COLUMBIA MQ31289 (1972?). *Antiphonal Music for Four Brass Choirs*. Columbia Brass Ensemble; Andrew Kazdin.
   Royal Fanfare (Vive le roy)
COLUMBIA M34554. *A Renaissance Christmas*. Waverly Consort; Michael Jaffee.
   Ave Maria
COLUMBIA 69693D (78 rpm; before 1939). Strasbourg Cathedral Chorus; Alphonse Hoch (coupled with Berlioz). Also issued as Eng. Columbia LX737, LWX296, and as French Columbia RFX59 (coupled with Mozart).
   Ave vera virginitas

COMPAGNIE INDUSTRIELLE DU DISQUE 33007 *see* ALLEGRO 17
CONCERT HALL SOCIETY *see* CHS
CONCORDIA 3 (1953-5). [Concordia Chorus, P.J. Christiansen].
    "Jesu Tu pauperum refugium" (sung in English)
CONNOISSEUR SOCIETY 2056 (1974?). *The Heavens Are Telling.*
    Hamilton College Men's Choir; John L. Baldwin.
    King's Fanfare (Vive le roy)
CONTREPOINT MC 20017 *see* ESOTERIC 514
COUNTERPOINT 601/5601 (1963?). *Music of the Renaissance.* Vocal
    Arts Ensemble; Levitt.
    Ave Maria
CROSSROADS 22 16 0093/4 (1 disc, S1967). *Josquin Desprez.*
    Prague Madrigal Singers, Musica antiqua Vienna; Miroslav
    Venhoda. Also issued as Supraphon 10553.
    M. l'homme armé st, Praeter rerum, Mille regretz (with
    pavane), Coeurs desolez, Tulerunt Dominum, Ave Maria

DA CAMERA MAGNA SM 94053 (1979?). *Josquin des Prez, Brumel.*
    Schola cantorum Sankt Foillan, Aachen; Wilhelm Esch-
    weiler.
    M. mater patris, O Domine Jesu Christe
DAS ALTE WERK *see* TELEFUNKEN
DECCA 9410/79410 (1961). *Josquin des Prez. Missa pange lingua;*
    Motets; Instrumental Pieces. New York Pro Musica; Noah
    Greenberg. Also issued as MCA 2507.
    M. pange lingua, Fanfare for Louis XII (Vive le roy),
    Fama malum, Dulces exuviae, La Bernardina, Tu solus
DECCA 9629 (1953-5). [French Renaissance Vocal Music]. Nadia
    Boulanger Ensemble. Also issued as Vox 6380.
    Mille regret
DECCA 79435 (1969). *Petrucci, First Printer of Music: Chansons,*
    Frottole, Popular Italian Dances and Sacred Compositions
    from the First Printed Collections (1501-1508). New
    York Pro Musica; John Reeves White. Also issued as
    MCA 2503.
    De tous biens playne, El grillo, M. ave maris stella
DECCA/OISEAU-LYRE 1288 203/6 (1975). *Musicke of Sundre Kinds:*
    Renaissance Secular Music 1480-1620. Consorte of
    Musicke; Anthony Rooley.
    Mille regret
DGG (Deutsche Gramophon) ARC 2533-110 (1973). *Marien-Motetten.*
    Hamburg Monteverdi Chorus; Jürgens.
    Benedicta es, Alma redemptoris, Illibata, O virgo virginum,
    Missus est Gabriel, Ave nobilissima creatura
DGG ARC 2533 145 (S1973). *Johannes Ockeghem: Missa pro defunc-*
    tis. Pro cantione antiqua, London; Hamburger Bläserkreis
    für alte Musik; Bruno Turner.
    Nymphes des bois

DGG ARC 2533 360 (recorded 9/20-24/76). *Josquin Desprez.*
    Missa "L'homme armé super voces musicales"; Motet: Huc
    me sydereo/Plangent eum; Laments on the Death of Josquin.
    Pro Cantiones Antiqua, London; Bruno Turner.
DGG ARC 3158/73159 (recorded 1959-60). *Josquin des Pres. Missa*
    pange lingua, 8 Secular Works. (Archive Production:
    History of Music Division of the Deutsche Grammophon
    Gesellschaft. IV. Research Period: The High Renaissance.
    Series A: The Netherlanders from Josquin des Prez). Pro
    Musica Antiqua; Safford Cape.
    M. pange lingua, N'esse pas un grant displaisir, Nymphes
    des bois, Fortuna d'un gran tempo, Bergerette savoyenne,
    Parfons regretz, Scaramella, Faulte d'argent, Baisez
    moy
DGG ARC 3223/73223 (recorded 1963). *Maximilian I Imperial*
    Chapel Repertory. Concentus Musicus, Vienna; N. D'Harnon-
    court.
    Comment peult
DGG 636501 (1966?). *Grand passé musical de Paris.* Ensemble
    instrumentale et soloists; J. Chailley.
    Mille regretz
DISCOPHILES FRANÇAIS 31-4 (set 7) (78 rpm; 4-record set; 1947?).
    La Chanson Français de la Renaissance. Vocal ensemble;
    Marcel Couraud.
    Allegez moy, Baisez moy (4 v., 6 v.), Coeur langoreulx,
    Incessament livré suis, J'ay bien cause, Je me com-
    plains, L'homme armé, Ma bouche rit, N'esse pas un
    grant displaisir, Parfons regretz, Plaine de deuil,
    Tenez moy
DISCOPHILES FRANÇAIS 84-7 (set 19) (78 rpm; 4-record set;
    1948?). [French Sacred Music of the Renaissance].
    Vocal ensemble; Marcel Couraud.
    Ave verum corpus, Vultum tuum
DISCOPHILES FRANÇAIS 330.111-4 (1961?) 3 discs. *Anthologie*
    de la chanson française de 1450 à 1550. Ensemble Vocal
    Roger Blanchard.
    Nymphes des bois, Plusieurs regretz
DISCOPHILES FRANÇAIS 730063/740015 (S1964). *Josquin des Prez:*
    Missa de Beata Vergine [*sic*]. Ensemble Vocal Roger
    Blanchard.
DONEMUS 6901 (1969). *Three Centuries of Netherlands Music:*
    Anthology for the Centenary of the Society for Nether-
    lands Musical History (Donemus audio-visual series
    no. 1).
    Benedicta es (recorded 1968; Netherlands Chamber Choir,
    Felix de Nobel; score included)
DOVER 95148-7 *see* PERIOD 597

ELECTROLA C91.107 *see* ANGEL 36383
EMS 213 (Series 1950 recordings). *Anthology of Middle Age and*
    Renaissance Music, vol. 13: Josquin des Prez Secular
    Works. Pro Musica Antiqua; Safford Cape. Recorded 1950
    in Brussels.
    N'esse pas ung grand displaisir, Parfons regretz, Ber-
    gerette savoyenne, Fortuna d'un gran tempo, Douleur me
    bat, Pour souhaitter, Faulte d'argent, Petite camusette,
    Incessament mon povre, Je me complains, La plus des
    plus, Allegez moy, Nymphes des bois, Baisez moy
EPIC 3045 *see* PHILIPS 00678
EPIC 3263 (1956?). [Choral music]. Netherlands Chamber Choir;
    De Nobel.
    El grillo
ERATO 2010 (1953-5?). *Josquin des Pres: Missa pange lingua*.
    Philippe Caillard Vocal Ensemble (recorded in the Church
    of St. Roch, Paris). (Cf. Musical Heritage 617, 1000.)
ERATO 3377/50277 *see* MUSICAL HERITAGE 894
ERATO 8026 (1967?). Same as Erato 42021, with title *Chansons*
    amoureuses et guerrières de la renaissance. (Collection
    fiori musicali 26).
ERATO 9070 *see* MUSICAL HERITAGE 617, 1000; ERATO 2010
ERATO 42021 (196-). *Chansons de la Renaissance*. Philippe
    Caillard Vocal Ensemble.
    Mille regretz
ERATO 42052 (before 1964). *Dix motets de la renaissance*.
    Petit Chanteurs de St. Laurent; Zurfluh.
    Ave verum
ERATO 70661 *see* MUSICAL HERITAGE 3859
ESOTERIC 514 (1953?). *Flemish Choral Works: 15th Century to*
    Modern. Ghent Oratorio Society; De Pauw. Also issued as
    Contrepoint MC 20017.
    Mille regretz
ESOTERIC 546 (1954?). *15th and 16th Century Motets*. Renais-
    sance Chorus of New York; Harold Brown.
    Misericordias Domine (parts 1, 2)
ETERNA 730002 (1953-5). [Choral music]. U.S.S.R. State Chorus;
    Shveshnikov.
    Et incarnatus est (M. pange lingua?)
EVEREST 3174/6174 (1967?). *Plainsong to Polyphony*. Carmelite
    Priory Choir; McCarthy. Also issued as Odéon 1895/3519.
    Nymphes des bois
EVEREST 3193 (S1968). *Concert at the Vatican*. Sistine Choir;
    Bartolucci.
    Ave Maria
EVEREST 3210 (S1968). *Choral Music of the Renaissance and the*
    Baroque. UCLA Men's Glee Club and Collegium Musicum;

Donn Weiss. (Musica ficta and text underlay by Edward E.
Lowinsky.)
Fama malum, Dulces exuviae, Huc me sydereo, O Domine Jesu
Christe
EVERYMAN *see* VANGUARD

FESTIVAL 70-202 (10" disc; 1951?). *Pre-Baroque Sacred Music.*
Harvard University Choir, Radcliffe Choral Society;
William F. Russell.
"Veni creator spiritus" (= Ave vera virginitas)
FOLKWAYS 3651 (1965?). *Music for Brass Quintet.* American
Brass Quintet.
Vive le roy

GRAMOPHON GY 213 (10" 78 rpm; 1936?). *Josquin Des Pres: Ave
Christe.* Montserrat Monastery Chorus; Pujol.
GRAMOPHON W.1514 (78 rpm; 1940-42?). *Josquin Des Pres: Missa
l'homme armé (svm): Gloria.* Paraphonistes de St. Jean;
G. de Van. (Cf. BridgmanO 634.)
GRAMOPHONE SHOP CELEBRITIES (GSC) 53-5 in set IX (78 rpm; 3
sides; 1950?). *Josquin des Pres: Mass pange lingua*
(Kyrie, Sanctus, Agnus Dei). Danish Radio Madrigal
Choir; M. Wöldike.
GREGORIAN INSTITUTE OF AMERICA (GIOA) Set PM 1 (78 rpm; 1948).
Polyphonic Masters of the XVIth Century. Gregorian In-
stitute Graduating Class (1948); Vitry. Reissued 33 1/3
rpm as GIOA PMLP1.
M. ave maris: Kyrie, Agnus Dei; Ave vera virginitas
GREGORIAN INSTITUTE OF AMERICA BF 1 (1953-5?). [Biggs Family
ensemble].
Ave vera virginitas
GREGORIAN INSTITUTE OF AMERICA EL 17, in set EL 100 (S1960).
Thirteen Centuries of Christian Choral Art, Vol. I.
Peloquin Chorale.
Ave verum

HARMONIA MUNDI 20339 (1972?). [Motets]. Soloists of Tolzer
Knabenchor, Pro Cantione Antiqua, Collegium Aureum,
Hamburg wind ensemble; Bruno Turner. Also issued as
BASF 20339.
Benedicta es, Tu solus, Dominus regnavit, Ave Maria ...
virgo serena, Miserere mei, Inviolata
HARMONIA MUNDI 21443. [Choral music]. Aachener Domchor; Pohl.
Also issued as BASF 21443 with title *Ave Maria Kaiserin.*
Tu solus
HARMONIA MUNDI 21513: same contents as Harmonia Mundi 20339.
HAYDN SOCIETY AS *see* ANTHOLOGIE SONORE

HAYDN SOCIETY 9038/2071 (1953-5). *Masterpieces of Music before 1750*. (Recordings for Carl Parrish anthology of the same title.)
Side 2: Ave Maria (Copenhagen Boys' and Men's Choir; Niels Møller)
HÉBERTOT 2046 (78 rpm; between 1936 and 1950). *Josquin des Pres: Mille regretz*. T. Filliol soprano, 2 gambas [*sic*].
HMV 1041 (1970?). *French Songs*. Elizabethan Consort; Nesbitt.
Coeurs desolez, Mille regret
HMV 3738 *see* ANGEL 36926
HMV 3766 (1975?). [The King's Singers].
Baisez moy, Petite camusette
HMV *see also* VICTOR
HUNGARITON 11633 *see* QUALITON 11633

INÉDITS RTF dist. Barclay 995 001 (1970). *Musique française des XVe et XVIe siècles*. Ensemble polyphonique de l'Office de Radiodiffusion-Télevision Française; Charles Ravier.
L'homme armé, Petite camusette

[J] Recording of Josquin Festival Conference Performance Workshops; a supplement to book J. 3 7" discs.
Absalon fili mi (Capella Antiqua, Munich; K. Ruhland, and Schola Cantorum, Stuttgart; C. Gottwald), Adieu mes amours (CAM; Ruhland, and New York Pro Musica; Paul Maynard), Fortuna d'un gran tempo (Prague Madrigal Singers; M. Venhoda), Je ne me puis tenir (CAM; Ruhland, and NYPM; Maynard), M. l'homme armé svm: Kyrie, Agnus 2 (4 versions) and Agnus 2-3 (PMS; Venhoda), M. malheur: Et in spiritum (PMS; Venhoda), Monstra te esse matrem (CAM; Ruhland, and SCS; Gottwald), Plus nulz regretz (CAM; Ruhland, and NYPM; Maynard), Stabat mater, part 1 (CAM; Ruhland, and SCS; Gottwald)

LONDON DUCRETET-THOMSON 94007 (1952-5). [French choral music].
Paris Vocal Ensemble; Jouve.
Ave Maria
LUMEN 4 *see* MUSICA SACRA 4
LYRICHORD 52 (1954?). *Motets of the 15th and 16th Centuries with Easter Themes*. The Welch Chorale.
Ave verum
LYRICHORD 109/7109 (S1964). *Music of the Pre-Baroque*.
Ave verum (unidentified performers)
LYRICHORD 775 (1958?). *Italian Music in the Age of Exploration*.
Fleetwood Singers.
El grillo

LYRICHORD 7214. Recorded 1968-9 at Yale University. *Josquin des Prez: Missa sine nomine; motets, chansons.* Capella Cordina; Alejandro Planchart.
   M. sine nomine, Faulte d'argent, Plusieurs regretz, Baisez moy, Benedicite omnia opera, Laudate pueri
LYRICHORD 7265. Recorded 1972 at Yale University. *Josquin des Prez: Missa gaudeamus, In exitu Israel, Dominus regnavit, Nymphes des bois.* Capella Cordina, A. Planchart.

MACE 9030 (S1966). *Sacred Music of the Masters.* Aachen Cathedral Chorus; Graff.
   M. Hercules: Sanctus
MACE 9078 (S1967). *Chamber Music for Voices.* Klagenfurt Madrigal Chorus; Mittergradnegger. Also issued as Musical Heritage 3683.
   Tulerunt Dominum
MCA 2503 *see* DECCA 79435
MCA 2507 *see* DECCA 79410
MUSIC GUILD 7/134 (1961). *Josquin Des Pres: Missa "Hercules dux Ferrariae."* Ensemble Vocal Roger Blanchard.
MUSIC GUILD 120 (1965?). *Fanfares from Six Centuries.* Paris Brass Ensemble. Also issued as Musical Heritage 1785.
   Royal Fanfare (Vive le roy)
MUSIC LIBRARY 6995 (S1967). [Stanford University Chorus].
   Tu pauperum
MUSIC LIBRARY 7075 (S1958). *Bach, Josquin, and Hindemith.* Berkeley Chamber Singers; Donald Aird.
   M. Hercules
MUSIC LIBRARY 7085 (1956). [Choral music]. Catawba College Choir; Robert Weaver.
   M. pange lingua
MUSICA SACRA 4. Recorded 1957. *Josquin des Pres: Missa Hercules dux Ferrariae; Misericordias Domini (part 1).* Chanteurs St. Eustache; E. Martin.
MUSICAL HERITAGE 617. *Josquin des Prez: Missa pange lingua.* Philippe Caillard vocal ensemble (coupled with LeJeune). Cf. Erato 2010, Musical Heritage 1000.
MUSICAL HERITAGE 713 (1966?). *Secular Music of the Renaissance.* Cappella Monacensis; Kurt Weinhoppel. Also issued as Amadeo 5043.
   El grillo
MUSICAL HERITAGE 894. *Music in Reims Cathedral.* Also issued as Erato 3377.
   Vive le roy (organ)
MUSICAL HERITAGE 929. *Sacred and Secular Music of the Renaissance.* Walther von der Vogelweide Chamber Choir; Othmar Costa. Also issued as Amadeo 5043.
   Tu pauperum refugium

MUSICAL HERITAGE 1000. *Josquin des Prez: Missa pange lingua,*
   Miserere mei Deus. Philippe Caillard Choir. Cf. Erato
   2010, Musical Heritage 617. This pressing issued (1969?),
   reissued 1972.
MUSICAL HERITAGE 1125 (1971?). *La chanson et la danse, Paris,*
   ca. 1540. Vocal Ensemble of Lausanne; Michel Corboz,
   and Ricercare ensemble of Zurich; Michel Piguet.
   Mille regretz, with pavane
MUSICAL HERITAGE 1442 (1972?). *French Music of the Middle*
   Ages and Renaissance. Studio für alte Musik, Düsseldorf.
   La plus des plus
MUSICAL HERITAGE 1716 (1973?). *Music at the Court of Maximilian*
   I. Concentus Musicus of Vienna; N. d'Harnoncourt.
   Vive le roy, Adieu mes amours, Baises moy, De tous biens
   playne
MUSICAL HERITAGE 1785 *see* MUSIC GUILD 120
MUSICAL HERITAGE 1804 (1974?). *Tower music.* Salzburg Tower
   Brass; S. Dörfner.
   Fanfare (Vive le roy)
MUSICAL HERITAGE 3411 (1976). *Choirs, Strings, and Brass.*
   Philippe Caillard vocal and instrumental ensemble.
   Fanfare (Vive le roy), O Jesu fili David (Comment peult),
   Requiem (Nymphes des bois)
MUSICAL HERITAGE 3558 (1977?). *Ars perfecta: Motets for Male*
   Voices. Harvard Glee Club; Adams.
   Alma redemptoris (no.38), Absalon fili mi, Domine ne in
   furore, O Domine Jesu Christe
MUSICAL HERITAGE 3682 *see* MACE 9078
MUSICAL HERITAGE 3729 (1978?). *Josquin Des Prez: Missa da*
   pacem. Karlsruhe Chamber Choir, Hamburg Wind Ensemble,
   Splenger Gamba Consort.
MUSICAL HERITAGE 3859 (1978?). *From Guillaume Dufay to Josquin*
   des Pres: Love Songs of the XVth Century. Ricercare
   ensemble of Zurich; M. Piguet.
   A l'heure, Si j'ay perdu, Bergerette savoyenne
MUSICRAFT 212 (10" 78 rpm; 1939?). *Vocal Music of the Renais-*
   sance. The Madrigalists; Lief.
   Baisez moy (6 v.)

NONESUCH 1010 (S1964). *Court and Ceremonial Music of the Early*
   16th Century. Roger Blanchard Ensemble.
   Allegez-moy, Adieu mes amours, Vive le roy
NONESUCH 1084/71084 (1965). [Choral music]. Kaufbeurer
   Martinsfinken; Ludwig Hahn.
   Ave Christe
NONESUCH 1095/71095 (S1966). *Renaissance Choral Music for*
   Christmas. N.C.R.V. Vocal Ensemble, Hilversum: Marinus
   Voorberg.
   Praeter rerum

NONESUCH 1216/71216 (S1969). *Josquin Desprez: Missa ave maris stella; Four Motets*. University of Illinois Chamber Choir; George Hunter.
   Tu solus, Mittit ad virginum, Absalon, Salve regina (5 v.)
NONESUCH 71261 (S1972). *Josquin Des Prez: Secular Music*. The Nonesuch Consort; Joshua Rifkin.
   Recordans de my segnora, Ile fantazies, Que vous madame, Cela sans plus, La plus des plus, Scaramella, De tous biens playne, La Bernardina, Qui belles amours, Comment peult, Quant je vous voy, Baisez moy, Entré suis, Una musque, Si j'ay perdu, In te Domine

ODÉON EMS 48 (10" 78 rpm; 1938?). (Société de l'Édition de Musique Sacrée: Musique au Vatican). *Josquin des Pres: Ave Maria*. Julian Chapel Choir; Boëzi.
ODÉON 1895/3519 *see* EVEREST 6154/3174
ODÉON 91.107 *see* ANGEL 36373
OISEAU-LYRE LD81 (1953-5). *Musiciens de la cour de Bourgogne, Vol. II*.
   Si j'ay perdu
OISEAU-LYRE 1288 203/6 *see* DECCA 1288 203/6
OVERTONE 2 (1953?). *Hymns of Praise*. Yale Divinity School Choir; Borden.
   Ave verum

PARLOPHONE 1016/27 (10" 78 rpm set, 1931?). *Two Thousand Years of Music*, edited by Curt Sachs. Issued under several other numbers and labels; see CloughW 713. Also issued as 33 1/3 rpm on Parlophone/Decca P 525.
   Record 1019: Et incarnatus est (M. pange lingua) (Berlin State Academy Chorus; Kalt)
PATHÉ X 93055 (78 rpm; before 1936). *Josquin Des Pres: Ave vera virginitas*. St. Léon XI Choir; Gaudard.
PATHÉ-FRANCE 2084 (1962-7). *Celebration chorale en l'ancienne église St. Philibert de Dijon*. Joseph Samson Ensemble.
   Ave verum
PELCA 40607 (1976). *Meisterwerk der Motettenkunst: Chormusik aus fünf Jahrhunderten*. Evangelische Jugendkantorei der Pfalz; Heinz Markus Gottsche. Recorded 1976.
   Tu pauperum refugium
PERIOD 535 (1951?). *Choral Masterpieces of the Renaissance*. The Nonesuch Singers; Ronald Dale Smith.
   Ave Maria, Ave verum (part 1)
PERIOD 597 (cop.1956). *Anthology of Renaissance Music*. The Primavera Singers of the New York Pro Musica Antiqua; Noah Greenberg. Later reissued as Dover 95248-7.
   Tu solus, Ave Maria ... virgo

PERIOD 746 (S1959). *Easter at Grailville*. Grail Singers;
    Miller.
    Ave verum
PHILIPS 00678. [Sacred and secular songs of the Renaissance].
    Netherlands Chamber Choir; De Nobel. Reissued as Epic
    3045.
    Ave Maria, El grillo
PHILIPS 00994 (1953-5). *Chansons polyphoniques français*.
    Roger Blanchard Vocal Ensemble.
    Bergerette Savoyenne
PHILIPS 4FM 10017 (1969?). [Madrigals]. I Madrigalisti di
    Roma; Domenico Cieri.
    El grillo.
PLAISIR MUSICAL 30308 (1964?). *De Josquin des Prés à Igor*
    Stravinsky. Maîtrise RTF; Besson.
    Mille regretz.
PLEIADES 252 (S1970). *Late 15th Century and Early 16th Cen-*
    tury. (Recordings of Davison-Apel *Historical Anthology*
    of Music). University of Chicago Collegium; H.M. Brown,
    and Southern Illinois Collegium Musicum.
    Agnus Dei (M. l'homme armé svm, Agnus 2), Tu pauperum,
    Faulte d'argent

QUALITON 11633 (1974?). *Josquin Des Pres: [Secular works]*.
    Liszt Music Academy Choir; Parkai.
    Allegez moy, Coeurs desolez, Nymphes des bois, Je ne me
    puis, Mille regretz, Petite camusette, Regretz sans
    fin, Si congié prens

RECORD SOCIETY 29 (1961?). *Josquin des Prés: Missa Hercules;*
    Miserere mei, La Bernardina. Roger Blanchard Vocal
    Ensemble.

SERAPHIM 6052 (S1969). *The Seraphim Guide to Renaissance*
    Music. Syntagma Musicum of Amsterdam; Kees Otten.
    Side 6: Agnus Dei (2 v., from Glareanus), La Bernardina,
    Baisez moy
SERAPHIM 6104 (cop.1976) 3 discs. *The Art of the Netherlanders*.
    Early Music Consort of London; David Munrow.
    Side 1: Scaramella, Allegez moy (vocal and lute duet),
    El grillo. Side 2: Guillaume s'en va, Adieu mes amours
    (vocal and keyboard versions), Fortuna desperata. Side
    3: Vive le roy, La Spagna, La Bernardina. Side 4: Credo
    de tous biens playne. Side 5: De profundis (5 v.),
    Benedicta es, Inviolata
SPECTRUM 114 (1980?). *Josquin des Pres: Missa de Beata Virgine;*
    Secular Works. West Virginia University Collegium
    Musicum; Harry Elzinga.

M. de Beata Virgine, Adieu mes amours, Baisez moy, De
    tous biens playne, La Bernardina, Mille regretz, La
    plus des plus
STUDIO 25-03 (before 1962). [Choral music]. Roger Blanchard
    Ensemble.
    Ave Maria, Stabat mater, Praeter rerum, Benedicta es
STUDIO 33-41 (before 1964). *Motets polyphoniques du XVIe
    siècle.* Schola du Grand Scolasticat des Pères du St.-
    Esprit de Chevilly; Deiss.
    O Domine Jesu Christe
STUDIO 33-60 (before 1964). *Motets de la nativitie.* Ensemble
    Vocal Blanchard.
    In principio
SUPRAPHON 111.2126 (1978?). *Le jardin musical.* Musica antiqua,
    Vienna.
    El grillo

TELARC 5024 (S1977). [Choral music]. Canby Singers; Edward
    Tatnall Canby.
    In Domino confido, Jubilate Deo, O bone et dulcissime
    Jesu, Tribulatio et angustia
TELEFUNKEN 8008 (45 rpm; 1959?). *Musik der alten Niederlander.*
    Musiekkring Obrecht.
    De tous biens playne
TELEFUNKEN 9480 (S1967). *Josquin Desprez: Motetten um 1490-
    1520.* Capella Antiqua, München; Konrad Ruhland.
    Ave Maria ... virgo, Stabat mater, Alma redemptoris/Ave,
    Benedicta es, Ave Christe, Ave verum corpus, Planxit
    autem
TELEFUNKEN 9561-2/16250/2 (S1971). *Staatsmusik der Renais-
    sance.* Capella Antiqua München; Konrad Ruhland.
    Absolve quaesumus, Coeurs desolez (5 v.), Carmen
    gallicum (Guillaume s'en va)
TELEFUNKEN 9595/641259 (S1974). *Josquin Desprez: Missa pange
    lingua; Alma redemptoris/Ave regina; Planxit autem David;
    O virgo virginum.* Prague Madrigalists; Miroslav Venhoda.
TELEFUNKEN 11515/1-2 (S1972). *Musik der Dürerzeit.* Josquin
    contents identical with Telefunken 9561-2.
TELEFUNKEN 641917 (1977?). Prager Madrigalisten; Miroslav
    Venhoda.
    Mille regretz (with Morales: M. mille regretz)
TITANIC 22 (1979?). *Josquin des Pres: Missa fortuna desperata;
    In principio.* Boston Camerata; J. Cohen.
TURNABOUT 34380 (S1971). *Love & Dalliance in Renaissance
    France.* The Cambridge Consort; Joel Cohen.
    Mille regretz, Una mousse de Biscaye, Allegez moy,
    Adieu mes amours

TURNABOUT 34431 (S1971). *Josquin des Pres: Missa pange lingua*.
Spandauer Kantorei; Martin Behrmann.
TURNABOUT 34437. Reissue (1971?) of M. de Beata Virgine from
Vox 600 with Dominus regnavit, Ave Christe, and Tulerunt
Dominum from Vox 580.
TURNABOUT 34485 (S1973). *Kissing, Drinking, and Insect Songs*.
The Sine Nomine Singers; Harry Saltzman.
Baises moy, El grillo
TURNABOUT 34512 (S1973). *The Wandering Musicians: Flemish
Composers in Renaissance Italy*. The Boston Camerata;
Joel Cohen.
Scaramella

VANGUARD/BACH GUILD HM 3 (S1972). *Historical Anthology of
Music II. The Renaissance (Early); C. The Flemish
Masters; 7. The Mass/5. Motets: Josquin des Pres*.
The Josquin Choir; Jeremy Noble.
Mass l'homme armé sexti toni, Regina caeli (6 v.),
Absalon fili mi, Illibata
VANGUARD 298/BACH GUILD 671 (1969?). *Madrigal Masterpieces,
Vol. 3*. The Deller Consort. Also issued as Everyman
298SD.
Nymphes des bois, Parfons regretz
VANGUARD 71223 (1980?). [Music for brass]. Canadian Brass.
Royal Fanfare (Vive le roy)
VERVE 2137/6151 (S1960). *Music for Antiphonal Choirs*. The
Gregg Smith Singers.
Nymphes des bois
VICTOR 1231 (1967?). *Sixteenth-Century Love Songs*. Rome
Polyphonic Chorus; Q. Petrocchi.
El grillo
VICTOR LM 6016-2 (1954). *History of Music in Sound, Vol. III:
Ars nova and the Renaissance*. Originally issued as
78 rpm, HMV 28.
Side 3: El grillo, Je ne me puis tenir (Pro Musica
Antiqua; S. Cape). Side 4: M. l'homme armé svm: Sanc-
tus, Tribulatio et angustia (Schola Polyphonica; Henry
Washington)
VICTOR 11677 in set M212 (78 rpm; before 1936). Dijon
Cathedral Choir; Joseph Samson.
Ave verum corpus; Ave caelorum domina (= Ave vera
virginitas)
VOX DL580 (1960). *Josquin des Pres: Choral Works*. The Dessoff
Choirs; Paul Boepple.
Dominus regnavit, Ave Christe, Tulerunt Dominum, O Jesu
fili David (= Comment peult), La plus de plus, De tous
biens playne, Parfons regretz, Bergerette savoysienne

VOX DL600 (cop.1962). *Josquin Des Pres: Missa de Beata Virgine.*
    The Dessoff Choirs; Paul Boepple.
VOX 6380 *see* DECCA 9621

B. INDEX OF RECORDED WORKS

    It has not been possible to determine in every case which
of identically named works has been recorded. I have assumed
the obvious work (e.g., Ave Maria ... virgo rather than Ave
Maria ... benedicta), and the genuine (e.g., Coeurs desolez
for 5 v. rather than 4 v.) unless the record expressly indicates otherwise.

A L'HEURE
    (1972?) Mus. Her. 3859 Piguet
ABSALON FILI MI
    S1969 None. 71216 Hunter
    1971 J Gottwald
    1971 J Ruhland
    S1972 Van. 3 Noble
    cop.1975 Argo 793 Morrow
    S1977 ABC 67017 Ruhland
    (1977?) Mus. Her. 3558 Adams
ABSOLVE, QUAESUMUS
    S1971 Tele. 9561 Ruhland
ADIEU MES AMOURS
    S1963 Angel 36379 Arndt
    S1964 Nonesuch 1012 Blanchard
    1971 J Maynard
    1971 J Ruhland
    S1971 Turn. Cohen
    (1973?) Mus. Her. 1716 D'Harnoncourt
    cop.1975 Argo 793 Morrow
    S1977 ABC 67017 Ruhland
    S1977 Seraphim 6104 Munrow
    (1980?) Spectrum 114 Elzinga
ALLEGEZ MOY
    (1947?) Disc. Fr. 17 Couraud
    1950 EMS 213 Cape
    S1964 Nonesuch 71012 Blanchard
    S1971 Turn. 34380 Cohen
    (1974?) Qualiton 11622 Parkai
    S1977 Seraphim 6104 Munrow
ALMA REDEMPTORIS MATER (no.38)
    (1977?) Mus. Her. 3558 Adams

ALMA REDEMPTORIS MATER/AVE REGINA
    S1967 Tele. 9480 Ruhland
    (1972) Tele. 9595 Venhoda
    (1973) DGG 2533-110 Jürgens
AVE CHRISTE IMMOLATE
    cop.1960 Vox 580 Boepple
    (1965) Nonesuch 1084 Hahn
    S1967 Tele. 9480 Ruhland
    S1971 Turn. 34437 Boepple
AVE MARIA ... BENEDICTA
    1953-5 Haydn Soc. 9038 Møller
AVE MARIA ... VIRGO SERENA
    (1938?) Odéon 48 Boëzi
    (1949?) CHS 47 Boepple
    (1951?) Period 535 Smith
    (1953-5) Lon. Du. Th. 94007 Jouve
    (1954?) Philips 00678 De Nobel
    (cop.1956) Period 595 Greenberg
    (before 1962) Studio 25-03 Blanchard
    (1963?) Counterpoint 5601 Levitt
    S1967 Tele. 9480 Ruhland
    (1967) Crossroads 22 16 0093 Venhoda
    S1968 Everest 3193 Bartolucci
    S1973 Har. Mun. 21513 Turner
    (1977?) Col. 34554 Jaffee
——, Part 2 only: AVE VERA VIRGINITAS
    before 1936 Pathé X93055 Gaudard
    before 1936 Victor 212 Samson
    before 1939 Col. 69693 Hoch
    1936-50 Chant d. M. 540 Annecy Lycée
    1948 GIOA 1 Vitry
    (1951?) Fest. 70202 Russell
    1953-5 GIOA BF1 Biggs
    S1959 Cap. 8060 Wagner
    cop.1967 Av. Garde 129 McCarthy
——, 6 v. version
    cop.1971 Argo 681 Burgess
AVE MARIS STELLA, Part 4: MONSTRA TE ESSE MATREM
    1971 J Gottwald
    1971 J Ruhland
AVE NOBILISSIMA
    (1973) DGG 2533-110 Jürgens
AVE VERA VIRGINITAS *see* AVE MARIA ... VIRGO SERENA
AVE VERUM CORPUS
    before 1936 Victor 212 Samson
    (1948?) Disc. Fr. 19 Couraud
    (1951?) Period 535 Smith

(1953?) Overtone 2 Borden
(1954?) Lyr. 52 Welch
S1959 Period 746 Miller
S1960 GIOA 17 Peloquin
1962-7 Pathé 2084 Samson
before 1964 Erato 41052 Zurfluh
S1964 Lyr. 109 (unidentified)
S1967 Tele. 9480 Ruhland

BAISEZ MOY
    (1939?) Musicraft 212 Lief (6 v.)
    (1947?) Disc. Fr. 7 Couraud (4 v. and 6 v.)
    1950 EMS 213 Cape
    1960 DGG 3159 Cape
    S1969 Lyr. 7214 Planchart
    S1969 Seraphim 6052 Otten
    cop.1971 Argo 681 Burgess
    S1972 Nonesuch 71261 Rifkin
    S1973 Turn. 34485 Saltzman
    (1973?) Mus. Her. 1716 D'Harnoncourt
    (1975?) HMV 3766 King's Singers
    (1980?) Spectrum 114 Elzinga
BENEDICITE OMNIA OPERA
    S1969 Lyr. 7214 Planchart
BENEDICTA ES, CAELORUM REGINA
    before 1962 Studio 25-03 Blanchard
    S1967 Tele. 9480 Ruhland
    1968 Donemus 6901 De Nobel
    S1973 Har. Mun. 21513 Turner
    (1973) DGG 2533-110 Jürgens
    S1977 Seraphim 6104 Munrow
BERGERETTE SAVOYENNE
    1950 EMS 213 Cape
    (1953-5) Philips 00994 Blanchard
    1960 DGG 3159 Cape
    cop.1960 Vox 580 Boepple
    (1972?) Mus. Her. 3879 Piguet
    cop.1975 Argo 793 Morrow

CELA SANS PLUS
    S1972 Nonesuch 71261 Rifkin
COEUR LANGOREULX
    (1947?) Disc. Fr. 7 Couraud
COEURS DESOLEZ, 5 v.
    (1949?) Allegro 17 Calder
    (1967) Crossroads 22 16 0093 Venhoda
    (1970?) HMV 1041 Nesbitt

    (1970?) Qual. 11663 Parkai
    S1971 Tele. 9561 Ruhland
    cop.1971 Argo 681 Burgess
——, 4 v.
    cop.1975 Argo 793 Morrow
COMMENT PEULT AVOIR JOYE
    1964 DGG 3223 D'Harnoncourt
    S1972 Nonesuch 71261 Rifkin
—— as O Jesu fili David
    cop.1960 Vox 580 Boepple
    (1973?) Cantate 658236 Popp
    (1976) Mus. Her. 3411 Caillard
CREDO DE TOUS BIENS PLAINE
    S1977 Seraphim 6104 Munrow

DE PROFUNDIS
    (1949?) CHS 47 Boepple
    S1962 Bach G. 620 Gillesberger
    (1973?) Cantate 658 236 Popp
    S1977 Seraphim 6104 Munrow
DE TOUS BIENS PLAYNE
    (1959?) Tele. 8008 Musiekkring Obrecht
    cop.1960 Vox 580 Boepple
    S1969 Decca 79435 White
    S1972 Nonesuch 71261 Rifkin
DOMINE NE IN FURORE (no.39?)
    (1973?) Cantate 658 136 Popp
    (1977?) Mus. Her. 3558 Adams
DOMINUS REGNAVIT
    cop.1960 Vox 580 Boepple
    S1971 Turn. 34437 Boepple
    1972 Lyr. 7265 Planchart
    S1973 Har. Mun. 21513 Turner
    (1973?) Cantate 658 236 Popp
DOULEUR ME BAT
    1950 EMS 213 Cape
DULCES EXUVIAE
    S1968 Everest 3210 Weiss
    (1971) Decca 79410 Greenberg

EL GRILLO
    (1954?) Philips 00678 De Nobel
    (1954) Victor 6016 Cape
    (1956?) Epic 3263 De Nobel
    (1958?) Lyr. 775 Fleetwood
    (1967?) Victor 1231 Petrocchi
    S1969 Decca 79435 White

    (1969?) Mus. Her. 713 Weinhöppel
    (1969?) Philips 10017 Cieri
    cop.1971 Argo 681 Burgess
    1972 Turn. 34485 Saltzman
    cop.1975 Argo 793 Morrow
    S1977 ABC 67017 Ruhland
    S1977 Seraphim 6104 Munrow
    (1978?) Supraphon 111.2126 Mus. Ant. Vienna
ENTRÉE SUIS EN GRANT PENSÉE
    S1972 Nonesuch 71261 Rifkin

FAMA, MALUM
    (1961) Decca 79410 Greenberg
    S1968 Everest 3210 Weiss
FAULTE D'ARGENT
    1950 EMS 213 Cape
    1960 DGG 3159 Cape
    S1969 Lyr. 7214 Planchart
    S1970 Pleiades 252 Brown
    cop.1975 Argo 793 Burgess
FORTUNA DESPERATA
    cop.1971 Argo 681 Burgess
    (1975) Collegium 116 Blachly
    S1977 Seraphim 6104 Munrow
FORTUNA D'UN GRAN TEMPO
    1950 EMS 213 Cape
    1960 DGG 3159 Cape
    1971 J Venhoda
    S1977 ABC 67017 Ruhland

GUILLAUME S'EN VA CHAUFFER
    S1971 Tele. 9561 Ruhland
    S1977 Seraphim 6104 Munrow

HUC ME SYDEREO
    S1968 Everest 3210 Weiss
    1976 DGG 2533 360 Turner

ILE FANTAZIES
    (1949?) Allegro 14 Vielle trio
    S1972 Nonesuch 71261 Rifkin
    S1977 ABC 67017 Ruhland
ILLIBATA DEI VIRGO
    S1972 Van. 3 Noble
    cop.1972 Argo 793 Morrow
    (1973) DGG 1533 110 Jürgens
IN DOMINO CONFIDO
    S1977 Telarc 5124 Canby

IN EXITU ISRAEL
    1972 Lyr. 7265 Planchart
IN PRINCIPIO ERAT VERBUM
    S1962 Bach G. 620 Gillesberger (parts 1-2)
    before 1964 Studio 33.60 Blanchard
    (1974?) Titanic 22 Cohen
IN TE, DOMINE, SPERAVI
    S1972 Nonesuch 71261 Rifkin
    cop.1972 Angel 36926 Munrow
    cop.1975 Argo 793 Morrow
INCESSAMENT LIVRÉ SUIS
    (1947?) Disc. Fr. 7 Couraud
INCESSAMENT MON POVRE COEUR
    1950 EMS 213 Cape
INVIOLATA, INTEGRA ET CASTA
    S1973 Har. Mun. 21513 Turner
    S1977 Seraphim 6104 Munrow
    S1977 ABC 67017 Ruhland

J'AY BIEN CAUSE
    (1947?) Disc. Fr. 7 Couraud
    S1963 Angel 36379 Arndt
JE ME COMPLAINS
    (1947?) Disc. Fr. 7 Couraud
    1950 EMS 213 Cape
JE NE ME PUIS TENIR
    (1954) Victor 6016 Cape
    1971 J Maynard
    1971 J Ruhland
    S1977 ABC 67017 Ruhland
JUBILATE DEO
    S1977 Telarc 5014 Canby

LA BERNARDINA
    before 1962 Rec. Soc. 19 Blanchard
    (1961) Decca 79410 Greenberg
    S1969 Seraphim 6052 Otten
    cop.1971 Argo 681 Burgess
    S1972 Nonesuch 71261 Rifkin
    S1977 ABC 67017 Ruhland
    S1977 Seraphim 6104 Munrow
    (1980?) Spectrum 114 Elzinga
LA PLUS DES PLUS
    1950 EMS 213 Cape
    cop.1960 Vox 580 Boepple
    (1971-2?) Mus. Her. 1442 Düsseldorf Studio
    S1972 Nonesuch 71261 Rifkin
    S1977 ABC 67017 Ruhland
    (1980?) Spectrum 114 Elzinga

LA SPAGNA
   S1977 Seraphim 6104 Munrow
LAUDATE PUERI
   S1969 Lyr. 7214 Planchart
L'HOMME ARMÉ
   (1947?) Disc. Fr. 7 Couraud
   (1970) Inédits 995 001 Ravier
   (1975) Collegium 109/10 Taruskin
LIBER GENERATIONIS
   (1975) Collegium 111 Blachly

MA BOUCHE RIT
   (1947?) Disc. Fr. 7 Couraud
MAGNUS ES TU, Part 2 only: TU PAUPERUM REFUGIUM
   1939/40? Col. 71 Hoch
   1953-5 Concordia 3 Christiansen
   S1967 Mus. Lib. 6995 Stanford U.
   S1970 Pleiades 252 Brown
   (1970?) Mus. Her. 929 Costa
   1976 Pelca 40607 Gottsches
MILLE REGRETZ
   1936-50 Héber. 2046
   1950-51 Acad. 308 Westergaard
   (1953?) Esoteric 514 De Pauw
   (1953-5) Decca 9629 Boulanger
   (196-) Erato 42021 Caillard
   (1964?) Amadeo 6326 Caillat
   (1966) DGG 636501 Chailley
   1967 Crossroads 22 16 0093 Venhoda
   1970? HMV 1071 Nesbitt
   S1971 Turn. 34380 Cohen
   (1971?) Mus. Her. 1125 Corboz
   cop.1975 Argo 793 Morrow
   (1975?) Decca 1288 203/6 Rooley
   (1977?) Tele. 641917 Venhoda
   (1980?) Spectrum 114 Elzinga
MISERERE MEI DEUS
   (1940?) Anth. Son. 107-8 de Van
   (1955) BAM 022/9022 Martin
   before 1962 Rec. Soc. 29 Blanchard
   (1963?) Argo 90 Martin
   (1969?) Mus. Her. 1000 Caillard
   S1973 Har. Mun. 21513 Turner
   S1977 ABC 67017 Ruhland
MISERICORDIAS DOMINI
   (1954?) Esoteric 546 Brown (parts 1, 2)
   1957 Musica Sac. 4 Martin (part 1)

MISSA AVE MARIS STELLA
    1948? GIOA 1 Vitry (Kyrie, Agnus)
    S1969 Decca 79435 White
    S1969 Nonesuch 71216 Hunter
MISSA DA PACEM
    S1962 Bach G. 620 Gillesberger (Et incarnatus)
    (1978) Mus. Her. 3729 Karlsruhe Chamber Choir
MISSA DE BEATA VIRGINE
    cop.1962 Vox 600 Boepple
    S1964 Disc. Fr. 730063 Blanchard
    (1969?) Seraphim 6052 Otten (Agnus 2)
    S1971 Turn. 34437 Boepple
    (1975) Collegium 102/3 Taruskin (Credo)
    (1980?) Spectrum 114 Elzinga
MISSA FORTUNA DESPERATA
    (1979?) Titanic 22 Cohen
MISSA GAUDEAMUS
    1972 Lyrichord 7265 Planchart
    (1975) Collegium 102/3 (Kyrie)
MISSA HERCULES DUX FERRARIAE
    (1938?) Anth. Son. 73 de Van (Kyrie)
    (1955) Mus. Lib. 7075 Aird
    1957 Musica Sac. 4 Martin
    (1961) Music G. 7 Blanchard
    S1962 Bach G. 620 Gillesberger
    S1966 Mace 9030 Graff (Sanctus)
MISSA LA SOL FA RE MI
    S1977 ABC 67017 Ruhland
MISSA L'HOMME ARMÉ SEXTI TONI
    (1967) Crossroads 22 16 0093 Venhoda
    S1972 Van. 3 Noble
MISSA L'HOMME ARMÉ SUPER VOCES MUSICALES
    (1940?) Gramophon 1514 de Van (Gloria)
    (1954) Victor 6016 Washington (Sanctus)
    S1970 Pleiades 252 Brown (Agnus 2)
    1971 J Venhoda (Kyrie, Et in spiritum, Agnus 2, 3)
    1976 DGG 2533 360 Turner
MISSA MATER PATRIS
    1961 Carillon 124 Forbes
    (1979?) Da Camera 94053 Eschweiler
    (1979?) Mus. Her. 4077 Adams (Gloria)
MISSA PANGE LINGUA
    (1931?) Parlophone 1017 Kalt (Et incarnatus)
    before 1936 Christschall 119 Berberich (Sanctus)
    (1951) Gramophone Shop IX Wöldike (Kyrie, Sanctus, Agnus)
    1953-5 Erato 2010 Caillard
    1953-5 Eterna 73002 (?) Shveshnikov (Et incarnatus)

(1956) Mus. Lib. 7085 Weaver
1959 DGG 3159 Cape
(1961) Decca 79410 Greenberg
(1965?) Mus. Her. 617, 1000 Caillard
S1971 Turn. 34431 Behrmann
(1972) Tele. 9595 Venhoda
MISSA SINE NOMINE
1968-9 Lyr. 7214 Planchart
(1972) Arno 101-3 Hömberg (Sanctus)
MISSA UNA MUSQUE DE BISCAYA
(1959?) Baroque 9002 Brown
MISSUS EST GABRIEL
(1973) DGG 2533 110 Jürgens
MITTIT AD VIRGINEM
S1969 Nonesuch 71216 Hunter
MONSTRA TE ESSE MATREM *see* AVE MARIS STELLA

N'ESSE PAS UN GRANT DISPLAISIR
(1947?) Disc. Fr. 7 Couraud
1960 DGG 3159 Cape
NYMPHES DES BOIS
1950 EMS 213 Cape
1960 DGG 3159 Cape
S1960 Verve 2137 Smith
(1961?) Disc. Fr. 330223-4 Blanchard
S1964 BAM 040 Martin
(1967?) Everest 617 McCarthy
(1969?) Bach G. 671 Deller
cop.1971 Argo 681 Burgess
1972 Lyr. 7265 Planchart
cop.1973 DGG 2533 145 Turner
cop.1975 Argo 793 Morrow
(1976) Mus. Her. 3411 Caillard

O ADMIRABILE COMMERCIUM
(1975) Collegium 111 Blachly
O BONE ET DULCISSIME JESU
S1977 Telarc 5024 Canby
O DOMINE JESU CHRISTE
(1939-40?) Col. 73 Hoch
before 1964 Studio 33-41 Deiss
S1968 Everest 3210 Weiss
(1977?) Mus. Her. 3558 Adams
(1979?) Da Camera 94053 Eschweiler
O JESU FILI DAVID *see* COMMENT PEULT
O VIRGO VIRGINUM
(1964) Camerate 30031 Voorberg
(1973) DGG 2533 110 Jürgens
S1974 Tele. 9595 Venhoda

PARFONS REGRETZ
    (1947?) Disc. Fr. 7 Couraud
    1950 EMS 213 Cape
    1960 DGG 3159 Cape
    cop.1960 Vox 580 Boepple
    S1969 Bach G. 671 Deller
PETITE CAMUSETTE
    1950 EMS 213 Cape
    (1962?) Disc. Fr. 330222-4 Blanchard
    (1970) Inédits 945001 Ravier
    cop.1971 Argo 681 Burgess
    (1975?) HMV 3766 King's Singers
PLAINE DE DEUIL
    (1947?) Disc. Fr. 7 Couraud
    cop.1975 Argo 793 Morrow
PLANXIT AUTEM DAVID
    S1967 Tele. 9480 Ruhland
    S1974 Tele. 9595 Venhoda
    S1977 ABC 67017 Ruhland
PLUS NULZ REGRETZ
    S1963 Angel 36379 Arndt
    1971 J Maynard
    1971 J Ruhland
PLUSIEURS REGRETZ
    (1962?) Disc. Fr. 330222-4 Blanchard
    S1969 Lyr. 7214 Planchart
POUR SOUHAITTER
    1950 EMS 213 Cape
PRAETER RERUM SERIEM
    S1960 Nonesuch 71095 Voorberg
    before 1962 Studio 25-03 Blanchard
    (1964?) Camerate 30031 Voorberg
    (1967) Crossroads 22 16 0093 Venhoda

QUANT JE VOUS VOYE
    S1972 Nonesuch 71261 Rifkin
QUE VOUS MA DAME
    S1972 Nonesuch 71261 Rifkin
QUI BELLES AMOURS
    S1972 Nonesuch 71261 Rifkin
QUI VELATUS
    S1977 ABC 67017 Ruhland

RECORDANS DE MY SEGNORA
    S1972 Nonesuch 71261 Rifkin
    cop.1975 Argo 793 Morrow
REGINA CAELI, 6 v.
    S1972 Van. 3 Noble

REGRETZ SANS FIN
     cop.1975 Argo 793 Morrow

SALVE REGINA, 5 v.
     S1969 Nonesuch 71216 Hunter
SANCTUS DE PASSIONE
     S1977 ABC 67017 Ruhland
SCARAMELLA
     1951-3 Anth. Son. 5 Raugel
     1960 DGG 3159 Cape
     S1972 Nonesuch 71261 Rifkin
     1973 Turn. 34512 Cohen
     cop.1975 Argo 793 Morrow
     S1977 ABC 67017 Ruhland
     S1977 Seraphim 6104 Munrow
SI CONGIÉ PRENS
     (1942?) Anth. Son. 108 de Van
SI J'AY PERDU
     (1953-5) Oiseau 81 Recorder trio
     (1953?) Classic 1018 Recorder consort
     S1972 Nonesuch 71261 Rifkin
     (1972?) Mus. Her. 3859 Piguet
STABAT MATER
     (1938?) Anth. Son. 73 de Van
     before 1962 Studio 2503 Blanchard
     S1967 Tele. 9480 Ruhland
     1971 J Gottwald (part 1)
     1971 J Ruhland (part 1)

TENEZ MOY EN VOS BRAS
     (1947?) Disc. Fr. 31-4 Couraud
     cop.1975 Argo 793 Morrow
TRIBULATIO ET ANGUSTIA
     (1954) Victor 6016 Washington
     S1977 Telarc 5024 Canby
TU SOLUS QUI FACIS MIRABILIA
     cop.1956 Per. 597 Greenberg
     (1961) Decca 79410 Greenberg
     S1969 Nonesuch 71216 Hunter
     (1972?) Har. Mun. 21443 Pohl
     S1973 Har. Mun. 21313 Turner
     S1977 ABC 67017 Ruhland
TULERUNT DOMINUM MEUM
     cop.1960 Vox 580 Boepple
     (1967) Crossroads 22 16 0093 Venhoda
     S1967 Mace 9078 Mittergradnegger
     S1971 Turn. 34437 Boepple

UNA MUSQUE DE BUSCAYA
    S1971 Turn. 34380 Cohen
    S1972 Nonesuch 71261 Rifkin

VENI SANCTE SPIRITUS
    S1962 Bach G. 620 Gillesberger
VIRGO PRUDENTISSIMA
    (1975) Collegium 102/3 Taruskin
VIVE LE ROY
    (1942?) Anth. Son. 108 de Van
    (1961) Decca 79410 Greenberg
    S1964 Nonesuch 1012 Blanchard
    (1965?) Folk 3651 American Brass Quintet
    (1965?) Music G. 120 Paillard
    cop.1971 Argo 681 Burgess
    (1972) Col. 31289 Kazdin
    (1973?) Mus. Her. 1716 D'Harnoncourt
    (1974?) Connoisseur 2056 Baldwin
    (1974?) Mus. Her. 1804 Dörfner
    (1976) Mus. Her. 3411 Caillard
    S1977 Seraphim 6104 Munrow
    (1980?) Van. 71223 Canadian Brass
VULTUM TUUM
    (1948?) Disc. Fr. 19 Couraud

V. BIBLIOGRAPHY

AdamsT   Adams, Courtney S. "The Three-Part Chanson during the Sixteenth Century: Changes in Its Style and Importance." Diss., University of Pennsylvania, 1974.

AdyM   Ady, Cecilia M. *A History of Milan under the Sforza*. New York: G.P. Putnam's Sons, 1907.

AfMw   *Archiv für Musikwissenschaft.*

AgricolaCW   Agricola, Alexander. *Opera omnia*, ed. Edward E. Lerner. CMM 22

AlbrechtH   *Hans Albrecht In Memoriam: Gedenkschrift mit Beiträgen von Freunden und Schülern*, hrsg. von Wilfried Brennecke und Hans Hasse. Kassel: Bärenreiter, 1962.

AlbrechtZ   Albrecht, Hans. "Zwei Quellen zur deutschen Musikgeschichte der Reformationszeit." Mf 1 (1948):242-85.

AM   *Acta musicologica.*

Ambros   Ambros, August Wilhelm. *Geschichte der Musik.* Dritte ... Auflage, besorgt von Otto Kade. Leipzig: F.E.C. Leuckart, 1891.

AMMM   *Archivium musices metropolitanum mediolanense.* Milano: Veneranda· Fabbrica del Duomo, 1958- .
     Vol. 15: Josquin des Pres e Vari. *Messe, magnificat, motetto e inno.* Trascrizione di Amerigo Bortone.
     Vol. 16: *Liber capelle ecclesie maioris. Quarto codice di Gaffurio*, a cura di Angelo Ciceri e Luciano Migliavacca. [Facsimile].

AnglésA   Anglés, Higinio. "El archivio musical de la catedral de Valladolid." AM 3 (1948):59-108.

AnglésMC   ———. "La musica conservada en la Biblioteca Columbina y en la catedral de Seville." *Anuario musical* 2 (1947):3-39.

AnglésMI   ———. "Un manuscrit inconnu avec polyphonie
                du XVe siècle." AM 8 (1936):6-17.

AnglésMME   *La música en la corte de los reys católicos*
                (MME 1, 5, 10, 14). Barcelona, 1941-51; 4 vols.

AnglésT   Anglés, Higinio. "El tesoro musical de la
                Biblioteca Vaticana." *Collectanea vaticana*
                (1962):23-53.

AntonowyczC   Antonowycz, Myroslaw. "Criteria for the De-
                termination of Authenticity. A Contribution
                to the Study of Melodic Style in the Works of
                Josquin." TVNM 28 (1977-8):51-60.

AntonowyczI   ———. "'Illibata Dei virgo': A Melodic Self-
                Portrait of Josquin des Prez." J 546-59.

AntonowyczJ   ———. "Die Josquin-Ausgabe." TVNM 19 (1960-
                61):6-31.

AntonowyczM   ———. *Die Motette Benedicta es von Josquin*
                des Prez und die Messen super Benedicta von
                Willaert, Palestrina, de la Hêle und de Monte.
                Utrecht, 1951.

AntonowyczMP   ———. "Die Missa mater patris von Josquin des
                Prez." TVNM 20 (1966-7):206-18.

AntonowyczP   "Das Parodieverfahren in der Missa mater
                patris von Lupus Hellinck." LenaertsFs 33-8.

AntonowyczPS   "The Present State of Josquin Research."
                IMG: Report of the Eighth Congress, New York,
                1961, 1:53-65. Ed. Jan LaRue. Kassel: Bären-
                reiter, 1963.

AntonowyczZ   "Zur Autorschaftsfrage der Motetten *Absolve,*
                quaesumus, Domine und *Inter natos mulierum.*"
                TVNM 20 (1966):154-69.

AtlasC   Atlas, Allan. *The Cappella Giulia Chansonnier*
                (Rome, Biblioteca Apostolica Vaticana, C. G.
                XIII. 27). Musicological Studies/Wissenschaft-
                liche Abhandlungen, 17. Brooklyn, N.Y.: Insti-
                tute of Mediaeval Music, 1975.

Bain   Bain, S.E. "Music Printing in the Low Countries
                in the Sixteenth Century." Diss., Girton
                College, Cambridge University, 1974.

BakerU   Baker, Norma Klein. "An Unnumbered Manuscript
                of Polyphony in the Archives of the Cathedral
                of Segovia: Its Provenance and History." Diss.,
                University of Maryland, 1978.

Bank   Bank, J.A. *Tactus, Tempo and Notation in Mensural Music from the 13th to the 17th Century.* Amsterdam: Annie Bank, 1972.

BankH   ————, ed. Josquin Des Prez. *Missa Hercules dux Ferrariae.* Amsterdam: A. Bank, 1950.

BankP   ————, ed. Josquin Des Prez. *Missa pange lingua.* Amsterdam: A. Bank, 1950.

Barber   Barber, Elinore Louise. "Antonio de Cabezón's Cantus-firmus Compositions and Transcriptions." Diss., University of Michigan, 1960.

BarbieriC   Barbieri, Francisco. *Cancionero musical de los siglos XV y XVI.* Madrid: Tip. de los Huérfanos, 1890.

Barblan   Barblan, Guglielmo. "Vita musicale alla corte Sforzesca." *Storia di Milano* 7:787-872. Milano: Fondazione Trecani degli Alfieri, 1961.

Barclay-Squire   Barclay-Squire, William. "Petrucci's Motetti de Passione." MfMg 27 (1895):72-5.

BarthaB   Bartha, Dénes von. "Bibliographische Notizen zum Repertoire der Handschrift Cambrai 124 (125-128)." ZfMw 13 (1931):564-6.

Bautier-Regnier   Bautier-Regnier, Anne-Marie. "L'Édition musicale italienne et les musiciens d'outremonts au XVe siècle (1501-1563)." In Renaissance 27-49.

BecheriniC   Becherini, Bianca. *Catalogo dei manoscritti musicali della Biblioteca Nazionale di Firenze.* Kassel: Bärenreiter, 1959.

BecheriniM   ————. "I manoscritti e le stampe rare della Biblioteca del Conservatorio L. Cherubini." *La bibliofila* 66 (1964):255-99.

Benoit-Castelli   Benoit-Castelli, G. "L'Ave Maria de Josquin des Prez et la séquence 'Ave Maria ... virgo serena.'" *Études grégoriennes* 1 (1954):187-94.

BenteW   Bente, Martin. *Neue Wege der Quellenkritik und die Biographie Ludwig Senfls.* Wiesbaden: Breitkopf & Härtel, 1968.

BenthemC   Benthem, Jaap van. "Die Chanson *Entré je suis* a 4 von Josquin des Prez und ihre Überlieferung." TVNM 21 (1970):203-70.

BenthemE   ————. "Einige Wiedererkannte Josquin-Chansons im Codex 18746 der Österreichischen Nationalbibliothek." TVNM 27 (1971):18-42.

BenthemF   ——. "Fortuna in Focus: Concerning Conflict-
                    ing Progressions in Josquin's *Fortuna d'un
                    gran tempo.*" TVNM 30 (1980):1-50.

BenthemFE   ——, ed. *Fortuna d'un gran tempo.* Het orgel
                    50 (1864):170-74.

BenthemJ   ——. "Josquin's Three-part 'Chansons Rus-
                    tiques': A Critique of Readings in Manuscripts
                    and Prints." J 421-45.

BenthemK   ——. "Kompositorisches Verfahren in Josquins
                    Proportionskanon *Agnus Dei* (Antwort an Edward
                    Stam)." TVNM 26 (1976):9-16.

BenthemM   ——. "Einige Musikintarsien des frühen 16.
                    Jahrhunderts in Piacenza und Josquins Pro-
                    portionskanon *Agnus Dei.*" TVNM 24 (1973):
                    97-111.

BenthemZ   ——. "Zur Struktur und Authentizät der
                    Chansons a 5 und 6 von Josquin des Prez."
                    TVNM 21 (1970):170-88.

BergquistM   Bergquist, Peter. "Mode and Polyphony around
                    1500, Theory and Practice." *Music Forum* 1
                    (1967):99-161.

Bernet-   Bernet-Kempers, Karel Ph. "Accidenties."
  Kempers   LenaertsFs 51-9.

BernsteinC   Bernstein, Lawrence F. "Cantus Firmus in the
                    French Chanson for Two and Three Voices, 1500-
                    1550." Diss., New York University, 1969.

BernsteinCF   ——. "*La Corone et Fleur des Chansons a Troy*:
                    A Mirror of the French Chanson in Italy in the
                    Years between Ottaviano Petrucci and Antonio
                    Gardano." JAMS 26 (1973):1-68.

Berz   Berz, Ernst-Ludwig. *Die Notendrucker und ihre
                    Verlager in Frankfurt-am-Main von den Anfängen
                    bis etwa 1630. Eine bibliographische und
                    drucktechnische Studie zur Musikpublikation.*
                    Catalogus musicus, 5. Kassel: Bärenreiter,
                    1967.

BesselerA   Besseler, Heinrich, ed. *Altniederlandische
                    Motetten von J. Ockeghem, Loyset Compère und
                    Josquin des Prez.* Kassel: Bärenreiter, 1948.

BesselerC   ——, ed. *Capella: Meisterwerke mittelaltlicher
                    Musik.* Kassel: Bärenreiter, 1959.

BesselerM	———. *Die Musik des Mittelalters und der Renaissance*. Handbuch der Musikwissenschaft, 1. Potsdam: Akademische Verlagsgesellschaft, 1931.
BlackburnJ	Blackburn, Bonnie J. "Josquin's Chansons: Ignored and Lost Sources." JAMS 29 (1976): 30-76.
BlumeJD	Blume, Friedrich. "Josquin des Prez." Verlags-Jahrbuch Kallmeyer "Drachentöter," 1929.
BlumeJJ	———. "Josquin des Prez: The Man and the Music." J 18-27.
Böker-Heil	Böker-Heil, Norbert. "Zu einem frühvenezianischen Motettenrepertoire." *Helmuth Osthoff zu seinem siebzigsten Geburtstag*, pp. 59-88; in Verbindung mit Wilhelm Stauder, hrsg. von Ursula Aarburg und Peter Cahn. Tutzing: Hans Schneider, 1969.
Boer	Boer, Coenraad L.W. *Chansonvormen op het einde van de XVde Eeuw*. Amsterdam: H.J. Paris, 1938.
Boetticher	Boetticher, Wolfgang. "Zu inhaltlichen Bestimmung des für Laute intavolierten Handschriftenbestands." AM 51 (1979):193-203.
BohnM	Bohn, Emil. *Die musikalischen Handschriften des XVI. und XVII. Jahrhunderts in der Stadtbibliothek zu Breslau*. Breslau: J. Hainauer, 1890.
BolteC	Bolte, J. "Eine Choralsammlung des Jakob Praetorius." MfMg 25 (1893):37-44.
BoormanC	Boorman, Stanley, and Herbert Kellman. "Czech and Hungarian Manuscripts" (Section IX:15 of "Sources, MS"). G 17:687-9.
BoormanF	Boorman, Stanley. "The 'First' Edition of the Odhecaton A." JAMS 30 (1977):183-207.
BoormanJ	———. "Josquin and His Influence." *Musical Times* 112 (1971):747-9.
BoormanP	———. "Petrucci at Fossombrone: The Motetti de la corona." *IMS: Report of the Eleventh Congress, Copenhagen 1972* I:295-301. Copenhagen: Wilhelm Hansen, 1974.

BoormanPD   ——. "Petrucci at Fossombrone: A Study of
                   Early Music Printing with Special Reference
                   to the Motetti de la corona (1514-1519)."
                   Diss., London University, 1976.

Bordes   Bordes, Charles. *Anthologie des maîtres
                   religieux primitives des XVe, XVIe, et XVIIe
                   siècles*. Paris: Édition Schola Cantorum,
                   1893-8. Reprint. New York: Da Capo Press,
                   1976.

BorrenA   Borren, Charles van den. "A propos de quelques
                   messes de Josquin." *IMG: Report of the Fifth
                   Congress, Utrecht, 1952*, 179-84. Amsterdam:
                   G. Alsbach, 1953.

BorrenE   ——. "L'enigme des credo de village." Al-
                   brechtH 48-54.

BorrenH   ——. "Une hypothèse concernant le lieu de
                   naissance de Josquin des Prez." *Festschrift
                   Joseph Schmidt-Görg zum 60. Geburtstag ...*,
                   pp. 21-25, hrsg. von Dagmar Weise. Bonn:
                   Beethovenhaus, 1957.

BorrenI   ——. "Inventaire des MSS de musique poly-
                   phonique qui se trouve en Belgique." AM 5
                   (1933):66, 120, 177; 6 (1934):23, 65, 116.

BragardM   Bragard, Anne-Marie. "Un manuscrit florentin
                   du quattrocento: Le Mag. XIX.59 (B.R.229)."
                   Revue de musicologie 52 (1966):75-112.

BraithwaiteI   Braithwaite, James. "The Introduction of
                   Franco-Netherlandish Manuscripts to Early
                   Tudor England." Diss., Boston University,
                   1967.

BrenneckeH   Brennecke, Wilfried. *Die Handschrift A.R.
                   940/41 der Proske-Bibliothek zu Regensburg*.
                   Schriften des Landesinstituts für Musikfor-
                   schung Kiel, 1. Kassel: Bärenreiter, 1953.

Bridge   Bridge, John S.C. *A History of France from
                   the Death of Louis XI*. Oxford: Clarendon
                   Press, 1924. 5 vols.

BridgmanA   Bridgman, Nanie. "The Age of Ockeghem and
                   Josquin." *Ars Nova and the Renaissance*, 239-
                   302. Ed. Dom Anselm Hughes and Gerald Abraham.
                   New Oxford History of Music 3. London: Oxford
                   University Press, 1960.

BridgmanAL ————, and François Lesure. "Une anthologie 'historique' de la fin du XVIe siècle: le manuscrit Bourdeney." *Miscelánea en homenaje a Monseñor Higinio Anglés*, 1:161-74. Barcelona: Consejo Superior de Investigaciones Cientificas, 1958.

BridgmanC Bridgman, Nanie. "Christian Egenolff, imprimeur de musique." *Annales musicologiques* 3 (1955):77-178.

BridgmanM ————. "Un manuscrit italien du début du XVIe siècle à la Bibliothèque nationale (Département de la musique, Rés. Vm⁷ 676)." *Annales Musicologiques* 1 (1953):177-267.

BridgmanO ————. "On the Discography of Josquin and the Interpretation of His Music in Recordings." J 633-41.

BridgmanV ————. *La vie musicale au quattrocento et jusqu'à la naissance du madrigal (1400-1530).* [no place]: Editions Gallimard, 1964.

Brockhoff Brockhoff, M.E. "Die Kadenz bei Josquin." *IMS: Report of the Fifth Congress, Utrecht 1952*, 186-91. Amsterdam: G. Alsbach, 1953.

BrownA Brown, Howard Mayer. "Accidentals and Ornamentation in Sixteenth-Century Intabulations of Josquin's Motets." J 475-522.

BrownCF ————. "Chansons for the Pleasure of a Florentine Patrician: Florence, Biblioteca del Conservatorio di Musica, MS Basevi 2442." ReeseFs 56-66.

BrownCM ————. "Choral Music in the Renaissance." *Early Music* 6 (1978):164-9.

BrownGC ————. "Chanson." G 4:137-40; bibliography 144-5.

BrownGG ————. "A Guardian God for a Garden of Music." GilmoreFs 2:372-7.

BrownGP ————. "Performing Practice: 4." G 14:377-83; bibliography 390-91.

BrownI ————. *Instrumental Music Printed Before 1600, A Bibliography.* Cambridge, Mass.: Harvard University Press, 1965.

BrownIO   ————. "Improvised Ornamentation in the Fif-
                   teenth-Century Chanson." *Memorie e contributi
                   alla musica dal medioevo all'età moderne
                   offerti a F. Ghisi nel settantesimo compleanno
                   (1901-1971)*, 1:235-68. Bologna: Antiquae
                   Musicae Italicae Studiosi, 1971.

BrownIV   ————. "Instruments and Voices in the Fifteenth-
                   Century Chanson." CurrentT 89-137.

BrownMF   ————. *Music in the French Secular Theater
                   1400-1550*. Cambridge, Mass.: Harvard University
                   Press, 1963.

BrownMR   ————. *Music in the Renaissance*. Englewood
                   Cliffs, N.J.: Prentice-Hall, Inc., 1976.

BrownMRM   ————. [Edition of Florence BR 229 in prepara-
                   tion for MRM].

BrownMS   ————. "The Music of the Strozzi Chansonnier
                   (Florence, Biblioteca del Conservatorio de
                   Musica, MS Basevi 2442)." AM 40 (1968):115-29.

BrownOP   ————. "On the Performance of Fifteenth-Century
                   Chansons." *Early Music* 1 (1973):3-10.

BrownPC   ————. "The Parisian Chanson, 1500-1530." *Chan-
                   son and Madrigal 1480-1530: Studies in Com-
                   parison and Contrast (A Conference at Isham
                   Memorial Library September 13-14, 1961)*, pp.
                   1-50. Ed. James Haar. Cambridge, Mass.: Harvard
                   University Press, 1964.

BrownPE   ————. "Performing Early Music on Record, 2:
                   Continental Sacred Music of the 16th Century."
                   Early Music 3 (1975):373-7.

BrownTC   ————. "The Transformation of the Chanson at
                   the End of the Fifteenth Century." *IMS: Report
                   of the Tenth Congress, Ljubljana 1967*, pp. 78-
                   96. Kassel: Bärenreiter, 1970.

Buggert   Buggert, Robert W. "Alberto da Ripa: Lutenist
                   and Composer." Diss., University of Michigan,
                   1956.

BurckardC   *Johannis Burckardi liber notarum*, a cura di
                   Enrico Celani. Rerum italicarum scriptores:
                   raccolta degli storici italiani ... ordinata
                   da L.A. Muratori. Nuova edizione ... T.XXXII.
                   Città di Castello: S. Lapi, 1906-11; 1940- .

BurckardT   *Johannis Burchardi diarium sive rerum urbanarium
                 commentarii.* Ed. L. Thuasne. Paris: Ernest
                 Leroux, 1883-5. 3 vols.

Bussi   Bussi, Francesco. *Piacenza, Archivio del Duomo.
                 Catalogo del fondo musicale.* Bibliotheca musi-
                 cae, 5. Milano: Istituto editoriale italiano,
                 1967.

Callahan   Callahan, Virginia Woods. "'Ut Phoebi radiis':
                 The Riddle of the Text Resolved." J 560-63.

Canova da Milano *see* Francesco Canova da Milano

CarpentrasCW   *Carpentras opera omnia*, ed. Albert Seay. CMM
                 58.

Casimiri   *Societas Polyphonica Romana: Repertorium* ...;
                 a cura ... Raph. Casimiri. Roma: Edizioni
                 Psalterium, 192-, vol. 1.

CasimiriC   Casimiri, Raffaele. "Canzoni e mottetti del
                 sec. XV-XVI." *Note d'archivio per la storia
                 musicale* 14 (1937): 145-60.

CC   *Census-Catalogue of Manuscript Sources of
                 Polyphonic Music.* Compiled by the University
                 of Illinois musicological archives for
                 renaissance manuscript studies. Renaissance
                 manuscript studies, 1. Vol. 1: A-J. Neuhausen,
                 Stuttgart: Hanssler Verlag, 1979.

CDMI   *I Classici della Musica Italiana.* Milano:
                 Istituto editoriale italiano, 1918 et seq.
                    Quaderni 23-7: G. Cavazzoni, *Dal I e II
                    libro di intavolature per organo.*

CEKM   *A Corpus of Early Keyboard Music.* [no place]:
                 American Institute of Musicology, 1963- .
                    6:3: Jan of Lublin. *Motet Intabulations*,
                    ed. John R. White.

CEMF   *Corpus of Early Music.* Bruxelles: Éditions
                 culture et civilisation, 1970.

Černý   Černý, Jaromir. "Soupnis Hudebnich Rukopisu
                 Muzea v Hradci Krǎlové." *Miscellanea musico-
                 logica* (Prague) 19 (1966):9-240.

CesariM   Cesari, Gaetano. "Musica e musicisti alla
                 corte Sforzesca." Malaguezzi-Valeri 4:183-
                 254; also RMI 29 (1922):1-53, lacking illus-
                 trations and musical examples.

Chapman   Chapman, Catherine Weeks. "Andrea Antico."
                     Diss., Harvard University, 1964.

Chorwerk   *Das Chorwerk*. Berlin: Kallmeyer, 1929- .
                       Vol. 1: Josquin Des Pres. *Missa pange lingua*,
                       hrsg. von F. Blume.
                       Vol. 3: *Weltliche Lieder von Josquin Des
                       Pres und andere Meister*, hrsg. von F. Blume.
                       Vol. 18: Josquin Des Pres. *Vier Motetten zu
                       4 und 6 Singstimmen*, hrsg. von F. Blume.
                       Vol. 20: Josquin Des Pres. *Missa da pacem*,
                       hrsg. von F. Blume.
                       Vol. 23: Josquin Des Pres: *Drei Evangelien-
                       Motetten zu 4, 6, und 8 Stimmen*, hrsg. von
                       F. Blume.
                       Vol. 30: *Acht Lied- und Choralmotetten zu
                       4, 5, und 7 Stimmen*, hrsg. von H. Osthoff.
                       Vol. 33: Josquin Des Pres. *Drei Psalmen zu
                       4 Stimmen*, hrsg. von F. Blume.
                       Vol. 42: Josquin Des Pres. *Missa de Beata
                       Virgine*, ed. F. Blume.
                       Vol. 54: *Fünf Vergil-Motetten zu 4-7 Stimmen*,
                       hrsg. von H. Osthoff.
                       Vol. 57: Josquin Desprez. *Drei Motetten zu
                       4-6 Stimmen*, hrsg. von H. Osthoff.
                       Vol. 64: Josquin Desprez. *Zwei Psalmen zu
                       4-5 Stimmen*, hrsg. von H. Osthoff.

Ciminelli, Serafino *see* Menghini

Clarke   Clarke, Henry Leland. "Musicians of the
                     Northern Renaissance." ReeseFs 67-81.

Clercx-   Clercx-Lejeune, Suzanne. "Fortuna Josquini.
  LejeuneF   A proposito di un ritratto di Josquin des
                     Prez." *Rivista musicale italiana* 6 (1972):
                     315-37.

Clercx-   Clercx, Suzanne. "Introduction à l'histoire
  LejeuneI   de la musique en Belgique: II." RB 5 (1951):
                     114-31.

Clinkscale   Clinkscale, Edward H. "Josquin and Louis XI."
                     AM 38 (1966):67-72.

Clough   Clough, Francis F., and G.J. Cuming. *The
                     World's Encyclopedia of Recorded Music*. Lon-
                     don: Sidgwick & Jackson, 1952.

CMM   *Corpus mensurabilis musicae*. [no place]:
                     American Institute of Musicology, 1947- .

CMP   *Choral Music in Print. Volume I: Sacred Choral Music; Volume II: Secular Choral Music*, ed. Thomas R. Nardone, James H. Nye, Mark Resnick. Philadelphia: Musicdata, 1974.

Coclico   Coclico, Adrian Petit. *Compendium musices, Nuremberg 1552*. Facsimile, ed. Manfred F. Bukofzer. Documenta Musicologica, 1:9. Kassel: Bärenreiter, 1964.

CoclicoT   ———. *Musical Compendium*. Translated by Albert Seay. Colorado College Music Press Translations, 5. Colorado Springs: Colorado College, 1973.

CollinsC   Collins, Michael Bruce. "The Performance of Coloration, Sesquialtera, and Hemiolia (1450-1570)." Diss., Stanford University, 1963.

CollinsP   ———. "The Performance of Sesquialtera and Hemiolia in the 16th Century." JAMS 17 (1964): 5-18.

Columbro   Columbro, Sister Mary Electa. "Ostinato Technique in the Franco-Flemish Motet: 1480-ca. 1567." Diss., Case Western Reserve University, 1971.

Constant   Constant, John G. "Sixteenth-Century Manuscripts at the Cathedral of Padua." Diss., University of Michigan, 1975.

Coover   Coover, James B., and Richard Colvig. *Medieval and Renaissance Music on Long-playing Records*. Detroit Studies in Music Bibliography, 6. Detroit: Information Service, Inc., 1964.

     ———. ———. *Supplement (1962-71)*. Detroit Studies in Music Bibliography, 26. Detroit: Information Coordinators, Inc., 1973.

Coussemaker   Coussemaker, Edmund de. *Notice sur les collections musicales de la bibliothèque de Cambrai*. Paris: Techener, 1843.

CrawfordS   Crawford, David. *Sixteenth-Century Choirbooks in the Archivio Capitolare at Casale Monferrato*. Renaissance Manuscript Studies, 2. [no place]: American Institute of Musicology, 1975.

CrawfordV   ———. "Vespers Polyphony at Modena's Cathedral in the First Half of the Sixteenth Century." Diss., University of Illinois, 1966.

CrétinD   Crétin, Guillaume (Dubois). *Déploration de Guillaume Crétin sur le trépas de Jean Ockeghem, musicien, premier chapelain du roi de France et trésorier de Tours* ..., précedée d'une introduction biographique et annotée par Er. Thoinan. Paris: A. Claudin, 1864. Reprint. London: H. Baron, 1963.

CrétinO   ———. *Oeuvres poétiques* ..., publiées avec une introduction et des notes par Kathleen Chesney. Paris: Firmin-Didot, 1932.

CrevelA   Crevel, Marcus van. *Adrianus Petit Coclico: Leben und Beziehungen eines nach Deutschland emigrierten Josquinschülers*. Haag: Nijhoff, 1940.

CrevelS   ———. "Secret Chromatic Art in the Netherlands Motet?" TVNM 16 (1946):253-304.

CrevelV   ———. "Verwante sequensmodulaties bij Obrecht, Josquin en Coclico." TVNM 16 (1941):107-24.

CummingsF   Cummings, Anthony Michael. "A Florentine Sacred Repertory from the Sixteenth Century: Ms II.I.232 of the Biblioteca Nazionale Centrale, Florence." Diss. in progress, Princeton University.

CummingsT   ———. "Towards an Interpretation of the Six-teenth-Century Motet." JAMS 24 (1981):43-59.

CurrentT   *Current Thought in Musicology*, ed. John W. Grubbs, Rebecca A. Baltzer, Gilbert H. Blount, and Leeman Perkins. Symposia in the Humani-ties, 4. Austin: University of Texas, 1976.

Curtis   Curtis, Alan. "Josquin and 'La belle tricotée.'" PlamenacFs 1-8.

Cusick   Cusick, Suzanne G. "Valerio Dorico, Music Printer in Sixteenth-Century Rome." Diss., University of North Carolina, 1975.

D'Accone   D'Accone, Frank A. "The Performance of Sacred Music in Italy during Josquin's Time, c.1475-1525." J 601-18.

DahlhausO   Dahlhaus, Carl. "On the Treatment of Dissonance in the Motets of Josquin des Prez." J 334-44.

DahlhausS   ———. "Studien zu den Messen Josquins des Pres." Diss., Göttingen University, 1952.

DahlhausT ――. "Tonsystem und Kontrapunkt um 1500." *Jahrbuch des staatlichen Instituts für Musik-forschung, Preussischer Kulturbesitz, 1969*, 7-18.

DahlhausZ ――. "Zur Akzidentiensetzung in den Motetten Josquins des Prez." *Musik und Verlag: Karl Vötterle zum 65. Geburtstag am 12. April 1968*, pp. 206-19. Hrsg. von Richard Baum und Wolfgang Rehm. Kassel: Bärenreiter, 1968.

DammannS Dammann, Rolf. "Spätformen der isorhythmischen Motette im 16. Jahrhundert." AfMw 10 (1953): 16-40.

Darvas Darvas, Gábor, ed. Josquin Des Pres. *Missa l'homme armé sexti toni.* London: Boosey & Hawkes, 1971.

DavidS David, Hans Theodore, ed. Josquin des Pres. *Salve Regina, a Five Part Motet. Edited for Voices and Instruments ad lib.* New York: Music Press, 1947.

Delporte Delporte, J. "Un document inédit sur Josquin Desprez." *Musique et liturgie* 22 (1939):54-6.

Delpuech Delpuech, L. Ch. *Josquin des Prés.* St. Quentin: Imprimerie générale du "Gutteur," 1945.

Diehl Diehl, George K. "The Partbooks of a Renaissance Merchant: Cambrai, Bibliothèque Municipale MSS 125-128." Diss., University of Pennsylvania, 1974.

DisertoriF Disertori, Benvenuto. *Le frottole per canto e liuto intabulate da Franciscus Bossinensis.* Istituzioni e Monumenti dell'Arte Musicale Italiana, nuova serie, 3. Milano: Ricordi, 1964.

DisertoriS ――. "Una storica mistificazione mensurale de Josquin des Prés: sue affinità con Leonardo da Vinci." *Liber amicorum Charles van den Borren*, pp. 49-57. Anvers: Lloyd Anversois, 1964.

Dixon Dixon, Helen M. "The Manuscript Vienna, National Library 1783." MD 23 (1969):105-16.

Drake Drake, George Warren. "The First Printed Book of Motets, Petrucci's *Motetti A numero trentatre A* (Venice, 1502) and *Motetti de passione de cruce de sacramento de beata virgine et huiusmodi* (Venice, 1503): A Critical Study and Complete Edition." Diss., University of Illinois, 1972.

DunningJ   Dunning, Albert. "Josquini antiquos musae,
                memoremus amores." AM 41 (1969):108-16.

DunningS   ——. *Die Staatsmotette 1480-1555*. Utrecht:
                A. Oosthoek, 1970.

EDM   *Das Erbe deutscher Musik: Abteilung Motette
                und Messe*. Lippstadt: Kistner & Siegel.
                    Vol. 21: *Georg Rhau Sacrorum Hymnorum Liber
                    Primus. Erster Teil: Proprium de Tempore*,
                    hrsg. von Rudolf Gerber, 1961.

EitnerB   Eitner, Robert. *Bibliographie der Musik-
                Sammelwerke des XVI. und XVII. Jahrhunderts....*
                Berlin: Trautwein, 1877. Reprint. Hildesheim:
                Olms, 1963.

EitnerF   ——. "5 Briefe von Lucas Wagenrieder von
                1536-38." MfMg 8 (1876):28-36.

EitnerH   ——. "Ein handschriftlicher Codex in der
                Bibliothek Maglibechiana in Florenz." MfMg 9
                (1877):31-6.

EitnerV   ——. *Verzeichniss neuer Ausgaben alter
                Musikwerke....* MfMg Beilage 3 (1871).

EldersJ   Elders, Willem. "Josquin des Prez in zijn
                motet *Illibata Dei virgo*." *Mens en melodie*
                25 (1970):141-4.

EldersP   ——. "Plainchant in the Motets, Hymns, and
                Magnificat of Josquin des Prez." J 522-42.

EldersST   ——. *Studien zu Symbolik in der Musik der
                alten Niederländer*. Utrechtse Bijdragen tot
                de Muziekwetenshap, 4. Bilthoven: A.B.
                Creyghton, 1968.

EldersSY   ——. "Das Symbol in der Musik von Josquin
                des Prez." AM 41 (1969):164-85.

EldersZA   ——. "Zur Aufführungspraxis der altnieder-
                ländischen Musik." LenaertsFs 89-104.

EldersZZ   ——. "Zusammenhänge zwischen den Motetten
                Ave nobilissima creatura und *Huc me sydereo*
                von Josquin des Prez." TVNM 22 (1971):67-73.

Elliot   Elliot, Kenneth. "Church Musick at Dunkell."
                ML 45 (1964):228-32.

EngelM   Engel, Hans. *Das mehrstimmige Lied des 16.
                Jahrhunderts*. Das Musikwerk, 3. Köln: Arno
                Volk Verlag, 1952.

Facsimilia   *Facsimilia musica neerlandica.* Buren: Frits
                  Knuf, for Vereniging vor nederlandse muziek-
                  geschiedenis.
                      Vol. 1: *Occo Codex. Facsimile Edition*, his-
                      torical introduction by Bernard Huys, 1979.

Faider   Faider, Paul, and Pierre van Sint Jan. *Cata-
                  logue des manuscrits conservés à Tournai
                  (bibliothèques de la ville et du séminaire).*
                  Gembloux: J. Duculot, 1950.

FAM   *Fontes artis musicae.*

FeldmannA   Feldmann, Fritz. "Alte und neue Probleme um
                  Cod. 2016 des Musikalischen Instituts bei der
                  Universität Breslau." *Festschrift Max Schneider
                  zum Achtzigsten Geburtstag*, pp. 49-66. Hrsg.
                  von Walther Vetter. Leipzig: Deutscher Verlag
                  für Musik, 1955.

FeldmannC   ———. *Der Codex Mf.2016 des Musikalischen
                  Instituts bei der Universität Breslau: eine
                  paleographische und stillistische Beschreibung.*
                  Breslau: Priebatsch, 1932.

FellererA   Fellerer, Karl Gustav. *Altklassische Poly-
                  phonie. Das Musikwerk*, 28. Köln: Arno Volk
                  Verlag, 1965.

FellererJ   ———. "Josquins Missa faisant regrets in der
                  Vihuela-Transkription von Mudarra und Narvaez."
                  Spanische Forschungen der Görresgesellschaft,
                  Reihe 1: Gesammelte Aufsätze zur Kultur-
                  geschichte Spaniens 16:179. Münster: Aschen-
                  dorff, 1960.

FinscherH   Finscher, Ludwig. "Historical Reconstruction
                  versus Structural Interpretation in the Per-
                  formance of Josquin's Motets." J 627-32.

FinscherW   ———. "Ein wenig beachtet Quelle zu Johann
                  Walthers Passions-Turbae." Mf 11 (1950):189-
                  95.

FinscherZ   ———. "Zur Cantus-Firmus Behandlung in der
                  Psalm-Motette der Josquin-Zeit." AlbrechtH
                  55-62.

FinscherZS   ———. "Zu den Schriften Edward E. Lowinskys."
                  Mf 15 (1962):54-77.

FinscherZV   ———. "Zum Verhältnis von Imitationstechnik
                  und Textbehandlung im Zeitalter Josquins."
                  OsthoffFsr 57-72.

FischerK   Fischer, Hans. *Katalog der Handschriften der
                  Universitätsbibliothek Erlangen, Neuarbeitung.
                  II. Die lateinischen Papierhandschriften.*
                  Erlangen: Universitätsbibliothek, 1936.

Formen   *Formen und Probleme der Überlieferung mehr-
                  stimmiger Musik im Zeitalter Josquins Desprez,*
                  hrsg. von Ludwig Finscher. Wolfenbütteler
                  Forschungen, 6; Quellenstudie zur Musik der
                  Renaissance, 1. München: Kraus International
                  Publ., 1981.

Forney   Forney, Kristine Karen. "The Netherlandish
                  Chanson in the Early Sixteenth Century: A
                  Critical Study of the Secular Publications
                  of Tylman Susato, 1543-1550." Diss., University
                  of Kentucky, 1979.

Foss   Foss, Julius. "Det Kgl. Cantoris Stemmebøger
                  A.D. 1541." *Dansk aarbog for musik* (1923):
                  24-40.

Fox   Fox, Sister Bertha Mary. "A Study of Renais-
                  sance Polyphony in the Bártfa Mus. Pr.6 (a-d),
                  National Széchényi Library, Budapest." Diss.,
                  University of Illinois, 1977.

FrancescoL   Francesco Canova da Milano. *The Lute Music of
                  Francesco Canova da Milano (1497-1548),* ed.
                  Arthur Ness. Harvard Publications in Music, 4.
                  Cambridge, Mass.: The Harvard University Press,
                  1970.

FrancescoO   ———. *Opere complete per liuto.* Trascrizione
                  in notazione di Ruggero Chiesa. Milano:
                  Edizioni Suivi-Zerboni, 1971. Vol. 2.

Frati   Frati, Lodovico. "Per la storia della musica
                  in Bologna dal secolo XV al XVI." RMI 24
                  (1917):449-78.

Frei   *Bicinien aus Glareans Dodekachordon zum
                  Singen und Spielen auf Zwei Melodie-Instru-
                  menten,* hrsg. von Walter Frei. Hortus Musicus,
                  187. Kassel: Bärenreiter, 1965.

FryeCW   Frye, Walter. *Collected Works,* ed. Sylvia
                  Kenney. CMM 19.

G   *The New Grove Dictionary of Music and Musicians.*
                  Ed. Stanley Sadie. London: Macmillan Pub-
                  lishers Limited, 1980. 20 vols.

Gaehtgens	Gaehtgens, W.F. "Die alten Musikalien der Universitätsbibliothek und die Kirchenmusik in Alt-Rostock." *Beiträge zur Geschichte der Stadt Rostock* 2 (1941).
GallicoJ	Gallico, Claudio. "Josquin's Compositions on Italian Texts and the Frottola." J 446-54.
GallicoJG	——. "Josquin nell'Archivio Gonzaga." *Rivista italiana di musicologia* 6 (1971):105-10.
GanassiF	Ganassi, Silvestro, dal Fontega. *Opera intitulata fontegara....* Venetia: Sylvestro di Ganassi, 1535. Facsimile, Milano: Bollettino bibliografico musicale, 1937.
GanassiT	——. ——. *A Treatise on the Art of Playing the Recorder and of Free Ornamentation*, ed. Hildegard Peter. Eng. trans. from the German ed. by Dorothy Swainson. Berlin: Lenau, 1959.
Garbelotto	Garbelotto, A. "Codici musicali della Biblioteca Capitolare di Padova." RMI 53 (1951): 389; 54 (1952):218, 289.
Gaspari	Gaspari, Gaetano. *Catalogo della bibliotheca del Liceo Musicale di Bologna*. Bologna: Libreria dall'Acqua, 1890-1943. 5 vols. Reprint. Bologna: Forni, 1961.
Gatti-PererA	Gatti Perer, Maria Luisa. "Art and Architecture in Lombardy at the Time of Josquin des Prez." J 138-47.
Geering	Geering, Arnold. *Die Vokalmusik in der Schweiz zur Zeit der Reformation*. Schweizerisches Jahrbuch für Musikwissenschaft 6. Basel: Helbing & Lichtenhahn, 1933.
GehrenbeckM	Gehrenbeck, David Maulsby. "Motetti de la Corona: A Study of Ottaviano Petrucci in His Four Last-Known Motet Prints." Diss., Union Theological Seminary, 1951.
GerberR	Gerber, Rudolf. "Römische Hymnenzyklen des späten 15. Jahrhunderts." AfMw 12 (1955): 40-73; also in his *Zur Geschichte des mehrstimmigen Hymnus: gesammelte Aufsätze*. Musikwissenschaftliche Arbeiten. Kassel: Bärenreiter, 1965, pp. 63-95.
Gerhardt	Gerhardt, Carl. *Die Torgauer Walter-Handschriften: eine Studie zur Quellenkunde der Musikgeschichte der deutsche Reformationszeit*. Kassel: Bärenreiter, 1949.

Gerle

Gerle, Hans. *Musica Teusch*.... Nürnberg: Author, 1532. Facsimile, MMMF 2:101.

GhislanzoniD

Ghislanzoni, A. "Des Prés (Josquin)," in *Larousse de la Musique*, publié sous la direction de Norbert Dufourcq ..., I:262-3, 580. Paris: Larousse, 1957.

GiesbertA

Giesbert, F.J. *Ein altes Spielbuch ... Liber Fridoline Sichery*. Mainz: B. Schott, 1936. 2 vols.

GilmoreFs

Essays Presented to Myron P. Gilmore, ed. Sergio Bertelli and Gloria Ramakus. Villa I Tatti: The Harvard University Center for Italian Renaissance Studies, 2. Florence: La Nuova Italia Editrice, 1978. Vol. 2.

GlareanusD

Glareanus, Henricus. *Dodecachordon*. Basel: Petri, 1547. Facsimile, MMMF 2:65.

GlareanusM

Glarean, Heinrich. *Dodecachordon*. Translation, transcription, and commentary by Clement A. Miller. Musicological Studies and Documents, 6. [no place]: American Institute of Musicology, 1965. 2 vols.

GodtM

Godt, Irving. "Motivic Integration in Josquin's Motets." *Journal of Music Theory* 21 (1977): 264-93.

GodtR

———. "The Restoration of Josquin's *Ave mundi Spes, Maria*, and Some Observations on Restoration." TVNM 26 (1975-6):53-83.

Göllner

Göllner, Marie Louise. *Bayerische Staatsbibliothek. Katalog der Musikhandschriften 2: Tabulaturen und Stimmbücher bis zur Mitte des 17. Jahrhunderts*. Kataloge Bayerischer Musiksammlungen, 5/2. München: G. Henle, 1979.

Gomart

Gomart, Ch. *Notes historiques sur la maîtrise de St. Quentin et sur les célébrités de cette ville*. Annales de la Société academique des sciences, arts, belles-lettres et agriculture de Saint-Quentin, ser. 2, v. 8. St. Quentin, 1851.

GombosiB

Gombosi, Otto. *Bakfark Bálent élete és müvei*. Musicologica hungarica, 2. Budapest: Orsz. Széchenyi, 1935.

GombosiC   ——. *Compositione di Meser Vincenzo Capirola.*
                  Neuilly-sur-Seine: Société de Musique d'Autre-
                  fois, 1955.

GottwaldH   Gottwald, Clytus. *Die Handschriften des Würt-*
                  tembergischen Landesbibliothek Stuttgart I.
                  1. Codices Musici. Wiesbaden: Breitkopf &
                  Härtel, 1964.

GottwaldM   ——. *Die Musikhandschriften der Staats- und*
                  Stadtbibliothek Augsburg. Wiesbaden: Breitkopf
                  & Härtel, 1974.

GottwaldMM   ——. *Die Musikhandschriften.* Die Handschriften
                  der Universitätsbibliothek München, 2.
                  Wiesbaden: Otto Harassowitz, 1968.

Grasberger   Grasberger, F. *Die Musiksammlung der Öster-*
                  reichischen Nationalbibliothek. Vienna: Bundes-
                  kanzleramt, Bundespressedienst, 1970.

Gregorovius   Gregorovius, Ferdinand. *History of the City*
                  of Rome in the Middle Ages. Eng. trans. by
                  Annie Hamilton. London: George Bell & Sons,
                  1909. Vol. 7:1 (1421-96), 2 (1497-1503).

Haar   Haar, James. "Some Remarks on the 'Missa la
                  sol fa re mi.'" J 564-88.

Haarlem   Haarlem, Rob van. "The 'Missa de Beata Virgine'
                  by Josquin Used as a Model for the Mass of
                  the Same Name by Arcadelt." TVNM 25 (1974):
                  33-7.

HaberlR   Haberl, Franz X. "Die römische Schola
                  Cantorum' und die päpstlichen Kapellsänger
                  bis zur Mitte des 16. Jahrhunderts." VfMw 3
                  (1887):189-206. Also in *Bausteine für Musik-*
                  geschichte, 1888.

HaberlV   ——. *Katalog der Musikwerke welche sich im*
                  Archiv der päpstlichen Kapelle im Vatikan zu
                  Rom. MfMg *Beilage,* 1888.

HallM   Hall, Thomas. "*Musica Ficta* in the Josquin
                  Masses: A Source-Analytical Study." Diss.,
                  Princeton University; in progress.

HallS   ——. "Some Computer Aids for the Preparation
                  of Critical Editions of Renaissance Music."
                  TVNM 25 (1975):38-53.

Halm
: Halm, August. *Katalog über die Musik-Codices des 16. und 17. Jahrhunderts auf der König- lichen Landes-Bibliothek in Stuttgart.* MfMg *Beilage*, 1902.

HAM
: *Historical Anthology of Music: Oriental, Medieval, and Renaissance Music*, by Archibald T. Davison and Willi Apel. Cambridge, Mass.: Harvard University Press, 1946.

HammM
: Hamm, Charles. "The Manuscript San Pietro B 80." RB 14 (1960):40-55.

HammS
: ———, and Call, Jerry. "Sources, MS: Renais- sance Polyphony." G 17:668-702.

Han
: Han, Kuo-Huang. "The Use of Marian Antiphons in Renaissance Motets." Diss., Northwestern University, 1974.

Harrán
: Harrán, Don. "Burney and Ambros as Editors of Josquin's Music." J 148-77.

HeartzC
: Heartz, Daniel. "The Chanson in the Humanist Era." CurrentT 193-230.

HeartzP
: ———. *Pierre Attaingnant, Royal Printer of Music.* Berkeley: University of California Press, 1969.

HeikampZ
: Heikamp, D. "Zur Struktur der Messe l'homme armé super voces musicales von Josquin Des- prez." Mf 19 (1966):366-84.

Hertzmann
: Hertzmann, Erich. "Zur Frage der Mehrchorigkeit in der ersten Hälfte der 16. Jahrhunderts." ZfMw 12 (1929/30):138-42.

HewittC
: Hewitt, Helen, ed. *Ottaviano Petrucci Canti B numero cinquanta, Venice 1502.* With an in- troduction by Edward E. Lowinsky; texts edited and annotated by Morton W. Briggs, translated by Norman B. Spector. MRM 2.

HewittO
: ———. *Harmonice musices odhecaton A.* Edition of the literary texts by Isabel Pope. Cam- bridge, Mass.: The Mediaeval Academy of America, 1942.

Heyden
: Heyden, Sebald. *De arte canendi.* Nürnberg, 1540. Facsimile, MMMF 2:139.

: ———. ———. Translation and transcription by Clement A. Miller. Musicological Studies and Documents, 21. [no place]: American Institute of Musicology, 1972.

Heyer   Heyer, Anna Harriet. *Historical Sets, Collected Editions, and Monuments of Music: A Guide to Their Contents*. 3rd ed. Chicago: American Library Association, 1980. 2 vols.

Hilton   Hilton, Ruth B. *An Index to Early Music in Selected Anthologies*. Music Indexes and Bibliographies, 13. Clifton, N.J.: European American Music Corporation, 1978.

Hoffmann-ErbrechtD   Hoffmann-Erbrecht, Lothar. "Datierungsprobleme bei Kompositionen in deutschen Musikhandschriften des 16. Jahrhunderts." OsthoffFs 47-60.

Hoffmann-ErbrechtF   ———. "Ein Frankfurter Messen-Codex." AfMw 16 (1959):328-34.

Hoffmann-ErbrechtM   ———. "Miszellen zur Frankfurter Musikgeschichte." *Helmuth Osthoff zu seinem Siebzigsten Geburtstag*, pp. 51-8. Hrsg. Wilhelm Stauder, Ursula Aarburg, Peter Cahn. Tutzing: Hans Schneider, 1969.

Hoffmann-ErbrechtO   ———. "Das *Opus Musicum* des Jacob Praetorius von 1566." AM 28 (1956):96-121.

Hoffmann-ErbrechtP   ———. "Problems in the Interdependence of Josquin Sources." J 285-93.

HolzmannH   Holzmann, K. "Hieronymus Formschneyders Sammeldruck Trium vocem carmina, Nürnberg 1538." Diss., University of Freiburg, 1957.

Homoly   Homoly, István, and Daniel Benkö. *Bakfark opera omnia*. Budapest: Editio Musica, 1976- .

HoneggerM   Honegger, Marc. "Les messes de Josquin des Prés dans la tablature de Diego Pisador (Salamanque, 1552)." Diss., University of Paris, 1970.

HoneggerT   ———. "La tablature de Diego Pisador et le probleme des altérations au XVIe siècle." *Revue de musicologie* 59 (1973):38, 191; 60 (1974):2.

Hudson   Hudson, Barton. "A Neglected Source of Renaissance Polyphony: Rome Santa Maria Maggiore JJ.III.4." AM 48 (1976):166-80.

Hüschen   Hüschen, Heinrich. *Die Motette. Das Musikwerk*, 47. Köln: Arno Volk Verlag, 1974.

Hughes-Hughes   Hughes-Hughes, Augustus. *Catalogue of Manu-script Music in the British Museum*. London: The Trustees, 1906-9 . 3 vols. Reprinted 1964.

Huys   Huys, Bernard. "An Unknown Alamire Choirbook ('Occo codex') Recently Acquired by the Royal Library of Belgium." TVNM 24 (1973):1-19.

IM   *Instituta et monumenta, serie I*. Cremona: Athenaeum Cremonense, 1954- .
                 Vol. 1: *Le frottole nell'edizione principe di Ottaviano Petrucci. Tomo 1: Libri I, II e III*, nella trascrizione di Gaetano Cesari; edizione critica di Raffaello Monterosso, precede uno studio introduttivo di Benvenuto Disertori, 1954.

Ingram   Ingram, Sonja Stafford. "The Polyphonic *Salve Regina* 1425-1550." Diss., University of North Carolina, 1973.

InskoC   Insko, Wyatt M. "The Cracow Tablature." Diss., Indiana University, 1969.

Israel   Israel, C. "Übersichtlicher Katalog der Musikalien der ständischen Landesbibliothek zu Cassel." *Zeitschrift des Vereins für hessische Geschichte und Landeskunst*, n.s. supp. 7. Kassel, 1881.

J   *Josquin des Prez. Proceedings of the Inter-national Josquin Festival-Conference Held at The Juilliard School at Lincoln Center in New York City, 21-5 June 1971*. Edited by Edward E. Lowinsky in collaboration with Bonnie J. Blackburn. London, New York, Toronto: Oxford University Press, 1976. 1 vol. with recordings (3 7" discs).

JacksonT   Jackson, Philip T. "Two Descendants of Jos-quin's 'Hercules' Mass." ML 59 (1978):188-205.

JacobsC   Jacobs, Charles, ed. *Antonio Cabezón: The Collected Works*. Collected Works/Gesamtausgaben, 4. Brooklyn, N.Y.: Institute of Mediaeval Music, 1964.

JacobsO   ———. *Miguel de Fuennlana. Orphénica lyra (Seville, 1554)*. Oxford: Clarendon Press, 1978.

James   James, Montague Rhodes. *Biblioteca Pepysiana: A Descriptive Catalogue of the Library of Samuel Pepys. Part III: Medieval Manuscripts.* London: Sidgwick & Jackson, 1923.

JAMS   *Journal of the American Musicological Society.*

JefferyC   Jeffery, Brian. *Chanson Verse of the Early Renaissance.* London: Tecla Editions, 1976.

JefferyL   ———. "The Literary Texts of Josquin's Chansons." J 401-20.

JeppesenD   Jeppesen, Knud. "Die drei Gafurius-Codices der Fabbrica del Duomo, Milano." AM 3 (1931): 14-28.

JeppesenF   ———. *La frottola. Bemerkungen zur Bibliographie der ältesten weltlichen Notendrucke in Italiens.* Kφbenhavn: Einar Munksgaard, 1968. 3 vols.

JeppesenM   ———. *Die mehrstimmige italienische Laude um 1500.* Leipzig: Breitkopf & Härtel, 1935.

JohnsonM   Johnson, Alvin. "The Masses of Cyprian de Rore." JAMS 6 (1953):117-39.

JonesF   Jones, George Morton. "The First Chansonnier of the Biblioteca Riccardiana, Codex 2794. A Study in the Method of Editing 15th-Century Music." Diss., New York University, 1972.

Joseph   Joseph, Charles M. "Architectural Control in Josquin's *Tu pauperum refugiam.*" *College Music Symposium* 18 (1978):139-45.

JosephsonK   Josephson, Nors S. "Kanon und Parodie: Zu einigen Josquin-Nachamungen." TVNM 25 (1974): 23-32.

JosephsonM   ———. "The Missa de Beata Virgine of the Sixteenth Century." Diss., University of California, Berkeley, 1970.

JustM   Just, Martin. *Der Mensuralkodex Mus. Ms. 40021 der Staatsbibliothek Preussischen Kulturbesitz Berlin: Untersuchungen zum Repertoire einer deutschen Quelle des 15. Jahrhunderts.* Würzburger musikhistorische Beiträge, 1. Tutzing: Hans Schneider, 1975. 2 vols.

       ———. [Ed. of Berlin 40021 in preparation, as EDM vol. 76-8].

JustR

———. [Review of Josquin CW, af1.49 (Motets, vol. 5, Bundel 23, nos.82-5: Absolve, O virgo, Inter natos, Responsum acceperat)]. Mf 18 (1965):109-10.

Kämper

Kämper, Dietrich. *Studien zur instrumental Ensemblemusik des 16. Jahrhunderts in Italien.* Analecta musicologica, 10. Köln: Bölau, 1970.

Kastner

Kastner, M.G. "Los manuscritos musicales ns. 48 y 232 de la Biblioteca General de la Universidad de Coimbra." *Anuario musical* 5 (1950):78.

KellmanJ

Kellman, Herbert. "Josquin and the Courts of the Netherlands and France: The Evidence of the Sources." J 181-216.

KellmanO

———. "The Origins of the Chigi Codex: The Date, Provenance, and Original Ownership of Rome, Bibliotheca Vaticana, Chigiana C.VIII.234." JAMS 11 (1958):6-19.

Kindermann

Kindermann, Jürgen. "Verzeichnis von Konkordanzen zu Kompositionen aus den Annaberger Chorbüchern Ms 1126 und Ms 1248." Mf 27 (1974):86-92.

KirschJ

Kirsch, Winfried. "Josquin's Motets in the German Tradition." J 261-78.

KirschM

———. *Die Motetten des Andreas de Silva: Studien zur Geschichte der Motette im 16. Jahrhundert.* Frankfurter Beitrage zur Musikwissenschaft, 2. Tutzing: Hans Schneider, 1977.

KirschQ

———. *Die Quellen des mehrstimmigen Magnificat- und Te Deum-Vertonung bis zur Mitte des 16. Jahrhunderts.* Tutzing: Hans Schneider, 1966.

KirschZ

———. "Zur Funktion der Tripeltaktigen Abschnitte in den Motetten des Josquin Zeitalters." OsthoffFsr 145-58.

Kohn

Kohn, Karl. "The Renotation of Polyphonic Music." MQ 67 (1981):29-49.

Kopff

Kopff, René. "Bernard Jobin, luthiste et imprimeur strasbourgeois de la seconde moitié du XVIe siècle." Diss., Strasbourg University, in progress.

KotterbaO — Kotterba, Karin. "Die Orgeltabulatur des Leonhard Kleber. Ein Beitrag zur Orgelmusik der erste Hälfte des 16. Jahrhunderts." Diss., Freiburg im Breisgau, 1958.

KrautwurstC — Krautwurst, Franz. "Codex Pernner." MGG 10, cols. 1075-6.

KrautwurstH — ———. "Die Heilsbronner Chorbücher der Universitätsbibliothek Erlangen (MS 473, 1-4)." *Jahrbuch für frankische Landesforschung* 25 (1965):273-324; 27 (1967):263-82.

Krings — Krings, Alfred. "Untersuchungen zu den Messen mit Choralthemen von Ockeghem bis Josquin." Diss., University of Cologne, 1952.

KuhnB — Kuhn, F. *Beschriebendes Verzeichnis der alten Musikalien, Handschriften und Druckwerke, des Königlichen Gymnasium zu Brieg.* MfMg *Beilage*, 27 (1897) [in vol. 28 of reprint ed.].

LagasM — Lagas, R. "Het Magnificat IV Toni van Josquin des Prez." TVNM 20 (1964-5):20-36.

LandK — Land, J.P.N. "De Koorboecken van de St. Pieterskerk te Leiden." *Bouwsteenen* 3:37-8.

Leichtentritt — Liechtentritt, Hugo. *Geschichte der Motette.* Kleine Handbücher der Musikgeschichte nach Gattungen, 2. Leipzig: Breitkopf & Härtel, 1908.

Lemaire — Lemaire, Jean, de Belges. *Oeuvres, III,* ed. J. Stecher. Louvain: Lefever, 1885.

LenaertsC — Lenaerts, René B. "Contribution à l'histoire de la musique belge de la renaissance." RB 9 (1953):103-21.

LenaertsFs — *Renaissance-muziek 1400-1600: donum natalicium René Bernard Lenaerts,* onder redactie van Jozef Robijns. Musicologica lovaniensia, 1. Leuven: Katholieke Universiteit Seminarie voor Muziekwetenschap, 1969.

LenaertsK — Lenaerts, René B. *Die Kunst der Niederländer.* Das Musikwerk, 22. Köln: Arno Volk Verlag, 1962.

LenaertsM — ———. "Musical Structure and Performance Practice in Masses and Motets of Josquin and Obrecht." J 619-26.

LenaertsMS ────. "Les MSS polyphoniques de la Bibliothèque Capitulaire de Toledo." *IMS: Report
of the Fifth Congress, Utrecht 1952*, pp.
172-7. Amsterdam: G. Alsbach, 1953.

LenaertsZ ────. "Zur Ostinato-Technik in der Kirchen-
musik der Niederlander." *Festschrift Bruno
Stäblein zum 70. Geburtstag*, pp. 157-9.
Hrsg. von Martin Ruhnke. Kassel: Bärenreiter,
1967.

LesureA Lesure, François, and Thibault, G. *Bibliographie
des éditions d'Adrian Le Roy et Robert Ballard
1551-1598*. Paris: Heugel, 1955.

LesureN ────. "Bibliographie des éditions musicales
publiées par Nicholas du Chemin." *Annales
musicologiques* 1 (1953):269; 4 (1956):251;
6 (1958-63):403.

Lichtenhahn Lichtenhahn, Ernst. "'Ars perfecta': Zu
Glareans Auffassung der Musikgeschichte."
Festschrift Arnold Geering zum 70. Geburtstag,
pp. 129-38. Hrsg. von Victor Ravizza. Bern:
Paul Haupt, 1972.

LippmannM Lippmann, Friedrich. "Musikhandschriften und
Drucke in der Bibliothek des Fürstenhaus
Massimo, Rom." *Analecta musicologica* 17
(1976):254-73.

LippmannU ────. "Eine unbekannte römische Musiksamm-
lungen: Bibliothek des Fürstenhauses Massimo."
*Gesellschaft für Musikforschung: Bericht über
den Internationalen Musikwissenschaftlichen
Kongress Berlin 1974*, pp. 310-12. Kassel:
Bärenreiter, 1980.

LitterickM Litterick, Louise. "The Manuscript Royal
20.A.XVI of the British Library." Diss., New
York University, 1976.

LitterickP ────. "Performing Franco-Netherlandish
Secular Music of the Late Fifteenth Century."
Early Music 8 (1980):474-85.

LlorensC Llorens, Josephus M. *Capellae Sixtinae codices
musicis notis instructi sive manu scripti
sive praelo excussi*. Studi e testi, 202.
Città di Vaticano: Biblioteca Apostolica
Vaticana, 1960.

LlorensCC ———. "El códice casanatense 2856 idendificado como el Cancionero de Isabella d'Este (Ferrara) esposa di Francesco Gonzaga (Mantua)." *Anuario musical* 20 (1967):161-78.

LlorensO ———. *Le opere musicali della Cappella Giulia: ... I manoscritti e edizione fino al '700.* Città del Vaticano: Biblioteca Apostolica Vaticana, 1971.

LoachA Loach, Donald. "Aegidius Tschudi's Songbook (St. Gall Ms 463): A Humanistic Document from the Circle of Heinrich Glarean." Diss., University of California, Berkeley, 1969.

LockwoodA Lockwood, Lewis. "Aspects of the 'L'homme armé' Tradition." Proceedings of the Royal Musical Association 100 (1974):97-122.

LockwoodG ———. "Mass II: 6-7." G 11:784-9; 790.

LockwoodGM ———. "Musica ficta: 1 (v)-2." G 12:806-8; bibliography by Stanley Boorman 810.

LockwoodJ ———. "Josquin at Ferrara: New Documents and Letters." J 103-37.

LockwoodJM ———. "Jean Mouton and Jean Michel: New Evidence on French Music and Musicians in Italy." JAMS 32 (1979):191-246.

LockwoodMF ———. "Music at Ferrara in the Period of Ercole I d'Este." *Studi musicali* 1 (1972): 101-32.

LockwoodMG ———. "'Messer Gossino' and Josquin Desprez." *Studies in Renaissance and Baroque Music in Honor of Arthur Mendel*, pp. 15-24. Ed. Robert Marshall. Kassel: Bärenreiter; Hackensack, N.J.: Joseph Boonin, 1974.

LockwoodS ———. "A Stylistic Investigation of the Masses of Josquin Desprez with the Aid of the Computer: A Progress Report." *Musicology and the Computer: Three Symposia*, ed. B.S. Brook, pp. 19-27. New York: City University of New York Press, 1970 (American Musicological Society Greater New York Chapter Publications, 2).

LockwoodV ———. "A View of the Early Sixteenth-Century Parody Mass." *Queens College of the City University of New York Twenty-fifth Anniversary Festschrift (1937-1962)*, pp. 53-78. Ed. Albert Mell. New York: Queens College Press, 1964.

Lodi

Lodi, Pio. *Catalogo delle opere musicali.*
Città di Modena, Biblioteca Estense. Bollettino
dell'Associazione del Musicologi Italiani,
Serie 8. Parma, 1923. Reprint. Bologna: Forni,
as Biblioteca musica 1:2.

Loewenfeld

Loewenfeld, Hans. *Leonhard Kleber und sein
Orgeltabulaturbuch als Beitrag zur Geschichte
der Orgelmusik im beginnenden XVI. Jahrhundert.*
Berlin: R. Boll, 1897.

LogeM

Loge, Eckhard. *Eine Messen- und Motettenhand-
schrift des Kantors Matthias Krüger aus der
Musikbibliothek Herzog Albrechts von Preussen.*
Kassel: Bärenreiter, 1931.

López-Calo

[Catalogue of Valladolid MSS in preparation].

LovellM

Lovell, John Harrison. "The Masses of Josquin
des Prez." Diss., University of Michigan,
1960.

LowinskyA

Lowinsky, Edward E. "Ascanio Sforza's Life: A
Key to Josquin's Biography and an Aid to the
Chronology of His Works." J 31-75.

LowinskyF

———. "The Goddess Fortuna in Music." MQ 29
(1943):45-77.

LowinskyJ

———. "Josquin des Prez and Ascanio Sforza."
MilanoM 2:17-22.

LowinskyM

———. "The Medici Codex: A Document of Music,
Art, and Politics in the Renaissance." *Annales
musicologiques* 5 (1957):61-178.

LowinskyMB

———. "A Music Book for Anne Boleyn." *Flori-
legium Historiale: Essays Presented to Wallace
K. Ferguson*, pp. 160-235. Ed. J.G. Rowe and
W.K. Stockdale. Toronto: University of Toronto,
1971.

LowinskyMC

———. "Music in the Culture of the Renaissance." *Journal of the History of Ideas* 15
(1954):509-53.

LowinskyMRM

———, ed. *The Medici Codex of 1518.* Chicago:
University of Chicago Press, 1968. 3 vols.
MRM 3-5.

LowinskyMV

———. "Music of the Renaissance as Viewed by
Renaissance Musicians." *The Renaissance Image
of Man and the World (Fourth Congress on the*

Humanities, *Ohio State University, 1961)*, pp. 129–77. Ed. Bernard O'Kelly. Columbus: Ohio State University Press, 1966.

LowinskyN ———. "A Newly Discovered Sixteenth-Century Motet Manuscript at the Biblioteca Vallicelliana in Rome." JAMS 3 (1950):173–232.

LowinskyO ———. "Ockeghem's Canon for Thirty-six Voices: An Essay in Musical Iconography." PlamenacFS 155–80.

LowinskySC ———. *Secret Chromatic Art in the Netherlands Motet.* Columbia University Studies in Musicology, 6. New York: Columbia University Press, 1946. Reprint. New York: Russell & Russell, 1967.

LowinskySCR ———. "Secret Chromatic Art Re-examined." *Perspectives in Musicology*, pp. 91–135. Ed. Barry S. Brook, Edward O.D. Downes, Sherman Van Solkema. New York: W.W. Norton, 1972.

LowinskySR ———. "Scholarship in the Renaissance: Music." *Renaissance News* 16 (1963):255–62.

LowinskyT ———. *Tonality and Atonality in Sixteenth-Century Music.* Berkeley: University of California Press, 1961.

Maas Maas, Chris. "Josquin-Agricola-Brumel-De la Rue. Een authenticiteitsprobleem." TVNM 20 (1966): 120–39.

McMurtryB McMurtry, William Murl. "The British Museum Manuscript Additional 35087: A Transcription of the French, Italian, and Latin Compositions with Concordance and Commentary." Diss., North Texas State University, 1967.

Maderna Maderna, Bruno. *Magnificat quarti toni* [by Josquin] *dall'originale quatuor vocibus messo in partitura per coro misto, e tre gruppi di instrumenti....* Milano: Edizioni Suivini Zerboni, 1967.

Maier Maier, Julius Joseph. *Die musikalischen handschriften des Kgl. Hof- und Staatsbibliothek in München. Catalogus codicum manu scriptorum Bibliothecae regiae monacensia*, tomi 8, pars 1. München: Palm'schen Hofbuchhandlung, 1879.

Malaguezzi-   Malaguezzi-Valeri, Francesco. *La corte di*
  Valeri   *Lodovico il Moro*. Milano: Ulrico Hoepli,
                  1923-9. Reprint. Nendeln, Liechtenstein:
                  Kraus, 1970. 4 vols.

Maleady   Maleady, Antoinette A. *Record and Tape*
                  Reviews Index. Metuchen, N.J.: Scarecrow
                  Press, 1971- (annual).

Mallett   Mallett, Michael. *The Borgias*. New York:
                  Barnes & Noble, 1969.

ManiatesC   Maniates, Maria. "Combinative Techniques in
                  Franco-Flemish Polyphony: A Study of Mannerism
                  in Music from 1450 to 1530." Diss., Columbia
                  University, 1965.

MarxN   Marx, Hans Joachim. "Neues zur Tabulatur-
                  Handschrift St. Gallen, Stiftbibliothek, Cod.
                  530." AfMw 37 (1980):264-91.

MattfeldC   Mattfeld, Jacquelyn Anderson. "Cantus Firmus
                  in the Liturgical Motets of Josquin des Pres."
                  Diss., Yale University, 1959.

MattfeldS   ———. "Some Relationships between Texts and
                  Cantus Firmi in the Liturgical Motets of
                  Josquin des Pres." JAMS 14 (1961):159-83.

MattfeldU   ———. "The Unsolved Riddle: The Apparent Ab-
                  sence of Ambrosian Melodies in the Works of
                  Josquin des Prez." J 360-66.

MD   *Musica disciplina*.

MeierM   Meier, Bernhard. "Melodiezitate in der Musik
                  des 16. Jahrhunderts." TVNM 20 (1964):1-19.

MeierMR   ———. "The Musica Reservata of Adrianus Petit
                  Coclico and Its Relationship to Josquin." MD
                  10 (1956):67-105.

Meissner   Meissner, Ute. *Der antwerpener Notendrucker*
                  Tylman Susato. Berliner Studien zur Musik-
                  wissenschaft, 11. Berlin: Merseberger, 1967.
                  2 vols.

MendelT   Mendel, Arthur. "Towards Objective Criteria
                  for Establishing Chronology and Authenticity:
                  What Help Can the Computer Give?" J 297-308.

Menghini   Menghini, Mario, ed. *Le rime di Serafino de'*
                  Ciminelli dall'Aquila. Collezione opere in-
                  edite o rare dei primi tre secoli della lingua,
                  77. Bologna: Romagnoli Dall'Acqua, 1894.

Mf   *Die Musikforschung.*

MfMg   *Monatshefte für Musikgeschichte*, 1869-1905.
                      Reprint. Scarsdale, N.Y.: Annemarie Schnase,
                      1960.

MGG   *Die Musik in Geschichte und Gegenwart. All-*
                      gemeine Enzyklopädie der Musik.... Kassel:
                      Bärenreiter, 1949- . 14 vols.

Milano, Francesco *see* Francesco Canova da Milano

MilanoD   *Il Duomo di Milano: Congresso internationale*
                      ... settembre 1968: Atti, a cura di Maria
                      Luisa Gatti Perer. Monografie di arte Lombarda,
                      I monumenti, 3. Milano: Edizioni La Rete,
                      1969. 2 vols.

MischiatiA   Mischiati, O. "Un'antologia manoscritta in
                      partitura del secolo XVI: Il MS Bourdeney
                      della Bibliothèque Nationale di Parigi."
                      RMI 10 (1975):265-328.

ML   *Music and Letters.*

MME   *Monumentos de la musica española.* Barcelona:
                      Consejo Superior de Investigaciones Científicas,
                      1941- .
                         Vols. 1, 5, 10, 14: *see* AnglésMME
                         Vol. 2: Luys de Narvaez. *Los seys libros*
                         del delphin ..., ed. E. Pujol.
                         Vol. 6: Alonso de Mudarra. *Tres libros de*
                         música ..., ed. E. Pujol.
                         Vols. 22-3: Enriques de Valderràbano.
                         Libros de musica de vihuela ..., ed. E.
                         Pujol.
                         Vols. 27-9: Antonio de Cabezon. *Obras de*
                         música ..., ed. H. Anglés.

MMMA   *Monumenta monodica medii aevi....* Kassel:
                      Bärenreiter, 1956- .
                         Vol. 1: *Hymnen (I). Die mittelaltlichen*
                         Hymnen-melodien des Abendlandes, ed. B.
                         Stäblein.

MMMF   *Monuments of Music and Music Literature in*
                      Facsimile. New York: Broude Brothers, 1965- .

MoerkS   Moerk, Alice. "The Seville Chansonnier: An
                      Edition of Seville 5-I-43 and Paris n.acq.fr.
                      4379 (Part I)." Diss., University of West
                      Virginia, 1971.

MohrH   Mohr, Peter. *Die Handschrift B.211-215 der*
                 Proske-Bibliothek zu Regensburg mit kurzer
                 Beschreibung der Handschriften B.216-219 und
                 B.220-222. Schriften des Landesinstituts für
                 Musikforschung Kiel, 7. Kassel: Bärenreiter,
                 1955.

MolinetF   Molinet, Jean. *Les faictz et ditz*, ed. Noel
                 Dupire. Société des Anciens Textes Français.
                 Paris, 1936. Vol. 1.

Monnikendam   Monnikendam, Marius, ed. *Missa "Hercules dux*
                 Ferrariae" van Josquin des Pres, ca. 1450-
                 1521. Musica sacra "Sancta sancte" Jaarg.
                 61:1, 39-43.

MonteCW   Monte, Philippe de. *Opera*, vol. 38. Ed.
                 Charles van den Borren, A. Smijers....
                 Bruges: Desclée, 1927-39.

MoserG   Moser, Hans Joachim, ed. *Gassenhawer und*
                 Reutterliedlin. (Facsimile of [c1535][13].)
                 Augsburg, Köln: Dr. Benno Filser Verlag, 1927.
                 Reprint. Hildesheim, New York: G. Olms, 1970.

MoserM   ———. "Eine Musikaliendruckerei auf einer
                 deutschen Ritterburg." ZfMw 17 (1934-5): 97-
                 102; also in *Festgabe für Hans Joachim Moser*
                 zum 65. Geburtstag.... Kassel: Hinnenthal,
                 1954.

MottaM   Motta, Emilio. "Musici alla corte degli
                 Sforza." *Archivio storico lombardo* 14 (1887):
                 300-527.

MQ   *The Musical Quarterly.*

MRM   *Monuments of Renaissance Music*. Chicago: Uni-
                 versity of Chicago Press, 1964- .

Müller-   Müller-Blattau, Joseph, ed. *Musica reservata*
   Blattau   [choral collection]. Kassel: Bärenreiter,
                 1952- .

Müller-   ———. "Die musikalischen Schätze der Staats-
   BlattauM   und Universitätsbibliothek zu Königsberg
                 i.Pr." ZfMw 6 (1924):215-39.

Murányi   Murányi, R.A. [Thematic catalogue of Budapest,
                 Bártfa MSS in preparation].

Myers   Myers, Kurtz. *Index to Record Reviews*. Boston:
                 G.K. Hall, 1978.

NagelJ   Nagel, Wilibald. "Johann Heugel (ca. 1500-1584/5." *Sammelbände der Internationale Musikgesellschaft* 7 (1905-6):80-110.

NAWM   *Norton Anthology of Western Music (in Two Volumes).* Vol. 1, ed. Claude V. Palisca. New York: W.W. Norton & Company, 1980.

Nef   Nef, W.R. "Der St. Galler Organist Fridolin Sicher und seine Orgeltabulatur." *Schweizerisches Jahrbuch für Musikwissenschaft* 7 (1938):3-215.

Newsidler   Newsidler, Hans. *Ein newgeordent kunstlich Lautesbuch.* Nuremberg: Author, 1536. Facsimile. [*Instituto pro Arte Testudinis*, ser. A:1. Neuss: GbR-Junghänel], 1974.

Newton   Newton, Paul G. "Florence, Biblioteca del Conservatorio di Musica Luigi Cherubini, Manuscript Basevi 2439: Critical Edition and Commentary." Diss., North Texas State University, 1968.

NobleJ   Noble, Jeremy. "Josquin Desprez:8-11." G 9: 718-36.

NobleN   ———. "New Light on Josquin's Benefices." J 76-102.

NobleNM   ———. "A New Motet by Josquin?" *Musical Times* 112 (1971):749-52 and Supplement, August 1971 (MT 1542).

NobleO   ———. "Ottaviano Petrucci: His Josquin Editions and Some Others." GilmoreFs 2:433-45.

NobleS   ———. "Sixteenth-Century Music on Records. I: Sacred Music." ML 39 (1958):154-5.

NoblittC   Noblitt, Thomas. "Das Chorbuch des Nikolaus Leopold (München Staatsbibliothek Mus MS 3154) Repertorium." AfMw 26 (1969):169-208.

NoblittD   ———. "Die Datierung der Handschrift Mus. Ms. 3154 der Staatsbibliothek München." Mf 27 (1974):36-56.

NoblittMD   ———. "Manuscript Mus. 1/D/505 of the Sächsische Landesbibliothek Dresden (*olim* Annaberg, Bibliothek der St. Annenkirche, Ms. 1248)." AfMw 30 (1973):275-310.

NoblittR   ———. "A Reconstruction of Ms. Thomaskirche
                51 of the Universitätsbibliothek Leipzig
                (*olim* A. alpha 22-23)." TVNM 31 (1981):16-72.

NovackF   Novack, Saul. "Fusion of Design and Tonal
                Order in Mass and Motet: Josquin Desprez and
                Heinrich Isaac." *Music Forum* 2 (1970):187-263.

NovackT   ———. "Tonal Tendencies in Josquin's Harmony."
                J 317-33.

NowackiL   Nowacki, Edward. "The Latin Psalm Motet 1500-
                1535." OsthoffFsr 159-84.

Nowak   Nowak, Leopold. "Eine Bicinienhandschrift der
                wiener Nationalbibliothek." ZfMw 14 (1931-2):
                94-102.

Obst   Obst, L.D. "Die Psalm-Motetten des Josquin
                Desprez." Diss., Frei Universität Berlin,
                1957.

Orf   Orf, Wolfgang. *Die Musikhandschriften Thomas-*
                kirche MSS 49/50 und 51 in der Universitätsbiblio-
                thek Leipzig. Quellenkataloge zur Musikgeschichte,
                13. Leipzig: Deutscher Verlag für Musik, 1977.

Osthoff   Osthoff, Helmuth. *Josquin Desprez.* Tutzing:
                Hans Schneider, 1962-5. 2 vols.

OsthoffB   ———. "Besetzung und Klangstruktur in den
                Werken von Josquin des Prez." AfMw 9 (1952):
                177-94.

OsthoffFs   *Festschrift Helmuth Osthoff zum 65. Geburtstage.*
                Hrsg. von Lothar Hoffmann-Erbrecht und Helmut
                Hucke. Tutzing: Hans Schneider, 1961.

OsthoffFsr   *Renaissance-Studien: Helmuth Osthoff zum 80.*
                Geburtstag.... Hrsg. von Ludwig Finscher.
                Frankfurter Beiträge zur Musikwissenschaft, 2.
                Tutzing: Hans Schneider, 1979.

OsthoffJ   Osthoff, Helmuth. "Ein Josquin-Zitat bei
                Henricus Isaac," pp. 127-34. *Liber Amicorum*
                Charles van den Borren. Anvers: Lloyd Anver-
                sois, 1964.

OsthoffM   ———. "Das Magnificat bei Josquin Desprez."
                AfMw 16 (1959):220-31.

OsthoffP   ———. "Die Psalm-Motetten von Josquin Desprez."
                Bericht über den Internationalen Musikwissen-
                schaftlichen Kongress Wien Mozartjahr 1956,
                pp. 452-7. Graz, Köln: Hermann Böhlaus, 1958.

OsthoffR ——. "Renaissance-Tendenzen in den Fortuna desperata Messen von Josquin und Obrecht." Mf 11 (1956):1-26.

OsthoffV ——. "Vergils Aeneis in der Musik von Josquin des Prez bis Orlando di Lasso." AfMw 11 (1954): 85-102.

OsthoffW ——. "'Wohlauf, gut G'sell, von hinnen,' ein Beispiel deutsch-französischer Liedgemeinschaft um 1500." *Jahrbuch für Volksliedforschung* 8 (1951):128-36.

OsthoffZ ——. "Zur Echtheitsfrage und Chronologie bei Josquins Werke." *IMS: Report of the Fifth Congress, Utrecht 1952*, pp. 303-10. Amsterdam: G. Alsbach, 1953.

Pannella Pannella, Liliana. "Le compositioni profane di una raccolta fiorentina del cinquecento." *Rivista italiana di musicologia* 3 (1968): 3-47.

PAPTM *Publikationen älterer praktischer und theoretischer Musikwerke*. Berlin: Leipmannsohn, Trautwein, 1873-1905. 29 vols.
Vol. 6 (Jg. 5): Josquin Deprès/Jodocus Pratensis. *Eine Sammlung ausgewählter Kompositionen zu 4, 5, und 6 Stimmen* ... in Partitur gesetzt und mit einem Klavierauszuge versehen unter Mitwirkung von Raymond Schlecht und Robert Eitner, veröffent von Franz Commer.
Vol. 16 (Jg. 16-18): Henricus Glareanus. *Dodecachordon*, in deutscher Übersetzung von Peter Bohn.

Pastor Pastor, Ludwig. *The History of the Popes*. English translation by F.I. Antrobus. St. Louis, Mo.: B. Herder, 1898. Vol. 5.

PatrickC Patrick, Philip Howard. "A Computer-Study of a Suspension-Formation in the Masses of Josquin Desprez." Diss., Princeton University, 1973.

Pease Pease, Edward. "A Report on Codex Q 16 of the Civico Museo Bibliografico Musicale." MD 20 (1966):57-94.

PedrellC Pedrell, Felipe. *Catàlech de la Biblioteca musical de la Disputació de Barcelona*. Barcelona: Palau de la Disputació, 1908-9. 2 vols.

PedrellM   ——, ed. *Músicos contemporaneos y de otros tiempos. Estudios de vulgarization.* Paris: Ollendorf, 1910.

PerformanceJMa "The Performance and Interpretation of Josquin's Masses." J 696-719.

PerformanceJMt "The Performance and Interpretation of Josquin's Motets." J 646-62.

PerformanceJS "The Performance and Interpretation of Josquin's Secular Music." J 663-95.

PerkinsG   Perkins, Leeman J. "Motet II: Renaissance." G 12:632ff.; bibliography 646-7.

PerkinsM   ——. "Mode and Structure in the Masses of Josquin." JAMS 26 (1973):189-239.

PetrucciCB   *Canti B* (Facsimile). MMMF 1:23.

PetrucciCC   *Canti C* (Facsimile). MMMF 1:25.

PetrucciH   *Harmonice musices odhecaton A* (Facsimile). Milano: Bolletino bibliografico musicale, 1932; and MMMF 1:10.

PetrucciJ   *Missarum Josquin liber secundus* (Facsimile). Monumenta musica typographica vetustiora: Italica, 8. Bologna: Antiquae Musicae Italicae Studiosi, 1971.

PickerC   Picker, Martin. *The Chanson Albums of Marguerite of Austria: MSS 338 and 11239 of the Bibliothèque Royale de Belgique, Brussels. A Critical Edition and Commentary.* Berkeley: University of California Press, 1965.

PickerJ   ——. "Josquiniana in Some Manuscripts at Piacenza." J 247-60.

PickerJG   ——. "Josquin and Jean Lemaire: Four Chansons Re-examined." GilmoreFs 447-56.

PickerJP   ——. "A Josquin Parody by Marc Antonio Cavazzoni." TVNM 22 (1972):157-9.

PickerM   ——. "The Motet Anthologies of Andrea Antico," pp. 211-37. *A Musical Offering: Essays in Honor of Martin Bernstein.* Ed. Edward H. Clinkscale and Claire Brook. New York: Pendragon Press, 1977.

PickerP   ——. "Polyphonic Settings of c. 1500 of the Flemish Tune 'In meinen sin.'" JAMS 12 (1959): 94-5.

Piqueras *see* Rubio Piqueras

Pirro   Pirro, André. *Histoire de la musique de la fin du XVIe siècle à la fin du XVe*. Paris: Librairie Renouard, 1940.

PirrottaD   Pirrotta, Nino. "Despres, Josquin." *La Musica. Parte Prima: Enciclopedia Storica*. Torino: Union Tipografico-Editrice Torinese, 1966. 2:214-30.

PirrottaM   ——. "Music and Cultural Tendencies in 15th-Century Italy." JAMS 19 (1966):127-61.

Pisador   Pisador, Diego. *Libro de musica de vihuela*. Salamanca: Author, 1552. Facsimile reprint. Genève: Minkoff, 1973.

PlamenacFs   *Essays on Musicology in Honor of Dragan Plamenac on His 70th Birthday*. Ed. Gustave Reese and Robert J. Snow. Pittsburgh: University of Pittsburgh Press, 1969.

PlamenacP   Plamenac, Dragan. "A Postscript to the 'Second' Chansonnier of the Biblioteca Riccardiana." *Annales musicologiques* 4 (1956):261-5.

PlamenacR   ——. "A Reconstruction of the French Chansonnier in the Biblioteca Columbina, Seville." MQ 37 (1951):501-42; 38 (1952):85-117, 245-77.

PlamenacS   ——. "The 'Second' Chansonnier of the Biblioteca Riccardiana (Codex 2356)." *Annales musicologiques* 2 (1954):105-87.

PlamenacSP   ——, ed. *Sevilla, 5-I-43, Paris nuov. acq.fr. 4379* [facsimile]. Publications of Mediaeval Musical Manuscripts, 8. Brooklyn, N.Y.: The Institute of Mediaeval Music, 1963.

PowersG   Powers, Harold S. "Mode: III." G 12:397-414; bibliography 448-9.

Prod'homme   Prod'homme, J.-G. "Les institutions musicales (bibliothèques et archives) en Belgique et en Hollande." *Sammelbände der internationale Musikgesellschaft* 15 (1913-14):458-503.

Raugel   Raugel, F. "Josquin des Prés à la Collegiale de St. Quentin." *Actes du Congrès d'histoire de l'art ... Paris 1921*, pp. 807-10. Paris: Presses universitaires de France, 1922?

Ravizza   Ravizza, Victor. *Das instrumentale Ensemble*
               von 1400-1550 in Italien. Publikationen der
               Schweizerischen Musikforschenden Gesellschaft,
               Ser. 2:21. Bern, 1970.

RB   *Revue belge de musicologie*.

Rectanus   Rectanus, Hans. "'... Ich kenne dich, Josquin,
               du Herrlicher....' Bemerkungen zu thematischen
               Verwandtschaften zwischen Josquin, Palestrina
               und Pfitzner." OsthoffFsr 211-22.

ReeseFs   *Aspects of Medieval and Renaissance Music:*
               A Birthday Offering to Gustave Reese, ed. Jan
               LaRue. New York: W.W. Norton, 1966.

ReeseH   Reese, Gustave. "The Hewitt Edition of the
               Odhecaton." MQ 29 (1943):257-65.

ReeseJ   ———. "Josquin Desprez" (sections 1-7) in G
               9:713-8, 737-8.

ReeseMR   ———. *Music in the Renaissance*. New York:
               W.W. Norton, 1954.

ReeseP   ———. "The Polyphonic 'Missa de Beata Virgine'
               as a Genre: The Background of Josquin's Lady
               Mass." J 589-98.

Reeser   Reeser, Eduard, ed. *Drei oud-nederlandsche*
               motetten. Vereeniging voor Nederlandsche
               Muziekgeschiedenis, Uitgave 44. Amsterdam:
               G. Alsbach, 1936.

Reiffenstein   Reiffenstein, Helmuth. "Die weltlichen Werke
               des Josquin des Prez." Diss., Johann-Wolfgang-
               Goethe-Universität, Frankfurt am Main, 1952.

Renaissance   *La renaissance dans les provinces du nord*
               (Entretiens d'Arras 27-20 juin, 1954). Ed.
               par François Lesure. Paris: Éditions du
               Centre National de la Recherche Scientifique,
               1956.

Report   "Problems in Editing the Music of Josquin des
               Prez: A Critique of the First Edition and
               Proposals for the Second Edition." J 724-54.

Report 1   Willem Elders. "Report of the First Josquin
               Meeting (Utrecht 1973)." TVNM 24 (1973-4):
               20-82.

Report 2   ———. "Short Report of the Second Josquin Meet-
               ing (Utrecht, 1974)." TVNM 25 (1975):57-60.

Report 3   ———. "Short Report of the Third Josquin
               Meeting with a Proposal for an Ordering of

the Works in the New Josquin Edition." TVNM 26 (1976):17-40.

Report 4 ——. "Short Report of the Fourth Josquin Meeting (Dartmouth College)." TVNM 28 (1978):31-7.

Rhaw *Bicinia gallica, latina, germanica, Tomus I, II, 1545.* Hrsg. von Bruce Bellingham. Georg Rhau Musikdrucke aus den Jahren 1538 bis 1545, vol. 6. Kassel: Bärenreiter, 1974.

Richter Richter, Julius. *Katalog der Musik-Sammlung auf der Universitäts-Bibliothek in Basel.* MfMg *Beilage* 23 (1892).

Riemann Riemann, Hugo. *Handbuch der Musikgeschichte.* 2. Bd., 1. Teil: *Das Zeitalter der Renaissance.* 2. Aufl. Leipzig: Breitkopf & Härtel, 1920.

RifkinN Rifkin, Joshua. "A 'New' Renaissance Manuscript." *Abstracts of Papers Read at the Thirty-seventh Annual Meeting of the American Musicological Society*, Chapel Hill and Durham, North Carolina, November 11-14, 1971, p. 2.

RifkinP ——. "Pietrequin Bonnel and Ms. 2794 of the Biblioteca Riccardiana." JAMS 29 (1976): 284-96.

RifkinS ——. "Scribal Concordances for Some Renaissance Manuscripts in Florentine Libraries." JAMS 26 (1973):305-26.

RISM A1:4 *Einzeldruck vor 1800, Bd. 4.* Redaktion Karlheinz Schlager. Répertoire international des sources musicales, A/I/4. Kassel: Bärenreiter, 1974.

RISM-RI *Recueils imprimés, XVIe-XVIIe siècles.* Ouvrage publié sous la direction de François Lesure. Répertoire international des sources musicales. München: G. Henle, 1960.

RMI *Rivista musicale italiana.*

Robijns Robijns, Jozef. "Eine Musikhandschrift des frühen 16. Jahrhunderts im Zeichen der Verehrung unserer Lieben Frau der sieben Schmerzen (Brüssel, Kgl. Bibliothek, Hs. 215-216)." *Kirchenmusikalisches Jahrbuch* 44 (1960):28-43.

RobisonV Robison, John Orian. "Vienna, Nationalbibliothek Manuscript 18810: A Transcription of the Unpublished Pieces with Comments on Performance Practices in Early Sixteenth-Century Germany." Diss., Stanford University, 1975.

Roediger   Roediger, Karl Erich. *Die Geistlichen Musik-
                    handschriften der Universitäts-Bibliothek
                    Jena*. Textband, Notenverzeichnis. Jena:
                    Frommann, 1935. 2 vols.

Rosen   Rosen, Ida. "The Treatment of Dissonance in
                    the Motets of Josquin Desprez." Diss., Cornell
                    University, 1961.

RRMR   *Recent Researches in the Music of the Renais-
                    sance*. Madison: A-R Editions, 1974- .
                       Vols. 16-17: *Sixteenth Century Bicinia: A
                       Complete Edition of Munich, Bayerische
                       Staatsbibliothek, Mus. Ms. 260*. Ed. Bruce
                       Bellingham and Edward G. Evans, Jr.
                       Vol. 34: *see* WarburtonK.

Rubio   Rubio Piqueras, Felipe. *Códices polifónicos
   PiquerasC   toledanos, estudio crítico de los mismos con
                    motivo del VII centenario de la catedral
                    primada*. Toledo, [1925?].

RubsamenM   Rubsamen, Walter. "Music Research in Italian
                    Libraries." *Notes* 6 (1948-9):220-33, 543-69;
                    8 (1950-51):70-99.

RubsamenU   ———. "Unifying Techniques in Selected Masses
                    of Josquin and LaRue: A Stylistic Comparison."
                    J 369-400.

RuffF   Ruff, Lillian M. "Some Formal Devices in Jos-
                    quin's Motets." *The Consort* 25 (1968-9):362-72.

RuffJ   ———. "Josquin des Prez--Some Features of
                    His Motets." *The Consort* 28 (1972):106-18.

Sacerdote   Sacerdote, Gustavo. *Cesare Borgia*. Milano:
                    Rizzoli Editore, 1959.

Salzer   Salzer, Felix, and Schachter, Carl. *Counter-
                    point and Composition*. New York: McGraw-Hill,
                    1969.

SartoriB   Sartori, Claudio. *Bibliografia delle opere
                    musicali stampate da Ottaviano Petrucci*.
                    Florence: Olschki, 1948.

SartoriC   ———. *La cappella musicale del duomo di
                    Milano: Catalogo delle musiche d'archivio*.
                    Milano: Veneranda Fabbrica del Duomo, 1957.

SartoriJ   ———. "Josquin des Prés cantore del duomo di
                    Milano." *Annales musicologiques* 4 (1956):
                    55-83.

SartoriQ ———. "Il quarto codice di Gaffurio non ha del tutto scomparso." *Collectanea historia musices* 1 (1953):14-28.

Scharnagl Scharnagl, A. [Catalogue of the Proske-Musikbibliothek in Regensburg, in preparation].

ScheringG Schering, Arnold. *Geschichte der Musik in Beispielen.* Leipzig: Breitkopf & Härtel, 1931.

ScheringM ———. "Musikalisches aus Joh. Burckards 'Liber Notarum' (1483-1506)." *Musikwissenschaftliche Beiträge. Festschrift für Johannes Wolf zu seinen sechzigsten Geburtstag,* pp. 171-5. Hrsg. von W. Lott, H. Osthoff und W. Wolffheim. Berlin: M. Breslauer, 1929.

ScheringN ———. *Die niederländische Orgelmesse in Zeitalter des Josquin.* Leipzig: Breitkopf & Härtel, 1912. Reprint. Amsterdam: Frits Knuf, 1971, as Bibliotheca organologica, 1.

ScheringNG ———. "Die Notenbeispiele in Glarean's Dodecachordon (1547)." *Sammelbände der Internationale Musikgesellschaft* 13 (1911-12):569-96.

Scherrer Scherrer, G. *Verzeichnis der Handschriften der Stiftsbibliothek von St. Gallen.* Halle: Waisenhaus, 1875.

Schmidt Schmidt, Henry Louis III. "The First Printed Lute Books: Francesco Spinacino's *Intabulatura di Lauto, Libro primo* and *Libro secondo* (Venice: Petrucci, 1507)." Diss., University of North Carolina, 1969.

Schmidt-Görg Schmidt-Görg, Joseph. *Geschichte der Messe.* Das Musikwerk, 30. Köln: Arno Volk Verlag, 1967.

SchröderE Schröder, Otto. "Das Eisenacher Cantorenbuch." ZfMw 14 (1931-2):173-8.

SchulerS Schuler, Manfred. "Spanische Musikeinflusse in Rom um 1500." *Anuario musical* 25 (1970): 28-36.

Schwartz Schwartz, Rudolf, ed. *Ottaviano Petrucci. Frottole, Buch I und IV.* Publikationen älterer Musik, Jg. 8. Leipzig: Breitkopf & Härtel, 1935.

Seeley   Seeley, Ann Neely. "Motets for the Hungarian
                  Court: The Origin and Contents of Rome,
                  Vatican Library, Palatini Latini 1976-79."
                  Diss. in progress, University of California,
                  Berkeley.

Shepherd   Shepherd, John. "A Liturgico-Musical Ap-
                  praisal." *Current Musicology* 23 (1977):69-78.

SherrN   Sherr, Richard. "Notes on Two Roman Manu-
                  scripts of the Early Sixteenth Century."
                  MQ 63 (1977):48-73.

SherrP   ———. "The Papal Chapel 1492-1513 and its
                  Polyphonic Sources." Diss., Princeton Univer-
                  sity, 1975.

ShippC   Shipp, Clifford M. "A Chansonnier of the Dukes
                  of Lorraine: The Paris Manuscript Fonds
                  Français 1597." Diss., North Texas State
                  University, 1960.

Siegele   Siegele, U. *Die Musiksammlung der Stadt Heil-
                  bronn: Katalog mit Beitragen zur Geschichte
                  der Sammlung und zur Quellenkunde des 16.
                  Jahrhunderts.* Veröffentlichungen des Archivs
                  der Stadt Heilbronn, 13. Heilbronn: Stadt-
                  archiv, 1967.

SillimanR   Silliman, A. Cutler. "'Responce' and 'Replique'
                  in Chansons Published by Tylman Susato, 1543-
                  1550." RB 16 (1963):30-42.

Skei   Skei, Allen B. "*Dulces exuviae*: Renaissance
                  Settings of Dido's Last Words." *Music Review*
                  37 (1976):77-91.

SMd   *Schweizerische Musikdenkmäler.* Kassel:
                  Bärenreiter, 1955- .
                  Vol. 5: *Das Liederbuch des Johannes Heer
                  von Glarus: Ein Musikheft aus der Zeit des
                  Humanismus (Codex 462 des Stiftsbibliothek
                  St. Gallen).* Ed. Arnold Geering, Hans Tümpy.
                  Vol. 6: *Tabulaturen des XVI. Jahrhunderts,*
                  Teil I: *Die Tabulaturen aus dem Besitz des
                  Basler Humanisten Bonifacius Amerbach.* Ed.
                  Hans Joachim Marx.
                  Vol. 7: *Tabulaturen des XVI. Jahrhunderts,*
                  Teil II: *Die Orgeltabulatur des Clemens
                  Hör (Ms. Zurich, Zentralbibliothek, Z.XI.301).*
                  Ed. Hans Joachim Marx.

SmijersJ   Smijers, Albert. "Josquin des Prez." *Proceedings of the Royal Musical Association* 53 (1927):102.

SmijersK   ———. "Een kleine bijdrage over Josquin en Isaac." *Gedenkboek aangeboden aan Dr. D.F. Scheurleer op zijn 70sten verjaardag*, pp. 313-9. 's-Gravenshage: Nijhoff, 1925.

SmijersU   ———. "De uitgave der werken van Josquin des Prés." TVNM 10 (1921):164-79.

SmijersV   ———, ed. *Van Ockeghem tot Sweelinck, Afl. 5.* Amsterdam: Vereniging voor Nederlandse Muziekgeschiedenis, 1954.

SmijersVZ   ———. "Vijftiende en zestiende eeuwsche muziekhandschriften in Italie met werken van Nederlandse componisten." TVNM 14 (1935): 165-81.

Smithers   Smithers, Don. "A Textual-Musical Inventory and Concordance of Munich University MS 328-331." *R.M.A. Research Chronicle* 8:34-89.

Snížková   Snížková, Jitka. "Josquin in Czech Sources of the Second Half of the Sixteenth Century." J 279-84.

SparksC   Sparks, Edgar H. *Cantus Firmus in Mass and Motet 1420-1520.* Berkeley: University of California Press, 1963.

SparksM   ———. *The Music of Noel Bauldeweyn.* American Musicological Society Studies and Documents, 6. New York: American Musicological Society, 1972.

SparksP   ———. "Problems of Authenticity in Josquin's Motets." J 345-59.

StaehelinF Staehelin, Martin. "Eine florentiner Musik-Handschrift aus der Zeit um 1500." *Schweizer Beiträge zur Musikwissenschaft* 1 (1972):55-81.

StaehelinG ———. *Der Grüne Codex der Viadrina: ein wenigbeachtete Quelle zur Musik des späten 15. und frühen 16. Jahrhunderts in Deutschland.* Akademie der Wissenschaft und der Literatur: Abhandlungen der geistes- und sozialwissenschaftliches Klasses, Jg. 1970, nr. 10. Mainz: Akademie der Wissenschaft und Literatur, 1971.

StaehelinM   ———. "Möglichkeiten und praktische Anwendung
                der Verfasser-bestimmung an Anonym über-
                lieferten Kompositionen der Josquin-Zeit."
                TVNM 23 (1973):79.

StaehelinR   ———. [Review of LowinskyMRM]. JAMS 33 (1980):
                575-87.

StaehelinW   ———. "Eine wenig beachtete Gruppe von Chor-
                büchern aus der ersten Hälfte des 16. Jahr-
                hunderts." IMS: Report of the Eleventh Con-
                gress, Copenhagen 1972, 2:664-8. Copenhagen:
                Wilhelm Hansen, 1974.

StaehelinZ   ———. "Zum Egenolff-Diskantband der Biblio-
                thèque Nationale in Paris: Ein Beitrag zur
                musikalischen Quellenkünde der 1. Hälfte des
                16. Jahrhunderts." AfMw 23 (1966):93-109.

StaehelinZS   ———. "Zum Schicksal des alten Musikalien-
                Fonds von San Luigi dei Francesci in Rom."
                FAM 17 (1970):125-6.

StamJ   Stam, Edward. "Josquin's Proportionskanon
                Agnus Dei und dessen piacentiner Überliefer-
                ung." TVNM 26 (1976):1-7.

StamQ   ———, ed. Josquin, "Qui habitat, 24 vocum."
                Exempla Musica Neerlandica 6. Amsterdam: Veren-
                iging vor Nederlandse Muziekgeschiedenis, 1971.

StamV   ———. "Die vierundzwanzigstimmige Kanonische
                Psalmmotette Qui habitat in adiutorio altissimi
                von Josquin des Prez." TVNM 22 (1971):1-17.

Stephan   Stephan, Wolfgang. Die burgundisch-nieder-
                ländische Motette zur Zeit Ockeghems. Kassel:
                Bärenreiter, 1937.

Steude   Die Musiksammelhandschriften des 16. und 17.
                Jahrhunderts in der Sächsischen Landesbiblio-
                thek zu Dresden. Quellenkataloge zur Musik-
                geschichte, 6. Wilhelmshaven: Heinrichhofen's
                Verlag, 1974.

StevensonJ   Stevenson, Robert. "Josquin in the Music of
                Spain and Portugal." J 217-46.

StevensonT   ———. "The Toledo Polyphonic Choirbooks and
                Some Other Lost or Little Known Flemish
                Sources." FAM 20 (1973):87-107.

Strunk   Strunk, Oliver. "Vergil in Music." MQ 16
                (1930):482-97.

Taricani   Taricani, JoAnn. "Munich, Bayerische Staats-
                bibliothek, Mus. Ms. 1508: A Study of the
                Dissemination of the Chanson in Germany in
                the Sixteenth Century." Diss., University of
                Pennsylvania, in progress.

ThibaultI   Thibault, G. "Instrumental Transcriptions of
                Josquin's French Chansons." J 455-74.

Tiersot   Tiersot, J. "Les Motets de Josquin des Près."
                Le Ménestrel 87 (1925):30.

TirroG   Tirro, Frank. "Giovanni Spataro's Choirbooks
                in the Archive of San Petronio in Bologna."
                Diss., University of Chicago, 1974.

TirroR   ———. [Renaissance Musical Sources in the
                Archive of San Petronio in Bologna. In prepara-
                tion for the series Renaissance Manuscript
                Studies].

TirroRG   ———. "Royal 8.G.Vii: Strawberry Leaves,
                Single Arch, and Wrong-way Lions." MQ 67
                (1981):1-28.

Titcomb   Titcomb, Caldwell. "The Josquin Acrostic
                Re-examined." JAMS 16 (1963):47-60.

Torner   Torner, Eduardo M., ed. Narvaéz, Luis de.
                El Delphin de Música 1538. Estudio y trans-
                cripción. Madrid: Union Musical Española,
                1965.

Treize   Treize Livres de Motets parus chez Pierre
                Attaingnant en 1534 et 1535, ed. Albert
                Smijers, A. Tillman Merritt. Paris: L'Oiseau-
                Lyre, 1960, 1963. Vols. 4, 12.

TurriniC   Turrini, G. Catalogo descrittivo dei mano-
                scritti musicali antichi della Società
                Accademia Filarmonica di Verona. Bolletino
                dell'Associazione dei Musicologi Italiani,
                Ser. 14. Parma, 1935.

TurriniP   ———. Il patrimonio musicale della Biblioteca
                Capitolare di Verona dal sec. XV al XIX.
                Atti dell'Accademia di agricoltura, scienze
                e lettere di Verona, ser. 6, v. 2. Verona:
                La Tipografica Veronese, 1952.

TVNM   Tijdschrift van de Vereniging voor Nederlandse
                Muziekgeschiedenis.

Ursprung   Ursprung, Otto. "Josquin Des Prés: Eine
                Charakterzeichnung auf Grund der bisher
                erschienenen Gesamtausgabe der Werke Josquin's."
                Bulletin de la Société Union Musicologique 6
                (1926):11-50.

VaccaroO   Vaccaro, Jean-Michel, ed. *Oeuvres d'Albert
                de Rippe. II: Motets, Chansons.* Paris: Éditions
                du Centre National de la Recherche Scien-
                tifique, 1974.

ValeC   Vale, M.G.A. *Charles VII.* Berkeley: University
                of California Press, 1974.

Van der Linden Van der Linden, Albert. "La nationalité des
                artistes des provinces du nord." RenaissanceR
                26-37.

Vanderstraeten Vanderstraeten, Edmond. *La Musique aux pays-
                bas avant le XIX siècle.* Brussels: Muquardt
                (vol. 1), van Trigt (vols. 2-7), Schott
                (vol. 8), 1867-88. 8 vols. Reprint. New York:
                Dover, 1969. With an introduction by Edward E.
                Lowinsky. 4 vols.

VaughanV   Vaughan, Richard. *Valois Burgundy.* London:
                Allen Lane, 1975.

VfMw   *Vierteljahrschrift für Musikwissenschaft.*

Vollhardt   Vollhardt, R. *Bibliographie der Musik-Werke
                in der Ratsschulbibliothek zu Zwickau.* MfMg
                Beilagen 25-8 (1893-6).

WagnerG   Wagner, Peter. *Geschichte der Messe. I. Bis
                1600.* Kleine Handbücher der Musikgeschichte
                nach Gattungen, 11. Leipzig: Breitkopf &
                Härtel, 1913.

Walker   Walker, Helen Margaret. "MS. London, British
                Museum, Royal 8.G.vii and Its Contents."
                Diss., University of California, Berkeley, in
                progress.

Wangermée   Wangermée, Robert. *Flemish Music and Society
                in the Fifteenth and Sixteenth Centuries.*
                Trans. Robert Erich Wolf. New York: F.A.
                Praeger, 1968.

WarburtonE   Warburton, Thomas, ed. Josquin des Pres.
                Missa pange lingua. Early Musical Masterworks,
                1. Chapel Hill: University of North Carolina,
                1977.

WarburtonF   ———. "Fridolin Sicher's Tablature: A Guide to Keyboard Performance of Vocal Music." Diss., University of Michigan, 1969.

WarburtonK   ———. *Keyboard Intabulations by Josquin des Prez.* MMMR 34 (1980).

WardJP   Ward, John. "Parody Technique in 16th-Century Instrumental Music." *The Commonwealth of Music: In Honor of Curt Sachs*, pp. 161–88. Ed. Gustave Reese and Rose Brandel. New York: The Free Press, 1964.

WardJU   ———. "The Use of Borrowed Material in 16th-Century Instrumental Music." JAMS 5 (1952): 88–98.

WardTP   Ward, Tom Robert. "The Polyphonic Office Hymn from the Late Fourteenth Century until the Early Sixteenth Century." Diss., University of Pittsburgh, 1969.

WardTPC   ———. [The Polyphonic Office Hymn from 1400–1520, a Descriptive Catalogue; in preparation].

Ware   Ware, John Marley. "Sacred Vocal Polyphony in More Than Five Parts to the Death of Josquin." Diss., Louisiana State University, in progress.

Weidensaul   Weidensaul, Jane B. "Early 16th-Century Manuscripts at Piacenza: A Progress Report." *Current Musicology* 16 (1973):41–8.

Werner   Werner, Theodor. "Anmerkungen zur Kunst Josquins und zur Gesamtausgabe seiner Werke." ZfMw 7 (1924):33–41.

WernerA   ———. "Anmerkungen zur Motettenkunst Josquins." *Bericht über den musikwissenschaftlichen Kongress in Basel ... 1924*, p. 375. Leipzig: Breitkopf & Härtel, 1925. Reprint. Wiesbaden: Dr. Martin Sändig, 1969.

Wexler   Wexler, Richard. "Newly Identified Works by Bartolomeo degli Organi in the MS Bologna Q17." JAMS 23 (1970):107–18.

Whisler   Whisler, Bruce Allen. "Munich, Mus. Ms. 1516. A Critical Edition." Diss., University of Rochester, 1974.

Williams   Williams, Isabelle. "Manipulation of Imita-
                    tive Temporal Distance in Textural Progressions
                    of Josquin des Prez." Diss., University of
                    Michigan, 1975.

WioraJ   Wiora, Walter. "Josquin und 'der Finken
                    Gesang.'" *Deutsches Jahrbuch der Musikwissen-
                    schaft* 13 (1960):72-81; also in *Historische
                    und systematische Musikwissenschaft*. Tutzing:
                    Hans Schneider, 1972, pp. 229-39.

WioraR   ———. "Der Religiöse Grundzug im neuen Stil
                    und Weg Josquins des Prez." Mf 6 (1953):
                    23-37.

WioraS   ———. "The Structure of Wide-Spanned Melodic
                    Lines in Earlier and Later Works of Josquin."
                    J 309-16.

WolfS   Wolf, Johannes. *Sing und Spielmusik aus
                    älterer Zeit*. Leipzig: Quelle & Meyer, 1931.
                    Reprint. New York: Broude Bros., 1947.

WolffC   Wolff, Arthur Sheldon. "The Chansonnier
                    Biblioteca Casanatense 2856: History, Purpose,
                    and Music." Diss., North Texas State Univer-
                    sity, 1970.

WolffM   Wolff, Helmuth Christian. *Die Musik der alten
                    Niederländer (15. und 16. Jahrhundert)*.
                    Leipzig: Breitkopf & Härtel, 1956.

WolffheimM   *Musikbibliothek Dr. Werner Wolffheim*. Berlin:
                    Martin Breslauer & Leo Leipmannsohn-Anti-
                    quariat, 1928.

Wooldridge   Wooldridge, H.E. *The Polyphonic Period*.
                    Oxford History of Music, 2. Oxford: Clarendon
                    Press, 1901.

Wright   Wright, Craig. "Performance Practices at the
                    Cathedral of Cambrai 1475-1550." MQ 64 (1978):
                    295-328.

Yong   Yong, Kwee Him. "Sixteenth-Century Printed
                    Instrumental Arrangements of Works by Josquin
                    des Prez: An Inventory." TVNM 22 (1971):
                    43-65.

YouensM   Youens, Laura. "Music for the *Gottesdienst*
                    in Mss. 49/50 of the Universitätsbibliothek,
                    Leipzig." Diss., Indiana University, in
                    progress.

YouensR   ——. [Review of Orf]. TVNM 29 (1979):59–62.

ZarlinoI   Zarlino, Gioseffo. *Le istitutioni harmoniche.* Rev. ed. Venetia: Senese, 1573. Reprint. Ridgewood, N.J.: Gregg Press, 1966.

——. *The Art of Counterpoint. Part Three of Le istitutioni harmoniche, 1558.* Trans. Guy A. Marco and Claude V. Palisca. Music Theory Translation Series, 2. New Haven: Yale University Press, 1968.

ZfMw   *Zeitschrift für Musikwissenschaft.*

INDEX

In this index, the citation "bibl." indicates that the name occurs in alphabetical order in the bibliography section, pp. 155-204 above. Only the principal page reference is given in those cases in which an entry is cross-referenced between different sections above.